The Wrong Side of Eternity

Mary Mendenhall

To Amber

Peace + Joy!

The Wrong Side of Eternity

A PRESENT-DAY PASSION

Mary Mendenhall

© 2016 *by Mary Mendenhall*

Printed by CreateSpace
North Charleston, South Carolina, USA

All rights reserved.
No part of this publication may be reproduced,
stored in a retrieval system, or transmitted
in any form by any means,
without the prior permission of the author,
as provided in US copyright law.

ISBN: 1519502605
ISBN 13: 9781519502605
Library of Congress Catalog Number 2016904441
CreateSpace Independent Publishing Platform
North Charleston, South Carolina

By the same author:

FICTION
Michael and the Ice Princess:
A Mystical Romance

NONFICTION
The Dream of St. Clare:
Reflections on Divine Dependence

With gratitude

for the lives of Janice Lynn Swanson,
Jessica Ntambara, and Earl Mueller—
unsung heroes all.

Program

—OVERTURE: Uganda—

—ACT I: West-Coast America—
Threshold
Two Worlds
Evasion
Deadlock

—ENTR'ACTE—

—ACT II: Rural Uganda—
Portal
Double Vision
Incursions
Rift

—OPENING NIGHT: West- Coast America—
House Lights Down
Offstage
Curtain
Exit Music

Acknowledgments, Glossary, and Quotation Sources

Dramatis Personae
In Order of Appearance

Charity Ntambara	a Ugandan schoolgirl
Geoffrey Mahoro	her uncle and a school headmaster
Eva and Stan Thompson	missionary teachers
Stephen O'Connell	a Mexican-Irish American
Diane	his former girlfriend
Madeleine Benson	an administrative assistant at a Bible college
Sam Stuart	a professor of theology
Ted	a hospital orderly and all-around kind of guy
Father Theodosius	an Orthodox priest and chaplain
Bryce Everett	a musical genius from England
Julie Burns	a physical therapist
Roger Morris	a theology student at the seminary
Margaret Whitman	an Episcopal priest
Keith Hardesty	a professor of Bible
Elisabeth Hardesty	his wife
Cipriana	Stephen's mother
Sir Thomas Everett	Bryce's father
Joseph Wilson	a regional mission society director
Boniface Muneza	a Ugandan pastor
Ann Rourke	a New Zealander and missionary pastor
Phoebe Kizito	a promoter of women's development
Sam O'Connell	Stephen's son
Innocent Habimana	a Christian zealot
Gwen	Bryce's sister

Also Seen Throughout
students, nurses, bus drivers, soldiers, children,
musicians, villagers, dancers, and miscellaneous people
of a variety of color and creed

With the notable exceptions of the late Ugandan bishop Festo Kivengere and the dictator Idi Amin, all the major characters in this story are fictitious. Any resemblance to actual people, living or deceased, is unintended by the author. The events are drawn from the remembered experiences of real people, however, and reflect actual feelings and responses to true events. Many place names have been fictionalized to suit the story line.

PROLOGUE

—————

THE WINDS OF CHANGE HAD begun to blow again across the sultry face of the continent. Oh, they had been blowing for aeons, now a whispering breeze, another time a fiery whirlwind full of angry smoke and sulphurous fumes. They whipped the mountains and danced along over the wide plains, molding and shaping the lives at their mercy.

They had blown through tidal years of migration, settlement, conquest, and endless flights of refugees. One never knew where they would lead or what they would bring.

Now, nearing the close of what some called the twentieth century, they blew again, picking up speed at an unpredictable pace only to drop into deceptive pockets of calm. And borne upon these chaotic, primeval currents lay a tiny seed, frail and vulnerable, driven through fire and tempest to nestle somewhere in fertile and well-watered ground. A tiny pinprick of hope, meant to become a crimson blossom set against the black of cold, volcanic rock.

1

OVERTURE

"If I were to abolish human sacrifices," Kwaku Dua told a missionary,
"I should deprive myself of one of the most effectual means
of keeping the people in subjection."

—T. B. FREEMAN, PERSONAL JOURNAL, 1864

UGANDA 1970s

THE RUSTY BUS BOUNCED ALONG the tarmac, churning up a mixture of dust and sunshine. *It is always sunny out here*, thought the girl gazing out the window. Not like at home, where the clouds flew between the mountains chased by merciless winds. Where the air stayed cool and didn't even feel equatorial because of its high elevation. On the threshold of the sky...

A pothole jarred her back to the present, and she settled herself on the worn Naugahyde seat.

Charity spent the whole bus ride thinking about home. Pleased as she was with her marks—she had placed third in her class of over a hundred—she ached for the moment her dusty feet reached the shamba. Her nephew would just be bringing in the goats for the night; already the charcoal fire would be lit and the dinner begun. School life receded into the distance until the holidays were over. Had Mama been well? She'd had so much trouble with her stomach lately...

The bus slowed down. Charity glanced nervously out the window to note one of the barricades that sprang up in different locations every morning: police check. The government troops were trying to flush out rebels again. She sighed and checked the time. At this rate, it would be too late to find a pickup taxi in Kabiizi. She would have to stay with Uncle Asaph that night. She wished she were home.

The Wrong Side of Eternity

She clutched her school bag and waited for the cursory inspection to end. Several soldiers mounted the bus and ambled down its cluttered aisle. No one looked up to meet their gazes. No one spoke. Someone with shoes on was being hassled at the back; they didn't usually bother you if you were barefoot. Charity's heart pounded in her chest. The black boots stopped next to her seat, and the smell of tobacco and days of sweat drifted over her like a mouldy blanket. He poked her in the shoulder with the butt of his Kalashnikov, motioning her to get up, to move out of the bus. *God, no*, she thought, but out of fear she mechanically obeyed. Another woman was roused out of her seat, a smartly dressed secretary kind of person who probably had four or five children at home. Picked at random, like a chicken in the marketplace. A second soldier breathed heavily and pushed her out the door.

Out of the corner of her eye Charity took in the dry terrain, sprinkled with an occasional bush and fig tree. Her clothes were still on the bus. She hoped they wouldn't take long. Then she realised that another soldier—lower rank, she supposed—was waving the bus on through the roadblock. Without her. She must have paused, because a rifle barrel prodded her to keep walking. Into the bush. *My God*, she breathed, *do not forsake me now*.

The two guards chatted in Swahili, then separated at an unseen fork in the path. Her guard swiftly tripped her with his rifle and towered over her, silhouetted against the afternoon sun. He grinned and threw down his cigarette. She looked away, gritting her teeth. *It is death to resist*, she reminded herself, as at that moment she heard scuffling and screaming a few yards away. They were stronger, and they had every right while you had none. If you wanted to stay alive, you had to co-operate.

She wasn't sure she wanted to stay alive, not now. Distantly she felt her school bag grabbed away, and the smothering weight of her assailant. She squeezed her eyes so tight it hurt—harder, and she wouldn't feel anything else. There was a banging and a ripping and a sharp pain, and she must have wriggled because he hit her in the face, hissing an epithet she didn't understand but could guess at. She lay still, concentrating on the bits of gravel jabbing into her back, and prayed for it to be over.

The other soldier appeared; she thought he was drunk. There was anger in his face, and he barked an order in a language strange to her, perhaps one of the northern dialects. The words would find her later, in her nightmares. The soldiers traded places, adding the weight of panic and despair to her pain. She wished the earth would open up beneath them, to swallow them whole…

The sunny world slipped away into darkness, and Charity Ntambara, seventeen-year-old schoolgirl, lay senseless in the dirt.

———————

Gunfire peppered the capital throughout the night. Things always happened at night. In the country, if you felt unsafe, you slept in the darkness of a banana plantation until morning dispersed the shadows. Even in the backwaters of the borderland villages, fear trickled in through rumour.

Where could she be? pondered a care-worn mother, grinding peanuts into flour with the rhythmic thud of a heavy wooden pestle. The usual daily worries of where to get sugar, flour, and soap paled against the thought of what might have happened to Charity, her firstborn. She stopped to wipe her forehead with the edge of her *kitenge* when her husband, grim-faced, staggered into the confines of the shamba. He tossed his hoe into the corner and threw himself onto the nearest stool. She smelled the hard work of digging, and went on with her pounding, but waited for him to speak first.

"We must go to the football pitch this afternoon. Everyone must go." He waited a moment, fidgeting. "There's to be an execution."

"What?" Her hands stilled.

"Someone was caught stealing a fish from the market. Others were arrested on the same charge, Graciano and Habyarimana—"

"Our neighbour?"

The Wrong Side of Eternity

"Yes." He covered his face with his hands. "They're to be buried alive."

Under the tyranny of the New Regime, as everyone so politely called it, a law against thieving had come down without question. Everyone knew the military was somehow exempt. But no one protested; no one spoke. People in the cities disappeared from their workplaces or were taken from their homes by masked gunmen at night, thrown into the boot of a 504 Peugeot and never seen again.

He made his lament quietly, to himself: "They say that one stole a fish from the market. A fish! But he is a wealthy man, an influential man. He wouldn't try to take anything."

"His wife and children! *Aii, Data weh!*" She wrapped her arms around herself to keep out the cold of pain. "Can we not try to talk to the soldier in charge?"

"We have no voice. Who will listen to us? We will only become the next target."

Silence fell over them as the sun beat down in a brief spotlight between the passing clouds. In spite of its warmth, they shivered and clenched their teeth. The daily chores continued, but their hearts were not in them.

Their hearts were nowhere at all.

The clouds threatened rain while the accused dug their own common grave. Now and again one of them stopped shoveling to plead tearfully with the soldier who guarded him. The response was always the same: the barrel of a rifle in the face, and the accused one's return to stifled obedience. The guards chewed on sugarcane and spat while the men in the pit sweated and begged for their lives. There had been no hearing, no inquiry; the sentence had been passed. No one had a voice, not the rich, not the educated, not the leaders of the community. Only the gun spoke. The gun and the fear it brought.

At ten minutes past three, a brooding shadow fell on the village of Rutoki. Some official made a lofty speech about crime and its prevention,

8

that those who died today would serve as an example to anyone who broke the law (*Arbitrary as it is*, Charity's father thought silently).

The five prisoners were ordered into the pit by some loud officer, a big man. The wealthy one, who they said stole a fish, cried out for deliverance—his wife and children shouldn't have to suffer such an outrage. He was shot first, his appeal cut short by the report of an AK-47. Frothy red bubbles gurgled out his mouth. A little girl screamed. After a terrible second of realisation, the others followed. Down they tumbled, one after another, gravity sucking them into the hole. And as they grabbed at their bleeding wounds or the sparse grass that lined the pit and called upon God, soldiers took up shovelfuls of earth and tossed gritty dirt into their open mouths. The sky bolted earthward, and the executioners cursed and spat and hurried to finish their assignment before rainwater drenched their fatigues.

The crowd stood motionless as the thick drops struck their downcast heads, watching as gray rivulets of mud seeped into the footprints of the men who lay suffocating below. Silence and terror would overrule the day; no one could possibly get anything done now. They could only go to their impoverished homesteads, to huddle and talk, to drown their agony in banana beer, or to pray.

What could they have possibly died for? thought Charity's father in fury, as he took the arm of his wife, rather roughly, to turn her homeward. But he dare not speak. He had no voice. And where in heaven's name was his daughter?

————◆————

The ground was too wet. If he could just manage another kilometer, he would meet the pumice gravel road that ran homeward, to the mountains where freedom still nested amid a growing chaos. Past the border, maybe, to accept that scholarship he'd been offered in America... Geoffrey Mahoro gripped the handles of his bicycle and headed southwest and away from the soggy ground, up into the hills where shadows

The Wrong Side of Eternity

lay thicker and the roads were drier. Early this morning, he had woken to a beautiful day. He had walked next door to ask for some sugar for his tea. They were friendly, as usual: the kind of Muslims you liked to have as neighbours. Most of his people wouldn't talk with them since the previous year when the leader of the country had proclaimed himself President for Life. All of a sudden, normal, everyday Muslims had things no one else could get: white flour, soap, meat. Beneath the civil façade, they were generally resented and seldom trusted by the Protestants of Ankole.

As headmaster, Geoffrey enjoyed a mild public status. His school was open to boys from any tribe or religion. He knew he was a maverick, trying to modernise when the country was slipping so far toward doom. But something inside him couldn't help it: he was no fair-weather Christian.

He had been home reviewing some papers when a student came to his house at noon. Lunch wasn't served until one; the boy had apparently left class hurriedly to bring him a message.

"Sir, I don't mean to trouble you, but you must know..."

"Take it easy, Gad, and sit down a moment. You're out of breath— you must have run!"

"Sir, you must leave. I heard men, men in town, talking about you. Someone has accused you to the army commander..."

"They must be mistaken," he answered irritably, without looking up. "Accused of what? I have done nothing out of the ordinary—"

"I'm afraid for you, sir. And so many others. The archbishop is in big trouble, everyone knows that. They broke into his house to search for hidden weapons. People talk, sir. And they've started to talk about you." Nervously he shifted his feet and waited for a reply, glancing over his shoulder at the flimsy curtains that danced before the open window. Geoffrey tossed his pen onto the sheaf of documents and looked up.

"You believe this to be serious." *Of course it is serious,* he thought. The world had gotten too much serious. He had hoped that trouble wouldn't find its way into the backcountry, where schools were small and poor, where nobody cared about what went on in the backstreets of the capital. But it had. Just now. "All right, back to class. Hold your stomach and looked pained, and explain that you had to spend extra time in the latrine. Go out the back, so you can look as if you've been there." The headmaster stood, weighing his options. There weren't many to weigh. "And thank you, Gad, for the news."

"Certainly, sir. God strengthen you, sir."

"You as well, Gad." He smiled weakly as the boy dashed out the door, looking sick. He didn't have to try to look pale; fear had already done that. Geoffrey sighed and began to look for things to take with him.

He'd gone through the rest of the day in his most normal, even cheerful, manner. All the time he thought about nightfall. Things always happened at night. He had to go during the fellowship meeting, in the late afternoon when students were revising their notes or people were occupied with business or housework. When people were still in the fields, digging, and the town was quiet. He left at tea time, explaining that he had to visit a village where a student's mother was dying. It lay in the opposite direction from his real intentions.

His clothes were damp even though the evening was cool. He'd been pushing the bike for eight miles now. On the rack over the rear wheel were tied his most vital possessions: an extra shirt and socks, two notebooks, a bible, his identity papers and qualifications, a small knife. The nightmare, more than the journey, made him stop. He leaned over his bicycle, wracked with stifled sobs.

As darkness fell, he turned off the road, praying for enough starlight to guide the bicycle tires but not enough to give him away. If he skirted the swamp, he could get to the footpath heading to the border of Rwanda. The tires slogged down in the mud and sweat poured down from his armpits inside his suit coat. His shoes slipped on the papyrus reeds that had fallen, and more than once he had to lift the bicycle out of a hole. How much farther? He heard shouts from a small trading center a few hundred meters behind him, and looked back.

The Wrong Side of Eternity

A red sheen filled the sky behind him. The sharp report of gunfire blended with cries of alarm and the loud boom of an exploding shell landing somewhere amid the poor mud shops. He dropped his bike and threw himself onto the dank soil. There was a banana plantation just ahead; if he could just crawl there he might be safe...

He untied his bundle and pushed the bike into the swamp; depending on what happened, he could retrieve it come morning or leave it to sink. On his way into the shadows he slipped in a slimy puddle. *Cow dung*, he thought. No, it shone wrong in the dim light. Something else, something with familiar shapes. The stench hit him like a sledge-hammer. Tufts of hair. A bone. More than one. Not animal.

Stories of soldiers dumping their victims in the swamps flooded his mind, and he bolted, stomach coming into his mouth. The banana leaves arched overhead like angels' wings, and he fell, exhausted, beneath the shadowed canopy that hid the light. He didn't want to sleep, but he couldn't help it. Too much fear, too much tiredness. He listened intensely for voices, for footsteps, for any sound at all. He thought he heard a distant crackling before the darkness went from the outside to within him, to chill his hope and extinguish his future.

The headmaster knew he was in exile, and he didn't know whom to trust. If someone had accused him, he couldn't afford to travel as himself. In the darkness, he wadded up his qualification papers and identity card and stuffed them into his underwear. At first light, he copied the numbers, just the numbers, into his notebook and tossed it between the worn pages of his bible. If he had to lose the papers, perhaps this way... someday he could retrieve a copy of his records tucked away in some official's dusty files.

He deliberately tore his coat and dirtied his trousers even more, scuffed his shoes in the dirt, and started to walk. It was over fifty miles to the borderlands, where his homestead lay cradled against the winding hills amid volcanic cinder cones and steep gardens. He assumed the careless frivolity of a fool; it was all that would save him. If you could read or write in this world, your life was in danger. If you had money and you weren't a government official, your life was in danger. If you were a Christian, your life was in danger. If you were a woman…well, he wouldn't think about that. He had four sisters at home.

Now, two days later, as he stumbled along the dirt road into the rising hills, he was approached by a young man. Not a soldier, just a boy. He winced and squinted, trying to recognise the face.

"Sir?" a timid voice asked. "Master Mahoro?"

"Gad!" His voice sounded far away, squeaking and dry. There were others with Gad, two or three—he couldn't even count—tutors and another student.

"Thank God we found you," said the deputy headmaster, a young man named Byiringiro. "It's not safe to be going alone. Not now." He glanced around them, then laid a hand on Geoffrey's quaking shoulder. "We brought some food, a mattress." The tutor gestured toward a laden bicycle. "I've relatives near here. My wife and children are staying there. You can rest for a while."

Geoffrey nodded numbly. He had never needed such help before; always, it had been he who had helped others. He had helped his parents work their farm. He had even worked in other fields during term breaks to help pay his school fees.

"What news of the school?" he managed to ask.

"Burnt, along with your house. And mine."

"Any students hurt?"

"A few beaten up. Nobody said where you had gone."

No, thought Geoffrey, nobody had known. He hadn't told anyone. It wouldn't have been safe to tell anyone.

The deputy head spoke softly in the borderland dialect in case they were overheard. "Most of them just ran off."

They huddled silently under a drizzly sky. Byiringiro gently took Geoffrey by the arm and led him toward a shamba between the hills. The kraal was big enough for twenty head of cattle.

The Wrong Side of Eternity

"What other news?" Geoffrey asked, his heart beating so that his head pounded.

"It's bad."

"I still need to hear."

"The archbishop's dead. They said it was a motor-vehicle accident, in the papers. He was arrested the day before, when he went to talk with the president." Grainy photos of the archbishop and the president walking together amicably shimmered in Geoffrey's memory. But he knew there was little trust between them. There was little trust between anyone. No: the church leader had either been shot or clubbed to death. Everyone knew that's what really happened.

The group walked on silently, choking on emotions they had never admitted having before. The shock gave way to a numb determination to reach home.

"Any soldiers nearby?" Geoffrey whispered.

"We haven't seen any—today. We went around the roadblocks with the cattle boys. Once, we prayed our way through: it was as if they didn't even see us."

"Maybe they were just too drunk to see anything," Gad offered with the ripple of a smile. Geoffrey stopped and looked into the faces of his friends.

"I'll spend the night. But before it's light, I want to go on. I have to go on."

They looked around at one another, nervous. A man alone with a bicycle—a refugee...

"We'll go with you," Gad said. They held hands and headed toward the shamba in the spreading evening twilight.

———◆———

Over four thousand people had gathered on the sultry hilltop, where a light breeze made things barely tolerable in the equatorial sun. The rainy season would be starting again soon, but everyone was glad for the dry morning. They needed to see one another, to talk.

A clump of well-dressed Africans stood next to an open pit, freshly dug in response to the terrible news. It lay between the graves of Bishop Hannington and Alexander Mackay, revered pioneer of the gospel. The Protestant cathedral loomed up behind them in the morning light, a massive brick monolith able to accommodate crowds such as this one. Into this little group walked a middle-aged *bazungu* couple. Teeth clenched, the woman grasped her handbag tightly but kept to the niceties of civil behaviour in spite of the turmoil she felt inside.

She had first come to Africa to work for the archbishop, back when he was only an education officer in a small country diocese. She had admired his gentle calmness in the face of almost any tension, his gracious smile, his humility. He had moved on, reluctantly, into greatness, while she and her husband stayed within the rural confines of the church-school compound. The archbishop had so much to offer the world, so much gospel, so much hope. She was furious he was dead. It was premature; he was so young. So gifted, so capable. Such a pastor! How could they murder a *pastor*? Those people, those terrible people.

Eva Thompson had thorns in her heart.

Her husband, Stan, greeted the group cordially as the drums began to sound for the morning's service. Slowly they turned their backs on the grave and headed toward the great church. When next they raised their eyes, they saw that they were surrounded.

Soldiers were everywhere, clutching rifles, driving up in jeeps and lorries. Their faces were stone, but they moved quickly. They hopped off their vehicles and stood sentinel en masse, waiting for some sort of order.

Bishop Festo gave it, unexpectedly.

"If you gentlemen would like to join us for our Sunday worship, you're more than welcome," he announced, opening his arms to beckon them in. "But you'll have to put your guns down before you come inside." He walked toward them, almost laughing, exultant.

15

The soldiers looked at one another, men just wakened from sleep. A commander took a deep breath, about to respond, but then his shoulders slumped, and he motioned the troops away without a word. The worshippers watched them go. It was they, the soldiers, who looked like they were going to a funeral. In the memory of many, it seemed that they had simply fled.

Festo joined the Thompsons as they continued to walk toward the portal. "You see," he explained, rather nonchalant, "for the Christian, living in danger is liberating. You are no longer imprisoned by your own lack of security—because there is none." A slight pause, a lowering of his voice. "I shall miss seeing the two of you." He patted them both on the back and went to get robed for the procession.

Eva stared after him. Of course he would slip away into exile: he had to. She was still in Uganda; she had remained when others left. She was ready to give her life. If only she had an opportunity, she would! She looked back at the open grave, which lay like a gaping wound baring the red earth beneath the green hilltop. She knew the president would never release the body. It would disappear, secreted away or dumped in the Nile to cascade down the falls with hundreds of other mutilated corpses. The archbishop! How dare they!

A little group of mourners hovered over the hole in the ground, softly singing the martyrs' song. She could just make out the Lugandan words from where she stood on the pavement: "Oh, that I had the wings of angels; I would fly away to be with God."

An old man wearing a tattered suit knelt at the brink of the hole. Tears streamed down his wrinkled face. But he was smiling, even chuckling to himself. He touched the ground and held up his hand. His soft pronouncement fell on the ears of only a few, but it spread in ripples through the crowd to shake the foundations of the cathedral. People took it up, daring to speak it aloud, on and on. They shouted it, clasping one another in congratulation and exhilaration.

"He is not here: he is risen!"

Overture

When she remembered that day, Eva Thompson had to admit that this particular sunny morning in February was Easter that year, for all of Uganda.

ACT I
WEST COAST AMERICA
LATE 1970S

THRESHOLD

Education, *noun*. That which discloses to the wise and disguises from the foolish their lack of understanding.

—AMBROSE BIERCE

1. AT THE EDGE OF THE DESERT

STEPHEN GLANCED BACK TO SEE the gray stretch of road snaking away behind him. It folded its way to the horizon, a ribbon of gray velvet. Even in the rearview mirror, the mirages of puddled water sparkled atop the pavement, shimmering with late-morning light. He gripped the steering wheel and took a deep breath, exhaling slowly while letting go the tension in his shoulders and fists. *Good riddance.*

The breeze whipped through the open window at sixty-five miles per hour, evaporating the sweat that dampened his shirt. It felt so good to be going away. His heart set on the future, he didn't even mind the heat. Everything would be different now. He glanced at his watch. Five more hours of hard driving, if Diane was on time. Well, *he* was going to be punctual: he had altered his life's course since high school. Diane hadn't. It was pure and amazing coincidence that they were pursuing their studies in the same town.

He had to stop thinking like that. "Town" was much too small a word for the city, that bastion of culture and threshold to the career world.

He would be such a small fish in such a big pond! All the better. He was tired of being known.

The well-dusted pickup veered off the highway onto an exit leading toward a clump of wooden false-front buildings and weatherworn shops. He filled the tank at the gas station, where he used the men's room and lathered his hands. Two minutes later, he pulled onto the packed-dirt parking lot of the Desert Edge Café, a tumbledown place known far and wide to travelers in need of a wake-up. Its legendary cup of coffee was rumored to be so stiff that a spoon would stand up straight in the middle, and that was with no sugar on the bottom.

Diane had told him on the phone that the bus would drop her thereabouts around eleven. He took off his driving glasses and cupped his hand over his eyes to scan the mirrored windows, but he could see only gingham curtains until he stepped inside. It took him a moment to adjust to the dim light. The newspaper stand offered yesterday's paper, its headline forecasting doom for the new peace treaty in the Middle East. He looked around, and she was there all right, waving at him from a corner booth, cigarette smoke wafting about her face in a whirling cloud.

"Stephen, you hot dog! You made it! Didn't think you'd get here so early—thought you'd keep to a pokey fifty-five."

"Hi, Diane." He cleared his throat and joined her at the square wooden table, softly mentioning to the waitress that he'd like a cup of coffee, please, black, and a BLT. "There wasn't much in the way of traffic."

"I'm surprised," she answered, looking up from her second Budweiser. "I'd've thought the road'd be choked with college students." She was studying political science. It figured. A serious student of human nature, Diane learned everything experientially. She scowled as his coffee arrived. "Guess you're not gonna let me drive that clunker of yours, now that you caught me drinkin' in broad daylight."

"You're right." He hadn't seen her for several months but marveled at how she had aged in that short time. Maybe she was doing drugs.

22

He folded up his sunglasses and deftly slid them into his shirt pocket. "Where are you staying tonight?"

"I was hoping it might be somewhere with you," she cooed, leaning forward. "Don't know an awful lot of people near *the city*. That's what they call it, y'know. Sounds more sophisticated that way."

"Mm-hmm," he said, consulting his wristwatch. "I'm due to check into the dorms tonight, and I seriously doubt they would let us share a room." He smiled grimly at the thought of cohabitation at a conservative bible college. "I thought you signed up to stay at a sorority house near the university."

"Yeah," she sighed, sounding extremely worn out and disappointed. "Yeah, I did. I guess you can drop me there."

He sipped the bitter brew in silence as she toyed with the fringe on her suede jacket. He thought it might be a bit hot for that thing, but then again she might be wanting to hide the state of her arms, if she was using needles now.

"Diane, I hope you can get enough space to, uh, try to take a good look at where your life is heading."

Her mouthful of beer just about exploded in his face.

"Christ, Stephen, cut the crap. Ever since you got 'saved' or whatever weird thing happened to you, you've been preachin' at everybody in sight. Seems you can't help tellin' us poor lost folks to shape up. Well, my dear ol' buddy, we all have our own time to get good, and mine's just not come yet. Get that into your stuck-up head and let's just get on with our lives, okay?"

"All right." He sighed. "But I'm going to leave a phone number with you, in case you ever change your mind and want to talk about things that really matter."

She guffawed and looked up from the checkered tablecloth, her eyes full of pity and disappointment. He could read her skepticism that he would never make it, not in the city. What a way to start out a long drive alone together. He felt her eye on him as he devoured the sandwich,

The Wrong Side of Eternity

potato chips, and rubbery pickle, washing it down with that god-awful coffee. Her tone shifted.

"Whatever transformation you've undergone, Stephen, it didn't hurt your bod. You still look damn sexy in those tight jeans. Dead giveaway you're from the boonies. That and the truck."

"Maybe I should change the style."

"Don't. Even good boys need a *little* attention when they get to the city."

"You haven't changed."

"Damn right I haven't. Don't know why *you* had to, so much. God, Stephen, you used to be so much fun! You and your dark looks. I remember when you danced Bernardo in *West Side Story*, and I got to be Anita..."

"That was before." A fleeting memory of their intimacy assailed him, but he pushed it aside.

"You were a helluva good actor, that's all I have to say." She stubbed out her cigarette in the tin ashtray. "And afterward, at the cast party, when you..."

His censorial look silenced her. She sighed. He wiped his mouth with his paper napkin and tried to find someone to bring the bill. "I only hope you're actin' now, that all this niceness will wear off sometime. That you'll do some dancin' again. Hell, Stephen, you're *good* at it."

He grunted and waved to get the waitress's attention, a gentleman flagging down a Victorian carriage.

"Shit," she mumbled, slowly standing and shouldering her heavy patchwork bag. "It's going to be a helluva drive." She would either try to put up with his new-found gentility or go to sleep. *Yeah.* A sleep probably sounded pretty good to her, about now.

The bright sunlight stunned them both as they left the café. He flung her large canvas duffel into the truck bed, then opened the cabin door for her. She laughed at his chivalry. They climbed up into the aging Ford and started off.

24

"Good-bye, cactus country!" she shouted out the window toward the desert as they picked up speed, heading west toward the state border.

"Amen," Stephen sighed reverently.

2. AT A BIBLE COLLEGE ON A HILL OVERLOOKING THE CITY

Stephen stepped into the reception hall, feeling dirty from the long drive. A chandelier hung over his head, scattering crystal-clean light around the already sparkling room. Portraits of serious-faced men lined the white walls, in a diagonal parallel to the winding staircase that led to the balcony. Scholars Bible College, at long last. His application had taken so much time; they had written back with so many questions! Both he and his pastor had to convince them that he had truly changed, that he was really converted, that he was ready to be a serious Christian. Apparently they had succeeded, for here he was.

A pleasant secretary in a modest suit led him into a new-smelling lounge and motioned him to take a seat. She reminded him vaguely of his mother. Very vaguely—his mother was a dumpy Mexican, and this lady was a WASP.

"You're a little early, Mr. O'Connell. Most of the out-of-town students won't be in till tomorrow. But we know it's been a long trip, and you'll want to rest up. I'll just check with hospitality to find out if your room is ready. Shall I find you here?"

"Yes, that would be fine," he said politely, trying not to behave like a cowboy from the sticks. With that, she nodded her bespectacled face and left him alone to take in the surroundings. Her low-heeled shoes tapped efficiently over the polished floor on their way back to her office.

He glanced through the spacious room's large plate-glass windows overlooking a marginal neighborhood some distance from the bay. Low-lying clouds hid the rest. A grand piano sat poised in a corner, and judging by its shine and luster, it was hardly ever used. Dark red carpet

The Wrong Side of Eternity

blanketed the floor in every direction, practical and institutional rather than cozy, with a symmetrical tile-like design.

On the glass tabletop in front of him lay a tidy selection of magazines, the latest edition of the *Bible Times* and some expository notes on Galatians. The more sordid fare hid underneath: *Newsweek* and *Time*, and it was for these he reached. A huge face stared at him from beneath a decorated soldier's cap. He had heard the radio broadcasts of what was happening out there in Uganda—he didn't even know the exact geographical location, somewhere in Africa—to the point where he no longer bought a newspaper because it made him so sick. But the face challenged—no, *dared* him—and he opened the magazine and began to read.

He scanned several headlines and recent black-and-white photos of freshly executed African men tied to tree trunks. He found his speed slowing as the words pounded themselves into his head.

The reign of terror began almost immediately after Amin seized power in a lightning coup six years ago, and it has been the predominant fact of life ever since. At first, the outside world recoiled in horrified disbelief at the tales of bodies—often hideously mutilated—floating in the Nile, of prominent citizens disappearing and of ghastly scenes of torture and execution in Uganda's dank prisons. But the refugees streaming out of Uganda—soldiers, civil servants, intellectuals, businessmen, professional people, and even cabinet ministers purged by Amin—were weighted with an abundance of grisly detail.

The major bloodletting occurred in 1971 and 1972, when Amin was consolidating his hold on power by purging the army of men suspected of loyalty to President Milton Obote, whom Amin had overthrown. According to one reputable account, as many as 3,000 Acholi and Langi tribesmen, mostly Christians from the northern part of the country—the traditional backbone of the army—may have died in the first terrible purges.

26

Act I

One of the first to die was Brig. Gen. Muhammed Hussein, the army chief of staff who had led attempts to thwart Amin's coup. Hussein, according to reports at that time, was killed by Nubian soldiers, his crotch and stomach smashed by rifle butts. Later, a servant at the "command post"—as Amin's house in Kampala is known—claimed that Hussein's severed head was brought to Amin, who placed it on a table and berated it—then put it in the refrigerator overnight. Among other officers liquidated then, one was disemboweled, others were herded into a room that was blown up with explosives, and another was suffocated with his own genitals.

Stephen swallowed hard and read on, while the pristine room engulfed him, its walls perceptively closing in.

One appalling story told by a former Uganda diplomat who was forced into exile concerns Amin's wife Kay, a Christian and one of the three wives he abruptly divorced in 1973. (As a Muslim, Amin is allowed by his religion to have as many as four wives.) Because she was pregnant at the time, Kay had an abortion rather than give birth to a child out of wedlock. When Amin heard of what she had done, he was so enraged, the exile claims, that he had Kay's doctor slain as well as the doctor's wife and two children. Kay was also slain, and her arms and legs were cut off—then sewn back on, but in the opposite way: the right leg on the left side, and so on. Amin, according to this exile's report, then had his two children by Kay brought into the room to view the hideously deformed body, and warned them, "See what happens to bad mothers!"

Stephen looked up suddenly, but the room, the light, the piano, the carpet were all the same. He hadn't heard any thunder or seen any lightning in the dimming sky outside the plate-glass window. But from

The Wrong Side of Eternity

halfway across the world something had resonated somewhere, a jangling alarm that wouldn't stop. Could words do so much? Was it true? He knew how sensational those secular journalists could be these days, writing anything to sell a magazine. President Carter had publicly criticized this brutal tyrant, but what good did that do? What good could *anyone* do in the face of such a monstrosity?

He stuffed the magazine beneath the others and rose mechanically to seek refuge among the piano music dormant in the corner of the lounge. He sighed as he sat on the varnished bench, raised the lid covering the keys, and began to play as if the piano would collapse under his softest touch.

The "Largo" from Dvorak's *New World Symphony* oozed out from the tiny space above the strings, falling note by note on the red carpet and staining his fingers with sorrow. Numbness overcame the stinging after a minute or so. It was only when he let the last chord die away that the tomb-like quality of the room faded.

"That was beautiful." A woman's voice spoke, a voice that belonged on stage: rich, deep, lustrous. He blinked and raised his eyes to a spotless specimen of purity and refinement, sitting where he had but a moment ago. A lifetime ago. She sat erect, her legs together in a composed and modest manner.

"Thank you," he responded, looking down at the keys.

"Did you write about your music ability on your application?"

"I mentioned it under the heading of hobbies. I didn't think there were any music opportunities here. It's a seminary."

"Bible college," she corrected. "But if you can do the same thing with hymns, we're always in need of good pianists for chapel."

"Hymns are kind of new to me. I'm used to praise choruses. But I could try."

"Good," she said, satisfied. "I'll tell the dean I heard you play. Oh," she continued, almost as an afterthought, "I'm Madeleine Benson, his personal assistant and sometime student."

Act I

He tried not to look at her legs as she rose to extend her hand. "Sometime?"

"I audit some courses out of pure interest. I already have several degrees."

He was sure she wasn't lying.

———————

The next few days were a whirlwind of activity. Mrs. Williams, the secretary who had first met him, took a few of them to a nice secondhand shop in a big church basement to find appropriate attire for SBC. Jeans weren't allowed, she casually explained, nor were open collars unless you wore a white crew-neck T-shirt underneath. Ties and knit slacks were the accepted uniform for proper bible school students, she said, as she went on to detail other standards of behavior. It was all in the manual, she explained, but new students, God bless them, didn't always take the time to read the fine print.

Stephen, with his AA degree behind him, found all this amusing. He had never been so aggressively parented in his life. His mother never told him how to dress, unless they were going to someone's First Communion or a wedding, and even then she wasn't that picky.

"Estevaníto," she would explain to him, "you always look so good anyway." And he would blush and offer her his arm, feeling like a million bucks.

He made a pretense of looking through a rack of long-sleeved shirts. Mama. She hadn't even been that upset when he had left the Church; she just waddled up the plaza as usual the next morning at six to pray. He never caught her praying at home, but the little lighted corner in the bedroom where she kept her statue of the Virgin never got dusty, either. She prayed better, he guessed, when she was surrounded by the Spanish mystique of shadow and arch, incense and votive, and garishly painted statues in various poses of supplication and holiness. How fake, how unlike real life it all seemed to him now.

When he had told her he was born again, she smiled—a warm, pitying motherly smile not unlike Mrs. Williams's when she first noticed his tight jeans. Then she had said, "Sí, míjo. I am happy for you. But there is more to life than being saved." He had questioned her with what Diane called one of his dark looks, and she simply went on to ask, "What are you saved *for?*"

That question burned within him, even now, in this moldy church basement. He vowed he would answer it by studying the Bible and discovering its timeless truths in a world full of compromise. He would show her that being born again was way beyond her little trips to church to pray—that you could grow out of that sort of religion if you wanted to.

He knew he had to leave home to find out where he really belonged. Anywhere but home. At home, he couldn't be himself. He wasn't Mexican and he wasn't Irish. He loved the theater and the studio, and his father continually put him down in public for it. Once, in a drunken furor, he had beaten Stephen up after jazz class, just because having a son who danced brought so much shame. Stephen found himself perpetuating the lie the next day: when the guys asked him about his swollen eye, he joked that he'd tried out boxing at the gym and decided it wasn't his thing. But he wouldn't think of Da, not now. He'd practically kicked Stephen out of the house. After he got saved, he couldn't be Catholic either, and he was not yet used to being a Protestant. His mother—well, she would be Catholic forever. And he prayed daily for her salvation.

It struck him that perhaps his little Mexican mother prayed for him too. He resented her gossiping to God. How in heaven's name could his mother pray for *him?* Why should she, anyway? There were other souls to be saved, millions all over the world: his was finally safe. He was on the right road, the way of salvation. Where in God's scheme of things was she?

At SBC, he would find out.

"Ah, Mr. O'Connell, here we are. This looks to be your size."

Act I

A gray double-breasted pinstripe suit. Something you would wear if you were in the Mafia, wearing a fedora with a cigar hanging out the corner of your mouth.

He thanked her and dutifully tried it on. He almost cursed aloud when he found that it fit, and that he felt compelled to buy it. Out of gratitude for her help.

The power of an older woman had foiled him again.

———◆———

He peered at his schedule and around the classroom. Printed on the chalkboard were the words INTRO TO BIBLICAL STUDIES, PROF. SAM STUART. After tiresome hours of A Christian View of History and Introductory Ethics, this is what he had come for. He'd learned some acronyms already—like "ITS" meant International Theological Seminary and was the grad school at the university—but still he felt a stranger. A younger student stood with one foot on a chair, talking glibly to a well-known peer. Stephen pretended to order his course overviews while he eavesdropped on their conversation.

"Prof Stuart isn't like the others. You can get away with things in his class."

"Like what?"

"Oh, rolled-up shirtsleeves, crossed-out words on your papers. But they say he's tricky."

"Who says?"

"The grads. None of them could figure out just what he was after on a test. Asked lots of questions and left you to sweat out the answers in the library. And he would never mark you right or wrong, just scribble more and more questions on your essays. Rick says he never could figure out just what he had learned in this course."

"Rick's got a church now."

"Yeah, lucky him. Half a year after getting his M. Div., he's already an assistant pastor in a mega-church. I bet someone pulled strings for him..."

The professor quietly stepped in through a side door and interrupted the rustle of waiting students.

"Let us pray." The whole class in unison bowed their heads and closed their eyes, including Stephen, who had learned the proper form in his meager time as a true believer. "God, good morning. Thank you for these students. Be their teacher here so that they in turn might become teachers. Send to your church teachers who will build and not destroy, who have courage to challenge the intellect, and who remind themselves that the heart has reasons of its own. Amen."

"Amen," came the preconditioned chorus.

"That was *weird*," someone whispered behind Stephen.

No it wasn't, he thought. But it was certainly different. It had *thought* in it, along with respect. You got the feeling that Professor Stuart actually considered God a person. And that *was* a pretty weird thing at Scholars Bible College, as Stephen had yet to discover.

After class, he paused to look at his hastily scribbled notes to make sure they were legible, simultaneously wondering why it mattered so much. It was easy to take notes in the other classes: the lectures had predictable outlines. Here, it seemed, Stephen had wanted to grab everything word for word:

Reading the scriptures is not as easy as it seems since in our academic world we tend to make anything and everything we read subject to analysis and discussion...Instead of taking the words apart, we should bring them together in our innermost being; instead of wondering if we agree or disagree, we should wonder which words are directly spoken to us...Only then can we really 'hear and understand'—Matthew 13:23.

It would never do for study.

"Enjoy the class?"

God, it was Professor Stuart himself, addressing him. "Yes, sir. Very much."

"Are you what they call a new believer?"

"Yes, sir."

"What were you before?"

"A nominal Catholic, sir."

"Oh. Like to hear your testimony sometime." Professor Stuart opened up a datebook covered with paisley designs. "Lunch tomorrow? In the cafeteria?"

"Uh, yes, sir."

"About 12:30."

"Fine."

"See you then, Mister—"

"O'Connell. Stephen O'Connell."

"Lovely. I'm Sam." He reached out his hand, which was warm, and shook Stephen's, which was cold and sweaty. "See you tomorrow."

Amazing, thought Stephen happily as the professor walked out the door.

———————

It was quasi-roasted chicken. Roasted because the skin was a nice, barbecued hue of brown and black, and *quasi* because the insides of his drumstick were still pink, with an offensive uncooked blood vessel running next to the bone. But Stephen, in his navy blazer, found it somehow tolerable, for he was having a conversation with a wise man only a decade older than himself, who put him at ease.

"What exactly do you want to get out of bible school, Stephen?" Sam asked through a mouthful of coleslaw.

"I feel called to be a pastor."

"To whom?"

Well, you don't think about things like that, Stephen thought. *You just get ready and become a pastor.*

"I mean, do you feel more of a pull toward evangelism, or church work?" Sam continued. "Or inner-city missions? Or are you more interested in anthropology and the foreign field?"

"I don't really know yet," was all he could say.

"Good. You don't know. That's honest, and it'll get you farther than having all your sights fixed and goals set. This is an exploration for you, then?"

The Wrong Side of Eternity

An exploration. It sounded so tentative. "Yes, I guess so, Professor."

"*Sam* outside of class, please." He stabbed another forkful of the coleslaw and eyed it warily before he put it in his mouth. "How are you funded? Scholarship?"

"Only partly. Savings, summer jobs, that sort of thing."

"Ever think about working while you're in school?"

"I didn't know if that was allowed. Off campus, I mean."

"Why off campus? Isn't there anything you'd like to do here?"

"Not really, sir."

"Sam."

Stephen paused, thinking. "Maybe gardening."

"Tell me what you like to do, the kinds of jobs you've enjoyed before."

This was getting awkward. Soon he would have to talk about the past. "Physical jobs, like..."

"Like construction?"

"Not really," answered Stephen, growing more comfortable. "I dug ditches once but couldn't stand it."

"Ah. Something cleaner, like coaching swimming at the Y."

"Yeah, that or gymnastics."

"You teach gymnastics?"

"I only assisted one summer."

"I doubt that would get you very far. Here they want certification." He leaned back in the plastic chair and eyed Stephen's physique. "Digging ditches didn't give you all that lower-body strength, did it?"

"No." Stephen laughed and looked around a little in embarrassment.

"What did?"

"Dance."

The gracious professor didn't bat an eye. "Ballet?"

"Some. Mostly jazz. Show dancing."

"Do you still do it?"

"Here? Are you kidding, sir?"

"Sam."

"Sam. I'm in bible school now. According to the manual, it would be, uh, wrong."

"You have a point. But putting that aside, it seems you've made quite a sacrifice to study here."

"Maybe so. But isn't it worth it, to learn God's word?"

Sam Stuart smiled a little and pulled a worn New Testament from his tweed jacket pocket. He deftly flipped through some pages. "Maybe you should look up First Corinthians six later. The last part. And next." He eyed Stephen's hands. "No offense, but those are not ditch diggers' hands. Artist?"

"No, not really."

"Musician, then."

"Yeah, but not much of a singer." He was afraid Sam would suggest that he join the gospel quartet, and Stephen loathed that sort of music. "Percussionist."

"Really? My uncle was a percussionist, in the symphony." He paused. "A dancer and a musician too! Are you any good?"

"Great sense of pitch. Made the timpanist position in the Desert Sands Youth Orchestra."

"There are occasional music jobs around. Not much consistency, though. Hey," Sam said, pricked by an idea, "have you thought about the hospital?"

Stephen frowned, distracted. The elegant Madeleine Benson stood at the counter, showing her meal card to the cashier, her white blouse frothing with ruffles. *God, she's immaculate,* thought Stephen, before he remembered that he wasn't alone.

"Huh?"

"The hospital. Getting some work there."

"The university hospital? I didn't know they offered music jobs."

"They don't, unless it's therapy for the mental patients," Sam commented wryly, though he seemed not to have noticed Stephen's distraction. "But you'd need a teaching qualification for that. No, I was thinking

The Wrong Side of Eternity

of an evening or part-time night job as an orderly. The hours won't cut into your studies too much, and you'd stay in shape—in case you ever wish to go back to more physical forms of work—you know, like foreign missions..." His eyes were twinkling now as he washed the dinner roll down with milk. "They could use some sensitive people in that place."

"You mean—ah, Sam—that it would be like a mission field, working in the hospital?"

"Yeah, sort of. Anyway, it's a great way to test your call, if you're to be a pastor. Meeting people at their worst. And I'm not just talking about the patients. They pay pretty well, too, and there are usually openings."

"Okay, I'll apply. Will I need permission from the dean to work off campus?"

"Yes, of course. But in light of your present financial situation, I should think he would consider it good initiative. And if you worked in the university hospital..."

"Yeah?"

"You might be able to get access to the campus gym, to do a workout once in a while."

"Oh." What kind of a Christian *was* this man?

But Sam was looking at his watch, a practical, twelve-dollar off-brand.

"I've got a theology discussion group over at ITS in a few minutes. Will you excuse me?" He stood. "Let me know how things work out, will you?"

"All right. Uh, Professor?" They had reverted to formal roles; Sam's smile indicated that his timing was perfect, that he hadn't missed a step.

"Mr. O'Connell?"

"I'm curious why you chose to take an interest in a new student like me."

"I've got Irish blood in me, too. Grew up hearing about that hero Daniel O'Connell. Your name brought back memories of some glorious stories." He picked up his tray.

"Is that all?"

Professor Stuart answered only with a backward glance and a furtive smile.

36

Act I

3. ON THE UNIVERSITY CAMPUS

The bus rolled to a smooth stop just inside the campus common, and Geoffrey warily negotiated the steps down to the pavement after the short ride from the airport. He collected his worn suitcase from the driver and, copying those around him, handed the man a dollar. People gave you so much space here! No one pushed, even when they rushed. And they *did* rush; everyone was heading for something, somewhere, someone. The headmaster was headed to the seminary, and tried to stop about twenty young people to ask for directions before he got any help whatsoever.

It was a longish walk, with his baggage, but he had no money for such frivolities as taxis. Besides, he wanted to feel this new wind on his face, take in the strange environment. The green hills surrounded him with the comfort of his homeland, but there were new things in the air. Smells were different. A stiff breeze blew toward him from the bay—he had never in his life seen the sea—there was a hint of salt in it. There were trees and flowers planted everywhere, guiding pedestrians toward walkways and away from the broad stretches of neatly trimmed grass. He shuddered as a thought of the golf course in the capital back home invaded his thoughts. It was where President Amin or his media men used to casually meet with European visitors and convince them that all was well in Uganda.

Geoffrey sighed and forced himself to walk faster, away from there, away from the thoughts. He would outdistance them. *How can I?* he mused. *I'm already halfway around the world.*

This was a promised land, he remembered, where anyone could get an education if he wanted one. Where people believed in God to the extent that they printed it on their money. Its arms were open to refugees like Geoffrey. He walked without concern; no thugs would jump him from a passing Mercedes and push him into its black, yawning boot. Blacks were safer now, in America. It had been bad, he was told, ten, fifteen years ago. Americans were more tolerant nowadays.

He laughed inside to realise that his old suitcase got more stares than he did. And as he walked, he began to whistle.

The Wrong Side of Eternity

Twenty minutes later, a bit damp from sweating in his suit jacket, he reached the International Theological Seminary. It truly looked like a respectable fortress of knowledge and tradition, set amid rolling hills and the brightest of green grass. Old buildings, gray weathered stone, sprouting ivy arms. They beckoned to him to come inside, away from the fog encroaching from the Bay. Geoffrey was cold—it went through you, deeper than the mountain winds back home in Rutoki. He pulled his collar around his neck. *Home.* When would he go back? He thanked God he had no wife, no children to worry about. He wished his niece Charity could be here! She was bright; she should attend university in America when her secondary studies were over. Her British teachers had only glowing reports of her potential. There was little left in Uganda to stay for: many of the professors had left or disappeared. She should study law in the modern world, that bright girl, and take some enlightenment back home when the troubles died down. He made a mental vow to seek out someone who could sponsor her, some good Christian soul who cared about the people in his country, some rich American who had the means to turn potential into reality, who could make dreams come true.

His feet ached, used to dirt paths and not hard sidewalks. This embarrassed him; he felt a weakling in spite of years of hard toil digging beans in the fields near his family's shamba.

Geoffrey stepped into the seminary office, where the trappings seemed a little less glamorous. The stone and woodwork were old and re-worked to accommodate the modern conveniences of desks with electric typewriters and metal filing cabinets. He placed his bulky bag out of the way and sauntered to where lists hung on the large cork-covered bulletin board, looking for his name and perhaps some other direction as to what he was supposed to do next. People began to approach him with welcomes that were warm as well as polished. Someone offered him a cup of coffee. He was sure he was in America now: they hardly ever drank tea here! He began to relax a little, and suddenly he felt tears dampening his cheeks.

Act I

He tried to stop them, to reach for his handkerchief and feign that the travel and distance had wearied his eyes, that was all. But they would not stop. His shoulders began to spasm, and he wrapped his arms around his sides to keep his body from blowing apart like a bomb. The one who had brought the cup of coffee steered him into the refuge of a deep leather chair, which faced a glass case full of antique books near a cold stone hearth away from the door. It was darker there. The stranger sat with him and was silent.

Across the quadrangle in the library, Madeleine stared down at the pages before her, trying to comprehend what the author had in mind. She came here on occasion to do research, always alone. She made a wonderful detective, perusing books her colleagues would consider heretical. It was not that she couldn't be social; her people skills were highly developed. It was something that ran deep in her veins, the need to find out the truth no matter what, even if it meant mixing with, or reading, people who lived and thought differently from her. Inclusive language…feminist theology…the ERA…pagan rituals…some horrific thing called the "Religious Coalition for Abortion Rights"…Nothing was out of bounds for her.

Well aware of the time, she knew exactly how many minutes were left before she needed to stand up, return the volumes to the librarian, make a graceful exit, and walk across the parking lot to her car. There was just enough time remaining to look at one more section, and she set her jaw to plow through it.

Commentary on Genesis 1:27: Whatever the social and legal system may have looked like in the context in which these words gained their authority two and a half thousand years ago, the text talks of man and woman together as the human being. Any

The Wrong Side of Eternity

fundamental subordination of woman to man is thus invalidated by "the word of God," even if Judaism and, succeeding it, the Church for a very long time confirmed in practice the existing superior status of the male and not infrequently proclaimed it as part of the divine order...If the churches had concentrated on their role of proclaiming the Gospel instead of maintaining positions that were already lost, then they would have been able to make their contribution to the emancipation of woman that would do justice to the nature of woman—earlier and better than has occurred.

"That's all *you* know," she sneered, as she snapped closed the tome and pushed back her chair. She had come for this very purpose, to undergird the positions she held with academic facts. "Already lost, indeed."

But she had gathered some valuable notes for her next presentation.

4. UNIVERSITY HOSPITAL, NIGHT SHIFT

Stephen still felt a bit self-conscious in the hospital's uniform—white pants and shirt—but he also felt much, much better than he ever had on the construction crew. Even though Stephen sometimes heard the words "bible student" whispered behind his back the first week, the night nurses seemed to really appreciate his help. Besides, the hospital paid a nice differential for working the late shift. He made the rounds, jogging silently on padded shoes through the glistening halls, past cleaning ladies who always greeted him in Spanish, turning bedridden patients every two hours, lifting warm slippery bodies off soiled linens, wheeling gurneys between the operating room and the floors and the emergency department. It was nice to be doing something *physical* after sitting in class all day taking notes. He met paramedics and policemen and thought that people were generally nicer at night, when the world and the bulk of its business had shut down. It was also a great place to think over Sam's lectures, the state of the world, the priceless value of people.

The only one who didn't seem to care much for him was Ted, the other orderly. Ted drove a Thunderbird with a rosary hanging from the rearview mirror along with some large furry dice. He was about Stephen's age but seemed much older; he was always giving advice. They were often on duty together but rarely saw one another except when passing in the hallway during their rounds.

"If there's one thing I can't stand, it's a born-again Christian," he once confided to Stephen during their lunch break at 2:30 in the morning. Maybe it wasn't just a remark, maybe it was a challenge. It could be, coming from Ted. Stephen wasn't sure.

"Yeah? Why's that?"

"They're so goddamned stuck up. Pisses me off." But, thankfully, Ted knew little of Stephen. Stephen had heard it all before, from his Da.

"And nobody else is?"

"Not like *they* are, no way. They think they know everything. I'd like to find myself in a dark alley some midnight, after getting drunk..."

"If you talked like that about blacks, you'd be jumped."

"Well, that's because niggers aren't in season right now, sweetie pie. It's all about *timing*. You gotta pick on somebody."

They heard an approaching siren as a code blue came over the loudspeaker. The siren died as an ambulance pulled up outside of the ER. Ted jumped to his feet.

"Action!" he bellowed. "CPR, anyone?" He left his tray on the table and bolted for the glass doors. Stephen followed, trying to catch up.

The curtains were drawn around the cubicles, with their usual occupants with chest pain or drug overdose, but there was a rush for the trauma center; all Stephen could see were the flying tails of white lab coats and green scrubs. He waited in a corner to be ordered about as a gurney rolled through the automatic doors.

"What's her pressure?"

"Sixty over thirty."

The Wrong Side of Eternity

"Speed up that drip. Get bloodwork to lab, stat, for typing and cross match."

"Aye aye, captain."

"Why aren't you wearing gloves, for Chris'sake?"

"No time."

"You keep up that line of thought, you'll either never be a resident, or you'll be dead before you're thirty."

"Very funny, Doctor."

"You there, take the bag and breathe for her until this jerk gets a blood sample, okay?"

Stephen nodded and stepped up behind the head of the intubated patient, a victim of someone's uncontrolled temper. He steadied the taped shaft of the plastic tube with his left hand and took the black rubber bag into his right, counting in measured whispers to keep the respirations regular. And he thanked God for blessing him with a cool head.

The woman was pale from shock, her skin an ivory hue. She looked like a figure from a wax museum, except that blood dribbled darkly out of two holes in her side. Other things stuck in his memory as the staff cut off her clothes. The curve of her breasts, the angry redness of the wounds, the bruises. She'd been beaten before she was shot. Maybe. He couldn't think why someone would want to beat her afterward…The staff moved in slow motion as he counted off the seconds. His right hand was cramping.

"Thanks, man, you can sit out now," came another order, which Stephen promptly obeyed with relief. He melted away to become once again a spectator of high-tech machinery and silver needles sheathed in plasticized rubber, and an efficient medical team fighting furiously for the life of someone they'd never met. The Roman Colosseum, in reverse.

Ted found him in the men's room minutes later, bent over the toilet, retching.

"The police said it was her boyfriend. Some boyfriend. Hey, what the hell's the matter with you?"

Act I

"My Da used to beat up my Ma. But he never shot her. He'd've never shot her."

"Liked to use his fists, huh? Look, Steve, you gotta get used to this shit, 'cause it happens a lot. It happens all the time." He lit up a cigarette and offered it to Stephen, who turned it down with a flick of his hand. "Oh, yeah, I forgot. You don't smoke." He inhaled deeply and blew the smoke out the side of his mouth, away from Stephen. "Pisses me off, shooting your own girlfriend." Further language followed as he drifted out the door. Stephen was just splashing cold water onto his face when Ted crashed through the door again.

"Shit, man, we've got rounds to do."

"Coming."

People at their worst. At their best. Both. Sam was right. This was a perfect place to test your calling. His wristwatch told him he was late for Sally's floor, and she would be mad. Didn't want any bedsores on her shift, she always reminded him when he was more than thirty seconds late. Well, things happened. They happened all the time.

The ER victim haunted him throughout the day's lectures. He could hardly wait to get back on duty, to find out what had happened to her. Why would someone beat her, shoot her? Had she insulted a man? She had some sort of Spanish surname, he overheard, once they finally got an ID. *Why should that matter?* he asked himself.

He was turning her that night, amid the tubes and wires that spilled like tentacles from sundry parts of her body. Ted had joined him, for a change—or was it curiosity?—and was helping on the other side of the bed.

"You treat her like an egg."

"She's a human being, Ted."

"Maybe, but she can't feel anything, she's unconscious. Not even a deep pain response." He pulled out a pair of bandage scissors from his pocket and pressed it against the base of one of her fingernails, hard. No shadow crossed her sleeping face. "See?"

"How do you know what she can feel? She's alive."

"Not for long." They finished and went to the nurses' lounge so Ted could have a cigarette.

"Why should you or anyone else treat her like a butchered carcass?"

"Face it, man. That's what she is."

Heat rose to Stephen's face but Ted ignored it. The two orderlies made a good team, in spite of their differences. The ICU staff liked Ted because he was quick and efficient, and they liked Stephen because he was gentle and thorough. The night dwindled on as they drifted between floors, down to ER and over to orthopedics to negotiate trapezes and sandbags. The only two areas they didn't cover were maternity and the neonatal intensive care unit.

The code came around three. They were tied up positioning some guy with a broken hip and didn't get upstairs and in on the "excitement," as Ted called it. But Stephen knew the room number. It was *her*.

Christ, have mercy, he breathed.

At Ted's insistence, they went up to the ICU to clean up. There were other lives to attend to, he said—the nurses shouldn't be bothered with removing all the tubes and stuff. Together they would pop her into a body bag in no time. He wanted to see if the coroner had ordered an autopsy. Ted liked to know about those sorts of things.

"Why the hell are you being so delicate, man? She's not alive now. She can't feel a damn thing."

"No."

"Hell, Steve, it's just a body."

"But it was *her* body."

"You are crazy, man. You didn't even know her, for Chris'sake!"

Ted jerked away the pillow and let her head drop a few inches with a dull thud. A dark figure stepped through the doorway of the room, and he pulled back with a start. Stephen looked up to see a tall, spare man dressed in something long and black. His cylindrical hat covered a head of wispy white hair, which flowed down into a beard frozen like a waterfall in winter. Thick glasses hid his eyes. He held up his hand and glided over to the bedside, a fleeting shadow on the threshold of death. Stephen watched, fascinated, as he pulled out a round silver container and used his finger to smear some ointment on the corpse's forehead. He touched her as if it was costly perfume and muttered some words in a language Stephen didn't know. Then he made the sign of the cross—backward—and left as quietly as he had come. Ted's sigh sliced through the silence.

"That," he said emphatically, "was Father Theo. How the hell did *he* get in here?" Ted called out the door to the nursing staff. "He shouldn't be here at this hour of the night. God, he makes my skin crawl!"

The nurses shrugged and let Ted go back to helping Stephen bag the body.

Stephen knew the answer. For people like Father Theo, there were no closed doors. He smiled softly to himself as the cooling skin of the murdered woman yielded to the handling of the orderlies.

5. SBC Men's Dorm

His homework was interrupted by the sound of the telephone down the hall, footsteps on linoleum, and a voice at his door. "For you, Señor Stephen." The answerer followed him back to the phone, and others poked their heads out of narrow doorways.

Diane's telephone voice was so loud that it nearly echoed through the hallway of the dorm. He pressed his face closer to the earpiece to muffle it.

"God, Stephen, you need a break from all that shit. Let's go do something decent." A pause, but Stephen had caught her stress on *decent* and smiled at her consideration. She resumed. "I know: they're doing *Messiah* at the university tonight. Some mixed group from the various churches. That should be safe enough."

He nearly whispered into the phone, so many eyes were on him. They knew he was talking to a woman. He had to appear godly. "That sounds very nice. Shall I see if some of the other students are interested?"

The Wrong Side of Eternity

"Hell no, Steve, I want you all to myself."

"I'm afraid that's simply not possible."

"Then you pick someone you like, even if it's another gal. I don't give a shit who it is, except for the dean of students or some pastor whose pants are so tight he can't even sit down. You gotta get outta that place."

"I'll see what I can do." Handel's *Messiah*. He loved it. With a gentlemanly touch, he returned the handpiece to its cradle on the hall pay phone. After getting permission to go from the residents' assistant, he walked back to his room to clean up, feeling, as his mother would say, like a million bucks.

6. University Auditorium, 7:45 P.M.

The auditorium was cool and clean, dimly lit with a high wood ceiling that glittered ever so slightly overhead. The floor sloped downward, but not too noticeably, not like the older theaters where the angular steps joined forces with gravity to pull you down like quicksand. The curtain in front was open, revealing a stage with a honey-colored floor strewn about with an array of stacking metal chairs, accessories for instruments, a few electric cords anchored with masking tape, and black music stands. Behind them stood risers and a deflecting screen to ricochet the vocals out into the vast hall above the sound of the orchestra. Stephen's eyes wandered left, to the percussion corner, his homesickness showing in his longing look at the polished tympani and the young man who was now tuning them with the help of a battery-powered pitch gauge. He could almost feel the tiny needle swing to the right when the note went sharp...

"Aren'tcha glad we came?" whispered Diane, hugging his arm and wiggling into the seat at his side. "God, Stephen, you needed to get out of that sterile prison!"

She didn't understand, so he just smiled in response. He had been relieved when she turned up at the dorm door: she had dressed so convincingly modest that the staff had given him permission to go without a chaperone—as long as he met the curfew. No cleavage—and a distant part of him added, *Darn it.*

"I *am* glad," he answered. "It brings back memories."

Stephen glanced around to take in the audience. A black man sat bewildered at the end of the row, looking nervous and disoriented as his eyes darted between the polished balustrades and sculpted plaster of the 1940s architecture. He snatched up his program and began to read as he noticed Stephen watching. A trim, blond fellow in a red sweater vest—not an usher—hovered angel-like next to him, as if the black guy had some sort of fatal disease and needed a caretaker.

Stephen sighed and relaxed when the lights dimmed.

The choir was composed of a wide selection of people who loved music but never had enough time to pursue it professionally. They were known as the Foothill Singers, Diane explained, and they were considered quite good. What they lacked in technical precision they made up for in enthusiasm and expression. They were housewives, doctors, electricians, piano tuners, secretaries, schoolteachers, students, and retirees. They had every imaginable figure, hair type, skin color, and facial shape. He loved them the second they stepped on stage, walking gracefully with a team instinct that you couldn't rehearse. It just happened over years of singing together.

They held their folders with appropriate reverence. Before the lights faded Diane mentioned that they were hardly all Christians: some were followers of Eastern mysticism, a couple of them were Mormons, many were agnostics, and a few were atheists. Maybe she thought it would bother him. But here, on the brink of the Christmas season, it didn't seem to matter. The magic of the music held them together; the discipline that Handel demanded was enough to hold any group of people together. You just couldn't sing *Messiah* and think about anything else.

Their quality was beyond anything he expected from an amateur group. Well, he hadn't been near the city long enough to realize that its artistic standard was beyond what he considered professional anyway.

The Wrong Side of Eternity

Diane had tried to tell him, but he wouldn't listen. Although she was far more cosmopolitan than he, she seemed to have lost her taste—or perhaps it was merely her sense of modesty—about the same time he found his faith. Inwardly he chided himself for being so ignorant, now that he really was a small fish in a big pond.

A hush fell over the audience just before the downbeat; the violins were superbly in tune and the conductor, a slight man, obviously in complete control.

"Comfort ye...comfort ye My people..."

He hadn't noticed the tenor soloist until the words drifted over him, a smooth silk sail made of pure sound. Stephen had never heard those words before, not like that. Not from a prophet. A prophet with honey-colored hair to match perfectly a honeyed voice, lilting and succulent. Clear desert honey, clean as light, or scented with jasmine, faint and exotic.

"God." Diane, too, was evidently impressed. "What a voice."

He agreed inwardly: *a voice to wake the dead.* Not a gong, ominously royal, but more like a mother's greeting on the morning after a bad fever. A voice you wanted to wake up to.

He resisted the temptation to grab his program and read about the musician who gathered up the empty spaces of the auditorium into the Holy of Holies with his solo. His mind played it over and over again so that by the time the intermission came, he hadn't really heard any of the others. When the lights rose, he thumbed through the little glossy booklet and found the list of performers. The head shot he recognized—the soloist attended an evening discussion group at Scholars.

Bryce Everett, tenor: Mr. Everett hails from Devonshire, England, where as a boy he sang in church choirs. His previous engagements with the Foothill Singers include solos in Haydn's *Creation* and Mendelssohn's *Elijah,* and with the Foothill Musical Theater Company, the roles of Skye Masterson *(Guys and Dolls)* and Jean Valjean *(Les Misérables).* Mr. Everett divides his time between

48

studying for his masters in music performance here at the university and working as choirmaster for Mercy Cathedral in San Francisco.

Bryce Everett, tenor. They failed to mention any connection with SBC. Perhaps it was a secret. Perhaps Mr. Everett was testing a call to the ministry and just audited courses, like Madeleine. Perhaps...But speculations could wait.

He must meet this Mr. Everett, the prophet.

Diane had slipped away to the refreshment table or to the ladies' room. Stephen looked around as if he had just woken from a deep dream. The lights were suddenly too bright, not matching the architecture. Something had happened to the room. People hovered in slow motion about him like drifting snowflakes. He shook himself and rose to stretch his legs. The black man at the end of the row hadn't moved. He sat staring at the floor, lost somewhere between this glorious musical taste of heaven and some hideous memory.

"Are you enjoying the performance?" Stephen ventured, as gently as he could.

"Pardon?" There was a slight accent, something like British.

"The singing. Are you enjoying it?"

"Yes, yes...I've never heard anything, ah, classical before. I'm not from here," he explained, distantly.

"Oh?" asked Stephen, sitting down again, curious enough to put off a trip to the men's room. A fellow stranger was welcome in this haute-couture world of the university auditorium. "Where are you from?"

He lowered his voice. "Uganda."

And what horrible thing happened to you there? Stephen didn't ask aloud.

The black man explained. "I'm here for studies, at the seminary."

"Ah." What could you say to such a shadow? The descriptions in *Newsweek* threw themselves back into the mainstream of his thoughts, and he pushed them violently aside. But curiosity overcame politeness. "What was your work in Uganda?"

49

"A schoolteacher," came the muffled reply. As if he was afraid he was being watched. "What about you?"

"Me? I'm studying too, at the bible college." He wondered if this guy was saved and figured he probably wasn't, not if he was at the seminary. He took a risk: "I want to be a pastor." Maybe it would lead to a deeper conversation, a chance to witness.

"You'll make a good one," the man answered, smiling and relaxing—or making an effort to smile and *appear* relaxed, Stephen couldn't tell which. He wasn't used to the manners of Africans. Cowboys' body language he could read, and Mexicans', and maybe one or two other American types. But not Ugandans. "You listen."

"Thank you," Stephen found himself saying, when the lights began to signal the end of intermission. He excused himself to walk up the aisle against the traffic to find Diane. He didn't want her to miss the second part of the program.

That's what he told himself later, anyway, when he was wide awake and the harrowed face of Geoffrey Mahoro intruded into his after-midnight thoughts.

7. AN ORTHODOX CHURCH, SUNDAY MORNING

The wooden church smelled at least a hundred years older than it really was. The gold paint was faded and peeling off altogether in some places; it reminded Madeleine of the dilapidated Russian synagogues following the Bolshevik Revolution. The stalls were taller than anything else she'd ever seen, built to support you, standing, through a wearying two or three hour service of the Divine Liturgy. Tiny tapering candles burned, set upright in giant ashtrays full of sand, and the too-fragrant smoke tickled her throat and threatened to drive her out of the holy space by making her cough aloud.

Madeleine stood quietly in the back, watching, making mental notes by the dozens and filing them away in her immaculate memory. She listened to the repetition of the Kyrie Eleison going past her in machine-gunfire succession; they couldn't seem to say it enough. The priests appeared and disappeared in the little doorway in the front, making their timed exits and entrances in the opening of the huge screen covered with icons piled three, four high. She laughed inwardly at such an inane, mindless form of 'Christian' worship. Religious Perverts, holding tenaciously to a form that had become extinct centuries ago, devoid of relevance.

She was glad she had thought to bring along her black shawl. It came in handy for blending in to this crowd full of old women, most of them looking like a funeral was the next thing on their agendas. During a long, tedious chant, she pulled out her dictation recorder from her pocket and turned it on, holding it to her lips in a demure pose of reverence as she made a few comments on the surroundings before tucking it back into her tapestry handbag. She looked around, wishing she could sit. Against the wall were some stalls with tiny seats built in, presumably to hold you up if you inadvertently fell asleep during the service. She crept over to one of these and with a delicate motion slowly settled onto the hard surface of the shelf.

A heavy velvet curtain opened, closed, and opened again, and at last an old priest stepped into the gap to hold up some bit of a sacrament. The long black cassock reminded her of gothic murder stories. His hair was stringy and white under his cylindrical hat, or cap, or whatever they called it. He peered out over thick glasses to spoon bread and wine into the open mouths of the old ladies; Madeleine thought of baby birds stretching upward to be fed. A bell rang, then there was some more chanting, and of a sudden—relatively speaking, it had all gone so slowly—the worshippers were slowly filing past her out the door.

She sighed and felt in her handbag for the keys to her car. *Orthodox, my eye.* Well, the English translation of the Divine Liturgy was all right, but the packaging it had been stuffed into was so ancient. So *old.* Who could go on living with a dead faith like that? But the women seemed happy enough, once they had kissed the icons good-bye and walked into the portico-laced courtyard, to savor the strong cups of coffee and sticky sweetbreads before heading home to prepare typical Greek delicacies like roast lamb or dolmades.

Madeleine tried to get an experiential angle on most of the denominations she felt compelled to counter. She had attended Pentecostal and Nazarene revivals, Roman Catholic weddings, Lutheran mixes of liturgy liberally sprinkled with modern language (which sounded like a lot of psychological rot to her), and feel-good Methodist services. She had endured a number of dry Presbyterian sermons, which were either shallow discussions of the sports page or commentaries on the personhood of the human Christ or contained quotes from Gandhi or other Religious Pagans. And she was ever so glad that she had been raised in a solidly Christian home, where she learned how to separate the good from the garbage at a tender age. How little people on the West Coast knew about serious matters! They *studied* back East, where she came from. That's why all the best schools were there. How did she ever get to a small-scale place like SBC? Well, they could learn something, lots of things, from someone of her caliber. Perhaps it was a mission field. She could return to the upper echelons another time.

She made a trip to the spotless, barren ladies' room to add some verbal notes to her recorder and make a short summary of the morning's experience. Then she straightened her black blazer, touched up her mascara, appraised herself in the mirror, and stepped out to politely greet a few Greek-speaking old ladies before walking smartly down the sidewalk to a lunch appointment.

Father Theodosius watched her go.

Whoever invented the term "the gentle sex" had obviously never met anyone like Madeleine Benson.

TWO WORLDS

It is usual for the Christian to be aware concurrently
of the presence of the never-fading celestial glory
and of the brooding cloud of death
hanging over the world…
The prayer throbbing within us sets us on
the frontier between two worlds,
the transient and the one to come.

—ARCHIMANDRITE SOPHRONY

8. SCHOLARS BIBLE COLLEGE

HE STARED AT THE DIAGRAMS on the blackboard. They were so tidy, so neat. They reminded him of his philosophy class at the community college. But this was a different scenario: the Biblical Model of Man. And the notes on the board bothered him.

Timidly, Stephen raised his hand. He was recognized by Professor Stuart.

"Excuse me, sir, but the models you've drawn…" His voice faded out to nothing.

"Yes, Mr. O'Connell?"

"They seem so, uh, flat. Two dimensional." The student in front of him turned around with raised eyebrows. Stephen cleared his throat. "I just thought, sir, that the Hebrew idea of a person—man—was a little more, uh, blended."

"Can you clarify your ideas, Mr. O'Connell, and articulate them a bit more concretely?"

"Well, it seems to me what you've got on the board, sir, is Platonism. Mind, will, emotions. Neat categories for the various bits of a man's soul. I don't find it when I read my bible, sir, I'm sorry to say. It doesn't look so, uh, *neat* to me."

"You've studied philosophy, in a secular institution." Sam's guess was dead on.

"Yes..."

"And Augustine, and Aquinas."

"A very little, sir, but I can't see how *any* of the models can be carried directly across to the scriptures. They are more, uh, three-dimensional." He noted a wry smile on the face of the teacher, and it gave him courage to continue. "You can cut and paste bible verses to support the Platonic model, among others, easily enough, but trying to build one directly from the word of God—well, sir, I don't think it would look like yours."

"Perhaps you would like to pursue your philosophical argument in a paper, Mr. O'Connell."

"I hardly think it's an argument yet. More of an observation."

The guy sitting in front of him rolled his eyes, and Professor Stuart resumed his lecture.

That afternoon there was great excitement in the quad, which used to be a parking lot until some wise board member saw a need for students to have space to sit and chat on campus. Students were setting up folding chairs for a presentation. It was a nice day, admitted Stephen, but presentations were usually held in the chapel or auditorium.

"What's the topic?" he asked.

"Haven't you seen the flyers? A couple of homos are coming over from the university. They say they're Christians, but we all know that's impossible. They're RPs of the first degree," Greg explained

Act I

between bites of his sandwich. He looked up to answer Stephen's expression of puzzlement. "Religious Prostitutes, this time. Sometimes it's Religious Pagan, sometimes it's Religious Pervert...it all depends on the context."

"Oh." *So that's why everyone's so nervous.* Homosexuals. He anticipated that once word got out, it would spread like wildfire. There would be pre-judgment from the student body and faculty at SBC. He felt his heart rate go up a notch, a big notch, as he recalled a stranger in a theater restroom, straightening Stephen's collar and lingering, commenting on his figure...How he had fled that place, could hardly remember what the second act of the play was about.

At 2:15 a bell rang, and pockets of men and women gathered to sit in the makeshift lecture space. Stephen opted to stand in the back, next to a young cypress tree. He picked that spot to see the reaction of the audience as much as the speakers. The dean announced the topic as "Alternate Lifestyles in our Community" and added a disclaimer that the speakers' views were not those of SBC, but that students would encounter all manner of lifestyles and beliefs in the world. He invited the students' polite attention and promised ample time for questions and comments following the presentation. He then introduced the guests only by their first names, Roger and Ben, university students studying theology and the liberal arts. Stephen noted that the dean put a slight emphasis on the word *liberal.*

The couple walked with confidence to a microphone set up for the purpose. One of them, Roger, looked vaguely familiar. Their presentation was polished and engaging; they alternated speaking after a paragraph or two to prevent boredom. Well, they would hardly have to do that to interest this audience. Stephen heard a guy in the last row whisper, "Who invited *them* here?" He didn't hear the answer but imagined that the invitation might have been issued by Professor Stuart, bridge builder. Or could it be that Bryce Everett was behind this dramatic act of hospitality? Nah—he would, as only an occasional guest, lack the needed influence on this campus.

As the speakers talked about gay life in different historical eras, the audience became subdued. The two men tried to reflect on the practice of homosexuality in the ancient world, the pagan world, and they admitted freely that there were some who still practiced that kind of abomination: selfish sex with strangers or slaves. Ben quoted the psychologist Adler, remarking on the possibility of thinly disguising accepted norms as the Truth: "'The truth is often a terrible weapon of aggression. It is possible to lie, and even to murder, for the truth.'"

At least ten students shook their heads.

When they began to share their own story, however, people began to fidget quietly. Pens emerged from purses and knapsacks, notes were scribbled on yellow pads. A guy two rows in front of Stephen was underlining a passage in his worn leather bible. The student council president was either grinding his teeth or clenching them; his jaw muscles twitched and bulged, and his arms were crossed against his chest. Stephen looked about and noted Madeleine standing too, but on the right side, where most of the women sat in well-groomed clusters. She looked, as always, calmly objective, measuring up potential opponents and capturing quotes in her amazing memory, to retrieve later in the form of verbal ammunition.

Roger explained that they were, and had always been, faithful partners, monogamous—that they knew God loved them and accepted them as they were. They fervently wished that all the children of God would do likewise, consider them fellow human beings in a fallen world, overcome historical prejudice to find fellowship with them beneath the cross of Christ...This last phrase met with a murmur throughout the audience; students exhaled in unbelief or disgust. Stephen noticed himself growing tense, and his thoughts turned inward. He'd encountered these reactions before: Weren't most male dancers gay? Weren't the arts and sexual preference intertwined? Was Stephen *okay*? Would he ever be tempted to experiment with his affections?

He combed through his list of friends, acquaintances, familiar faces for any sign of compromise, but nothing glared on his inner radar.

Then his mind wandered back to the present, where the audience was now pummeling the guests with questions and quotes from the Bible. He marveled at the men's grace in being so prepared for the assault, and their response: did not Jesus accept, even fellowship with those who knew they were not perfect, were so far from it that only God could overcome the gap? They reminded the audience that no conditions were given for baptism, other than belief in the Savior, period. Their faces stayed pleasant, but underneath the surface lay subtle lines of battle fatigue. The dean stepped in like a referee to blow a whistle, held up his hands to quiet the wound-up students, and offered a conciliatory but uncompromising prayer.

The audience rose to leave, still murmuring, but Stephen remained to watch the speakers go. They did not hold hands, but their steps were in sync. Roger and Ben kept their heads held up, but their sighs were visible even through their jackets.

"If a town does not accept you, wipe your feet as a testimony against them." The words from the gospel came clear into his head, drowning out the murmuring in the quad. Jesus had spoken them to the group of disciples he sent out to preach, cure, and cast out demons. *Two by two.* And in that moment, Stephen O'Connell wondered who was the sent, and who the mission, of this afternoon's exercise.

9. University Hospital, 3:30 p.m.

The West Coast was far more expensive a place to live than the dreary desert, where cups of coffee still went for twenty-five cents with free refills. Here you had to have *taste* or you couldn't get anywhere. Even Christians had to have *taste*. Stephen wore jeans once, on a Saturday, and didn't even get out the dorm door. And *taste* cost money.

He was doing a double shift and went in at three. He walked to the hospital these days; being in open air gave him time to think, time to adjust from one world to another. Very different worlds, each with an endless array of surprises or stumbling blocks. It depended on his mood, what he called these worlds. The evening staff was pleasant, and most of the frantic daytime treatments, lab draws, and transfers were winding down. Best of all, Ted wouldn't come on duty until eleven.

The hospital world was a messy one—there was no doubt about it. But it was full of fascinating people, like Green Thunder. She was a Sioux princess on the fourth floor who was somehow coping with stomach cancer. The nursing staff allowed her to smoke her pipe in her room. Judging by the acrid smell, he was sure it contained pot or peyote, but they explained that cultural values were much more respected by the administration these days—and besides, whatever it was kept the pain down and Green Thunder from living up to her name. *You should have seen her before,* they said.

You'd never get away with things like that in a hospital in Phoenix, thought Stephen.

He was paged to rehab, on the ground floor, where the physical therapists were winding down their day. A post-surgical patient needed wheeling back to his room upstairs; he weighed over two hundred pounds. At times like this, Stephen was thankful for his dance-borne fitness.

He was faster in answering the page than the regular afternoon orderly, getting there before he was actually needed. The patient still wobbled along the parallel bars, tubes dangling off him like fishing gear, when Stephen entered the PT department and looked around. The area was in dire need of a coat of paint or full remodel. The equipment looked donated, and the furniture moth-eaten. Obviously the PT department was not high on the priority list of University Hospital.

"A few more steps, Mr. Johnson, and then we'll get you back to bed. You're doing so much better today—it will really help to get those tubes out tomorrow."

The voice came from a young therapist who walked alongside the tottering man, minding his steps as she deftly kept the dangles out of his way. There was something remarkable about the timbre of her voice. Not fawning but respectful. And, hey, if she could respect Mr. Johnson in his feckless state and corpulent person, she might treat her boss like the king of France. He turned his gaze in her direction to see what went with the musical voice. She was small, taut like a gymnast, dwarfed by the patient but not appearing uncomfortable with the contrast. She had some sort of canvas belt around his ample waist, and her eyes were down, concentrating on his steps, although her head was up. Unself-conscious poise. What Stephen noticed most, though, was the red of her tied-back hair; it glowed like a mesquite ember, warmer by far than the fluorescent dinge of the lights overhead. It burned his vision with poetry:

O the sun flamed in her red, red hair
    and in her eyes danced stars of mirth,
Her body held the willow's grace
    and her feet scarce touched the springing earth...

The memory of his father's voice spouting Irish verse was interrupted by a splintering crack. The parallel bars shook and sundered at the corner, where they telescoped out from the base. Stephen rushed ahead, but no sprinter would have made it in time. Mr. Johnson uttered a cry of horror and went down like a beached whale. The PT's intention was to lower him gently to the ground, but the broken equipment had knocked her off balance too, and she ended up beneath him on the floor.

"Julie!" cried the department head, starting up from behind his desk where he had been writing the day's notes. Either a colostomy bag had burst or Mr. Johnson was shocked into incontinence, because the next thing that hit Stephen was the stench of human waste, the kind that comes from a hospital diet.

The junior therapist groaned from underneath the foul heap. Her fair hand gripped the broken metal bar, holding it away from both the patient and herself.

"God," she grunted. She paused to catch her breath. "Pardon my language, Mr. Johnson," she added, propping herself up on one free elbow so she could breathe better. "Anybody out there care to help us up?"

The Wrong Side of Eternity

The senior PT, a large African American man in his thirties, knelt down to assess the situation.

"Stupid maintenance department," he grumbled. "You hurt?"

"No."

Stephen stepped forward with a wheelchair to help him lift and transfer Mr. Johnson, leaving the soiled Julie on the floor staring at the broken bar.

"It's rusted through." Then, in a more irritated tone, "I thought you had asked for new equipment."

"I wrote three requisitions to replace it all, goddammit, and went to the office in person only last week. 'Budget limitations,' they told me."

Stephen was buckling a lap belt atop the clean towel he'd grabbed to place across Mr. Johnson's thighs; he fumbled twice to adjust its length before it would connect.

Julie rose to her feet, laying the rusty metal on the floor. "You won't mind if I go for a quick shower before I leave today, will you, Bob?"

"Not on your life, Miss Burns. Take your time." He stifled a giggle, and so did she. "In fact," he called after her, "claim some overtime— you've still got notes to finish." Stephen felt he was intruding and whisked Mr. Johnson out the door.

"Shit," the patient said, as the elevator doors closed.

The nurses on med-surg naturally asked what happened, and he told them in the most sober tones he could. "Poor Mr. Johnson!" they exclaimed, but no one blamed the PTs. They knew the state of affairs when it came to hospital equipment. They'd had experiences of their own.

He went to the staff restroom to use some of the blue soap; it worked so well to overcome stink. He recalled the color of her eyes, a brilliant green-brown, like the bottom of some warm pool in an enchanted forest. And the words came flooding back to his memory, like a song.

and in her eyes danced stars of mirth,
    Her body held the willow's grace
and her feet scarce touched the springing earth.

The night spread its star-tasseled shawls,
    The river gossiped to its stones,
She sat beside the leaping fire
    and sang the songs the tinker owns...

The songs as old as turning wheels
    and sweet as bird-throats after rain,
Deep wisdom of the wild wet earth;
    the pain of joy, the joy of pain.

I'm going nuts, thought Stephen. *I never liked it when Da quoted poetry. I never learned any; I didn't want to.* He dried his hands and slipped out into the corridor, checking his watch.

Very late that night, he was called back to rehab for a code blue. They weren't supposed to keel over, not in Rehab; they were supposed to be getting better, ready for discharge. Stephen was the first to arrive; it seemed most of the staff had gone to dinner. A petite nurse stepped eagerly aside for him to do chest compressions, but he asked her to continue until he got a board to put under the patient; the foam pad covering the mattress was making all the work ineffective. It took him almost a minute to find what he wanted; nobody in Rehab expected codes, so equipment was not at hand like it would be upstairs.

"What's her name?" he asked, as he slid the backboard into place, took his position, and began bearing down. The patient was such a frail thing, the ribs were so brittle. He heard two snap even before the nurse could reply.

"Constance. She didn't have a no-code written. We had no choice but to call one." She was apologizing, but Stephen smiled graciously. At least she had a conscience; some of the others might have just ignored the situation until it was far too late. Which, when he thought about it later, may have been the kinder thing to do, really. Constance's body was still warm.

"I'm so sorry, Constance," he said to the body, feeling another rib break. He tried to lighten up the compressions, but it was hopeless. The

The Wrong Side of Eternity

airway had collapsed by the time the ER team arrived, and they gave up easily. Anyway, she was old.

The ER doctor pulled the sheet over her head and got out his pen to note the time of death. Everyone stepped out of the room, except Stephen, who stayed a moment longer. He met a familiar face when he re-entered the hallway. Father Theodosius. Either God or one of the nurses had alerted him to the death. Stephen burned with shame that his compressions had been so hard, so he faltered to find a diversion.

"Was she a parishioner of yours, Father?" he asked, the title coming easy to his lips. The priest was elderly but hardly frail. He looked like a very trim Santa Claus. It was easy to call this man father, in spite of Stephen's new Protestant orientation.

"You could say that." He stopped before the door, turning back toward Stephen. "Although she wasn't Orthodox."

Orthodox, so that was it. The reason for the strange costume. No one talked about the Orthodox, neither the Catholics of his past nor the Protestants of his present. It was as if they didn't exist. A sting of curiosity prodded Stephen, and he ventured to ask.

"Could I come to visit your congregation sometime, Father?"

"There's no need, my son," said the priest, smiling. "They're here."

"Who?" He hadn't seen any Orthodox labels on the charts he'd read.

"The dying. They are my congregation." With that, he stepped inside to administer rites that no one else would.

Stephen stared a second, then looked up at the clock. Check-out time; dawn had caught him unawares. He would just have time to shower at the dorm and change his clothes before getting to his class on expository preaching.

10. THE NEIGHBORHOOD, THE FOLLOWING SATURDAY

Stephen needed some air and headed toward the university campus. "The Impossible Dream" played in his head while he jogged the undulating streets of the foothills. He always used some song lyric to regulate his breathing. Having Don Quixote's quest in his thoughts made him feel more at home in this place where you didn't make eye contact unless you either knew somebody or really wanted to. The air was heavy here, not dry like the desert. In the summer, that would be oppression, pure and simple. But in early March it was a cooling balm. A hint of spring was in the air, the chill of winter waning. He wore baggy sweats these days. Well, he had ever since he came to this damp, coastal climate. He had only tried running in shorts once, the first day, and almost died from embarrassment when someone wolf-whistled at him, and when he arrived back at the dorm, he was shivering from the cold.

Too early for study, exercising students ricocheted from garden path to coffee shop wearing everything imaginable. Here a miniskirt, there a track suit, and over there a shiny pair of tight black bicycle shorts.

They wouldn't survive ten minutes wearing that in his home town.

There was an awful lot to think about. Class lectures at SBC, getting a call from a friend of Professor Stuart's about playing *Academic Festival Overture* in a university orchestra concert two weeks from now, catching a glimpse of Bryce Everett seated at the back of an evening lecture and feeling his heart thump against his rib cage: *like a child in the presence of a saint*, Stephen thought. The splash of a puddle beneath his running shoes yanked him back to the present.

He passed a stone church neatly set on a grassy corner. It reminded him of pictures he'd seen of churches in England, sturdy Norman bulwarks set amid crumbling churchyards where tombstones tilted at asymmetrical angles. Ready for a breather, he stopped to read the sign: ST. SIMEON'S EPISCOPAL CHURCH. M. WHITMAN, RECTOR.

Something drew him in. He nervously ascended the low concrete steps and found the city ebbing away behind him as he entered the quiet, well-kept gardens of the courtyard. There was an aesthetic here he hadn't felt—or was it the quiet he hadn't heard?—since his childhood wanderings through the plaza in front of a deserted southwestern

The Wrong Side of Eternity

cathedral, though on a very small scale. The architecture was, well, cool—beckoning. Soothing, in a way.

The building was, to his amazement, open at this early hour. It smelled nice inside, a blend of fresh-cut flowers and clean carpet, with a faint suggestion of seasonal incense. A skirted figure wearing a sweater with the sleeves pushed up was arranging a bouquet on the altar table. She looked average and was taking her time. Stephen felt a surprising and urgent need to chat, so he carefully wiped his feet on the mat at the threshold and walked with a soft step down the aisle.

When the woman, maybe in her early forties, turned, he stood face to face with a clerical collar. *Dear God,* he thought with terror. *She's a priest.* He wanted to turn and run—or laugh and assault her with an admiring kiss, he couldn't tell which.

"Hello," she said, breaking the ice.

"I'm looking for, uh, Reverend Whitman."

"I'm Reverend Whitman." She wiped her hands on her woolen skirt and stepped down from the carpeted platform, offering him her hand. Most graciously. "Margaret."

He had this impression of a queen approaching her gardener with a friendly hello: she was tailored, elegant, and unassuming. He felt like bowing but stood there gawking instead, a silly smile on his face. "I was just running past, and the church reminded me of something I saw in a history book somewhere." He took his eyes off her to admire the liturgical artwork of the windows, the light-colored stone, the design of the sacred space.

She smiled and guessed, "Are you a student?"

"Well, yes. At the bible college." He waited for a reaction and got none.

"Would you like a cup of tea? I'm ready for one about now." She glanced at her wristwatch. "And there's just time before my morning bible study group."

Stephen had never experienced such a bible study: people of wildly differing ages and backgrounds actually talked to one another. They shared

Act I

their thoughts, their reactions, their feelings, and Rev. Whitman—everyone called her Margaret—didn't correct anyone. She just guided them back to the passage at hand and asked questions. That therapist from the hospital, Julie Burns, was there, the only person who didn't say a whole lot. She sat in the back corner, a slight wrinkle just above her eyes, as if she considered every word before either rejecting it or letting it take hold of her. Perhaps she applied as she listened, comparing her life's experience with the dialogue. She seemed a very practical sort. He was sure she didn't recognize him; she hardly ever looked up.

After an hour, the assortment of folks glided off to their respective lives. *Probably interesting lives*, mused Stephen, reflecting on some of the comments they'd made.

The morning melted into afternoon. An hour in the library, a midday nap. For some reason he wanted to avoid the chatter of the dorms, so he went outdoors again—this time bundled into a flak jacket and scarf. It dawned on him that he'd missed lunch altogether, and he suddenly felt hungry. His wallet held two dollars. Just enough for a croissant and a cup of coffee at the little shop down the block, flanked by cast-iron lions and a lamp post. He went inside and ordered at the counter.

Sam Stuart sat at a table with his back to the window, soaking up the sparse sunlight. He immediately caught Stephen's eye and motioned him over, wiping crumbs of rye bread from the corner of his mouth. Stephen collected his food and joined him.

"Take a seat. Now's a perfect chance to respond to the question you asked in class—informally, okay?"

Stephen nodded, staring into his cup as cream swirled into the coffee.

"You went a bit beyond their ken, Stephen. They *expect* two-dimensional models."

"It was a simple observation. I didn't mean to cause offense."

"Of course not. You just come from a different world is all. Philosophy is tough for people who've been brought up breathing organized

The Wrong Side of Eternity

religion. Because you're new, you ask things they've never thought of."
He suddenly smiled. "You shatter their assumptions, because you're
growing out of your own." He fidgeted with his pickle. "Some of them
won't like it."

"I always thought college was for people who want to discover
answers."

"Yes, you think right. It is. I'm afraid some colleges take a more didactic approach, though. The answers come from the books and the
professors. It's easier that way."

"Yes, that's how it was in catechism classes, too. I was too poor to go
to Catholic school, so I had to attend those propaganda meetings in my
free time."

"Did you get anything out of them?"

"They bored me stiff. The priest knew everything. He didn't like
anyone asking questions."

"Well, some of the SBC profs might not like it, either."

"You're kidding. They're committed Christians. They should
understand."

"They're *people*, too, Stephen. They don't always act like wise rabbis
grooming disciples. It's easier to formulate 'objective' exams. The kind
you can grade by scanning multiple choice forms into a machine." He
drummed his fingers on the worn wooden tabletop. "Write them down,
all your questions. They'll gel into some really great thoughts. But if I
were you, I'd keep them separate from your class notes."

"Yeah?"

"Yeah. Put them in a journal or something." Professor Stuart—
Sam—drained his teacup and climbed into his leather-patched blazer,
then hopped up to open the door. Stephen realized he had somehow
burst the label of first-year student. And that Sam liked him.

"Do you keep a journal, Professor?" he asked gingerly, as they stepped
out onto the sidewalk.

"Absolutely. And I keep it locked in a drawer," he whispered, then
winked, before he dashed off looking at the sky.

66

Act I

Stephen sighed and looked both directions, like a good boy, before he crossed the busy street. And now the evening was closing in on him from every direction. He would have to head back soon to meet the strict Saturday-night curfew. SBC didn't want any of its students falling asleep in church on Sunday morning.

Instead of turning up the hill toward SBC, though, he went the opposite direction. He needed some space to think. A journal. Somewhere to stuff his thoughts. He didn't have any more money with him; the pastry had consumed his day's supply, so he couldn't buy a blank book now. But he walked past the bookshops all the same, glancing into their mirrored windows and getting a whiff of their musty insides, where antique treasures hid on the shelves amid popular novels and out-of-print textbooks. He walked past the library and the public square, where people got off buses to enter that bastion of knowledge and accomplishment, the university. He walked right to the edge of the hill upon which the International Theological Seminary was built, and there he stopped. People huddled in their coats and hunkered along, keeping their eyes on the path instead of all the budding tree branches over their heads, or engaged in brisk, pedantic conversations that left him stymied as to their meaning. So many big words. He was after something simple, like God.

Yeah, right.

11. CENTER STREET CONVENIENCE MART, MONDAY, 6:00 P.M.

Fair weather or foul, Julie Burns loved walking home from work. Taking in the fresh air deep, deeper, then blowing it out with puffed cheeks: it helped her unload the day. Most seasons, she would wear a track suit underneath her clinic coat and jog the six blocks to her apartment. Climbing the hill left her winded but ready to relax.

It was cold out and starting to rain, so she stopped at the convenience store to get a cup of tea. The banks of industrial lights assaulted

The Wrong Side of Eternity

her senses, but she headed straight to the hot-water carafe, filled a large Styrofoam cup, and selected an herbal berry packet. Just the smell of the tea bag made her smile. She plunked it in and fixed a plastic lid to the top, wished the depressed clerk a nice evening as she paid, and turned to go.

An African American man stood with his back to her, staring at the newspaper. He was still as a statue and blocking the door. Not wanting to frighten him, she touched him lightly on the arm. He spun and faced her; she'd never seen such pallor on a person of color. Thin but well groomed, barely older than she. Gently, she steered him to the side, so other harried people could rush in and out, most of them heading home. He moved like a zombie.

It was then she looked at the newspaper. The headline read: LYNCHING AT SEVENTH STREET BRIDGE HORRIFIES CAMPUS. A black-and-white photo showed the silhouette of someone dangling from a rope.

"Sir," she addressed him. His eyes met hers, dull and scared.

"They are here. They have come all this way for us." An African accent.

The lights were too bright; he needed some privacy. She led him out the door—he was so docile—away from the newspapers and into the twilight. A sign read NO LOITERING, so she quickly scanned the vicinity and saw a café across the street with outdoor tables under an awning. Empty, of course. All the customers were inside, taking shelter. She led him there. The busy traffic provided just enough background noise to shield their conversation.

"I'm Julie," she said. "I work at the hospital. And you are?"

"David Orombi, madame...miss. I am a student at the university."

"You're from Africa."

He nodded.

"I spent my early years in Cameroon—I heard the music in your voice." She could just about hear his thoughts, judging from the look on

Act I

his face: *Music? Most people can hardly understand me, they say my accent is so thick.*

"What did you mean, what you said in there?" She noticed he had no raincoat and was beginning to shiver, so she handed him her cup. He took it gingerly, smiling his thanks, and looked about him warily, answering in a low voice.

"Do you know what is happening in Uganda?"

"A little. Did it happen to you? Your family?"

"I had to leave…they were killing many educated people."

"I'm glad you were able to get away."

"Yes. But when I saw that picture…"

She waited, while the rain began pelting the canvas cover above their heads. "Yes?"

"They have come to track us down."

"Who?"

"The president's agents…They do not want us to talk, to tell people here what is really going on."

She shivered inside her rain poncho. He did not have the look of the paranoid. Something about that photo *spoke* to him.

"They tried to make it look like a racial crime, but it is not. It is so public. It is meant as a warning…"

"Wait here. I'll be right back." Julie dashed back to the store and bought a paper. She returned to their table and found the article, scanning it in the dim light.

The victim had no identification on him…police suspect gang-related activity…He had unusual scars near his eyes…Seven knife wounds included deep cuts to the genitals…

"Do you have a safe place to live?" she asked.

"I live in the student dorm, the one near the sciences building. I'm studying physics," he explained.

69

The Wrong Side of Eternity

"You need to contact the campus police and let them know that anytime you are walking by yourself, you must have an escort. And you mustn't go out alone."

"You believe me?"

"Yes, yes I do." She wondered what she could do, now, for him. *If I were in his shoes, I would be terrified.* "Come home with me, it's only another block from here. I'll get you a taxi...you won't have to talk at all."

She stood up to go; he followed. Her conscience pricked at her, with her father's voice, to be careful. But she knew this man wasn't lying. She'd lived in Africa just long enough to know.

Julie took his arm and made him bend his elbow; she made a pretense of flirting with him all the way home. Thankfully, she could tell that he knew it was merely a ruse and, despite his tension, he smiled and played along.

He stood inside her door, a puddle growing at his feet. He apologized. She shook her head, smiled, and searched her closet, found a heavy canvas shirt, large enough to put over her clothes for chores... perfect. He took it with a look of tenderness, putting it on as she phoned the All-American Taxi. When she hung up the phone, he began to shake. She gestured toward a wooden kitchen stool and he obediently sat down.

"Just breathe, Mr. Orombi. Breathe slowly," she ordered, wrapping her arms around him. He obeyed and let her embrace him—something he probably never would have done if he were in Uganda. A *muzungu* hugging him...She knew what a scandal it would cause! A minute passed, and of a sudden she could hear the ticking of her kitchen clock. Two horn honks summoned them to the door. She exited with him, back in character, holding onto his arm. When they got to the taxi, she opened the back door.

"Hey, my sweetie's just had three teeth pulled, so take him to the dorm on Northern, okay? Here's enough for fare..." She handed the driver a ten dollar bill.

Act I

"And hurry, before he starts bleeding again. Bye, hon. I'll see you tomorrow. Get some ice on that." She leaned in and kissed him on the cheek, then stood back to wave them off.

Dear God, she prayed. *Keep him safe. Please.*

12. SCHOLARS BIBLE COLLEGE, WEDNESDAY MORNING

It was time for chapel, and the class flowed out the door. Stephen hurried across the walkway to hop up the concrete stairs, three at a time, to get to the piano before the leaders arrived. He opened his thick green folder and scanned the order of service before easing into a series of arpeggios based loosely on "When I Survey the Wondrous Cross" and glancing around as the students found their seats. Bryce Everett, did he ever come to chapel? Or did he only audit Contemporary Concerns on Tuesday nights, as the dean had mentioned when Stephen asked? He should sing a solo here sometime. *I wonder if I could be any good accompanying someone like that?*

The suave worship leader stepped up to the podium, and Stephen wound down his prelude with an elongated chord that invited a hush into what was now considered sacred space. He waited patiently through the introduction to the day's theme, but one announcement from the dean got his attention: three weeks from now, all students should avail themselves of an opportunity to hear a preacher in exile, a certain Festo Kivengere from Uganda. He'd be at Mercy Cathedral over in the city on Wednesday evening, and at Foothills Community Church the following Sunday. The dean was careful to explain that although the African bishop would be at the cathedral, he was a staunch evangelical whose preaching crossed denominational lines. Stephen wrote down the time on a receipt he found in his pocket. Then, the wind-up pitch (it all reminded him of baseball, somehow) into the next hymn, and he lifted his hands to play. His peripheral vision caught the appraising eye of Madeleine, clipboard in hand, half way back… There were three verses

The Wrong Side of Eternity

in this hymn; he could do some nice counterpoint for the second, and full chording, the way they liked it, for the final.

"Like a river glorious is God's perfect peace," they dutifully sang. He did a slight ritardando and crescendo into the chorus: "Stayed upon Jehovah, hearts are fully blessed; finding, as He promised, perfect peace and rest." Some advanced students smirked within his peripheral vision; they knew it wasn't biblically correct. There was no such word as "Jehovah," one of them had explained to him one day. It was a corruption of the Hebrew, a mongrel word that never belonged in an English translation of the Bible. Those religious perverts the Jehovah's Witnesses had it all wrong, as usual...

He forced himself back into the spirit of the song and went up an octave for the second verse, adding a touch of filigree for the intimacy that was there.

"Hidden in the hollow of His precious hand..."

A hollowed hand that held the ravine of a wound, a nail wound that would never fully close. A ragged scar that you could put your finger into. *A wound you could hide in,* hinted a whispered voice from the caverns of his memory, when the world ran you into the ground. He recognized it at last: the Irish voice of some effeminate, romantic priest who wept at the oddest places in Mass. When he was eleven, he'd heard that. Serving at the altar in a boy-sized robe. "Not a shade of hurry touch the spirit there..."

He finished with a flourish and sensed approval from the corner, where his glance met the steady gaze of Madeleine Benson. Then he wondered who he was really playing for after all.

He was glad the piano wasn't on the platform, so he didn't have to change seats; he wanted to be ready to play as the preacher finished, and he did his best to concentrate on the talk—they didn't call it a sermon, not for chapel, but that's what it was.

Holy Week was coming up, warned the speaker, except that for the *real* Christian, every week is holy week. For the *real* Christian, he said, Jesus hung on the cross framed by memory every hour of every day, calling sinners to himself. Exalted now above the heavens, he called still from the shadow of the cross. He called across the centuries, across the false measures of human time, across the vain liturgies of hypocritical worship. He called through the lives and the words of his faithful followers, who cherished his memory over every life and every love.

The preacher stopped to mop his forehead, then went on, on into the sweat and agony of Jesus's selfless passion, on into the cold judgment of a Roman governor against a man he thought was a misguided Jew upsetting the religious leaders of the day. On into the cries of some poor women, who didn't have a clue as to who he really was. They could only weep. "Women can be like that," the preacher said in a brief aside, dramatic, "bemoaning things they'll never understand."

Stephen thought suddenly of his own mother, fingering her rosary on Ash Wednesday, tears in her eyes and staring beyond the huge crucifix that hung above the altar. His thoughts drifted toward the cool-headed Madeleine, what her reaction might be to the preacher's comment.

If Jesus hangs always in our memories, he asked his heart, *why do some people so hate the crucifix?*

Why did they call it an idol? They despised anything even remotely Catholic. None of his dorm mates had even heard of the Second Vatican Council! And they dismissed imagination even more, even though the preachers heaped piles of combustible fuel on top of it, smothering it into red-hot flame. Stephen tried, fought, to keep the words from getting to him. He felt angry, invaded, hot. Something horrible had happened, and it never should have. It had to do, somehow, with him.

The preacher lowered his voice now and beckoned to his well-trained congregation to respond to that anguished call of God. To give their lives afresh to the one who never gave up, not for anything, to see them carried safely over the turbulent, waters of sin into the Father's arms. It was a splendid performance. Not prophecy, perhaps, like Bryce's singing had been, but it worked.

It worked too well on Stephen.

He took the cue to begin playing softly, caressing the preacher's words with an undercurrent of tenderness; he played to evoke feeling,

The Wrong Side of Eternity

desire. Desire crept out from between the keys of the piano to resonate through his fingers. A current crept up his arms and numbed his shoulders; it stung the muscles of his cheeks and salted his eyes with tears. The tempo grew slower, slower, sinking down into the warm dark of somewhere beyond reckoning.

Madeleine sat erect, willing him to pick it up, to keep going. A good performer should be able to do that—even though true worship was nothing so cheap as a mere performance. Her manicured fingers gripped the clipboard with the details of next week's chapel schedule on it, until her knuckles went white. *Don't just sit there, Stephen, you idiot.* Her directed energy did no good.

Several professors glanced warily at one another when the pianist stopped playing, and more crossed their legs the other direction when they heard him sob. Stephen missed the next cue, an announcement for a victory hymn designed to rouse the listeners back onto their feet and out into the world to proclaim the good tidings of the glorious gospel. He just sat there, shaking, his hands covering his eyes, tears dripping onto the keyboard.

What relief Madeleine felt as Professor Stuart walked up the aisle from way in the back to tap Stephen on the shoulder and guide him off the bench to a waiting chair. At someone's signal, a less-accomplished pianist slid in and picked up where he'd left off.

Madeleine was the first one out the door, shaking her head in embarrassment. He was one excellent hymn player. Heck, he was *good;* he could do it better than anybody—even in the East—and now he wouldn't be invited back to play for chapel. *What a dirty, rotten shame.*

13. INTERNATIONAL THEOLOGICAL SEMINARY

Roger found Geoffrey practically dozing over a pile of textbooks in the seminary's vast underground library. He tapped him on the shoulder and gestured 'Come with me.' Geoffrey shook his head and blinked, then rose to follow him up the stairs.

Once they had reached the open air of the courtyard, Geoffrey was fully awake. The tops of the skyscrapers were poking through the blanket of fog across the bay; a reprieve from rain gave the air a deceptive promise of summer. Roger was buying tea at the kiosk. The Ugandan closed his eyes and drank in the smells. He kept his eyes closed as he reminisced.

"It is like home, except there are odours missing: the smoke of poor charcoal, the mixture of smells from the market, the dust." He opened his eyes to see Roger leaning against the retaining wall, smiling at him, then handing him the steaming cup. Lots of milk and sugar, like the chai from home. "You have been so kind to me. How you welcomed me here, that first day…"

"Trite as it sounds, it is not so hard when you know how kind God is."

"How do you know this, my friend?"

"Books and books about it, and no one can describe the delicious feel of forgiveness."

At this Geoffrey merely smiled. *Would that it were so simple.* If he were back home, he might be accosted at night, have his ears or nose cut off. Or worse. And then? Would he be able to forgive those who committed atrocities, sometimes in the name of justice?

"I'm going to a new church across the bay," announced Roger. "They've asked me to help with preaching."

"That is wonderful! And you are such a fine preacher…"

"But?" asked Roger.

"But you have an even more wonderful voice for singing. You should use that too."

"I plan to. I take voice lessons after church. But music is my second love." *Or third,* thought Roger. *Geoffrey doesn't need to know everything.*

"What sort of church is this?"

"It is a welcoming church. It welcomes everyone, no matter where you come from, or what color you are, or what kind of lifestyle you have, or how much money you have in your pocket...I needed that kind of church."

"So what kind of preaching will they be wanting from you there?"

"Same as anywhere: love God because he loved you first, sin is bad, love your neighbor."

"You are good at that, Roger. Loving your neighbour."

"Yeah? You're not so bad at it yourself." And he clapped the African headmaster on the back.

"Anyone is welcome?"

"Yes, anyone."

"The 'fruits'?"

Roger laughed outright. "Fruits, nuts...all are welcome. This is California, my friend, the land of fruits and nuts—but even more than that, it is the kingdom of God."

"I would like to go with you sometime."

"Please do. It will be a change from here, you understand...they welcome *everyone*."

"I understand. I will come with an open mind and probably weep." It might be a taste of heaven. If not, it would be a wake-up call of some sort. Roger left him wondering, and Geoffrey savored the hot, sweet tea before descending into the labyrinth of the library again.

14. ST. SIMEON'S CHURCH, RECTOR'S OFFICE

Stephen fidgeted a little on the swivel chair, hoping Rev. Margaret didn't notice, while steam rose from his mug of herbal tea. Pachelbel's *Canon in D* whispered against the muted walls, drowning out the traffic noises that drifted over the hedge. The small talk was over.

"I know you're grilled regularly at SBC, so I won't treat you like a target—or an adversary in debate!" She smiled, and he relaxed a little, hugging the warm ceramic cup between his palms. "So what did you wish to see me about? Something specific?"

Act I

"Sure," he answered, trying to conjure up his practiced opening lines. He realized then that no one had uttered the magic words, "Shall we open with a word of prayer?" It sort of bothered him—and sort of excited him. This was new territory. "Reverend Margaret, sometimes I'm afraid."

"Good."

He braced himself for further probing. But there was none. Only the balm of measured music and, far in the distance, an ambulance siren.

"What do I *do* about it?"

"Do?" She laughed. "Well, what do you *do* about it now?"

He swallowed and furrowed his brow. "I recall that verse about perfect love casting out fear and pray that God would grow me in that kind of love."

"And your fear goes away."

"Uh, not really."

"You mean, it doesn't work? At least, not as quickly as you'd like it to."

"Yeah, something like that."

"You get afraid again."

"Yeah." There. He'd admitted it.

"Maybe you're being asked to walk *through* the fear, face it, rather than wait for it to go away or head in the opposite direction."

"Wouldn't that be like courting temptation?"

"Are fear and temptation the same thing?"

No, answered Stephen inwardly. Then why did he behave as if they were? Were people always—ever—afraid of what tempted them? If someone could actually learn to be afraid of that, maybe they would avoid it...

"Stephen?"

"Oh. No, I don't think so. If they were, it would be easy to conquer temptation."

"It's never easy." But she said it comfortably, not as a rebuke but as someone who knew, someone who had fought lots of battles in that

77

The Wrong Side of Eternity

arena. She sipped from her cup; it was a delicate thing, from Limoges or somewhere. "The psalmist admitted to being afraid. It drove him to trust. I don't recall the fear vanishing, from his point of view, but he somehow got beyond it."

"Can I have a reference for that?" Thirsty now, he leaned forward.

"Gosh, I'm bad at references. Let me check the concordance…" She stood and searched the bookshelf behind her. It took her a moment. Apparently she didn't consult the concordance often enough to know its exact resting place. And that, to his delight, didn't even bother him. *Canon* swelled and finished during the lull. She found a reference, then pulled out some modern translation of the bible from the laden shelves. "Okay, how about this: Psalm fifty-six, verse three: 'What time I am afraid, I will trust in thee.' Is that relevant?"

"Very."

"There're lots more like it. Psalm three seems to say that fear is really unnecessary if it immobilizes you, while anger is, well, better somehow."

He understood that she was still "in process" herself, and he liked that quality of Margaret's. "That's enough for me to chew on. Thank you."

She smiled. "Anything else?"

"Yeah." He squirmed a little. "I sort of fell apart, playing in chapel the other day."

"How so?"

"I just *felt* it, Reverend Margaret, the Passion stuff. I couldn't play."

"What was more embarrassing, Stephen—the intensity of the emotion or letting down on the performance?"

He looked at her with wide eyes.

"Ah." She smiled again. "Here's an analogy for you: when a football quarterback is sacked during a play, is he kicked off the team?"

"No," answered Stephen, hesitantly, for he was not an avid follower of the game. "It would just show a lack of defense, his own team failing to protect him."

78

Act I

"You mean, he's not the only person on the team?" she asked mischievously.

He saw where this was leading. "I take myself way too seriously."

"Yes, you do—but you also take God seriously. How different the entire world would be, if the crucifixion actually *meant* something to us."

"That's comforting, Reverend Margaret. Thank you...Is there, uh, anything else you want me to read?"

"You mean like homework?"

"Yeah."

"Are you kidding? You've got so many thoughts whirling around in that head of yours that the last thing on earth you need is more home-work. On second thought, how about a walk in the park, around sunset tonight?" She looked up at his puzzled face. "Sometimes a change of scenery does wonders."

He nodded.

"Did you want to close with prayer?" she asked.

"Why not?"

"Fine." And without closing her sparkling gray eyes, she glanced through the window at the mottled shadows of the tree beyond it. "Gracious God, thank you for such a glorious day. Kindly guide these humble sinners of yours—both of us—in our search for you. Amen."

He rose, almost laughing, and took her beautiful hand in a quick clasp of gratitude. Then he walked out the office door into the alcove, feeling just like he did when his little Mexican mother paid him a compliment.

Just like that.

EVASION

As long as a person can be categorized and explained,
his actions can be anticipated and dismissed.

—DAN B. ALLENDER

15. UNIVERSITY AUDITORIUM, 6:00 P.M. TUESDAY

HE'D LEFT THE GREENING OF the late afternoon, entering the auditorium
from the stage door. Stephen always liked to arrive early. He told himself that it was on account of his heightened sense of responsibility—he
knew some of the bizarre things that could go wrong: a tympani foot
slipping off the platform, a cable snapping in the middle of a long roll.
Even though it was only a rehearsal, he wanted to make sure everything
was set, tuned, positioned right. He wanted to make a good first impression so as to be invited back.

But the lodestone of his early arrival was the room itself. A light,
airy room with more an atmosphere of theater than auditorium: light,
well planned. The walls rose white—or perhaps a gentler shade of
ivory or marshmallow—to a high-paneled ceiling of rose-tinted wood
with a glimmer of sparkle. The lights, tucked into canisters flush with
the paneling, were an integral part of the décor and didn't detract
from the airiness above. A heavy short curtain above the stage area

Act I

hid floodlights suspended from scaffolding, those intense colors that made musicians and actors sweat even on wintry afternoons.

Stephen drank in the smells of wood polish, violin resin, and trumpet-valve oil mingled with a clean hint of someone's aftershave. The scents weren't distinct, even very noticeable: they were just part of the room, shadows of the music played there, soaked into the thick curtains and the upholstery of the metal seats.

The conductor would not arrive for half an hour yet, so Stephen busied himself with equipment. He passed a tall, gaunt gentleman, sagged in a front seat with his ankle draped on his knees, his arms dangling from the wooden armrests at either side. The man looked as if he wanted a cigarette, or a drink, or both. He didn't return Stephen's cheerful attempt at a greeting.

Stephen met the other percussionist in the hallway, struggling to keep a door open while pulling a xylophone through. He was the one who had gotten Stephen this job: the usual drummer, a self-styled tympani "expert," had absolutely no ear for pitch, he'd said. Together they made the short trip from music room to auditorium many times until their territory was staked out, sufficiently compact but containing the necessary space to move silently and quickly between instruments unimpaired. Both feared the percussionist's nightmare of stumbling between the chimes and the suspended cymbal right in the middle of Bach's *B Minor Mass*. The drummer, a bit fidgety, decided to take a brisk walk: it was, he said, his habit. Probably needed a smoke.

After comparing the piano to his pitch pipe and doing an initial tuning of the tympani, Stephen sat to enjoy the escape from the mad rushing home of all sorts of tired people outside, hurrying to beat the spring rainstorm in the gray light of dusk.

A quarter of an hour later, he sauntered up the aisle to the men's room. When he returned, the young harpist was trying to negotiate a path through the stage, around the wind players' platforms. An elderly man toiled to roll her canvas-covered instrument behind her. *A day late and a dollar short*, thought Stephen, who hurried forward to help. He

81

cleared away two black music stands, top heavy with their clipped-on lights, before taking over the harp itself from this perspiring father or uncle, and carefully rolling it into place.

"My arm thanks you, Dad—and you too," said the girl—*No*, Stephen corrected himself—*young woman*. Or perhaps not so young: one couldn't generally find a good harpist among undergraduates. Lots of makeup. She embraced the older man before dismissing him and then cast another grateful smile on Stephen. She distracted herself over the meticulous tuning of the myriad strings hanging, like threads from a weaver's loom, from the curved arch of the harp's towering wooden neck. He wanted to greet her more formally but could not engage her eyes. In spite of the stage lights, she wore long sleeves—maybe a bit bulky on the left upper arm? And, Stephen noticed throughout the first hour of rehearsal, she kept blinking as if something stung her deep-set eyes.

He saw her again during the break, wiping her eyes with a Kleenex and talking with another woman. He wanted to ask if she was all right, but he never got the chance—for Bryce Everett was walking toward him with an engaging smile on his face. The turtleneck he wore gave him an artist's aura.

"Very attentive playing on the tympani—most just bang the hell out of them at one dynamic. You seem to know what you're doing." That British lilt!

"Percussion sticks out—you have to," answered Stephen modestly; somehow Bryce's accent called forth the meek in him. They sat down with relief in the second row and launched into stories of origin. Both presented theirs with brevity. Bryce had this dream of writing cutting-edge moral theater—"so sordid no one will even know it's spiritual unless they think about it later"—and was in the process of getting the right credentials for it: theology classes during the day, performance gigs of all sorts at night. Tonight he was the tenor soloist, and he admitted that being pushed into the spotlight unnerved him; he'd rather sing with the chorus, but the conductors insisted. He asked Stephen for his address and phone number and felt his pockets for a pen.

82

Act I

"I've got a pen and notebook in my rucksack at the back," said Stephen, rising. He liked to store his things near the back row, so he could take in the pieces that needed no tympani, drinking in music while dozing or cursorily studying bible notes.

Outside in the gathering twilight, thin leather shoes pounded the dampening streets. The crunch of gravel on asphalt beat half seconds in the rhythm of the night. Geoffrey had just stepped out to get a cup of cheap coffee; he had been struggling with the completion of a paper on the Arian heresy and needed some help staying awake. He knew that *they* were about, trying to mix in with other American blacks, watching for self-conscious Ugandans—especially scholars in exile who would spread "lies."

He passed a tailor shop and noticed the glinting eyes of an Indian fellow leaning against the door frame. Anyone could finger him, anyone who'd heard him speak or knew the African slope of the shoulders—the way you walked, the way you carried yourself, the way you dressed. He knew by now that there were even white people who used illicit drugs, who were so desperate for bounty money that they would report on the likes of him to Amin's thugs, sent West in flashy suits to engage in manhunts for refugees.

He hadn't seen *them*, but he felt the moment *they* spotted him. A cold shiver went up his spine and down his legs, and every intention to remain calm deserted him. His feet hurled him down the sidewalk, across the street, propelling him back to the guarded enclosure of the gray-stoned walls of the university. He skidded and nearly went down just outside the gates—then heard the pumping of soldiers' feet behind him. He needed a public building, fast, somewhere where people were: his wild glance found the concert hall, its lights on. He spun toward the right and crossed the threshold like a sprinter finishing a race.

There was another set of doors; he threw himself against the steel bars, and they opened, spilling him into a dimly lit hall.

Stephen had tossed his book bag between the last row of seats and the wall. Now he went to fish through it for a pen. Amid the hum of quiet voices catching up on personal news, the doors flew open, and a dark streak flew in and huddled behind a column, panting wildly. His wide eyes darted around the open room, looking for a place to hide. Stephen immediately recognized the Ugandan, the one he had met briefly during *Messiah*. He was terrified: you could see his pulse pumping at the side of his neck.

The stillness of the air caught Geoffrey's breath, and he looked severely to the right, where a sweat-shirted fellow knelt near the back wall. Their eyes met: the young man he'd seen at that beautiful choral concert months before. He motioned Geoffrey down into the gap between the last row and the wood paneling. Without another thought, Geoffrey flung himself to the floor. He rolled under the folded-up seats, and the man's sweatshirt fell over what still showed of head and shoulder, followed by a knapsack against his legs. Geoffrey heard the thundering of feet as *they* barged into the hall. Though his heart felt like bursting inside his burning chest, he held his breath. He had to squeeze his eyes shut, the sweat pouring off his forehead stung them so.

Tightly, willing himself invisible.

The conductor called the start of rehearsal, and performers drifted back onto the stage.

Stephen had only just assumed an air of nonchalance when the group of black men plummeted through the doors. They wore Hawaiian shirts and sunglasses, which they didn't take off. They braked like renegade taxis catching sight of a patrol car and wandered down the aisles as if to see what curiosities were arranged on the stage, checking out the colored sconces on the high walls and ceiling. But Stephen saw them glance down the rows as they went, hands in pockets, and *knew*: the older Ugandan who clung to the back wall was their target.

Performers and stagehands turned to stare at the four intruders, who slid into seats to catch the rehearsal. But the conductor objected, pointing at the tourists and shaking his head. An assistant walked, cautiously cheerful, up to them to request that they come to the concert this weekend instead. They looked at one another and gave a sign so subtle that Stephen nearly missed it. Then they rose to bow slightly, shake the usher's slender hand or clap him good-naturedly on the shoulder, and saunter up the aisles again to the exit. The last one out kept looking back as he went.

Stephen was glad they hadn't taken their glasses off. They hadn't given their eyes enough time to adjust to the dim room, and they failed to catch their prey. *Thank God.* He instinctively knew that Geoffrey would remain behind the barricade of sweatshirt and day pack until the break at least, likely until the last musician left the hall, and then try to blend in with little groups as they left rehearsal. Perhaps he would fall asleep while strains of Brahms drifted like incense around the great room.

Although he made no glaring error, Stephen couldn't quite concentrate on the second half of the practice. He kept glancing toward the back of the auditorium, where the closed doors held potential assassins at bay. He found himself praying for the campus police to happen by and send packing any brightly dressed loiterers. And while his vigil lasted, he decided he would walk the cornered African back to his dorm before returning to SBC.

At 10:05, Stephen walked softly to the back where his backpack lay and once again reached inside it. Not saying a word, he jotted down his dorm address on a slip of paper and hurried to deliver it to Bryce, who lingered to chat with an attractive violinist. Without interrupting the conversation or taking his eyes off the woman, Bryce casually accepted the slip of paper from Stephen and tucked it into his trousers pocket. It took another fifteen minutes for Stephen to put the percussion gear away, and the dress rehearsal had already gone over by twenty minutes. It always did.

The stage manager yelled that it was time to clear out. People packed instruments away and left in little clusters, out every exit with cases in tow, and Stephen collected his day pack and helped Geoffrey to his feet, dusting off his jacket. He somehow knew better than to bring up what had almost happened.

The Wrong Side of Eternity

"How far away is your room?" he asked quietly. The Ugandan looked disoriented, and he had to stop and think.

"I'm not sure—it's near the seminary chapel."

"I think I know where it is...I often jog around the campus. I'll walk you there." Geoffrey was shaking, so Stephen took his elbow and guided him out the door. They talked of musical things while traversing the dark grounds. They positioned themselves amid other small groups wending their way to the western dorms. No shadows lurked on the edges that Stephen could tell.

Geoffrey made small talk about the music, but he couldn't seem to stay away from the topic of his homeland. "The singing in Uganda is a different style, and we have very few Western instruments. In the back country, they will build rattles from soda-bottle tops and sticks, or pluck an *ikidongo*"—he was searching for descriptive words— "a sort of bass fiddle that lies on the ground, but the big part is cowhide covering a wood frame."

"I'd like to hear one."

Geoffrey stopped abruptly and turned to face Stephen, smiling. "Come to see me sometime in future, and I will show you a whole family of them, all sizes!"

A generous invitation, thought Stephen, and one he would very much like to accept.

Geoffrey had retreated into a worried silence once again.

"Is everything all right, back at home?" Stephen asked him.

Geoffrey scanned the surroundings before softly answering. "No, no it is not. President Amin is hunting down all educated people..." Their footfalls were quiet now, measured and quick. "I only just received a letter from my sister—they live in a remote village, near the border with Rwanda. It did not bring good news." He winced and remembered the careful words, with so much behind them. One had to be cautious—so many letters were opened and read by the authorities...*Charity sends her loving greeting. Her studies have been delayed by some trouble at the end of last term. She is busy helping during the harvest and may go to secretarial school in Mukezi*...Not the university, but much closer to home. His heart sped up,

86

recalling his flight through the marsh. His beloved niece was far too intelligent, gifted even, for secretarial school. She must have done poorly on her A-level examinations. That would be unlike her. Or something else. What terrible thing had happened? Had she been hurt? Worse?

Stephen's voice pulled him back from the black hole of conjecture.

"Has something happened?"

"I cannot talk of it now. Another time."

Another pause. Stephen squinted. "I think that's the chapel ahead."

"Ah, yes, and to the right, another twenty meters, is my dorm." Just as they arrived at the door, it opened, and Bryce stood silhouetted just inside the threshold, bidding a younger choir-mate good night. Geoffrey went on. "Thank you—ah, Stephen, is it? You have done more for me this night than just providing a walk home. I think...you helped me to remember why I came."

"You're very welcome. I hope we can talk some more."

The Ugandan smiled gently. "That would be most enjoyable. You are a good listener. Good night." He shook Stephen's hand and walked into the light of the yawning dorm hallway, and the door closed. A good listener! But the man had said very little, really...

"If it isn't the percussionist!" greeted Bryce, stepping into the night air. "That was stellar! We're lucky to have you." He leaned over, conspiratorially. "You play in tune, as well as with *panache*." They turned in tandem and walked almost in step back toward the parking lot. Stephen dodged the compliment and remembered what the program had said about the man at his side.

"Choirmaster at Mercy Cathedral. Do you live in the city?" he asked.

"With the price of real estate over there?" he laughed. "No, dear fellow, I don't. Have a breezy little place around the corner. Wind howls through it, though—the windows aren't caulked tightly enough, even if they're slammed shut. I spend at least as much time on this side of the bay, anyway." He shrugged. "I agreed to get a master's as a condition for accepting the choirmaster position. Experience I had, but not quite enough of the qualification of which you Americans are so fond."

The Wrong Side of Eternity

"I'd love to come and hear them sometime. Your choir, I mean."

"Then do! In fact, join us. We're doing Fauré's *Requiem* just before the Great Vigil of Easter this year. Rehearsals are Thursday evenings. Oh, I'm sorry. I hadn't even asked if you sing." He grinned. "Just assumed you were interested or had time to add your baritone to our mix—we're usually short."

"No, I meant to just hear them. I wouldn't have time for another gig, with studies and work," said Stephen. Bryce just walked, nodding. "I'm full time at the bible college and work part-time night shifts at the hospital."

Bryce stopped and tilted his head. "I forget that people aren't well funded sometimes. Sorry...Maybe you've not time, but I'm sure you've talent. It just, ah, shows."

"I'm no triple threat, but I can keep a tune."

"So you act or dance, then. That explains the *panache* when you play. It's delightful to see a percussionist who even knows how to move—mostly they stand there like sticks. And because they're so visible, well..."

"I know what you mean," admitted Stephen, smiling. "But I prefer the privacy of the orchestra pit, where no one can see me at all."

"And why is that?"

"I get self-conscious. And I'd rather concentrate on making music."

"You are a rarity! A humble performer. In America!" Bryce laughed. It was like music, his laughter, resonant and sparkling, champagne bubbles lit by streetlights standing vigil over a damp parking lot. The fog was beginning to roll in to get tangled up with the architecture. It was invincible, like the tide.

They both kept busy schedules. Stephen saw his chance.

"I'm off tonight. Would you like to have a late coffee at the Corner Café?" It was a pub-like place close by, open all night to serve students and delivery drivers as well as the flotsam and jetsam of jazz performers and theater people after a show. Most of them went there to relax, not party, and the pastel neon colors that lit the place had a calming effect.

Act I

"I'm game. Never can settle down after a rehearsal or performance. Artistic temperament and all. I'm up half the night anyway." They had arrived now at Bryce's VW, the beetle practically glowing under the streetlamps' overlapping circles of yellow. Stephen couldn't tell what color the car really was—maybe a light blue? *And why would that matter?* he asked himself.

To spot the car in the daylight, his subconscious answered.

Bryce opened the passenger side door. "I'll drop you back here later, if that's all right."

"Sure."

Bryce was nursing his second cup of decaf, totally engaged in Stephen's history, especially fascinated by his recent morbid scenes at the hospital, and his less-recent drama experience. No one had taken this much time to listen to Stephen, ever. He kept talking, and Bryce didn't seem to mind at all. He interposed a question now and then, mostly having to do with the performing arts: could they be a better vehicle for sharing the gospel? There seemed to be a market for spiritual drama, he opined, judging from the success of *Jesus Christ, Superstar* and *Godspell*. What could be done to draw the audience closer to God? Without being overt about it, or seeming to be manipulative?

This was new and Stephen felt his heart rate increase, despite the fact that he was drinking Sleepytime tea. Dancing, acting, even the youth symphony; it all had fallen by the wayside when he gave his life to Christ. It was his past, and he'd been told it should be left to the nonbelievers, who reveled in entertainment to tickle the carnal side of their natures. That was what he had been taught. But here was Bryce, obviously saved, thinking otherwise. Innovative. His mind wandered into shadowy places where he had felt spiritual during a romantic song in some musical he'd done percussion for, replaying itself in his head:

"Without you near me,
I can't see.

When you're near me,
Wonderful things come to be.

"This has been so good for me," Bryce confessed. "I should love to find someone to chat with late at night like this, but at home."

"You mean like a roommate—or a girlfriend?"

"Well beyond that, mate." He looked a bit embarrassed. "Wife. A helpmate, lover." He leaned forward. "Don't you ever crave one?"

"Yeah, I do," he murmured, thinking now of waterfalls of red hair...

"It's terrible. In the city, I meet young ladies often, but their lives are so full of the pursuit of success. Climbing the corporate ladder, that sort of thing."

Stephen recalled how he had seen Bryce chatting amiably with the violinist during rehearsal. No, not just any violinist: the concert mistress.

"Girls here all fall for the accent. Well, sometimes they fall for the chivalry. But I've not found one yet that can follow my thinking or that has the same interests that I do."

Was Bryce actually seeking an opinion from a country boy? Seeing as how they'd only met in musical venues or scholarly circles, Stephen felt both complimented and cautious. This was such a fine person—he deserved the best. He should have a brilliant woman, beautiful inside and out. *Classy, that's what he needs.* She would have to have leadership qualities to attract him. It made sense, now. Though he felt he already partly knew the answer, Stephen ventured a question. "What kind of young lady would you like to meet?"

"Oh, a well-bred sort of person who would please my rather uppity parents. A passionate woman, about things that mattered. Someone with a sense of mission, even, who would be educated enough to appreciate my, ah..."

"Desire to work on this performing-arts thing?"

"Exactly."

Act I

"You'd like someone with brains as well as beauty."

"You are so direct, it's refreshing!"

"Ever meet Madeleine Benson?"

"Who?"

"Beautiful, brilliant, and way out of my league. Strong, capable, classy..."

"You need say no more, mate. But can you tell me where our paths might cross?"

"I think I can, Bryce," Stephen smiled.

16. SBC PARKING LOT, 6:00 A.M.

Stephen startled awake at someone tapping on the tempered glass; he couldn't see them clearly right away because the inside windows of the truck were all fogged up.

"Campus security," came the answer, with more knocking.

He groggily sat up and rolled down the passenger-side window.

"Miss the curfew?" It wasn't really a question, but the tone was polite.

"Yeah, I guess so. Late rehearsal..."

The uniformed officer, a third-year student doing work-study, checked his watch. "It's still pretty early—you might have time for a shower if I walk you straight to your dorm."

"That's awful kind of you. I thought you'd report me to the dean."

"I will. Later."

Stephen tumbled awkwardly out the door, his joints stiff, and twisted left, right. Then he reached inside to pick up his day pack. The guard watched him with attention.

"Well, I don't smell anything forbidden like cigarette smoke or alcohol, so you might get off with a warning. You Stephen O'Connell?"

Stephen nodded, then fell in step with the security guy. "You looked up my truck registration," he noted, smiling lightly to dispel the tension. The grass was soft and dew sodden; he wished they were using the

The Wrong Side of Eternity

sidewalk to spare the blades of green from being crushed, and to keep his one good pair of shoes free of mud.

"You should have called your resident assistant, notified him of your whereabouts. They get nervous when students don't show up."

"I'll be sure to apologize. I didn't have the dorm phone number with me."

"Take it next time. It's different here than where you're from. We're in the city. People freak out if you don't show up, their imaginations run wild. Doesn't take much if you read the local papers or watch the news. There're some weird people hanging about these days."

Stephen nodded again. He'd had a taste of that last night, considering what had almost happened to Geoffrey. He wondered why the guard seemed to think that things happened only in the city; maybe it was just that the concentration of people was greater...or that events in smaller communities never made it into the larger papers, where only government decisions affecting the urban populations were flaunted in bold print. Nobody here thought about small towns, except as places of holiday or escape, somewhere to go if you failed in your quest to contribute to society.

While Stephen mused, his uniformed escort fished out a master key from the collection that hung from his belt. They stood at the dorm entrance.

"Thanks."

"Sure. Have a good day." The key slid into the lock, and with a small amount of noise, Stephen was inside a quiet hallway. In the shared bathroom, someone was showering: the day had dawned. He tiptoed toward his room but was intercepted by Eric, resident assistant.

"Hey, Steve."

It was no time to remind him that Stephen preferred no nickname, so he stood still, lifted his head, and sighed.

"Where were you last night?" Eric asked.

"I had a late rehearsal in the university auditorium. I'm sure I told you. Afterward, I walked someone home. He needed to talk. By the time

92

I got here, the door was locked...I knew better than to bang on it once I noticed the time." Eric looked skeptical. "So I slept in my truck."

"Who did you walk home?"

"An African guy. He's here studying at the seminary." Inwardly he winced; he should have said, "studying Bible." Students here thought everyone at the ITS was a religious pervert.

"Why did he need walking home, huh?" probed Eric, definitely suspicious by now. But Stephen felt irritated and opted for honesty.

"There's almost a genocide happening in his home country, and he's here trying not to get killed. The leaders there target anyone who's educated. He was afraid—people there get slaughtered at night, or disappear."

It was not working. Stephen skipped telling about the next few hours with Bryce.

"Look, it was a chance to minister, to bring some blessing to someone who needed it, okay?" he said. "I'm sorry I didn't call in. I will be sure to next time."

"During this semester, there shouldn't be a next time, Steve. You need enough sleep if you're going to keep up with your studies." Eric looked so serious, ready to cross his arms and be parental, although he was two years Stephen's junior. Stephen thought this was getting ridiculous but avoided the temptation to roll his eyes.

He was sent to the dean, who gave him a lecture and a stern warning.

17. UNIVERSITY COMMONS

GOD BEYOND GENDER: THE SONG OF MARY FOR TODAY proclaimed the flyer, with a stained-glass virgin looking up and holding her hand to her breastbone. Bryce looked closer: the description fascinated him.

Tuesday, May 6th, 7:00 p.m., university auditorium. Listen in on a conversation between a Christian feminist, Ms. Clare Perkins, and an Evangelical traditionalist, Miss Madeleine Benson, as they discuss the Bible's relevance in our times.

And, in smaller print:

Donations accepted at the door to defray costs.

Yes, he would have to go. It was too good an offer to pass up. And the price, no one could beat.

18. FOOTHILLS COMMUNITY CHURCH, SUNDAY MORNING

Stephen sat in the box-like sanctuary and felt like he was missing something. What? Stained glass windows, the whiff of incense, bells...His mind wandered during the forty-five minute sermon, an exposition of the Old Testament book of Nehemiah. He'd read it himself the night before, and it bothered him that the main character would resort to beating others, yelling at them, pulling out their hair in order to make his point. "Thus I cleansed them from everything foreign...Remember me, O my God, for good." The zeal of some of these bible characters! They wouldn't fit in the modern world—they'd be locked up in the county jail. He smiled; he was aware that he'd had similar thoughts yesterday, noticing of a sudden that people seemed so easily to jump to amazing conclusions based merely on what they saw people wearing.

Following the service, he went with the others to the fellowship hall. Madeleine Benson found him there, sipping coffee.

"Hello, Stephen. How did you like the preaching today?" Was there a slight edge to her question, recalling his behavior in chapel? He'd become very careful since then not to emote too much in church. Intentionally detached. Thanks to drama training, he pulled it off.

"I don't know. This guy Nehemiah seems to have had a one-track mind." One track, like enforcing the law. A bible sheriff with a badge.

"Zeal. We could use some of that these days, don't you think? People seem so concerned about how others see them. Not with what's *right*. The world's not gray, it's black and white."

Act I

"He seemed kind of mean to me."

She wasn't used to being interrupted, obviously. Her face blanked before coalescing into a slight frown—which suited her, Stephen thought. Her lips pursed a little, and she was so pretty, tilting her head down like that before she regathered her thoughts. *How she loves a good discussion.* She lifted her gaze to respond.

"The behavior of the people of Israel warranted correction. They got it."

"I wonder if that sort of correction really changed their behavior, in the long run," he offered.

She looked directly into his eyes. "I'm sure it did, or the account would not have been made part of the canon."

Ah, yes. If it's in the Bible it must be true. *I'm glad you're sure*, thought Stephen, *because I'm not.* What a rebellious thought! Hadn't all his studies made him the more sure? He needed to find out where this came from, whether it was a weed or a good plant, and deal with it accordingly. He could do some journaling before starting his night shift at the hospital. He smiled and bowed, tossed his empty cup into the trash bin, and headed out the door.

Got him, thought Madeleine with pleasure. *I'm glad he came to SBC to have his thinking straightened out before it ruined him.*

19. University Hospital, Tuesday Early Evening

Stephen decided to walk to work early and stopped by the PT department just as the therapists were putting things away. Bob sat in the glass cubical they called an office while the fiery-haired Julie organized equipment. Strangely conscious of his hospital whites, Stephen approached her carefully.

"Miss Burns?"

She looked up curiously and, after a second or two, smiled. "Ah, Mr. Clean. I guess you got Mr. Johnson back to his room all right?"

95

"Yeah, but the nurses weren't thrilled. They don't usually give baths on the evening shift."

"Unless they have to. I'm sorry, but I didn't get your name." She was looking for a badge, and he was so low on the payroll that he didn't have one.

"Stephen, Stephen O'Connell. I actually work nights. I just came to ask you..."

"Yes?" She stopped moving, and although she still faced the shelves and had a medicine ball in her hands, she gave him full attention.

"Do you know any good hikes around here? I'd like to stretch my legs Saturday morning, and I'm not that familiar with the area."

"Really? You seem in pretty good shape. Like a climb?"

"Absolutely. And perhaps"—he knew he was smiling but couldn't help it—"a guide?"

"Well," she laughed, "I'm not much of a guide, but there's this great hill I like to climb, overlooking the bay. If you don't mind the fog."

"Not at all, I think it's kind of magical."

Bob looked up, lifted his eyebrows, and resumed his paperwork.

"I've no car, I use public transport," she added.

"I can pick you up." He saw her eyebrows lift and added, "at any spot convenient for you."

"Where do you live?" she asked.

"At Scholars. The bible college."

Her face fell, but she recovered almost immediately. "I can meet you at the corner of Chestnut and Sycamore, there's a small coffee shop there."

"I know the place. What time do you think we should start?" This was much easier than he'd imagined.

"Is seven too early?"

"Nope, that works for me. I don't have to work the night before."

"See you then, Mr. Stephen...what?"

"O'Connell."

"Irish."

Act I

"Half of me."

"Tell me about the other half on Saturday," she said.

"Sure. See you then." And he turned toward the evening, and the floors of patients needing to be repositioned, leaving her to end her day.

Bob lifted his head again and tilted it, smiling furtively. Julie shrugged and took her jacket off the hook behind the door. But before she left, she entered the cubical to give her boss a kiss on the cheek.

"Let me know how it turns out, or else," he said.

She laughed and headed toward the door.

Sleep deprived by midnight, Stephen found himself yawning and gulping coffee every chance he got. Ted commented on the puffiness under his eyes and teased him about partying too much, but Stephen found his colleague actually helping him through the night, thumping him good-naturedly on the back, pushing him along the hallway as they made their rounds.

During his break, he opted to keep walking rather than sit and risk falling asleep. He got a packet of M&Ms from the vending machine, tore it open, and poured them into his mouth. He wandered down to the lower floor to look through the window of the PT area; he could just see the outline of a new set of parallel bars. *Julie. Burns. Miss.* He imagined touching her, just holding onto her firm upper arms and looking into her face, searching those green eyes of hers for secrets. That was it, but it gave him a thrill. Beyond that he would not allow his imagination to go.

"C'mon, bro, break's over," said Ted from behind him.

"You scared me."

"Yeah. Adrenalin does wonders. You're dreaming about that foxy PT lady, huh? Aren't we all! But she's a cold fish, Stephen buddy. She grew up as a missionary kid, one of those born-agains. She won't have anything to do with the likes of you and me, I guarantee it."

Stephen found himself totally conflicted now: Ted seemed to have forgotten the fact that he was also in that category. Should he fess up or stay quiet, glad that Ted considered him one of the guys, and let the camaraderie continue since they were working together so well?

He opted for the latter.

"She is cute," he admitted.

"Hell no, Steve. She's red hot, just doesn't know it."

The page came around 4:00 a.m. Psych unit. The locked side. He met Ted in the hallway en route, grinning. Ted liked action. They hurried as quietly as they could through the double doors. Noise came from the other side of the nurses' station: yelling and thumping. The night tech, a slight man with a sallow face, pointed to a patient. "Carol's drawing up some Thorazine...he's got lycanthropy."

"What's that? It sounds dangerous." Ted was half joking. Stephen was recalling procedure for taking someone down; he'd never had to use it before.

"Werewolf syndrome. No, really," said the tech, noting their incredulity.

"Mr. Schwarz, settle down," he said to the psych patient, who now crouched in the corner. "No one's going to hurt you."

He may as well have been talking to a rabid dog. The color of gray slate, Mr. Schwarz put his head back and *howled*. When he saw them approach, he sprang at them clawing and biting. He did not yell, he growled. It sent shivers up Stephen's spine, but in tandem he and Ted tripped him and held his arms back; the three of them muscled him to the isolation room. Arms and legs flew about as they tied his limbs down with leather restraining belts. Five-point restraints and Stephen had his thrashing head. It took focus to cover the patient's forehead with the thick strap. Stephen had just cinched it into place and stood above him when Carol, the RN, came into the room, her face grim.

"He escalated so fast...Thanks for coming, boys." She pulled Mr. Schwarz's trousers over his right hip and jabbed a syringe fast, like a master throwing darts. The patient bared his teeth, his eyes boring into the orderly's. Stephen almost expected to see fangs. Carol kept explaining; she obviously relished a teaching moment. "He's from Germany, goes stark raving mad whenever there's a full moon." She looked up. "It's well documented. They think it has to do with neurosensitivity to the moon's gravitational pull, you know, that causes the tides." So matter of fact. The patient's head began to loll, and although he fought it, his eyes closed. "He'll sleep a few hours if we're lucky. Would hate to wake up Dr. Evans. Psychiatrists aren't used to being paged at night," she explained, smiling. "They hate it."

They retreated and locked him in. *Now I know why people in the Middle Ages did exorcisms,* thought Stephen. *That was terrifying.*

He got back at 7:45, fell into bed, and slept until 2:00 p.m., missing three classes. He was well aware they were keeping score now. But Eric the resident assistant had a copy of his work schedule, so he would be excused *this* time. Maybe.

20. Across the Bay, before Mercy Cathedral Choir Practice

Stephen and Bryce walked from the rapid-transit station up two blocks and over three; the wind scuttled by them with leaves in tow. Their hands were buried deep inside their coat pockets. Bryce wore a woolen pea coat and looked like a sailor, complete with a Greek fisherman's cap. Stephen felt quite out of fashion in his down jacket and ski hat from the thrift store, but his friend put him at ease. And he was talking in that magical lilt of a voice...

"Whatever works, that's what you wear. Unless you're in the theatre district, there's more of a dress code there. Well, on the 'high holy days' people tend to dress up a little more, but nothing like they used to, I'm told." He pulled open the glass doors on the side of the looming cathedral and ushered Stephen inside what turned out to be a corridor offset by office doors. Daytime was ebbing, and the late afternoon light, worn and thin, came streaming through the high windows. It felt both fresh and familiar, light walls interspersed with a hand-lettered parchment or antique stained glass honoring one of the founders. Construction had just rendered the ancillary rooms handicapped accessible.

After introducing Stephen to office workers exiting through the hallway, Bryce guided him into the nave. The roof settled high above their heads, nearly out of view in the muted light. Stephen noted the décor en route to the choir stalls: there was a rainbow-bordered poster set up on the side, with meeting times posted on it for some sort of support group. Arches everywhere—framing stained glass windows, which held their dark secrets now that dusk descended outside. Arches decorating the pulpit. Arches behind the altar, arches outlining niches in the front, to the left and right. He'd been in Catholic cathedrals, and it seemed to him that the arches were set up where pictures or statues of saints would normally be. It was a little less cluttered here. A vast mural covered the wall on the left, some saint coming to St. Francis at night—he could tell by the torches—a woman, maybe.

It was simply work space to the choirmaster, but to Stephen, the ambiance was magnificent: a holy hush hit him full force as he stepped into the area just before the chancel, where the organ was planted like a boulder between the nave and the choir stalls. Lots more room for a choir than the cathedrals he'd been in before.

Bryce slid onto the polished bench and reached up to set the organ stops, obviously at home. He unfolded some music and began to play, made a few errors, and looked up. "I'm not very good, not like the *real* organist, you know. I pick the easy stuff. Carl puts me to shame...I only play when he's not here."

Stephen just nodded, closed his eyes, and let the organ pipes blast him to another century.

21. SATURDAY MORNING, A HILLSIDE NORTH OF THE CITY

Stephen parked on a dirt embankment just north of the bridge, its red cables anchored to the headland by a building-size block of cement. He

Act I

looked at the soaring towers and thought briefly about the guys who climbed them, braving the sweeping winds and piercing fogs to repaint the metal structure every few years against rust. Julie was practically out of sight before he'd even locked the truck. Sprinting against a cold, stiff gale, she crunched fine gravel underfoot.

He hurried to follow her past the empty shells of deserted concrete bunkers, where military watchmen once monitored the sea at the Pacific gateway to thwart attacks during the Second World War, and the Cold War upon its heels. A smell of stale urine: perhaps the homeless took refuge up here when weather was really bad. It was a dismal place. She was well beyond it, heading up to the crest of a jagged hill. There was no trail, just a meandering empty patch of ground —probably a firebreak —that worked for one. There were other footprints in front of him: waffle stompers, tennis shoes. He looked up into the sky and saw only drifting mist above him; he would soon be in its wake.

The wind blew cold, right through his windbreaker, but the climb made him sweat. Half an hour later, he found himself at the top of a rocky crest with the fog blowing over him and Julie almost silhouetted in front of him, not ten yards away. She had taken off her shirt and was lifting it over her head like a banner or a signal flag on a ship. When he looked a little closer, he saw that she wore no bra.

"Oh, Stephen, this is so great. Just the wind to dry you off and the fog to wake you up!" The mist had gathered itself into droplets against her fair skin, but she seemed impervious to the chill. He blushed and felt relieved that a red face might be natural in this particular climate condition, while something deep and unmistakably pagan welled up inside him. His breath came short and shallow, but not because he was winded from the climb.

He was enthralled. She was a wood nymph, reveling in the spirit of the sea mist that wafted in over the coast. But he was no Apollo and would not give pursuit. Instead, he swallowed and nodded, directing his gaze southward toward the bay, where hazy sailboats glided beneath the red towers while the fog drifted over them, washing words and indecent thoughts away.

101

22. MERCY CATHEDRAL EVENSONG

Stephen drove over to ITS to pick up Geoffrey; they had run into one another in the coffee shop a few days ago, when news of the African bishop's arrival was buzzing around the campus. He was glad to go with someone apart from an SBC field trip, someone from Africa, someone to whom this mattered very, very much. Geoffrey stood outside the dorm, wrapped in a used leather jacket and scarf. Thrift-store apparel, like his own, but many of the university students wore a wide assortment. He waved at Stephen as he would an old friend. In the cool afternoon the exhaust trailed out of the old truck like brown mist, and the engine coughed in protest of both the temperature and the moisture in the air. Geoffrey climbed aboard, grinning.

"This is like a vehicle you would find in Uganda," he explained.

"Glad it feels like home!" answered Stephen, and then wondered if he was being insensitive. They sputtered their way to the rapid transit station and parked. Geoffrey watched with amazement as Stephen slid bills into the vending portion of the wall, and tickets popped out a lower slot. "This ride will actually take us below the bay, to the city," he commented, and watched the gears turn in Geoffrey's head: would they be able to look out the window, and see the fishes? "No view while we're underground, though," he added, smiling. Geoffrey shrugged, smiling back. They found the right platform, one flight up, and boarded the very next train.

"They run so often here!" remarked Geoffrey. "Only one train goes to Kenya, and not every day. It may shut down for weeks at a time."

"Yeah, lots of people use it instead of a car. Places are just too far to walk." Stephen glanced at his travel partner throughout the rumbly journey, marveling at his composure. *Such a long way from home.* It got dark.

"And now we are under the water?"

"Yeah. You can't tell, can you?"

Geoffrey shook his head, holding tightly onto the vertical pole.

They exited the train and Stephen checked the map: four block's walk uphill to Mercy Cathedral. The clock in the square showed 6:32.

Act I

They would just make it. Fog drifted past them, its fingers reaching toward some unknown, rendering the city both gray and alluring. The wind cut through Stephen's clothes, yet he found himself sweating as they neared the stone edifice near the city center—blocks from the original Catholic mission site but imposing nonetheless.

He removed his cap, and Geoffrey loosened his scarf, as they stepped inside the foyer; a musty smell of old flowers and the residue of incense met his nose, and the immensity of the place stretched before him past the double doors. A nicely dressed man handed him a bulletin, or program, or whatever they called it here. The order of service was printed out in clear type, presumably for those who did not care to juggle both the hymnal and the prayer book.

The place was packed; word had gotten out. They walked softly around a cluster of SBC students wearing ties and clutching bibles, who'd come to hear Festo Kivengere, the "Billy Graham of Africa." Stephen glanced at one or two of his classmates and nodded briefly in greeting, then steered Geoffrey to a spot behind a pillar two-thirds of the way back. As they headed up the side aisle, he could hear whispering behind him and caught a questioning remark about the negro he'd come with. He smiled bitterly and shook his head. He was tempted to turn around and casually mention that the sixties were long gone, and he was saved from doing so by the tolling of a bell.

A notice in the bulletin requested prayers for the souls of their mayor and a much-loved administrator, gunned down six months ago by a disgruntled politician. Stephen ignored other notices in order to take in the sights. People knelt in some pews and visited softly in others. A woman in a white vestment was up front, using some kind of pointer stick to direct a distinguished visitor to a reserved seat. The organ began to play, and Stephen turned his gaze to the front of the enormous church, where the handsome face of the choirmaster, Bryce Everett, was hidden from his view by one of the columns. It occurred to him that they three had been together once before, he and Geoffrey in the audience, Bryce up front. How long ago? Months? It seemed more than a year.

The Wrong Side of Eternity

Four pews up, and from across the aisle, a fair hand waved at him. Julie sat with Reverend Margaret, and others from their study group. Stephen smiled and blushed in return. Even though he was in a church, he could not get the picture of her on that hillside to leave his head.

This service was evidently more ornate than the usual Wednesday night fare; a procession flowed past him when the first hymn was sung. Assistants in white gowns, someone holding a cross aloft—people around him bowed as it passed—the robed choir, the priests; the African bishop was obvious, wearing a frilly-sleeved white garment with a long red vest and a black stole. Stephen guessed the outfit was adopted from British custom; Geoffrey had told him that Uganda was once a British protectorate. The bishop did not look as though he much enjoyed dressing up, but he moved with some fluidity. He kept smiling at the ushers, at the choir members as they took up their positions in the choir stall, at individual faces in the congregation. He was a handsome man with a beautiful smile, as if he harbored a happy secret. Kind of young, for a bishop.

Just seeing him, Geoffrey had tears coursing down both cheeks which he did not bother to wipe away. He had proudly told Stephen on the way over that Festo was his bishop back in Kabiizi, preparing to return from his exile now that Amin had at last been deposed. During the second hymn, Stephen stepped aside to plead with an usher, urging him to arrange a private meeting between the two Ugandans. It took all four verses to get a tepid agreement from the sidesman to try.

He resumed his seat just in time for the opening remarks. Like a well-bred visitor, Bishop Festo thanked the dean for inviting him to the cathedral, then led the congregation in prayer. The first words out of his mouth were of forgiveness for the political murderer. Audible gasps emerged from the nave, quickly stifled as people remembered they were in prayer. *A superb move*, thought Stephen: *he's got their attention now*. And he held their rapt attention throughout the remainder of his thirty-minute sermon, which contrasted the atrocities of Uganda's dictator with the plea of Jesus as Roman soldiers stripped him for crucifixion: "Father, forgive them, for they don't know what they're doing."

Act I

"I'm here today to assure you that we can be together in this house, that we can fellowship despite our backgrounds or what kind of church we were brought up in—or not, as the case may be," Bishop Festo said lovingly, in a polished and beautiful voice, the curve of his smile welcoming them all. "And I'm also here to tell you that whoever suffers for the sake of others, like our Lord Jesus, no matter what they believe, that person will find a welcome in heaven. That is the place where all divisions cease. Because it is God's place—and *only* God's place—to judge anyone. We people, we can't bless anyone and judge at the same time. It's obvious from the Gospels that God has called us to work at the one and forget the other."

You could be Baptist or Pentecostal, Catholic or Nazarene, and you might go along with this. It was gospel, not theology. It *worked*. Neither the bishop nor the dean gave a verbal invitation for people to come forward to make a Christian commitment. Instead, the service just went on. The choir sang an anthem; many bowed their heads, many closed their eyes, but Stephen watched Bryce conduct the choir. His hands moved dance-like through the phrases, which etched themselves in memory as much or more as the preacher's words:

Thee we adore, O hidden Saviour...
Increase our faith and love, that we may know
The hope and peace which from Thy presence flow.

O Christ, whom now beneath a veil we see,
May what we thirst for soon our portion be,
To gaze on Thee unveiled, and see Thy face,
The vision of Thy glory and Thy grace.

Just before the benediction, the dean invited the congregation to greet Bishop Festo in the parish hall; the service had lasted just over ninety minutes. *For an African*, thought Stephen, *he kept his address short*. Maybe he was just that in tune with his audience, knowing that the average

The Wrong Side of Eternity

Episcopal sermon lasted fifteen minutes at most. Still, he had wasted no words and held their full attention for a good half hour. *Amazing.*

People flowed out the door like sheep, following the recessing choir, but as they headed up the steps toward the waiting clergy, Festo looked back and cried out, "Geoffrey!" The headmaster ran forward to practically collide with the bishop in embrace. They launched into a melodic tribal dialect and withdrew to a corner of the hall, where they might have five minutes to catch up before the important visitor was called away to be introduced to other more important people.

Stephen stood at a distance, his gaze wandering over to the SBC students, who stood in a huddle, deciding whether to stay or not; Professor Collins was waiting for the bishop to answer an invitation to address the students on campus. In their territory, not in this foreign world of high church ritual. *What would Festo say there, to elicit gasps from the student body?* he wondered, as he sought out a hot cup of coffee for the journey back. He smiled as he sipped it; Bishop Festo would think of something gently provoking, of that he was sure.

DEADLOCK

Sticks and stones may break my bones,
But names will never hurt me.

—CHILDREN'S RHYME

Death and Life are in the power of the tongue...

—PROVERBS 18:21

23. SCHOLARS BIBLE COLLEGE

MADELEINE SAT BEHIND HER DESK and sighed. The weekend conversation with Susan Collins had unsettled her. She was so content and always fobbed off so many of the more tedious things onto her husband: auto repair, finances...Other desks in the admin section all held family photos, portraits of grown children and faculty couples smiling from the deck of a sailboat, posed in front of a ski resort...

A husband. It had been coming up a lot lately in the weekly phone chats with her parents. She was twenty-six—the timing was right, in their view. She would need someone who would give her freedom enough to pursue her work, researching and debating the correct side of women's rights: the freedom of submission in a confusing postmodern world. She would need someone who was financially secure, someone who had

The Wrong Side of Eternity

work of his own to attend to, a Christian calling and a modest, albeit tailored, lifestyle. Someone with impeccable manners. Someone who looked good, was her age or a bit older, someone who took vows seriously enough that she never need worry about infidelity. And someone from outside the established confines of the world of SBC, as dating anyone there would be a conflict of interest.

Bryce Everett, that handsome English fellow. He fit the bill. Even her parents would approve.

Only they had yet to formally meet.

Shortly after this reverie, she sat on a concrete bench in the quad and took a small lined pad from her purse to jot down her thoughts. She would watch him during the ITS seminar she audited. After that, she would become more proactive, make herself more available, become more visible to him. She would have to take cues from his conversation, note the tastes that appealed to him, align herself with those without being seen as the aggressor.

She would have to be intentional and take her time.

———◆———

Stephen held his breath as he ducked through the doorway into Pastoral Concerns. The class was beginning to make him nauseated.

"Gentlemen, put your notebooks away. Today's class will be discussion only." Professor Hardesty began with a serious flourish, his voice deepening as if he were about to embark on a mesmerizing sermon. "You brought up something the other day that needs further exploration. And I need your assurance that by discussing these rather sensitive matters, we will remain in a figurative holy of holies: private."

The class nodded unanimously in agreement.

"The wife, gentleman, is an indispensable part of your ministry. You must take great care in choosing her properly so that no one will have an occasion to slander the profession."

Act I

"You mean we must pick a wife according to our *job description?*" offered a timid voice from the back row. Stephen turned, not so much to pick out the speaker but to see how the women in class were dealing with this. Then he felt like an idiot: there *were* no women in this class.

"Absolutely. Search the scriptures, gentlemen, and find her defined in Proverbs thirty-one, and Ephesians six, and numerous other crystal-clear passages."

"My mom was a great hostess," offered a near-graduate who had somehow forgotten to shave that morning; the man winced at the disapproval of fifteen sets of eyes turning upon him. "But in private, she cried a lot. She was so frustrated sometimes. When no one seemed to notice, she'd go for long walks and come back with mascara stains all down her face."

"A woman is a human being, entitled to feelings," commented the professor. "But you must make good use of those feelings, even the negative ones."

"How?"

"Ah, I'm glad you asked. Take anger, for example. We've all seen women angry. They practically scare us to death." The class tittered. "But a woman well trained will know that she must use her anger *for good*—that is, make some use of it, turn it to a productive purpose."

"Like cleaning the house?"

"That is the best direction in which to steer a woman's anger. The entire family benefits from it. She is purged from her strong feeling, and gets something accomplished besides. And who doesn't feel better after that?"

Stephen could contain his rising temper no longer. He blurted, a little loudly, "You mean, Professor, that you use the scriptures to *manipulate* your spouse into feeling guilty so that she does what is of most benefit to you?"

"Now, Mr. O'Connell, I said nothing of the sort. And I note that you use the word 'spouse' instead of 'wife.' Why is that?"

The Wrong Side of Eternity

"I have no idea. It just seemed, uh, less demeaning in this particular context."

"I see. It implies *equality*. You wouldn't by chance have gotten involved in an illicit correspondence with Ms. Jane Fonda, have you?"

The class snickered.

"No, sir. It just seems wrong to make use of a woman just because you're married to her."

"Are you, by any chance, from a *dysfunctional* family, Mr. O'Connell? One that did not live by the teaching of the word of God?"

"If you mean, did my alcoholic father beat my immigrant mother, yes, he did. And he thought himself the most righteous asshole on the planet."

"You will refrain from speaking for the rest of the class, Mr. O'Connell, and you will meet with me and the dean this afternoon at four p.m. in order to get help in refining your vocabulary." He shuffled a pile of papers and his voice softened. "And, speaking of refinement, would you care to accept a personal invitation for tea at my home after church on Sunday so that you may meet an authentic godly woman—my wife?"

They all gasped. It was unheard of, extending a social invitation to a student right in the middle of class. Stephen knew what they were thinking: he should shut up and take the hint, not the invitation.

"Actually, sir, I would be happy to come. I've a lot to learn."

"Fine then, Mr. O'Connell." There was something odd in the professor's tone. He cleared his throat. "You'll stop by my secretary's office for the address. I shall have informed her of your reason for asking. Now, then, gentlemen, onward. We shall see what such a woman is made of. Open your bibles to Proverbs, chapter thirty-one."

Stephen declined to open his and heard nothing of what followed. Alternating shame and pride covered him like a polluted wave.

24. UNIVERSITY AUDITORIUM, MAY SIXTH

"My soul magnifies the Lord," began the feminist, opening the discussion. "It's all so familiar. We take the words for granted. They've been immortalized in music, in drama, in liturgy for centuries."

Act I

Millennia, thought Madeleine, seated politely on stage. The setting was like a late-night talk show: two comfortable chairs, a coffee table complete with tasteful mugs and coasters. *It's not a debate*, she reminded herself. *No need to attack, get aggressive, no matter how wrong she is.*

"Mary—in her own day it was more likely Miriam—praising God in the words of an Old Testament prophet. So many of her lines recall the song of Hannah, as remembered in the book of Samuel." Some members of the audience nodded, knowing the reference. Others, students from SBC, made notes. "But I want to take a close look at Mary's opening lines," remarked Clare Perkins. "Especially that word 'magnify.' Does it not mean, 'to make bigger'? 'To enlarge'? Mary was remarking, in great poetic style, that God was bigger than her wildest dreams, bigger than she'd ever thought. God's greatness had burst the walls of her soul, and out of the cracks poured forth this song."

Older men smiled. It was hard for Madeleine to deduce whether Ms. Perkins was being serious or facetious. She caught a brief glimpse of Stephen O'Connell, seated with that priest from St. Simeon's and a red-haired woman she had met several years ago at Foothills Community Church. But she returned her focus immediately to the speaker, looking very polite and appreciative, as the occasion called for.

"As we approach the feast of the Visitation between Mary and Elizabeth—which is the context in which this song occurs—I do hope that we will heed her young voice and make God bigger, 'magnify the Lord' as we journey toward understanding that God is just too overwhelming to begin to explain or define."

"That God is beyond gender, you mean," chirped Madeleine, her turn to speak now. "And what would happen to the strong, protective images of a Father in Heaven if we dispensed with the male pronoun for God?" She enumerated a few, tossing them as if skipping stones upon a still lake. "The Rock, the Good Shepherd, the Forgiving Father, the Husband of Israel. If we look back at Hannah's song, First Samuel chapter two, the speaker makes clear that she perceives God very much in the masculine: 'by Him actions are weighed…the pillars of the earth are the LORD's, and on them He has set the world…His adversaries shall be

111

shattered...He will give strength to His king, and exalt the power of His anointed.'" All this Madeleine recited from memory, emphasizing ever so slightly, the masculine pronouns. "Mary is even more pointed, more specific, in chapter one of Luke's gospel: 'His mercy...He has shown strength...He has scattered the proud...He has brought down the powerful from their thrones...' Both these women, and many more besides in the pages of scripture, referred to God as 'He.'"

In the midst of the attentive audience Bryce leaned forward, clasping his hands together. *Touché! And exquisitely delivered!*

Clare Perkins listened meditatively. She was Madeleine's equal in her use of dramatic gestures, that was for sure. She set her cup down, softly and with grace, on the lacquered table top.

"Of course, they were brought up that way, to think of God in terms of the masculine. Theirs was a patriarchal culture," she explained, patiently and without condescension, as Madeleine resisted the temptation to roll her eyes. "Anyone with power thought of God that way. Even the pagan religions had stories of any presuming female, human or goddess, being put in her place, which was below that of the male." The auditorium was quiet, with a barely whisper of carols being sung in the streets outside. "Sometimes with violence. For instance, in the Babylonian creation myths the goddess Tiamat was literally drawn and quartered by the male gods of the ancient sky. Other forms of spirituality present a warm, nurturing, feminine side to God. And the scriptures do not always present God in masculine terms. That phrase so often used in Genesis, in the Pentateuch, 'the Almighty,' 'el shaddai' in the Hebrew, can also be translated 'the many-breasted one.'"

*Everyone remembers that statue of Diana pictured in the art history books, covered with engorged breasts...*Clare's dramatic pause lasted just long enough for the image to flit across the imagination. *She's smart, to leave out the lurid details,* thought Madeleine, prompting herself to use that strategy in the future.

112

Act I

"The Shekinah presence so powerfully mentioned in the Hebrew scriptures is a feminine word. In modern Judaism there remain vestiges of a feminine divinity, in both the Talmud and the Kabbala."

Madeleine smiled patiently. "May we return to the field of scripture, Miss Perkins?" she urged, "Since our main focus is the magnificat."

"Absolutely, Ms. Benson," came the polite response, "as we could be here for hours otherwise."

Bryce nearly laughed aloud, to hear the women using the titles in paradoxical jest, a coffee-table tennis game that was highly entertaining.

Clare Perkins recovered smoothly. "Jesus himself used feminine imagery for God: the woman who'd lost a coin, for example, in Luke chapter fifteen."

"The parables are certainly powerful analogies, meant to convey the depth of emotion in this particular case," answered Madeleine. "But Christ," she purposefully used the more liberal term for the Messiah, to underscore her broad tolerance of the use of religious language, "never implied that God had particularly feminine qualities. He used the word 'Father,' or the more intimate 'Abba,' when addressing him, and always employed the masculine pronoun when addressing an audience about God."

And so it went, a polite discussion about the definitions of God in a season of rain and cold, a warm exchange of ideas between two apparently Christian women who believed obviously different things.

Stephen was amused and not the least bit surprised to see Bryce slip forward at the end, while Madeleine sat smiling in her chair after warmly shaking hands with the erudite Ms. Perkins, who had not quite bested her. *She looks relieved*, thought Stephen, as she responded warmly to Bryce's proffered hand. *They make a fantastic couple.* Why this alarmed him, he did not know.

As he and Julie exited the auditorium, they caught the sotto-voce conversation of other members of the audience. "She should have been harder on her."

The Wrong Side of Eternity

"It wasn't the right setting, you know that."

"Still, Madeleine could've run circles around that lesbian."

"Now, now. We don't know the woman's sexual preferences."

"Anyone who uses the title 'Ms.' is suspect to me."

Stephen recognized the voice, a student at SBC, and declined to turn around and stare at him.

"It would be interesting to see them in a real debate situation," the other casually remarked.

"We can only pray that this will lead up to that."

"Why?" whispered Julie in Stephen's ear, "So he can carve another notch on his bible belt?" Stephen smiled. She wasn't one to be inspired by debate, or scholarly exchange, as it was sometimes called as a courtesy. Hearing two people express different opinions would only tire her out. She always kept quiet during the bible study at St. Simeon's, keeping her own council. As they exited into the night air, she turned toward him and rhetorically asked, "Do you think God likes these exchanges? Is he Bored? Frustrated? Poor God! Do they actually make a difference to people in the audience, or are they just another form of entertainment?"

Stephen squeezed her arm, and she looked up at him and smiled. He never asked her what she thought. She told him, when she wanted to, without pressure or prompt. It was easy to talk to Stephen O'Connell. Uncomfortable as he may have been in his own skin, he let you be yourself.

25. THE HARDESTY HOME, SUNDAY AFTERNOON

Mrs. Hardesty was so decked out, Stephen felt as if he were in the theater, playing out an English high tea scene. Except that she had a fantastic southern accent.

"Mr. O'Connell, I'm so glad you could join us today." Her manners were impeccable, her grace unmistakable. Yet for all the layers of character, Stephen felt an underlying tone of her being, well, *haunted.* She wasn't being false; it was just that there was much, much more to her than she presented. He could just tell.

For years he had hated that sense, that almost subliminal sensitivity he had. He'd gone to a counselor once about it, but there was no empathy there; only Reverend Margaret seemed to be able to tolerate his attempts to describe it. Back in the desert, three years ago now, his youth pastor had overheard a girl use the words "psychic" and "creepy" and just stopped short of suggesting an exorcism. He held a late-night prayer session instead, with Stephen in the middle of a circle, surrounded by four sincere young people coming against the powers of darkness and evil. Stephen knew that he had to look as normal as possible now, in front of Professor Hardesty, so he could stay at SBC.

He smiled and shook her extended hand. "Thank you for inviting me." The role of gentleman, he was good at that. He would call upon his dramatic powers and play it through the whole visit. Yeah, and then Professor Hardesty would think he was a schizophrenic. *Oh, well.*

Noticing a baby grand piano in the corner of the living room, Stephen gravitated to it, a planet seeking its sun. It had such a high polish that the black luster practically reflected the room. But the instrument seemed forlorn, forgotten. Neglected?

"You're a musician?" he ventured to ask Mrs. Hardesty.

"Not really—not formally. I had some voice lessons in college."

"What kind of stuff do you sing?"

"Oh, safe stuff," she answered, casting a glance in the direction of her husband, who was watching the scene with some interest. "Old show tunes."

"Like Rodgers and Hammerstein?"

"*Carousel*'s my favorite," she admitted.

"Can we do one?"

"It's been a long time…"

"Go ahead, Elisabeth," Professor Hardesty offered. "I'd love to hear you sing again." He remained standing.

The Wrong Side of Eternity

Stephen pictured a groomed little dog just let off its leash. Mrs. Hardesty bent to look through a stack of music on the bottom shelf of the expansive bookcase. She stood up with a spiral-bound book, which she placed on the piano. Stephen smiled and pulled out the padded leather bench. It looked practically new.

"Did you say *Carousel*? What do you want to try?" he asked. God, she had such a lovely voice. Just hearing her talk was listening to music. The babble of a brook...

"I always liked 'What's the Use of Wonderin'.'"

"Me too. But I think it's a bit sad."

"Aren't all good love songs a bit sad?" she asked, smiling. He began to play and she to sing. She looked the while at the admiring professor, who remained standing.

Somethin' made him the way that he is,
Whether he's false or true.
And somethin' gave him the things that are his—
One of those things is you.
So, when he wants your kisses,
You will give them to the lad,
And anywhere he leads you, you will walk.
And anytime he needs you,
You'll go runnin' there like mad!
You're his girl and he's your feller—
And all the rest is talk.

Stephen had never cringed at the lyrics before, but they seemed to jangle, here in the Hardesty home. And though she sang sweetly and perfectly in tune, did he detect a hint of irony in her tone?

Two songs were deemed sufficient. The professor invited Stephen into his study, where he could resume the mission of the afternoon. Mrs. Hardesty was not invited to join them. Instead, the lord of the castle directed her to bring them tea.

116

Act I

"I'm on my way, Keith." She retired to the kitchen.

Stephen was not surprised. He had come prepared for some act of humiliation—but hated to see her subjected to it as well.

The man tried a smattering of small talk before launching into his crusade.

"So you see, Mr. O'Connell, the home can be not only a place of refuge but a bastion against corrupt worldly forces."

"And evil," Stephen offered agreeably.

"Yes, of course." The professor frowned. "Did you grow up with evil in your home?"

"You've probably read my file, and you know what I said in class."

"I've not read your file, young man, but I remember what you said in class. It seems a tragic way to begin a life."

"Tragic? I'm not sure. Da had his faults, but he could spout some terrific poetry. Like 'The Ballad of Reading Gaol.'"

This was met with silence, and he wondered if Professor Hardesty had many conversations with students, period. Stephen recalled seeing some gorgeous photos of younger people on the piano, one couple with a baby. They were all studio pictures, and they all looked very, very happy. "Do you have kids?"

"Yes, two boys and a girl. All quite successful."

I'm sure they are, thought Stephen. *They would have to be.*

26. ST. SIMEON'S RECTOR'S OFFICE

Stephen hadn't heard from Diane in months. He closed the door and dialed her number from Rev. Margaret's office phone, wanting privacy. The phone rang only twice before another girl picked it up.

"Hello, Bright Sisters Sorority."

"I'm trying to reach Diane."

"Diane? Hold on." She muffled the phone and called out, "Is there a Diane here?" Then he waited another minute or so, drumming his fingers on the desk, looking at the titles on Rev. Margaret's bookshelves.

The Wrong Side of Eternity

"Well, there *used* to be a Diane here. She, uh, moved...transferred to another college. Were you and she, uh, dating or anything? Because if you were, I could give you her number..."

"Yeah, we were dating." A long time ago, but she didn't have to know that.

"Okay then." She read the number and wished him luck reaching her at this time of the day, then hung up. *That was too easy*, thought Stephen. He dialed the number, its prefix in the city. It was two in the afternoon. Would she be working? A sleepy voice answered on the fifth ring.

"Hello?"

"Hello, Diane?"

"Yeah, who's this?"

"Stephen. Stephen O'Connell." Did she even remember?

"Oh, Stephen, you," she yawned. "The guy from the desert shit hole."

"If this is a bad time..."

"No, no, it's fine. I work nights."

"So do I. At the university hospital."

"Doing what?"

"I'm an orderly. It's nothing glamorous, believe me." The silence on the other end of the line indicated she did. "I heard you transferred."

"Yeah, I go to the performing arts academy now."

"Let me guess: dance."

"Yeah, with a smattering of vocals. I'm a dismal actress."

I never thought so, thought Stephen. *You always seemed pretty convincing.* "I'd like to see you perform sometime."

"No you wouldn't, Steve. You're way beyond my league now."

"We could meet at the wharf, catch up on things."

"Forget that. I'm swamped with working...and stuff."

"Mind if I ask where you work?"

"Yes, I do. It's none of your goddamn business. But I'll tell you anyway. The Saucy Serbian." She waited. "It's a nightclub," she explained with patient exasperation. "I didn't think you were that dense. You practically warned me about where I might end up."

118

Stephen paused. "I bet you're good."

"Hell, I am." Her voice broke. "I'm fucking fantastic. Have a nice Christian life, Steve. Don't waste your time on me. I am so fucked up."

"Diane, I—"

"Bye."

She hung up. He did not get to apologize. He had so badly wanted to. It was more than—what did they call it at AA?—restitution. He really did care.

He really did.

27. A COASTAL MOUNTAIN TRAIL, MID-MAY

They trudged up a shadowed path winding among oaks and bushes, the occasional eucalyptus standing like a lighthouse on a rocky promontory with a sea of space below. Bryce was airing his opinions, and Stephen felt honored.

"I've always thought that we're here to help one another along in what we believe."

"Wouldn't that make you a universalist? Where everybody's in and no one left out?"

"No, because lots of people decide they don't want any kind of *in*," Bryce explained. "They take faith in their atheism. Others just don't care, they're so swallowed up in busy this-and-that. Like the parable where the invitees were too occupied to come to the marriage feast…"

Their steps hit a rhythm; their day packs bounced jauntily at their backs.

"Parables are so rich," added Stephen. "You can read them one week and get one thing, then the whole meaning seems to shift when you read them again."

"Bingo, mate. And that's what's made Judaism so interesting over the past few millennia. Debate, interpretation. No one questions the teaching of the Torah, but I venture years have been spent discussing what it *means*."

The Wrong Side of Eternity

"Now you're sounding dangerously close to relativism."

Bryce turned to face him but kept walking, backward. He held out his hands, just like Christ welcoming the children in a stained glass window.

"Nothing's static, Mr. O'Connell. Everything's in flux. Changing, growing, maturing, evolving, withering, dying…Not even rocks hold their shape after a few weeks. Only one thing is changeless."

"The Almighty? The law of love? Holiness?"

"Yes, that." He turned back to engage the trail. "It seems odd, but our system has almost overpowered us. Since the Enlightenment, we've wanted to label and analyze and dissect everything. Some things don't lend themselves to being defined."

"I get what you mean. Every field of study is pretty much learning new vocabulary and categorizing things. Saint Paul's Greek, the nomenclature of the periodic table…"

"Yes! And since things aren't static, it doesn't work. Especially for people. It never works with people."

"I thought you were an academic, but you're talking like a philosopher or an artist."

"Everyone's got art in them, Stephen, my dear. For some, it's like a wild beast that you have to keep in the cellar. Not a fine horse you can train and show, that can carry you sailing over a stile on a blustery day."

"Now you're an Englishman in riding habit!"

"You should come over to the—what do you call it?—the old stomping grounds sometime. Catch some nice British countryside. The Lake District."

"I doubt I'd have funds for that anytime soon."

"True." Bryce looked pained, bringing up the difference in their resources. "So instead, sharpen your beady little eyes to see the glory right here."

"I'll never catch it, like you, and be able to convey it." He envied Bryce, being able to do what he loved so easily. Geniuses were lucky that way.

120

"You will. It's in you, too. You're an artist, Stephen. Just haven't found your medium yet."

"And yours is music?"

"Music, conversation, drama. It's all of a piece."

They stopped near the summit, out of the wind's way, to eat lunch. Stephen had a peanut-butter-and-jelly sandwich and a can of Pepsi; Bryce brought out a hard-boiled egg, croissant, packet of butter, and small bottle of wine. Each laughed at the other.

"I get weary of the debate, the answers to all the questions—some of them pretty silly. Everybody trying to figure out where you stand on any issue, trying to pin you down...Even the artist thing, Bryce—the word carries such, ah, *baggage* with it."

"Associations, you mean, like 'slovenly' and 'erratic'..."

"...and 'wild' and 'experimental'..."

"That's you, all right," Bryce said with sarcasm. "The trick is *being* what you are without letting the words stick. There are much more important things to get done besides trying to figure out where everybody stands."

"Now you're preaching to the choir." They ate, looking out over the vast plain and the valleys of fog beyond. "How do *you* stay out of trouble?" He had told Bryce what was happening at SBC, about the reactions of the professors and being put on probation.

"Now *that* is probably a matter of experience. I pick my environment to accommodate my eccentricities. I find a spot where there's room for me."

"Like the International Theological Seminary?"

"And Mercy Cathedral. Instead of a place that thinks it has all the answers."

"Surely there are arrogant profs at ITS."

"Well, arrogant in their open mindedness, perhaps! They judge the dear conservative scholars quite as much as they themselves are judged. Each finds the other wrong."

Yes, thought Stephen. *It's everywhere.*

"And how are you getting on with Miss Benson? I saw you flirting with her after that Magnificat thing a few weeks back."

Bryce lifted his head, his eyes twinkling with mirth. His memory flashed back to a mere week ago, when he stood at the rear of the auditorium, listening to Madeleine parry with another opponent in another debate. She was such a brilliant improviser; if he hadn't known better he would have thought she'd studied drama for years. It was effortless for her, the subtle pursing of her lips, the understated raising of an eyebrow...And such fire!

How would she fare with intimacy? This was an amusing speculation for him. He doubted she had had much in the way of experience. She carried herself so...elegantly. Pristine. Unless she was *very* good at hiding it, she'd never been sullied; never allowed herself to *compromise*. She was virginal, all right. The thrill of it! He strategized.

To unleash her passion in the intimacy of marriage, he would have to take a decisive lead but ever so gently. He would have to keep his voice low and calm. She deserved that much—perhaps she deserved more. You could hardly fail to respect her, this Madeleine Benson. Given enough time, would she trust him enough to let down her guard? He imagined her arching beneath him, groaning with pleasure...it would take a while. Maybe a year. Maybe more. *But boy, would it ever be worth it.*

Stephen seemed to be reading his thoughts and interrupted his reverie.

"You know if she ever catches you at it, she'll put on the brakes."

"I know," Bryce admitted.

"She'll probably run a background criminal check on you."

"She probably will. She won't find anything." They walked for a quarter mile farther, while the distant surf, thousands of feet below them, silently pounded the beach sand into smaller fragments. "She thinks me safe."

"Are you?"

Act I

"For such a damsel, yes indeed...Your first impressions of her were high?"

"Very."

"And now?" asked Bryce.

"She'll make somebody a fantastic wife. But it didn't take me too long to figure out that that lucky somebody could never be me."

No, thought Bryce. *You're way too soft. She'd run right over you...*

Stephen was still talking. "I'd love to know more about her story."

"Her past?"

"Yeah. She's so...*together.*"

Bryce only smiled, and the subject changed to other things.

During their descent, Bryce began singing songs from the Elizabethan era, including a few from Shakespeare.

Stephen picked up the thread and launched into his favorite quotes: "but he who filches from me my good name robs me of that which not enriches him, and makes me poor indeed."

Bryce laughed heartily—a sun-dappled Errol Flynn. They traded quotes back and forth. "How do you know so much Shakespeare, for a bible scholar?"

"Oh, I'm just full of surprises, Mr. Everett."

"I shall sleep well tonight," said Stephen, dusty and refreshed, when they got back to the truck.

"And I shall be sore tomorrow," admitted Bryce, not at all ashamed to admit it. "For I've not a dancer's legs." He paused to issue an invitation, just before opening the VW's door with his beautiful hand. "If you're ever in a pickle, Stephen, and need a refuge, there's a draughty little garret above my flat. It's free, I just use it for storage." He could tell that Stephen considered this a serious offer, which it was. "You could pretend you were a love-struck sop in a Dickens novel."

"That might be just the role for me."

123

The Wrong Side of Eternity

28. SCHOLARS BIBLE COLLEGE, FRIDAY

Later in the afternoon, Madeleine sat primly across the desk from Professor Collins, who was her best source when it came to checking her biblical references. She and his wife met regularly for coffee and fellowship, two women discussing the balancing act of holding orthodox values in a world fallen into compromise. But she had not initiated this meeting; Professor Collins had. He said he had a concern he wanted to share with her.

"Miss Benson, I've been enjoying both your immense knowledge and your spunk at the last two debates. Are you planning to continue this activity?"

"Absolutely, sir. The issues need a woman's voice, in light of the changes some churches are making in their practice." Women's ordination, mostly, but she needn't say this; Professor Collins was adept at grasping the subtle.

"I admire your courage, and you know I am always available to you for any questions you might have regarding your content."

"I very much appreciate that, sir."

He pressed his fingertips together and looked down briefly at the note on his desk. "You need to practice what you teach," he advised.

"Yes, of course, or else it would be hypocrisy."

He sighed, and looked up with sudden concern. "Miss Benson, you so capably advocate the biblical ideal of the married woman. Have you any prospects yourself?"

She smiled warmly but only to hide her embarrassment. "No, not at the present time."

"Anyone, ah, expressing interest in spending time with you?"

"Yes, sir, but the relationship is only in the beginning stages."

"I won't intrude on your privacy, Miss Benson, but I do wish to know if his theology is sound."

"He is an evangelical, sir."

"I'm relieved to hear it." An awkward pause ensued; the professor seemed to be trying to find just the right phrasing for his counsel.

124

Act I

"Please feel free to contact my wife, Susan, for help with the more personal matters. I do wish the best for you, you know," he said, looking over his glasses with fatherly affection. "It would be best for your public if you were to exemplify everything you so ably convey...that is, if you were to marry in the near future."

"Thank you for that. My parents have been encouraging me for two years now."

"They love you, of course."

"Of course." They also monitored her progress, kept clippings of any news articles with her name in them, no matter how brief. They wanted her to succeed. Her mother, a socialite, had given her poise; her father, a lawyer, had bequeathed a thirst for the truth, knowledge—and a passion to confront those in error. She was aware that her father and Professor Collins spoke occasionally on the phone—about her. She knew that the professor regularly asked him about her submission as a daughter.

"I wish you well in your courtship."

"Thank you, Professor," she said, rising to go. Some naughty part of her mind was telling her to curtsey before making her exit, but she ignored the temptation. He would interpret the gesture as mockery. Whether it was rebellious or not, she couldn't tell. She was too well bred to give it much thought.

Madeleine paused as the door clicked closed. She walked, slowly for a change, along the carpeted corridor and beyond, where the leaves were a brilliant green and the sunny air greeted her with a crisp coolness. Her eyes closed, she stopped, and took herself back home to New England, where the colors were deeper and more extensive in the autumn, where age-old traditions kept respect locked inside every human exchange.

Another book-learned memory intruded into her thoughts: selections from the trial of Mrs. Anne Hutchinson, who had acted in such a way as to subvert the Puritan community in the seventeenth century. The quote echoed with the voice of Professor Collins: "We have thought good to send for you to understand how things are, that if you be in an erroneous way we may reduce you that so you may become a profitable member

125

The Wrong Side of Eternity

here among us. Otherwise if you be obstinate in your course that then the court may take such course that you may trouble us no further..."

It was about the accused having the temerity to offer spiritual instruction to men who sought her counsel. The outcome, she recalled, was imprisonment and banishment and the conclusion that Mrs. Hutchinson's opinions were "different from the word of God," and therefore a stumbling block to believers. *Which they were, of course.* But the dear governor who passed judgment also said: "She was a woman of haughty and fierce carriage, a nimble wit and active spirit, a very voluble tongue, more bold than a man."

So there.

Sometimes the acuity of her memory was a painful gift. She sighed and proceeded with her walk, making plans.

She was lost in her thoughts and missed the gossip circulating around the campus, where students were beginning to pack up for the summer break.

"Did you hear what happened to Stephen O'Connell?"

"That Mexican leprechaun?"

"Yeah, him. They dismissed him, you know."

"I think he moved over to the city to live with some fairy."

"Figures."

29. UNIVERSITY HOSPITAL, 7:15 A.M. THURSDAY

In the early morning, as he was nearly stumbling toward the door just after the change of shift, Stephen ran into a group of white-coated medical students and their professor in the hallway. Their heads were bowed and their deliberations hushed—so like a football team in huddle, planning a play. He paused just around the corner to try to catch their conversation.

Act I

"…a rare form of cancer, Kaposi's Sarcoma. It's never heard of in the West…Had two cases like this, and several on the East Coast…some sort of immune deficiency. All the present victims seem to be gay men…"

Stephen knew that his fellow students would read about it in the newspaper while researching current events, amid the references to the nuns killed in El Salvador, reviews of *The Elephant Man*, the suicidal deaths of that Jonestown cult.

They would say the patients deserved what they got.

30. LUIGI'S RESTAURANT, 9:00 P.M. SATURDAY, THREE WEEKS LATER

Stephen helped Julie with her coat, hanging up both hers and his on the coat tree inside the restaurant door. He felt nervous but could not tell why. They found a roomy booth in the corner, one of the almost circular ones. Julie was telling him about her plans to travel up north, see her folks this summer; he could hear the wistfulness in her voice when she mentioned the trees, the rural hamlet where they decided to retire, their ongoing correspondence with friends from their mission days in both Africa and America.

Bryce and Madeleine entered, and Stephen watched bemused as they replayed the whole coat scene near the door. They made such a beautiful couple: well dressed, attractive, polished. Beautiful people. They could appear on the cover of a healthy-values magazine: *Godly Living*, he imagined its title. There would be pictures of an immaculate kitchen, a garden breakfast nook with an open bible set alongside a porcelain coffee cup, the text of a table grace on the wall in muted gothic letters…

"Happy to see you again!" clucked Bryce, clapping Stephen on the back. He reached across the table to shake hands with Julie. "Miss Burns, I assume?" She beamed, thoroughly enjoying the performance, and responded in kind.

"The illustrious Mr. Everett, how are you this evening?"

127

The Wrong Side of Eternity

"Very well, thank you. May I introduce the esteemed Madeleine Benson?"

"Pleased to meet you," Julie said.

Stephen barely caught her alarmed look of recognition. Had they two met before?

"I call her Maddy, just to get the color to rise to her face," he interjected.

"Everyone back East calls me that," admitted Madeleine, and it was up to each of the others to decide which name they would use. Bryce opted for the more sophisticated, of course.

"I heard you're registered at the university now," she said to Stephen.

"Yes. Studying people," Bryce said. "We're such a fascinating lot."

"Sociology," Stephen amended. "Professor Stuart wrote me a reference. I guess it was something, because they offered me a pretty decent financial-aid package."

Madeleine pursed her lips. *Sociology. Such a waste of potential. Such a loss.*

After a bottle of mid-priced table wine, the conversation lightened up a bit. Stephen sat back, enjoying the banter of the others.

"Hey, Maddy, you and I could go into business together," Julie said, embedding her tongue deeply into her cheek. "Benson and Burns."

"Really? In what capacity?"

"Cutting-edge prosthetics. That, or computer software for medical missions." She leaned forward, her eyes sparkling. "I hear you're amazing with the research."

"Passionate," echoed Bryce, ogling the bit of cleavage displayed by Stephen's date. His eyes turned quickly toward Madeleine. "There's no defeating her."

Stephen smiled imperceptibly. Bryce was a harmless, shameless flirt.

At the end of a lively evening, they walked from the restaurant in opposite directions. Julie leaned into Stephen, her arm hugging his elbow. "What a guy," she laughed.

Act I

"Bryce? Yeah…Jules, I hope you come to love him as much as I do."

At this she stopped and peered into his face. "That's impossible, Stephen," she merely said, and they walked on together.

ENTR'ACTE

———

Fire and Air, Earth and Water
Wander through silence, beyond tears and laughter
Be harrowed together, then harnessed and hurled
Through this portal, out into the world

Bear the burdens, bind the wounds
Of peasants, soldiers, merchants, crowns;
When at the loud summons, called back from war,
Return to no prison. Instead, find a Door.

Entr'acte

There is no soul such a giant that it does not
often need to become a child again.

—TERESA OF AVILA

31. IN THE FOREST

SO GOOD TO BE AWAY from the routine and bustle of hospital life. Julie
felt her limbs heavy with fatigue—not from overdoing but from a long,
sustained propulsion, the marathon of full-time employment. Her carry-on duffel felt dense as she heaved it into the overhead bin, and that
should not have been. It wasn't that heavy. The fatigue carried with it a
weight of living through things: hours of unpaid clinical practice, passing the certification board, transition from junior therapist to mentor,
exchanging reports on patients' progress, clinical notes.

She plopped herself into the narrow seat nearest the window and
looked out at the fresh morning, then pulled her itinerary out of her
pocket. To the northwest, the trees and her home; perhaps she'd borrow
a car and make a foray to the rocky coast to let the wind whip through
her hair, even if she'd have to spend nearly an hour untangling it at day's
end. The talk with the parents, at once longed for and dreaded. Then to
the desert, to meet that wondrous and melancholy Stephen O'Connell;
at the mere thought of him she smiled. Was he really what he appeared
to be, a considerate gentleman, a sensitive soul? She had no inkling as
to whether this was the right course of action or not. It was just how the
holiday was planned to happen. Would happen. Might happen...

She let her head fall back against the seat to savor the pressure build-
up as the plane sped skyward. The push of gravity in her lap—she relaxed, while others tensed up at the moment the great hunk of metal
and wiring became airborne. It was strange for her, wanting privacy,
solitude—and yet she craved it, shunning conversation with the woman
at her right, whose mouth was sealed shut in a tight line but who would
surely want to chat later. She seemed a nervous kind of person.

Julie needed a break. She opened a leftover popular novel, left abandoned in the seat pocket in front of her, and pretended to read. Maybe later she would sleep. But now she needed to just think, take an inner inventory.

Spiritual life, check. She'd always started there. St. Simeon's was the best thing that had ever happened to her. Margaret, she could talk to— an older sister you could share secrets with. The guilt at failing to have a daily quiet time was ebbing, and the scriptures grew and knocked and became living questions that danced inside her head, instead of rules to memorize or lessons to learn. She knew, without doubt or reservation, that she was eternally loved: it took all the pressure off, and just recalling the fact brought her to near laughter, right there in her airplane seat. She did find herself smiling, unable to stop the tide of grace.

Career, check. She'd gotten some good reviews from Bob during her first year. Commendations, even, for being creative when a treatment program seemed to be impossible for this diabetic with foot ulcers, that stroke patient with depression, and the guy with the mangled hand who wanted to exercise well before the draining wound had closed. She looked forward to going to work and gravitated to the "minority" folks who didn't seem to know what to do with an urban Western way of thinking. No, that was automatic, and she knew the needle in her inner compass would always swing around to the magnetic north known here as the Third World. She'd taken a class in medical anthropology and knew that someday she would leave the supposed safety of the University Hospital and reengage the overwhelming needs in Africa. She just knew it. How, she had no clue: she would let the tidal current carry her there in its own good time.

Adulthood, check. No, un-check. She still felt the stranger, although she'd lived on the West Coast now for over a decade. She had her own apartment, but it was a temporary shelter disguised as home; she'd not put down roots, not even been tempted to after being jettisoned like dangerous ballast in a storm by that self-righteous SBC prick Neil...No, she'd entered the relationship with her eyes open, even if her heart was naively full of stupid hope. She'd let him toy with her, make love to her while all the time maintaining an air of chastity, as if the laws of Moses were suspended if you were just holy enough. She clutched at her lower abdomen, and the pain bubbled up afresh to mock her own self-assessment. She dreaded facing her loving parents, dreaded not telling them. She would never tell them. Her eyes stung, and she grabbed the paperback tighter to compensate. She turned the page, not even seeing the printed words.

"C'mon, Sparky!"

The feisty little mongrel flew toward her, welcoming her home. He was scraggly, squat, and by some standards ugly, with bright brown eyes that really looked at you. She thought him clairvoyant, the way he picked up on her mood. He seemed relieved when she did not appear to want to go running, his doggy age catching up with him. She dropped her carry-on in her room, donned her hiking boots, and headed back out the door with him in tow.

They cut across the meadow behind her parents' homestead, heading toward Sliver Falls, two miles away. The small gravel parking lot was perpetually empty; decades ago, an inebriated sign painter had misspelled 'silver', and the Forest Service never replaced the faulty sign. So 'sliver' had eventually made its way into maps and booklets, and, lacking the exotic and enchanting reference to a precious metal, went unnoticed by the masses. But the locals knew better, and so Sliver Falls became a favorite haunt of souls seeking solace.

You could hear the water pounding away at volcanic rock more than half a mile before you could see it: a white, undulating plume of foam cascading down the broken face of a basalt cliff. The path was overgrown, but the well-shod locals had carved their own switchbacks alongside the riverbed. Sparky struggled at times to keep up but was too happy for the outing to lag behind for long. They ambled directly into the forest, where a green canopy shut out sound and where shadow hushed the sterile world of symmetry.

The Wrong Side of Eternity

She drank in the green: the aspens and cedars arching overhead, the ferns and wildflowers at her feet. Julie could tell a Douglas fir from a western hemlock, a maple from a red alder, but the more serious nomenclature had drifted right past her. Her first boyfriend had prided himself by knowing the Latin as well as the generic names of just about all the local fauna, the *Delphinium nuttallianum* of the forest floor, the *Pseudotsuga menziesii* of the towering trees. The *Alnus rubra,* he'd explained, was used by Native Americans for medicinal purposes. She found it all so boring. And still the Latin stuck in her memory! It was enough for her to savor the delicacy of a fern-like cedar frond or admire the translucence of a maple leaf, to study the tidal waving of the pines standing sentinel above her or contemplate the direction of the wind. Why ruin it by attaching a label?

After an hour's walk on old paths lined with lichen-covered rocks, she and the little dog arrived at a small stream, a babbling brook with just enough white water to fool you into thinking it was mist. She turned off the trail into a sheltered outcropping halfway to the top.

Overhead, the clouds softened contrasts, and she gathered up the little mutt into her lap for warmth. Then she nestled into a smooth rock hollow and fell into the embrace of the woods, letting her mind unravel, sinking into a light sleep. Tears glistened on her eyelids, and a smile lingered on her face.

Dusk had fallen. Bonnie stepped outside to greet Julie as soon as her footfalls could be heard crunching on the gravel of the driveway.

"You're out a bit late."

Her mom always was a worrier.

"I had vicious little Sparky with me," Julie answered.

"So I see."

"What, did you think Bigfoot would get us?"

All the news in the papers lately, Bonnie thought, *and she jokes about it.*

Entr'acte

Through the Thou, a person becomes "I."

—Martin Buber

32. In the Desert

Stephen picked her up at the airport, and they headed east that afternoon, winding their way up into the mountains just for the scenery. The planned route took them across the desert during the night, shaded by starlight against the glare of the day. Julie was an experienced car tripper; that was evident by the old metal thermos and the baggage with external pockets, making just about everything accessible within the minute cabin of the truck. He already knew she liked to walk, and he looked forward to stretching his legs himself out in open country. The sun lit up the road climbing up in front of them, and they began to relax.

She asked about him, his history, his family, and he replied generously, noticing that she was intensely attentive. Quiet gaps intersected with an occasional question. She sipped strong coffee and gazed at the highway, drinking in his story and, perhaps, mentally comparing it with her own. When he told her he'd been brought up on Irish poetry, she asked him for a sample.

"You're not serious."

"I am too. People have thought I was Irish my whole life because of my hair."

"Promise you won't laugh," he said.

"No, I won't promise that."

He swallowed hard. The meandering river to their left tumbled through granite pools, and the trees stretched straight upward. "All right, here goes:

Oh, to have a little house!
To own the hearth and stool and all!

The heaped-up sods upon the fire
The pile of turf against the wall!

Och, but I'm weary of mist and dark,
And roads where there's never a house or bush
And tired I am of bog and road
And the crying of the wind and the lonesome hush!"

She didn't laugh. After a thirty-second silence, she just turned and looked at his profile and smiled.

They stopped for soup and salad in a secluded alpine vale and stretched their legs beside the meandering river behind the lodge. He found her outside the ladies' room, admiring the black-and-white photos of a log building up to its eaves in snowbank, and sighing.

"Let's honeymoon here," she said and, without waiting for his answer, headed back to the truck.

"Your turn," he ventured, when twilight overshadowed them. He could just make out a slight frown on her face, and he guessed that she was trying to find a place to begin.

"My first memories were of Africa, and I'm always going back there in my imagination." The dimness softened her features, and her tone. She reminisced like an old woman tracing an edge of lace on an antique dress or tablecloth, telling him about the simple games she'd played with the local children. Her lullaby voice and the evening light wove together, warp and woof, and made magic in his senses. He could smell the cooking fires, hear the dancing music, feel the woven grass mat below his bare feet. Her homesickness infected him.

They reached the desert floor and turned south.

"It was more than a bit of a shock, arriving here. I was twelve, and unimaginably naive...No, not naive, just not cultured."

Not a West Coast American, he surmised, but an international child whose mind easily stretched well beyond the borders of the nearest mall. Wise, in an Old World sort of way.

"You seem pretty mature to me," he said.

"Well, those next five years were, ah, pretty formative. I had to put up with puberty at the same time as cross-cultural reentry, which is a greater trauma than anyone can know who hasn't been through it. It's worse, I think, for mission families than for the military ones. Most of the time they have the consistent culture of the base. Well, I've met missionaries who stay in a compound kind of mind-set, too, and they're a lot alike. The 'foreign culture' is outside, the 'home culture' inside the walls or fence or whatever. My folks refused to cordon themselves off like that. Anyway…"

He let the silence breathe between them while the stars came out and the lavender glow sank into the west, behind the gigantic wall of granite to their right.

"How did you find St. Simeon's?" he asked.

"Oh, I stumbled in there on the brink of suicide," she answered, and Stephen felt a wave of shock. "I'd gotten involved with a recent grad of SBC, happened to be the dean's son, who dumped me as soon as he found out I was pregnant." There was fear in her voice now, but only a little, and he realized once again that she trusted him. "Of course I thought that, being a born-again Christian, he would do the honorable thing and marry me. I'm actually glad he didn't or it would have been hell. Word spread fast enough that I'd seduced him…I still can't put into words all that happened, so fast, but it was like emotional or spiritual blackmail and I kind of lost myself."

Half a mile passed in silence.

"Well, the Church sort of just caught me exiting the back door of the clinic. I guess I wandered into it or something. I found myself making a mess on Mother Margaret's office chair; she got me a box of tissues and some pads for the bleeding." Another pause. "God, that was horrible."

The Wrong Side of Eternity

"I can't imagine," was all he could say, but the image struck deep in his mind's eye: She was pale, and scared, and lost, and some angel had taken her by the hand and led her into the embrace of a maternal priest. Exactly what she needed at the time. He heard her sniffle and knew that tears wet her face, as she sat next to him in the dark, the miles stretching on ahead of them.

Somewhere in the desert, they pulled off the highway at a rest stop. He pulled out a mummy bag from behind his seat and tucked it in around them; they slept a few hours.

The road stretched behind them along with their morning shadow. Stephen looked right to see her still sleeping and comfortable, folded up with her feet draped across the duffel bag on the floor in front. What dormant strength she had! She could face anything and come out the other side more herself than ever. Real, that's what she was. She could teach him a lot.

He turned directly east and the rays of the sun smacked them full in the face. She stirred, mumbled a readiness to drive, and reached for her thermos. He laughed.

"It's only another hundred miles or so. We'll stop for breakfast first." She acquiesced and set to the business of waking up: rubbing her eyes, brushing her hair. God, the way the sun danced in it, it fired him up. "There's this great truck stop up here. I had oyster stew for breakfast once, last time I came home."

"You're kidding."

"Nope."

She laughed. "Maybe I'll try it. It can't possibly be fresh, but if it's the local specialty, hey, I'm game."

The tires rolled across the dirt driveway and sighed. They were going bald and couldn't last the trip back. At least they'd carried them this far. He would buy some used ones from Santiago...It was kind of Julie to not mention it. She seemed happy enough that the venerable old truck engine just kept firing. If she thought of it at all. *She doesn't seem to concern herself with anything, really*, Stephen thought, as he exited the cabin. He watched her turn westward to stretch and to soak up the morning sun on her back. Her eyes were closed, and she lifted her head, breathed in deeply, and smiled.

"It's like breathing light," she marveled.

"Yes, it is," he answered, but he'd never thought of it that way before.

Cipriana bustled to prepare them coffee. While Stephen had unloaded the baggage, she had met his "lady friend" with a welcome embrace. He watched his little mother hold Julie at arms' length and beam up into her face while squeezing her upper arms. He nearly chuckled; she always used to do that to him, every time he came home from camp or a trip anywhere. Checking his weight without using a scale.

"Qué bonita," was all she'd said then.

They stood in the shade of the porch, watching Julie meander along the dry creek bed, picking up stones.

"I hope she does not meet a rattlesnake, your Julie."

"She's too careful for that, Mama. She lived in West Africa when she was a girl."

"People cannot be too careful, míjo," she simply said.

He told her of his plans to go to the university now, and she, as always, listened and nodded. She was good that way.

"And her?"

"We want to be together, Mama, get married."

"Where? When? In the church?"

"Our church, Mama, by a priest." At this, Cipriana beamed with rapture. A priest! He sat down on a rush chair, took her hands in his, and looked up into her face. "A lady priest, Mama." But Cipriana's smile did not fade.

The Wrong Side of Eternity

"A priest is a priest, Estevaníto. Womens have been priests for many hundreds of years, offering themselves up for their families, giving birth..."

He had never thought about it that way.

His mother went back in to get him some *horchata*, his favorite drink, and he followed her. The mariachi band on the radio colored the little sitting room with upbeat Mexican music. She went on.

"I am hope you want me there, at your wedding."

"Of course I do, Mama!" He wrapped his arms around her waist and hugged her so tight she began to giggle.

MOTHER LODE HOT SPRINGS, the tiny brown sign read, 10 MILES. The sky was porcelain blue, clear as crystal; the jagged horizon stood out in razor-sharp contrast, gray-brown, dotted with pinpoints of cacti and sage, the occasional yucca jutting spear-like from the desert floor. They followed the sign, turning off the highway onto a dirt track. Neither spoke, and both left the windows wide open. The hot springs were not developed; only well-versed travelers took advantage of their remote location. You could barely see the weathered outline of an outhouse a stone's throw from the rock-lined pool. No parking lot greeted them; they parked on the sandy gravel at the end of the track and sat in the truck while the dust settled.

Stephen got out and stretched, facing the far hills, before doffing his outer clothing. When he turned around, Julie was already in the slightly murky rock pool, her cast-off clothes a pile on the side. The steaming water lapped against her pale shoulders, the floating silt just hiding the details of her breasts. He forced his eyes to not go any farther.

What's with this girl? he wondered. She didn't strike him as promiscuous, but as almost too innocent. Vulnerable rather than seductive. Her eyes closed, she soaked up the heat of the pool into her skin, her nose; her head was tilted back. Her face reminded him of that Bernini sculpture in the library book on art history...

Entr'acte

He entered the pool softly so as not to disturb whatever communion she was having with nature. He didn't know what to say, but chose to sit opposite her, leaning back against the rough stone wall. He swallowed his pride and asked the obvious.

"Is this a habit of yours, stripping for the elements?" Despite the fact that they were totally alone, he spoke quietly.

"A habit?" she answered, her eyes still closed. "I don't know. I just want to feel it, the wind, the water, the breathing of the earth."

"In mixed company?"

She opened her eyes, which sparkled, and grinned. The steam rose between them. "You mean with men?" She laughed outright. "Goodness no, Stephen, I told you that before. I won't reveal myself to anybody but my husband."

But what about...? But he bit his tongue before he said it. All her little hints of proposal... "Isn't it a little early for that?"

"Are you kidding? I think of it more as an appetizer. Come on, mister, shed your shorts and enjoy the currents. They're delicious!"

He was sure she wasn't inviting him to touch, and he kept his arms glued to his sides. Soon enough, his board shorts lay alongside the edge of the pool, and he breathed deeply and let the warmth caress him. He kept the water moving with his legs, though, to keep the flow of water going in order to disrupt his view from the surface.

She seemed to be just fine with that.

We dance round in a ring and suppose,
But the Secret sits in the middle and knows.

—ROBERT FROST

33. WITHIN WALLS

Bryce had flown to London two weeks ago. Madeleine envied him, relaxing among the gentry in Merry Old England while she studied and prepared. In an odd way, she was glad for the seclusion: he was becoming awfully distracting.

She had gotten used to having him in the audience. It had been unsettling at first, but she found his feedback and comments encouraging, and, accepting his advice, she grew in confidence. It was like taking lessons from a gourmet chef: the *flavors* of her speeches were all there, but did a bit of presentation help! He was so good at suggesting nuance, inflection…So tonight, when he wasn't in his usual spot, two-thirds back, house left, she missed him.

And in less than a week she would be in England, with him.

The auditorium was half full, a good sign of interest. It would have held four or five full lecture halls at SBC. The event had been well publicized on kiosks at the university and bulletin boards at churches. The opponents were well matched and had parried before in smaller settings. Usually, a liberal woman took on a male conservative, challenging the perceived status quo. This time, the gender roles were reversed, and Madeleine embraced the onslaught.

She had become well known in Christian circles, although a few pastors had felt it their duty to meet with her in private to make sure she understood that the New Testament frowned upon women speaking in public in any capacity where teaching men was concerned. So she had developed a unique tactic, that of standing up for Women's Privilege, embracing the time-honored traditions of the church, promoting the

Entr'acte

biblical tenet of submission as influence, as outreach, as its own kind of evangelism. She had gone to women's shelters to minister and to listen to stories of abuse, and she concluded that if a man were truly born again, he would never beat his wife. Only men who were drug addicts, alcoholics, or prone to violence would dare cross that line.

In her own way, she admitted, she was as idealistic as Stephen O'Connell. Who was getting married! Feisty little thing, that athletic redhead gal. Despite growing up on the mission field and getting a certificate at SBC, she'd had quite the fall. Just goes to show you what a year or two in the world could do to a person...Well, at least Madeleine's future husband would be getting a virgin for a bride. She had it over Julie in purity: that was beyond doubt.

The debate rules tonight were unique in that they allowed the opponents to cite only from biblical sources, contrast biblical ideas with the scriptures of other world religions, or reference quotes from literature greats insofar as they were referring to the Bible. Madeleine was well prepared, with one exception: she was not well versed in that gray zone of scripture that Protestants called the Apocrypha and that Orthodox and Catholics in varying degrees accepted as the word of God. And Dr. Goodson pulled those out of nowhere, as a magician would pull white rabbits out of a top hat. He started off.

"We must remember that the didactic parts of the scriptures differ at times from the stories, the models presented. The teachings of the Jewish scriptures—formerly known as the Old Testament—are patriarchal, sometimes misogynist even. But then you have such stalwart heroes as Deborah, the judge of Israel; Jael, whose weapon of deliverance was a tent stake; Ruth and Rahab, both foreigners who embraced the faith of the Hebrews and became named ancestors in the genealogy of Christ. Huldah, the prophetess, consulted by King Josiah. Susanna and Judith, braver than the men of their day."

"However, in the writings of Paul," answered Madeleine, "it is quite clear that women are not to seek positions of leadership in the church. They are to work in tandem with their husbands and provide godly nurture to their children, to engage in hospitality and to serve."

He smiled. "And yet, the writer of the Acts names several women as peers of Saint Paul, who not only host worship but actively evangelize: Prisca and Lydia, for instance. The four daughters of Philip the evangelist, who had the gift of prophecy. Tabitha, considered a saint. And Junia, who Paul, in the sixteenth chapter of Romans, calls 'prominent among the apostles.' Such women are not always linked with a husband or influential father. Both Luke and John gave remarkable roles to women in their Gospels: women disciples are commended and sometimes set up as examples for righteous men who just aren't getting Jesus's message. The Samaritan woman, to whom Jesus first admitted he was Messiah. She went and evangelized a whole town."

"She did not assume the role of teacher, however," countered Madeleine, respectfully. "She merely testified, in public, as to what wonderful things God had done for her. As should all women."

"As did Mary Magdalene, the first witness to the risen Lord. The apostles, as the account goes, didn't even believe her. Why should they? She was a woman."

It was harder sometimes to hold her ground than to make a bold assault on the field of debate. And yet Madeleine could see, with Bryce's tender help, that the gentle approach would probably bear more fruit in the long run. So tonight was one of those. *Hold your ground—be gracious, courteous. Do not concede: aim for a draw.*

How tired she was when she reached her apartment! She put the kettle on, to make some tea, and took a yogurt out of the fridge. As she sipped and ate, she decided.

She pulled his card out of her purse and turned it over, then reached for the phone. *I don't know if I've ever dialed such a long number,* she thought, carefully punching in what he'd written on the back. She found herself holding her breath as the tone rang on the other side of

Entr'acte

the world, five thousand miles away. One…two…On the sixth ring, he picked up.

"Hello, four-one-seven-four."

"Bryce, it's me, Madeleine."

"And what prompts you to phone at six in the morning, love?" he asked through a yawn. She had forgotten all about the time difference. So unlike her, to miss a detail like that!

"Oh, I am *so* sorry, Bryce…I was so eager to talk with you, I didn't even think about it. Please forgive me," she pleaded.

He laughed. "Don't trouble yourself over it, at all. It's so lovely to hear your voice again! If I weren't already having the best dream in the world, you've woken me up to it now." Bryce, her heart's desire. "Say, didn't you have a debate this evening? Or rather, last evening?"

"Yes, and it went fairly well, but I did miss your presence." *More than you know.* "We ended up in the usual truce of agreeing to disagree, keeping an open mind."

"That's my girl, ever the polite opponent." There was a pause. "Father's looking *so* forward to meeting you."

"And my parents you, on the return journey. I'll be stopping there for a few nights en route," she explained. *Mother wants to take me shopping…give me some pointers on etiquette,* she wanted to add but chose not to. "I'm looking forward to meeting him as well. Any chance we'll get to see your mum?"

"None."

Case closed. It was a sore spot, and she wouldn't broach it again.

"I'll meet you at the airport," he went on. "It's a fairly quick run from Manchester over to the Lake District. I know all about jet lag, so when you tire of the scenery, you can have a chance to rest on my shoulder. We'll arrive in good time for you to catch a few winks, freshen up, before meeting the Old Man."

"That sounds wonderful," she admitted, already feeling the tide of sleep stealing over her. "I'll see you then, very soon."

"Yes, my dear. Very soon."

Yes.

Nec amor nec tussis celatur.
('Neither love nor a cough can be hidden')

LATIN PROVERB

34. IN THE GLEN

Bryce strolled up and down the garden path, happy to be home. He took in the rolling hills and inhaled deeply as puffy clouds drifted overhead; it was a beautiful day at the height of summer. He followed the footpath to the water's edge to watch the boats. So much of his core self was here, ambling along the many trails and skipping stones into the water. He closed his eyes and pictured Madeleine at his side, and couldn't help but smile. No, grin, actually.

She would love it here. And she needed a holiday, a real break from all the presentations. She needed to relax, in several different ways. He seemed to have earned her trust: perhaps she could unwind here a little, with him.

His father had grilled him shortly after breakfast, so some of the more awkward questions would be left behind.

"I've two lovely, brilliant children, and you both have to marry *Americans?*" Sir Thomas Everett had asked in polite exasperation, seated with his son in the glass-encased conservatory overlooking the courtyard. He stirred his second cup of tea and lowered the cup and saucer to his lap.

Bryce poured on the charm. "Well, Father, you always told us to follow our hearts. And if our prospective spouses—spice—are lovely and brilliant as well? Does not that somewhat offset the cultural inconvenience?"

Thomas placed his teacup on the glass top of the white wicker table, folded his hands over his elegantly crossed knees. His gaze drifted over the manicured gardens.

"Not merely the inconvenience of culture," he noted. "But the distance! Bryce, it's such a journey, and I'm not getting any younger." Sir

Entr'acte

Thomas was hale and hearty and had never complained about distance until his daughter, Gwen, got married. His wife had left years ago, and he was finding bachelorhood trying, even with all the service help.

"Gwen and her family come every other year to see you, for an extended visit. We could alternate, and then you'd have at least one yearly family gathering to look forward to," answered Bryce. He reached for more practical ammunition. "If I were working in London or York, visits with you here would still be occasional…We could settle in New England, where she is from. It's an easier journey from there to here."

"No, you've told me already that you've both plenty to do right where you are. God knows the West Coast could use more civilizing, at any rate. Have you heard about this new plague? AIDS, they're calling it in the papers. Spreading all over that fallen city right next door to you." He reached for his pipe. Bryce always thought it served more as an aromatic gentleman's prop, something to do with keeping his father's hands busy, than a tobacco habit. Sir Thomas would on occasion leave it in his mouth, but he only rarely lit it to take in a puff. He had often used it as a pointer in his architectural presentations.

"Yes, I have. But the research seems to be showing that apart from sexual intercourse, and perhaps blood transfusions, it's nearly impossible to contract."

Sir Thomas removed the pipe from his mouth. "She'll have to be tested."

"Father! She's a quintessential virgin!" he protested, while the older man smiled.

"Only checking your defensive impulses, Bryce. Of *course* she's a virgin, with her upbringing. And when did you say she committed her life to Christ? Ah, yes, when she was ten. You're obviously quite taken with her."

"As will you be, once you meet."

"This coming Wednesday, is it?"

"Yes, Father, she flies into Manchester. If I may borrow the car…"

"Which one?"

The Wrong Side of Eternity

"The Mercedes." Not too flashy.

Sir Thomas leaned back. "That will be satisfactory."

The morning of her arrival, Bryce expected his father to return to a certain topic, and he wasn't disappointed.

"I'm still wondering how I will cope with having two children-in-law in the States. Peter is actually considering coming over here to work, you know."

"Really? He and Gwen seemed so settled, last I saw them."

"You do realise, don't you, Bryce, that your sister moved west just to be closer to you."

"I doubt it. Peter merely took advantage of a great job offer. Happened to be close by." He tried a different tack. "You should pop over once in a while, see us both in our new environment. The city does have its more cultured places. It's not all decadent and bohemian, Father."

"Perhaps I will." Sir Thomas surveyed the landscaped terrace out beyond the wall of windows, clothed in morning light. "All right, you've shown me the photographs. She's absolutely beautiful. On the inside as well?"

"You mean her behaviour, Father?" asked Bryce, coming to the point.

"And her history. You know I'm not so much concerned with her pedigree as with her life experience," his father said. "Is she *quite* saved?"

Bryce laughed. "I don't know anyone more saved than she. She's practically an evangelist, you know."

"Has she told you her entire story? Her past dating life, for instance?"

"Really, Father, you are an obsessive old coot. I told you, she's only dated very casually, no serious relationship."

"Until you?"

"Until me."

Sir Thomas nodded, and Bryce knew where his thoughts lay: A Christian, an educated woman. Unsullied, attractive. With good taste, he hoped. He could possibly forgive her for being an American.

150

"Perhaps you had better go in the finer car, with Colin, instead of taking the Mercedes. I should like to make a good first impression on this prospective bride of yours."

Bryce smiled, knowing he'd won the match.

The Bentley pulled into the circular drive, and Bryce peered out the window. He was pleased to see his father standing in front of the stone portal, hands in pockets, as the driver opened the passenger door. It was no small shock of delight that appeared on the face of Sir Thomas Everett when he was presented with Miss Madeleine Benson of Vermont. She was in a tasteful linen suit, and wearing *gloves*.

"That was lovely, Sir Everett," said Madeleine, elegantly wiping her mouth. High tea, in England. She took to it like a fish takes to water, aware of Bryce's unspoken approval as to how she was conveying herself.

And the accent, more New England than he'd heard before? More endearing than the Midwestern speech that had spread with the wagon trains westward all the way to the Pacific. A master stroke. He would tell her later how proud of her he was.

"So happy you could come such a long way."

"I've always wanted to. I used to sit in the corner of my father's study as a child, looking at picture books of Europe. The British Isles were my favorite."

They rose to tour the house, not so ostentatious as some of its neighbours but, according to Madeleine's reaction, impressive enough for her. Bryce excused himself, knowing his father's need for the one-on-one interview. She was immaculate, thus far, and could manage well enough on her own.

They stood in the book-lined study.

"Bryce told me a little about how you came into your knighthood, Sir Everett," she commented, surveying the honors and certificates

The Wrong Side of Eternity

tastefully mounted in one corner of the wood-paneled room. "I should like to hear more about your work."

She gave her full attention to his evaluation of his few modest architectural contributions to society—how he had designed, pro bono, remodels for both orphanages and lunatic asylums all over the United Kingdom.

"They were so sterile-looking, so ugly," he explained. "To inspire the charitable donations necessary for their survival, they needed a more tasteful presentation." He took down and opened an album of before-and-after pictures, complete with smiling visages of esteemed officials cutting ribbons in front of the newly constructed façades.

She carefully avoided any and all references to Bryce's mother, having deduced that the story was a scandalous embarrassment to the family. As she sauntered around the great country house, she imagined herself visiting often, perhaps even one day living here.

Just before dinner, Bryce knocked gently on her bedroom door.

"Do come in."

He stuck in his head. "Ready? You look gorgeous."

"Yes, and thank you." She took his arm for their descent down the staircase.

"One small pointer, though, darling," he said softly.

"Oh?" *He called me darling.*

"He'd probably prefer 'Thomas.'"

"Is that the more proper title?" She blushed. Oops. Her first mistake. And hopefully her last.

The evening meal was superb. Bryce introduced her to the cook, a middle-aged sturdy woman who allowed her into the sacred domain of kitchen and pantry. She confided to Madeleine that Sir Thomas was hopeless in this women's world and had to hire a Spanish maid to clean the house twice a week. Her name was, of course, Maria.

"Shall we retire to the drawing room then?" asked Sir Thomas, as Madeleine thanked the cook and stepped back into the dining room. He led the way, asking, "And what can I get you to drink?"

152

Really, Father, testing her like this. But Madeleine rose to the occasion.

"A very little cognac, if that would be all right," she answered, demurely. His body language showed that it would be very all right. She smiled and followed him, looking back at Bryce who gave her a thumbs up.

"We've quite a different setup here, regarding religion, than you do in the United States," explained Sir Thomas, eagerly. "The state church is of course quite reprobate, having to service any citizen that wants a christening or wedding..."

Holy Moses, Father, you make it sound like a whore, thought Bryce, watching from the sidelines as Sir Thomas poured the drinks.

"It's only too bad that, for all its erudition, it couldn't have parted with Rome over purely theological matters," Sir Thomas said. "Perhaps that set a pattern in motion, because its leaders can't stop compromising. They're becoming so liberal."

"They've held out longer than the North Americans when it comes to ordaining women," said Madeleine, seating herself on the sofa.

"It's only a matter of time, of *political correctness.* They'll give in eventually," he said with a gentlemanly display of bravado. He set his glass down and filled his pipe. "And some of the independent churches have taken to running after the latest fads, speaking in tongues and all." He turned the conversation back her way. "And how have you escaped all the slings and arrows, my dear? You're well learned—I understand you engage in theological debate! I'm sure there are those who would love to see a dog collar around your neck."

Bryce cringed; he was not at all sure that Madeleine knew the idiom in England for a clerical collar. And he feared she would think his father a boor.

"I take the Bible as God's word."

"Simple as that."

"Yes, Sir Thomas: simple as that." Madeleine took a sip from the crystal liqueur glass. It was her turn. "So how do orthodox Christians here maintain their standards?"

"Doctrine, my girl. Sound doctrine. All the senior pastors are well trained in the original biblical languages. No compromise with either the state church or the world."

"If I may be so bold to ask, Sir Thomas, what is your position on women's ministry?" she inquired.

Thomas eyed with approval the way she sipped her brandy. "Women are capable leaders, able to reach a certain audience," he admitted, "although they are not allowed ordination, naturally, or positions of authority over men."

"Naturally," she agreed.

"But few have risen to the point of actually being able to promote the values that you are so ably, according to my son, communicating in your presentations and debate. You would be a welcome addition here."

"Thank you, Sir Thomas." She blushed.

Bryce sat beaming, thoroughly enjoying the show.

"Now, son, a song before we retire," commanded his father, and Bryce bowed. He lifted the lid of the piano bench and searched for something suitable, something romantic and relaxing, something classical...He did feel self-conscious, though, playing and singing for an audience of two. He was no longer used to accompanying himself, and his skills of expression were nothing like his friend Stephen's.

He found himself hoping that Madeleine would be so carried away by his vocal rendition that she wouldn't notice the difference.

Late the next morning, he took her boating, rowing about the small lake in the dinghy. They had luncheon in a classic pub; he relished showing her off to the locals. And in the afternoon, he led her behind the gardens, across the lane, and up into the hills. Madeleine breathed in deeply, dropping her shoulders and taking in the fresh air. She let her head fall back just as Bryce caught it against his hand, and she opened her eyes.

He smiled. *I hope she sees a gentleman. Safe, protective. Respectful.*

Entr'acte

They descended the meandering slope and entered an old church-yard where ancient tombstones tilted like dominos frozen in mid-fall. He sat her down on a sheltered moss-tinted bench and pulled out a ther-mos from his leather satchel—along with two porcelain cups blanketed in bubble wrap, shortbread, and linen serviettes.

"You think of everything, don't you?"

"Don't *you?*" he answered, pouring clear tea from the flask. The steam rose invitingly in the shadowed air. "I thought I'd save you some trouble, put that brilliant mind of yours to rest."

"Thank you," she said, taking the delicate cup to warm her hands. It had turned into a coolish sort of day. He took off his light jacket and placed it around her shoulders. She wasn't surprised when, teacups aside, he reached to touch her face, and she let him. His fingers brushed her hair off her forehead and glided down to caress her ear, her neck. She closed her eyes.

It's high time we seriously kissed, she thought.

And kiss they did, there among the peaceful dead.

ACT II

Rural Uganda, 1990s

PORTAL

Projections of all kinds obscure our
view of our fellow men,
spoiling its objectivity, and thus spoiling
all possibility of genuine human relationships.

—DR. MARIE-LOUISE VON FRANZ,
A COLLEAGUE OF CARL JUNG

35. CHURCH OFFICES, THE WESTERN BORDERLANDS

CHARITY HEARD A CRY OF delight escape from Bishop Ruzaza's office and rose to see what it was about.

"Your grace?" she asked, standing in the doorway.

"They're sending us missioners!" he answered, beaming. "A young family. He'll help with the grant proposals—he's had experience writing those. And she's a physio-therapist!"

"*Who's* sending us missioners?" The diocese had applied to several different agencies. She wanted to know which one.

"Oh, Outreach to Central Africa. That branch of evangelicals, from England. They're long-term. We'll have to make ready for them."

OCA. Like Reverend Ann. She liked Reverend Ann, a modest New Zealander who seemed to have some cultural sensitivity as well as a sense

The Wrong Side of Eternity

of humour. The bishop picked up the letter and read it like a cleric, peering down over it with his reading glasses.

"They're Americans."

"Americans?" *In OCA? Americans.* She sighed. Someone had shown her a *Newsweek* once detailing the horrors of the days of Amin. Horrors she knew only too well. They knew, those Americans, they knew all about it, and they did nothing to help. Just made money writing about other countries' tragedies in their glossy magazines...

"The new guest house is nearing completion, isn't it, Geoffrey?" the bishop asked. The diocesan administrator nodded in reply. "So they can move into the old one next door. And that would be most convenient, because they could entertain the other Westerners who come to review the projects."

Charity liked how the bishop thought aloud; it afforded him some self-regard and kept communications clear. You never had to guess what Bishop Ruzaza was thinking.

"They'll come with a vehicle, probably a container, so we'll need to upgrade the old guest house, build them a driveway..."

"OCA missioners, the ones I know, Bishop, tend to be modest," offered Geoffrey. "Do you think they'll really—"

"A young family? Of course." The bishop looked up. He'd been educated in the States, he should know. "Can you imagine them using our public transportation?" He smiled, knowing that meant riding in the back of a pickup lorry over three hours of bouncy, winding road. The highway to Rutoki meandered among the cinder cones of the Ibirunga volcanic chain, bearing overloaded trucks of people or supplies or, often in the same trip, both. "Geoffrey, we'll need to look at the budget, see what improvements we can make before they arrive."

"What are their names?" asked Charity.

"Their names?"

She nodded. The bishop looked back down at the paper.

"O'Connell..."

Geoffrey started, hope rising high. Charity caught this and marveled.

160

Act II

"…Stephen O'Connell. His wife, Julie, and a small son, Sam."

"I know them from my time at the university," admitted Geoffrey, aglow. "They're wonderful people, Bishop. They know how to listen."

We'll see, thought Charity, but she added nothing further.

She wondered what they would be like. Reverend Ann she treated as a headmistress, deferentially providing superb secretarial assistance. Since the revival had touched parts of her life, Charity had become an avid reader of scripture. Lately, Reverend Ann had taken her into her confidence; when Ann couldn't find a bible reference, the missioner would casually mention it to her, and Charity would pull verses out of her astute memory or scour the concordance to save the busy pastor time.

Poised, elegant, polished, and more competent than many an elected official, Charity Ntambara shone. Everyone respected her. They also became quiet when she entered a room. No one talked about what had happened fifteen years ago, but people guessed. It had happened to so many girls, most of whom had married, had taken up the semblance of normalcy. Charity had risen from the ranks of secretarial-school graduate to the manager of the local orphan-sponsorship project in little less than two years. Without a teaching credential, she tutored girls at the secondary school in English, girls who excelled during the examinations and who went on to the university in Kampala to study law.

Charity herself knew she was accomplished and professional while simultaneously polite and submissive; she never asserted herself in public but managed to convince many a leader to adopt certain policies and decisions that never failed to make him look good.

It was obvious to everyone that her life's calling was to serve.

She also knew what people said about her in the privacy of their homes. It was too bad that she would not marry. She had all the beauty of a queen, all the poise of a model. Her parents were so proud of her. They knew she was bright, but only Charity herself knew that she was not stupid. She had read Western novels and noted how women in them were treated. Not like African women, certainly, but little better. She knew the cards were stacked against her. And this one black mark in her history only served to underscore the simple fact that she was not *available*. At some point in the future, long after she had passed, they would call her the African Emily Dickinson. But she held no such high hopes for herself.

For herself, Charity was always on guard.

36. OCA HEAD OFFICE, LONDON

The O'Connells' time in the UK had flown by, spent on meetings at the mission office, an excursion to a museum, and a night in the theatre district with the couple that had so kindly put them all up for the week. Sam particularly enjoyed the rides atop the red buses, where he could see over everything. When they weren't meeting with supporting churches or out walking on the commons, Stephen sat upstairs gazing out diamond window panes over the rolling hills and meadows that stretched to the horizon. Eight hours of jet lag was no laughing matter, and they were all glad for the lull. And for a chance to begin adjusting their speech to the lilting dialects they were sure to find in post-colonial East Africa.

"You take it too personally, Stephen," remarked Julie, when another joke about "the colonies" set his jaw to grinding. "They're just trying to be friendly."

"Maybe I should try my Irish brogue—it might meet with better results."

"It might. It might not. Whatever you talk like, my darlin' laddie, you're sure to offend somebody. It's inevitable. Live and learn."

"You're right," he admitted. On even the grayest of days she seemed to cast little waves of sunlight from her hair and face. When he got cross, she merely grew quiet, directing her full attention to their three-year-old. It was the threshold of a new decade and the portal to a new life. *Get used to it, stay in the present*, he told himself.

162

Act II

They sat with Joseph and a small administrative team in the modest OCA office overlooking the brown-tinted Thames. Becky, the "everything gal," had taken Sam up to the roof to admire the view and feed pigeons. The group prayer time had just ended.

"Right, then. Did you have any further questions?"

Stephen shook his head, but Julie chose to speak up.

"Yes—but more comment than question."

"Fire ahead."

"We've done—all your missioners have done—so much in the way of evaluation and training. There's been so much encouragement to 'shed one's baggage' and heal from the past." They all nodded, apparently happy that she appreciated their costly investment. "But I am wondering if perhaps one of the magical things about mission is not the baggage that's *shed,* but the redemptive power of the baggage that's *kept.*"

Joseph leaned forward, looking intrigued. She hadn't said much until now. "Do go on, Julie."

"I mean, if a person is struggling to put some sort of trauma to rest and just can't, despite prayer sessions and reading the right sort of books and all, perhaps it is because God has a *use* for their baggage." She wiggled in her chair. Stephen alone knew what she was talking about. He loved her unconventional way of putting things. "Say, if a white missioner arrives in Uganda with loads of stuff, that might be off-putting, distancing. If they arrive with nothing at all, then they have nothing to share. But if they come with just the right, ah, *recipe* in their bag for a higher-protein diet, or maybe a particularly affordable new medication to fight AIDS or something, would that not be appropriate *baggage?*"

Joseph nodded, while others began to gather up files and folders, glancing at wristwatches, their thoughts already returning to the scheduled events of the day. He sat calmly, listening. Julie continued.

"So if a Christian carries a hurt, not out of a lack of forgiveness but just because they are a human being, could that not possibly be used of God to bring grace somehow?"

The Wrong Side of Eternity

"The hurt itself, you mean."

"Yes. And both directions—their hurts helping us too."

The mission director paused, and chose his words carefully. "Our biblical heroes all had plenty of baggage, Julie. It did not seem to have stopped God from using them. In spite of all our training and knowledge, there is always the mystery of human pain, human suffering, and the availability of God's redemptive grace in the middle of it. We have to believe that, it's why we exist. The people we serve have suffered so much...So yes, some things that we might regret in our lives might be powerful and of use, if they are united with the gospel. You never know with people."

They stood up together, and Joseph offered her his hand to wish them well, held hers a brief moment, and smiled.

37. EN ROUTE TO RUTOKI

The mission family stepped off the next plane into a different world. The air hung thickly about them, its haze a blend of dust and engine exhaust. Julie smiled: *the smell of Africa.* Well, one little slice of Africa, the emergence from Western civilization into the developing world, that part.

Stephen scowled: the earth was red, the sky a muddy pale blue, the heat a sticky layer that clung to his skin, his clothes. Sam hugged his little day pack and held his mother's hand, spellbound. They descended the rolling stairway to collect their five battered suitcases.

Their official letter of invitation to serve in the borderlands was reviewed, their visas issued, their passports examined and stamped. Armed guards stood about, looking bored. The customs officer with the mellifluous voice defied description: Stephen couldn't tell if the uniform disguised an effeminate man or a masculine woman. Or— was it even possible, here in Uganda—someone in between? They were ordered to open two of their suitcases, and the officers found nothing worth bothering about: clothes, camping gear, anti-malarial medications. Julie smiled at everyone, stuffing their belongings back inside their baggage so as not to hold up the line. Stephen piled the suitcases precariously upon a rusty cart, and with squeaking wheels they approached the airport's arrival lounge, a bland open space with dirty tiles on the floor.

A smiling fellow held up a sign reading O'CONNELL, and Stephen led his family over.

"Welcome! My name is Wilberforce," the fellow said, offering his hand. "Bishop sent me, Mr. O'Connell. I am to take you to the guest house in the capital, for two days' rest, and your things on to Rutoki. We should hurry," he said, less loudly. "There are thieves here, and we need to get there before dark." He glanced cautiously about while guiding the mission family over to a white Land Rover.

Stephen nodded. *Wilberforce? Oh, the British influence.* He helped the bishop's driver load their luggage into the back of the dust-coated vehicle; when they had settled Julie and Sam onto a back bench with no seat belts, Stephen climbed into the front passenger seat, and Wilberforce started the roaring engine. A cloud of diesel fumes billowed out the back. Their conversation was small talk and simple questions; the driver's English seemed fairly limited.

Stephen yawned. After an overnight twelve-hour flight, a couple days at the guest house and a hot shower—even a lukewarm one—sounded pretty good about now.

Stephen and his family walked as much as possible, from the guest house past the enormous brick cathedral to the bustling streets of the capital and back, taking in the noises of the taxi park, the smells of the markets, the brown dusty veneer covering all the bright colors. But they all soon learned that there was safety in numbers: anyone who tried to cross a busy street in the capital could tell you that. The traffic moved like darting schools of fish, and one couldn't predict anything.

The Wrong Side of Eternity

Six hours in a Land Cruiser with a young family. How convenient that the Thompsons just happened to be heading east to Kabiizi, so the newcomers could tag along. Eva pressed her lips together. She was used to traveling the long stretches of road with her subdued husband, perhaps with a house girl or a local pastor as passenger. She was not used to the *chattiness* of Americans. They had questions about everything: the safety of street food, the infection rates of HIV, the local politics. Questions that Stan sometimes answered, good humoredly, and when he was quiet, concentrating on avoiding the next pothole, she would venture to address. Except the one about the street food, for it was not their habit to eat it.

Eva reminded herself that everything was new to these people, and that she herself might be asking as many questions if, of a sudden, she found she were suddenly in the middle of Prague or, God forbid, Arkansas.

Everyone relaxed three hours later when the Range Rover left the half-paved highway and rolled onto pure tarmac; the jostling gave way to smooth road as they headed into what travel writers called the Switzerland of Africa.

They stopped just south of the equator at a roadside market for some vegetables. Julie smiled to see the tomatoes piled artistically alongside foodstuffs she recognized from her childhood: mangos, papayas, melons, a variety of bananas, the usual onions and the unusual breadfruit. The women vendors wore a blouse, t-shirt, or polo shirt and a *kitenge,* which looked to be a simple screen-printed cloth, wrapped around the waist and falling below the knees. Flip-flops or sandals made from strips of old tires were the standard footwear. Stephen and Sam wandered among the tables, set up beneath giant umbrellas of thatch, while the Thompsons picked out some produce. Only two days earlier, when they were running errands in the capital, the Thompsons had been informed by the mission that they would have the new recruits as overnight guests. Not much notice. The stop didn't take nearly as long as Julie wanted it to, but they had a ways to go before nightfall.

Act II

"So," asked Stan, looking in the rearview mirror. "When do you go back to collect your container?"

"Container?" asked Stephen.

"Shipment, then. Your other goods. Appliances and such."

"The suitcases were picked up—collected—by the diocesan driver at the airport and taken ahead of us."

"Really?"

"Yes," answered Julie. "We only brought the standard luggage allowance. Anyway, he met us in the diocesan Land Rover. We squished in the back seat from there to the capital."

Squished. How gauche, thought Eva, but Stan seemed to be impressed, so she held her peace. At least the new mission wife had the decency to be wearing a midlength skirt and not trousers. What did Joseph *see* in these people? They lacked the necessary drive, propriety, and, Eva suspected, discipline. They didn't know how it was: they would learn soon enough about the night dancers, the witch doctors, the tribalism disguised as politics. They were naive. So did it then fall to her and Stan to set them on a straight course? Or was it better to let them grope in their own haphazard fashion, seeking advice from the locals?

The young woman smiling delightedly in the back seat was hardly mission material. She was too light, too gay—such a redhead. She was having too much fun moving thousands of miles from home to a strange world. Perhaps she was here only for the adventure. *She'll never make it,* Eva decided.

———◆———

"Did you sleep well?" asked Eva, putting the finishing touches on the lunch table. Evidently these Americans had not yet completed their adjustment from jet lag. She had been moving quietly all over their Kabiizi house just to let them sleep in.

"*Very* well, thank you, Mrs. Thompson," answered Julie.

The Wrong Side of Eternity

Stan bid them come and sit, and said grace. Then he turned to Stephen. "Why don't you join me this afternoon? My world geography class convenes at two—you could be our guest speaker, talk about where you come from."

"Thanks, Stan, I would like that," Stephen answered, winking at Julie, who sat at the table drinking tea. She lifted her eyebrows in response, hiding a smile behind the brim of the chipped porcelain cup. Sam was looking out the window at the new world beyond.

"And while you're doing that, Sam and I will go exploring," Julie announced, and it was Eva's turn to lift her eyebrows. "There are beasts out there and new smells and things." The little boy's face lit up: he'd noticed the pointed long horns of the local cattle and Julie could tell that he couldn't wait to have a closer look.

"Mind you avoid the mud and dung," urged Eva as she cleared the table. "I won't have you tracking it into the house."

"We shall be very careful, won't we, Sam?" asked Julie. He nodded and held his empty plastic cup up to the nice British lady, who looked to him like she had walked out of a painting. Eva smiled and called the house girl in to do the washing up.

Stephen stood before a group of perhaps thirty black faces, poised over cheap blue notebooks with Bic pens. A map of the United States had been set up behind him by Stan, who had just introduced him as a professor from America. He slipped into a clearly Irish accent and commenced, while Stan stood at the back, his arms crossed, his expression attentively encouraging.

"Hallo, everybody." They looked around, wondering whether to answer him or not. "I said, 'hallo, everybody.'"

"Hello, Mr. O'Connell," came a hesitant reply from about half of the students.

"Well now, Mr. Thompson's given me the go-ahead to tell you about the Far West, and I'll be assurin' you, it won't be like anythin' you've seen in the books or at the cinema." Some of them smiled,

168

others looked puzzled. "I come from the wild, urban parts of coastal California," he said, stepping over to the map of the States. "Where the foghorns blow from the great ships and the Victorian houses line up along the hilly streets like the colors of a rainbow." He picked up a piece of chalk and sketched a quick view, complete with suspension bridge. "But I was born and reared in the dry and dusty Southwest, the land of cowboys and Mexicans." He swept his hand over the region, his Irish thick as ever. "The land of colored cliffs and rattlesnakes, of cactus and sagebrush." He returned to the blackboard and drew as he made his list, hearing some breaths when he finished the snake, and an "Ah!" or two when he'd done the cactus. "You've got to wear thick boots out in the desert, to keep from getting bit or stuck by somethin' or other."

Stan smiled and nodded from the back, evidently enjoying the show. He allowed him to talk for another fifteen minutes before giving the students a chance to ask questions.

"Sir, are all Americans rich or only the ones who come to visit us?"

"Well now, my mother grew up with a long-drop out in the back of her adobe house—adobe's sort of like plaster or wattle over a mud-brick frame, it keeps you warm in the winter and cool in the hot summers. She came from a village where there were only three automobiles, and me father came over from Ireland in his youth, with eighteen dollars—about twenty thousand shillings—in his pocket." He could tell by the look on their faces that it was still a lot of money to them. "And in the big city, people sometimes dig in the garbage bins for food." He'd noticed some local children doing the same, when they rolled into Kabiizi the day before. His eyes swept over the room. "Anybody out there study economics?" Four hands shot up. "Then you'll be knowin' somethin' about the cost of livin', and how you just can't compare the amount of dollars somebody makes there with the number of shillings they make here, without also thinkin' about how much a tin of peas costs in each place."

"Is America a Christian country?"

The Wrong Side of Eternity

"Is Uganda?" he answered, and most heads nodded, though some students screwed up their faces, recognizing that the question was a real one.

"What kinds of food do you eat?"

"Nothing so healthy as what you've got here. We eat far too much meat"—several students gasped, wondering if this was even possible—"which causes us heart problems, because we don't get enough exercise, so many of us are fat." Stephen paused; 'fat' was equivalent to 'healthy', he had learned from other missioners during orientation. "Fat but not *fit*, if you know what I mean. When I was young, we ate a lot of beans and rice, with chili peppers so hot they made you sweat."

"Why did you choose to come to Uganda, sir?" asked an earnest fellow in the front row.

Had he chosen? Or had he been chosen? He didn't know. The obvious answer came into his head but was bumped out of the way by another thought, and he opted to be honest.

"To meet you. To learn about how people here live. And to help if I can."

"Thank you, Mr. O'Connell, that was most enlightening," announced Stan, stepping back into his position at the front. The students nodded and some clapped. He gave the class instructions about preparing for an upcoming exam and dismissed them authoritatively but politely. One lingered to ask one more question. Stan motioned her away but Stephen prompted her to go on.

"Mr. O'Connell, are you here to get us saved?"

"That's none of me business," he answered, "for I'm only still bein' saved meself. I'll be helpin' out with an AIDS project in Rutoki. You can come visit me in a year or so to see how it's getting on."

"Perhaps I will."

Stephen smiled and Stan escorted the girl to the door.

"You didn't sound Irish at the house."

"No, Stan. I thought about it, though, walking over here, and on the way I thought I'd try it. The American accent seems to be difficult for

Act II

them to understand. I heard my father pound the fair speech into my head for more than a decade, and I wondered if they'd understand it better, being used to more 'proper' English."

"It worked quite well. I enjoyed it, and so did they. But Stephen," he said with some amount of gentle concern, "you don't have to put on a show. They'll like you more for being yourself. So when you get to Rutoki, I suggest you just slow down a bit and make sure the consonants are clear. That should do it."

"Thank you for the advice, Stan," he responded, humbly.

"Sure, mate, anytime. I'm about ready for a walk before I mark some papers. Care to join me? We may run into that splendid wife of yours."

"She is, isn't she?" Stephen smiled, and they exited the building and walked into the lane together, taking in a fresh-washed sky.

Julie offered to help the Thompsons' house girl with the evening meal preparations, but Eva shook her head and invited the young wife to join her in the sitting room for a cup of tea instead.

"I know you're newly arrived, but would you be willing to take on a spot of advice?"

"From a seasoned veteran like yourself, Mrs. Thompson?" asked Julie. "Absolutely. Fire away."

Eva winced. "Kabiizi culture is a bit different from where you're headed, but there are many similarities throughout the region," she began tactfully.

Julie readied herself for a lengthy history of the area, but she soon saw that Eva planned to keep things to a minimum. So that it would be easier to remember. Perhaps she thought red-headed women lacking in intelligence. "Go on."

"Well, my dear, I know that where you come from life is more, ah, *casual*. But simple things are easily misconstrued here. Initiating a conversation with a man, for instance, or whistling."

"The cattle herders seem to do plenty of the latter," answered Julie.

171

The Wrong Side of Eternity

"Yes, my dear, but they are *male*. They are allowed. It is not becoming for a woman to whistle here."

Julie nearly laughed aloud. Hadn't her grandfather scolded her for whistling, just after she'd learned to do so by copying her older brother? He'd even quoted her an old rhyme from the Midwest:

'Whistling girls and crowing hens
Always come to some bad end.'

What a silly world it was! "And chatting with the men?"

"They will see you as being too forward, I'm afraid."

"Oh. Deference. Maintaining the meekness of the woman's role and all."

"Exactly."

"Well, thank you, Eva, for setting me straight. It looks like I'll have to unlearn some habits, but I certainly will take your counsel to heart."

Eva smiled, satisfied, and poured out tea from the porcelain pot.

The next day Wilberforce showed up in the same battered Land Rover to drive them the final leg of the journey. He introduced them to Pastor Boniface Muneza, who led worship in the cathedral when the senior leaders were out on safari making confirmation visits. The tall pastor smiled gently and made a little bow. Little Sam looked up and took his hand as if they'd been related since birth, and together they walked to the car. Julie thanked Eva and said good-bye, while Stephen picked up their backpack and shook Stan's proffered hand.

Eva smiled and waved them off.

"Isn't Boniface a Catholic name?" asked Stephen, as the Land Rover pulled away.

"It is indeed, my friend. I was born in a Catholic household but converted during the revival."

I hope this isn't just a denominational tennis game, with one converting the other, thought Stephen. The OCA missioners from Ireland had sadly

172

admitted, during orientation, that the Brits and French had brought a divided church to Uganda over a hundred years before. Boy, did he still have a lot to learn. And a lot to overcome.

Bishop was so clever to arrange the missioners' trip in stages, thought Boniface, smiling. They would have adjusted some and be rested. The pastor had seen others make the grueling journey in two days, after who-knows-how-many hours of air travel before that. It was a sad way to introduce them to the beautiful country near the border. This family looked much more ready to go on. *Brilliant, Bishop.*

Unfortunately, they were delayed twice.

At the roadblock just this side of the bamboo forest, the soldiers took their time examining the visitors' papers. Stephen kept glancing at a camouflaged man with a chain of machine-gun ammo draped around his neck; he fingered the three-inch long bullets as if they were beads on a rosary. One of the soldiers seemed quite taken with Sam, who had to get out and pee; Julie accompanied him to a bush nearby, ignoring their stares. Boniface went with them, speaking in some tribal language respectfully to the soldiers who loitered nearby.

Halfway down the twisting road that wound among the volcanic cinder cones, the vehicle hit a sharp stone, which flattened one of the tires, so they had to stop to change it. The road tilted downward precariously, and there was little space at the edge where it fell precipitously steep. It took a while, even with both Stephen and the pastor helping Wilberforce to get the Land Rover level enough to place a jack.

So they arrived at their scenic destination after dark, when all that the missioners could see in the headlights was the dirt track in front of them.

"We have arrived," said Boniface, who helped them out and led the way into a sparsely furnished house lit only by kerosene lanterns. Three Ugandan couples sat on chairs and an old upholstered sofa, waiting to greet them with chai and speeches. They all stood as the door opened, and one stepped forward with open arms.

"Stephen, my friend! Welcome to Rutoki!"

He had to squint to see the face of Geoffrey Mahoro before him, beaming with delight.

38. Cathedral Grounds, Rutoki, Sunday Morning

He met Pastor Boniface, as arranged, just before the tiny English service began. The sun had not yet crested the embracing hills. Together they lugged two enormous drums out of the choir room; Stephen imagined twenty-gallon drums being sawn in two, then covered with two flaps of cow hide tied together with twisted bits of furry leather. They were not tympani, but they were beautiful. The pastor lifted one up to a sawn-off branch in the tree twenty feet from the side door and hung it by a leather strap. Stephen followed suit with his. Then he waited there while Boniface retrieved the drumsticks from inside. He returned with four sticks, and handed two to Stephen.

I can't use these—they're just sticks, he thought. Well, they had some uniformity: about an inch or so round, but they were hardly straight, having several jags and curves. Boniface gave instructions.

"Like this." And he banged on the lower drum: DA-dahm, DA-dahm, DA-dahm. "Just keep it regular."

Oh, I get it, thought Stephen. *I'm the basso continuo. What a relief. I can do this.* He lifted his bent sticks and started in: DA-dahm, DA-dahm.

Boniface smiled with approval.

"Now, just keep it going. I'll fill in the rest."

Stephen nodded. He had to concentrate, though, because what Boniface did next was just short of genius: da-DA-DA be DAH, be DA-DA-da-DA-DAH—an evenly syncopated pattern that Stephen could hardly follow. He closed his eyes and kept whacking away at the bass drum, DA-dahm, DA-dahm, DA-dahm, DA-dahm, DA-dahm, DA-dahm, and tried to imagine the other pattern written on manuscript paper. He failed, so he just opened his eyes and gave himself to drumming people to church. Sweat ran down from his armpits, but he didn't let up. The

Act II

drumming lasted minutes, maybe ten. Longer than the entire number of tympani solos he'd ever performed, combined. The natural undulating shape of the hills would amplify the sound, he imagined, for miles.

Years later, he would still hear Boniface's rhythm—da-DA-DA be DAH, be DA-DA-da-DA-DAH—in his dreams. Or it would become mixed in with the sound of waves crashing upon the beach. He knew he would never be rid of it, but since it was such a happy noise, he didn't mind.

From the outside, the arched windows of the large church appeared as gaping dark holes, lacking glass. But they were not menacing: the space contrasted with the white-washed plaster and was almost alpine in appearance, with the chain of volcanoes lending a scenic backdrop. The little family entered through double hardwood doors and was directed to a front bench, its narrow seat and vertical back looking far from comfortable. They took in the high arch twenty feet over their heads, which separated the chancel from the enormous space that would soon be filled with over four hundred people. To their right, a group of twenty-somethings started to sing Ugandan praise music. A robed woman priest came up behind them to introduce herself. She was white, with a farmer's physique, her bobbed hair a light brown.

"Sorry I couldn't meet you last night, when you got in. I was on a pastoral call. Welcome to the borderlands! I'm Ann, Ann Rourke, your fellow missioner," she announced in a broad accent. Stephen stood to extend his hand. Hers was a firm grip; this was probably a woman to be taken seriously. "Bishop'll be introducing you this morning, so be ready to be on display. They'll want to have a good look at you. And you're Julie, right? The MK from Cameroon. Does it feel like home to be here?"

"A bit," she answered, smiling. "Different language."

"I bet. And who's this little man?"

"Sam," he said fearlessly, happy to be acknowledged.

"Well, Sam, if your mummy and daddy let me, I should like to take you exploring into the hills behind my house. Then we could share some bickies. Whaddaya say?"

175

Dang friendly, this one. Stephen couldn't place the accent. South African? Australian? Never mind; he would find out soon enough. A sturdy build, quite the presence. She seemed to be genuinely happy to see other Westerners in the church, then excused herself to join the procession.

The hymn tunes seemed vaguely familiar, accompanied by drumming and some odd kinds of rattles and tambourines. He'd seen the *ikidongo,* described to him by Geoffrey over a decade before, lying on the floor in the choir room, but they were not being played. Perhaps they were used for only special occasions.

The hundreds of dark brown faces seemed to be very happy to be there; the air hummed with vibrancy. Was it just that people were so relieved to have a break from the monotonous digging that filled most of their lives, eking out the basic sustenance from their small farms? Or was it more? Boniface had told Stephen about the revival movement that had spread throughout this region during the past seventy years, at least twice now. Geoffrey sat at his left to act as his interpreter. Julie was on his right, left to fend for herself when it came to figuring out what was going on. As she seemed to be perfectly comfortable, he didn't trouble himself about it. And within minutes, a middle-aged Ugandan woman sidled up and began whispering a translated summary in her ear.

Ann was right: just before the sermon, which would be long, the bishop stood to introduce the O'Connells. He called them to stand at the front, along with Geoffrey, and said many words, inciting an awed response. Stephen imagined what he was telling them, and wished he wouldn't: *These people have come half way around the wide world to be of help to us here. They have given up houses and lands and riches and friends...* He swallowed. Their expectations would be so high. A woman of about thirty sat in the fourth row, along with a girl of about nine years, and met his gaze. Stephen couldn't read the expression on her face. Was it pity? A challenge? Both?

As the bishop droned on, a shout was heard in the far back of the church, over a hundred feet away. A little boy disentangled himself from

Act II

his relatives and came sprinting down the aisle. Stephen was holding Sam; Julie stooped down and opened her arms, and the boy threw himself into them. He couldn't be more than three or four, but he was so *light*. She stood up and he surveyed the great church crowd as if he had just been turned into a heroic marble statue.

A murmur spread through the congregation. Julie knew why: this was *bizarre*. People this far out would most likely fear the *bazungu*; she'd learned during their orientation that the early Protestant missionaries in this part of the country had been none too kind. After beaming at the audience, the boy turned to touch her hair. Maybe its color gave her some sort of magical status? The bishop concluded his remarks, Julie let the boy go, and the O'Connells resumed their seats of honor while the two-hour service continued.

Of course there was a celebratory meal afterward. The invited group of twenty or so trickled over to the back courtyard behind the regional church offices across the dirt road, where the speeches continued. They were introduced to local officials, teachers, project-development managers: Nyiramunezero, Bahizi, Mwizere...*How am I ever going to get all their names into my head?* thought Stephen. Two girls appeared with a pitcher, plastic basin, and a bar of soap, kneeling on the patchy grass. Stephen followed the example of the others and let them pour warm water over his hands while he washed, then rinsed the same way. He shook off the extra drops and was then presented with a cotton towel. A steaming bowl was handed to him containing deep-fried whole potatoes, rice, beef complete with tripe and a very thin gravy, and some yellow slippery stuff that was very dense. Julie had already begun to eat with relish, using her fingers like everyone else. She and Ann had begun to talk.

The bishop was grinning wildly; Stephen noticed the gap between his upper front teeth and vertical scars running next to his eyes. Tribal markings? He would ask about them later; Geoffrey wouldn't be offended if he asked questions like that. What a wonderful resource, to have someone there he knew, someone to explain things to him, help him understand!

The Wrong Side of Eternity

Had he imagined it would be anything like this? He didn't care for the celebrity status, and yet he knew that he would have to make use of it. He decided to take cues from Geoffrey and Boniface, and spend the first several months listening, learning. It was the only way forward, if anything was going to last from his long-term appointment here. His thoughts were interrupted as the bishop called him forward.

"He says you are to tell the staff about your assignment," translated Geoffrey, who had materialized beside him. Stephen nodded and began.

"I have my degree in sociology, the study of people," he explained, pausing every half sentence or so to let Geoffrey turn his words into the borderland dialect. "Bishop has invited me to undertake some work in the health sector, along with your outreach officer, James." He nodded at the medical assistant. "We have much to do together, but you will not see me busy right away, except to spend time learning about you, trying to explore..." He noted Geoffrey was having some trouble keeping up with the bigger words. "Trying to find what works best. Everybody learns a little differently," he explained, suspecting this might be a new idea for some of them, "so I'll need time to visit your schools and other places to see how I can fit in."

Geoffrey looked at him with a happy expression on his face. He muttered, in almost a whisper, "You are not telling them what they expected. It is a good surprise."

"So do my family the kindness, please, of helping us to understand you better. We do not want to think you are like something described in an old textbook"—he got a laugh at this— "and we, too, want to learn new things. Thank you, Bishop, for the honor of inviting us here. May we do good things for God, together."

The speech was short, but the applause was sincere, and after three more welcome speeches the women began to clear up. The Mothers Union president had made one, but no one had asked Julie. The party was over.

Now the work begins, thought Stephen, as Geoffrey walked back with the O'Connells to their bare but—by local standards—luxurious house.

No plumbing, but Wilberforce drove a team of workers down to the local spring to pick up jerry cans of water every day. No electricity, but no real need to heat or cool the house either. It would be fine. They spent the rest of the day unpacking and greeting the many well-wishers who came to the door.

"What was that yellow stuff?" he asked his wife that evening, once the lanterns had been lit and Sam put to bed. "You sure seemed to be enjoying it."

"*Matoki,*" she answered. "Steamed bananas. It tasted fine with the gravy, but along with that sorghum brew, I thought it smelled a little like vomit." She saw his look of alarm. "I'm sure we'll get used to it, darlin'. They seem to be staples here."

39. Native Anglican Church Guest House, Rutoki, Tuesday

Stephen stepped outside for a breath of air. The fragrance from cooking fires hazed the little valley; the light had begun to lessen. Julie sat on the concrete step just outside the front door with a neighbor child, perhaps seven years old. They were giggling and talking. Sam was playing with an enormous black millipede not ten yards away. It must have been eight inches long.

"Don't try to eat that," cautioned Stephen. Sam looked up in horror—the thought had clearly not even crossed his little mind.

Julie took six of the small red lava stones from the driveway and placed them in a line in front of her. She picked up one and looked at the girl sitting next to her, who seemed delighted to be in the presence of such an odd lady. A lady who couldn't even count!

"One." Julie picked up another piece, and held them both in her hand. "Two." The little girl laughed.

"Ebiri."

"Yeah? And for one?" She dropped a rock.

The Wrong Side of Eternity

"Imwe."

"Imwe, ebiri…"

The little girl caught on. Fast. "Imwe, ebiri, itatu, enyeh, itanu, itandatu…"

"Whoa, hold on, not so fast!" cried Julie, laughing. They were using their fingers now, and made it all the way to fifteen before the little girl ran back home to her family.

40. CHURCH OFFICES, WEDNESDAY MORNING

"You're comfortable?"

"Very, Bishop. The house is more than we hoped for."

"We had it upgraded for you. And now I'd like to introduce you to my office assistant, Charity Ntambara."

Julie recognized her from the cathedral service and extended her hand. Charity took it graciously, but her expression was unreadable. The remainder of the meeting consisted mostly of introducing themselves and drawing a broad outline of Stephen's initial responsibilities. She was proud of the way he kept insisting on a lengthy orientation period.

"So, Julie, Charity here can be your language teacher. Her English is of a very high standard," Geoffrey announced.

The women were left alone in the large room to formulate plans.

"The diocesan offices are fairly busy," remarked Charity. "Perhaps we could find a place at the secondary school or in the vestry of the church."

"You are welcome to come to our house." Julie's offer was sincere; she could keep an eye on Sam and not feel so schoolified if she met Charity at home.

Oh dear, thought Charity, skeptically. *I shall maintain my professional role, it shall not turn into a casual visit…*They spent the next ten minutes setting times on a calendar.

180

Act II

"Of course, I understand this is only a tentative schedule," commented Julie. "I spent my early years in Cameroon and know how life can get in the way."

"Did you? Then you speak French."

Julie laughed. "It's very rusty. I've not spoken French in years."

This is an intelligent woman, thought Charity, *for all her gaiety.* Perhaps a bright person didn't have to be so serious all the time. "I'm sure it would come back quickly. That language would come in handy if you ever went to Rwanda." The border was only four miles away.

"I doubt it," answered Julie. "Anyway, I hope my rusty French doesn't get tangled up with your borderland dialect. Charity?"

"Yes?"

"Would you be willing, when you come over, to spend a few minutes of our lessons discussing some of the local history and customs? I tend to trip over my own feet when it comes to the nuances."

"Such as?"

"Oh, whistling."

"You *whistle*?"

"Tunes and things. I've heard it could be a problem."

Charity paused for half a second. "Yes, I could help you with that." *Some.* She pursed her lips. "There is a Mothers Union dancing competition next week. You could attend."

"That sounds like a perfect place to start!" Julie extended her hand. "I'm glad. We gals, we have to talk. It's the only way to survive."

Charity stifled her horror, hearing the echo of a scream inside her head. "For us women here," she answered, "sometimes we have to be silent. In order to survive." With this remark, she gathered up her files and left, preparing herself for a twice-weekly meeting at the *muzungu*'s home.

41. Rutoki Environs, 9:00 a.m. Friday

Wilberforce opened the door of the Land Rover for Stephen, who politely asked him not to. Geoffrey was already seated in the back. Stephen pushed the front seat forward and climbed in next to the diocesan administrator. Geoffrey wore his clerical collar and suit jacket, and the newly arrived missioner a tweed blazer, against the cool of the mountain climate.

Amazing, thought Stephen, *one degree south of the equator and I'm chilly.* It was the dry season, so everything was sprinkled with dust.

"How was the night?" inquired Geoffrey.

"Fine." Stephen liked this morning greeting. And the other standard, of saying "you have worked" to people seen out and about, instead of "Hi." The phrases made so much sense, in context.

Geoffrey launched in with the day's agenda. "We'll meet the local MP—it's a woman, you'll be interested to know—and some of the community project leaders. Then we shall stop at the AIDS clinic so you can see what's going on there."

"Is it near the hospital?"

"Yes—but they hold it at the Catholic parish offices. I've notified them, they are expecting you. I told them you grew up Roman Catholic." Geoffrey beamed.

And God forbid that they consider me a traitor. "Like Boniface. I hope that will go down well with them?"

"They are so happy for any help, they will be glad to see you. And it is the first time we have worked on a project together."

"Really?"

Geoffrey nodded.

"So who's been running the AIDS project?" Stephen asked.

"A couple of Germans, but they left last year. They call it RACIS, which stands for"—he paused to remember—"Rutoki AIDS Counseling and Information Service."

Kind of long, thought Stephen. RACIS. Not a good association, for the Germans. "Do they know that Americans are not Germans?"

"You are all *bazungu,* Stephen—they won't care." He appeared happy they were together again and gave more than his usual rendition of the local history. "Only a few years ago, the politicians were

182

denying that AIDS was even a problem here. Uganda has led the efforts to educate the people, once the infection rate topped eighteen percent."

"Eighteen percent?"

"Yes. They could no longer deny it was a problem then. And the country has almost a million orphans from AIDS alone."

Wilberforce turned onto the main road, an asphalt-strewn wider stretch of volcanic dirt. The largest volcano stood sentinel above them, poking its pointed crest through the drifting clouds.

"At the top, the borders of Uganda, Rwanda, and Zaire meet," explained Geoffrey.

"Have you ever climbed it?"

"No, my friend. It is in the gorilla reserve. Only the tourists and the soldiers go up there."

"Geoffrey, could you tell me what made those marks on Bishop's face?"

Wilberforce looked back at him in the rearview mirror and scowled.

"The scars?"

"Yes."

"They are from the old way of treating eye infections. Hot metal bars, laid alongside…"

"Cauterization?"

"Such a big word, Stephen!"

"Where they treat a wound or infection by burning it."

"Yes. That was the old way."

Like St. Francis in the Middle Ages, thought Stephen. "And the new way?"

"Antibiotics," Geoffrey answered. "They work better, and they do not cause so much pain."

The staff of the honorable Phoebe Kizito consisted of two people, a driver who apparently doubled as a bodyguard and an office assistant. The

The Wrong Side of Eternity

young woman, perhaps in her twenties, served the local chai—a sweetened hot milk boiled with tea leaves and strained into mugs or a large thermos flask—along with small bananas, dry white bread, margarine, and jam. The member of parliament wore a long dress with high shoulders, which Stephen had seen in the capital far east of here. She was obviously fluent in the local dialect, however, chatting amicably with Geoffrey. Her English was excellent, her manner polished. She had the usual poster of the president above the filing cabinet, a cross in one corner, a crucifix in another. In a prominent place on the bookshelf stood a Koran, among other books on the history of the region. She obviously did her best to appear interested in all parties. Perhaps it was for the best, her wearing a different style from the locals…gave her more clout, in a way. Stephen could not figure out if she was single, divorced, or widowed, and he told himself, *It doesn't matter, you idiot, as long as she has the people's respect.*

"Fill me in, Geoffrey, on your life since you were at ITS," requested Stephen as they started toward the clinic.

"I do not know where to begin," he stammered. "You started to study at the university just as I graduated. I came back here straightaway, and the bishop ordained me deacon. Amin had gone into exile by then."

"Fortunately," said Stephen.

"Somewhat fortunately. His successor wasn't much better."

"Oh. That didn't make the papers back in America."

"No, it did not." He did not sound bitter about it. "Then I had a time finding my betrothed, a teacher. When I disappeared, she ran to her family in Rwanda. It was more stable there, then. I have you to thank that I came back at all."

"I never knew you had a fiancée! She must have been sad to be apart from you for so long."

"Grace was safe, and, God bless her, she waited for me. She found work in the church offices. The language here in the borderlands is nearly the same as in Rwanda."

"So you were married and priested and then had a parish?"

184

Act II

"Yes, but because my English had become so good, from being in America, Bishop kept promoting me until he had me in the office, doing the—what do you call it?—the 'diplomacy thing' with the Western visitors." He paused as the Land Rover stopped in front of the RACIS office. "Stephen, did you ask to be sent here?"

"Why?"

"Because I remember inviting you! That night, when you so bravely hid me from… "

"No. The mission matched my skills with what the bishop requested."

"God brought us back together, my friend."

"Indeed. Praise God," Stephen ventured in Kinyarwanda.

"Praise him." Geoffrey smiled broadly.

"And what about your niece, the one you were so worried about?"

"You have met her, Stephen. She is the bishop's office assistant, Ntambara Charity." He looked straight ahead. "I worry about her still."

Their tour was cut short; Geoffrey directed the driver toward a back road, and they parked at the edge of a field. Villagers were streaming to a compound on the far side of it; Stephen could hear soft singing wafting their direction. The whole town seemed to have materialized, spreading across the field before a burial service began. Nothing stopped the daily routine like a funeral, as the responsibilities to the dead were great. Even for Christians.

"We have a proverb here: 'A dead person speaks louder than drums,'" Geoffrey told Stephen. "I promised Pastor Ann I would translate for her."

When they arrived, Julie and Sam were already there. They had walked with their neighbors. One of the secondary teachers had succumbed to malaria; his simple coffin lay next to an oblong hole. Charity stood under the eaves of the square house, staring at the hole in the ground, holding the hand of the widow, who looked to be still in her twenties.

The Wrong Side of Eternity

"In the old days, they would dig down and then a bit over to the side, to make a little shelf," said Geoffrey, making his way toward the front of the gathering.

"Why?"

"It was to give the dead one a better rest, so the ground above them was less disturbed, I think, but I am not sure. In our traditional religion, the dead journey to somewhere beneath the volcanoes for a sort of after-life. It is at this stage that a kind of ancestor worship takes place."

Stephen filed the information under African Tribal Religion in his mind. He had already learned that divination involved the shedding of blood.

Some women close to the home were wailing until Ann stepped forward to give an address. Stephen stood with Wilberforce a respectful distance from the gravesite. The hymns were all being sung by memory: Ann held the only prayer book in sight. The service, too, seemed to have been memorized, or else was more casual and extemporized for the occasion.

Ann would shed her clerical robes afterward and join the family for a simple meal, explained Geoffrey, eating in silence until the sun set. As they climbed once again into the Land Rover, he beckoned to Julie to join them. She shook her head and headed over to explain that the walk would do her and Sam good, and she was working at "cracking" the local dialect. Better to be within the sphere of conversation. Geoffrey looked down at her shoes and judged them sufficiently sturdy to manage the sharp volcanic rocks that protruded from the dirt pathways. She blew a kiss toward Stephen, who winked and smiled back.

I think they will be happy here, hoped Geoffrey, watching her go.

———◆———

"I love Ann's New Zealand accent," confessed Julie, as they ate rice and beans flavored with onions and tomatoes in the fading light. Their new house helper, Esther, was a capable cook, and despite initial protests, she had quickly become accustomed to Julie's presence and help in preparing the evening meal. Charity had explained to her that the seasons were marked by wet and dry, each twice a year; there was no winter or spring, summer or fall. This close to the equator, each day seemed to be as long as the next.

"I had trouble making out one particular word, hearing Ann talk," said Stephen. "I'm so dense, it took me a while."

"What was that?"

"'Deeth.'"

"Oh. I heard 'dith.'"

But you got it right away, you bright linguist, you, he didn't say aloud.

42. The Following Wednesday

The day of the Mothers Union gathering dawned clear and cool. Even in the dry season, the winds that blew through the volcanic mountain corridor could bring a chill. Stephen donned a sweater vest atop his dress shirt before adding the wool blazer he'd found in the market with Esther's help. He took his cues for dressing from the local pastors, and Julie was proud of him.

"You look so professional, Stephen."

"I want them to feel like they're getting their money's worth," he joked.

"I'm sorry you won't be here for the competition."

"Me too. But the AIDS clinic is being held today at the Catholic parish office, and I want to see how they do things. No point in reinventing the wheel." He took another sip of the chai and made a face. "I think I'll switch to coffee, support the Ugandan industry, unless I'm a visitor somewhere. But I like the *posho* Esther makes. It reminds me of Cream of Wheat."

Julie stepped into the *huaraches* she wore in the dry season and walked down the hall. "Any idea where Sam's got to?"

The Wrong Side of Eternity

Esther looked frightened and shook her head. "I did not lock the door, madam."

"Oh, Esther, please call me Julie. We are on level ground, you and me. And you don't need to lock the boy in the house, he's not *that* wild." She laughed.

Esther went to the front door, Julie to the back, while Stephen washed the chai down with some fresh water from the filter. The sound of bugles and drums wafted through the open kitchen window.

"What's that?" Stephen asked.

"It is the Boys' Brigade," explained Esther. "They are invited to begin the gathering this morning."

"I bet they're glad for a break from school, but they could use some practice."

"They're not *that* bad, darlin'," said Julie, heading to the door.

A column of about eighteen boys in scouts' uniforms and caps marched from the direction of the primary school, led by a drum major brandishing an African-style baton. The old snare and bass drums were Western made, but the tom-toms were the heavy local ones made with wood and cowhide, fitted with a strap. Where they got the brass bugles was anybody's guess: perhaps a remnant of the days of the British Protectorate? They had come to a halt in front of the guest house.

"Stephen, look!" exclaimed Julie, grinning as she stood on the front steps. He came at her bidding, much to the delight of Esther, who caught sight of little Sam standing smack in the middle of the column, waving his arms as the old bugles blared the semblance of a tune.

The house helper ran out to retrieve Sam.

"No, Esther, let him," called Julie after her. "He's having fun, and they obviously don't mind." No, the Boys Brigade looked very amused to have such a young recruit. When they began marching again, Sam kept up. "I hope he doesn't ask for a uniform. He's a little young yet, for that group," remarked Julie. Most of the boys were at least eleven; Sam was three and a half. She walked to the street where they were passing

Act II

by and motioned him to come. He did, strutting like a little peacock, a big grin on his face.

We're off to a good start, thought Julie. *He wants to belong.* She recalled her earliest memories of life in West Africa and picked up her son to kiss him proudly. "You'll need to stay with Miss Esther now, Sam. Mummy's got a meeting to go to."

Charity met her at the door and they walked down together. Clumps of women gathered at different spots in the cathedral: in the transept, near the choir room at the back, and in the middle of the large church. A table had been set up in front of the concrete steps that led to the altar area, where the choir normally sat on each side. Three men in suits sat there, writing tablets and ball-point pens at the ready.

"They take this pretty seriously," Julie said.

"Yes, but it is fun. You will see." Charity could tell that her language pupil was taking in the differing colours of the teams of women and had already concluded that the older ones who wore blue and white were the Mothers Union senior members. She wondered if Julie would feel compelled to join. And what the women would have to say about her, this *muzungu* with the very red hair, so thin in comparison with most of them.

The four teams each had a drummer, and two of them had additional members who played bamboo-covered rattles and string instruments. One of the teams offered a solo dancer, explained Charity, a young woman from the secondary school who'd come from the area near the capital. She had a very different technique. Faster, wilder than the leaping borderland style, with much in the way of hip wiggling, similar to the Tahitians.

After each dance, the audience clapped enthusiastically, followed by the men giving their opinion or critique on the piece and the teamwork. Then, a number score.

The Wrong Side of Eternity

"They always say mostly good things," whispered Charity. "But the ones who get the highest marks are the ones who use the most energy, who do not hold back...The method is not so important here."

Pastor Boniface stood to give the final result, and the winning team jumped up and down, slapping one another like football players after a dramatic touchdown.

"Now there is one more dance, a traditional borderland one, and everyone is invited to join in," he announced, as the music began. A three-man *ikidongo* band struck up a lively rhythm.

Julie stood up immediately, trying the steps carefully, swinging her trim arms out to the side as she had seen the others do, leaping and stomping. *She is as strong as a man,* thought Charity, who, like Pastor Ann, did not participate. This Julie, she could not manage the complicated steps—but could she ever *jump.*

———◆———

From the first days of arrival in Kampala, and ever since, it seemed to Stephen that women clustered everywhere, gathering to work, to pray, to sing. He stepped inside the embracing space of the Catholic cathedral, and there were twenty, chanting an Ave Maria in unison, and in a far more African tune than he was used to hearing in any of the Protestant churches. Few wore religious dress. He thought of his mother, attending Mass practically every day. She probably still did. Across the street from the dentist's office, a loudspeaker carried the gospel voice of a Pentecostal songstress: her backup choir sounded totally female.

Am I in the wrong place? Stephen had thought, entering the Native Anglican Church cathedral the day after they'd landed in Uganda, to find a woman washing floors, another wiping cobwebs from a high corner with an extended broomstick, another just sitting with bowed head in the middle of the huge church. A woman pecked on a manual typewriter in a tiny office—it looked like a coat closet—just off the nave. No pastor was in sight.

Act II

And then, on the way to Rutoki, he'd seen women in the fields, chopping up the grass-knotted stony ground with hoes that looked like they were made a decade ago. They bustled in the shambas, pounding peanuts into flour, shelling beans, fanning charcoal fires, and trying to keep toddlers from falling into the glowing coals.

Where were all the men? In positions of authority. He had watched them sitting proudly behind desks, stamping papers, or leading church services with smooth, mechanical certainty. The telephone operator who connected your calls, the postal worker who stamped your letters, the hotel managers who rented your room: all men. He had seen some poorer men working in the fields or transporting enormous clay pots or gigantic hands of bananas precariously perched atop wobbling bicycles, or laying bricks. The bars were full of men drinking, the roads full of barefooted men, walking two by two and chatting.

There was no question that in *this* world, if you were male, you had power as well as freedom. Unless you happened to be a *muzungu*, like Reverend Ann, your white skin providing a passport to worlds unheard of by the majority of educated Ugandan women. Charity was *brilliant*; Geoffrey had said so, those long years ago. Stephen and she had exchanged some pleasantries containing references to literature, history, even philosophy. Not only brilliant, but elegant, regal even. And yet she served as an undersecretary to VIP males. With downcast eyes.

He sighed. He'd overheard the opinions. No one disagreed that women were spiritual, influential. Not fit to pastor, not really. Let the ordained ones work in the schools as chaplains, or visit the sick, the culture practically screamed. But there was something, well, *receptive*, about a woman. Endurable. Comfortable. And those who attended the RACIS clinic—all women. Where were the men?

Reverend Margaret, he said inwardly, beseeching her counsel. *What have I gotten myself into?*

DOUBLE VISION

We must learn to live together as brothers
or perish together as fools.

—MARTIN LUTHER KING, JR.

43. THE HOME OF PHOEBE KIZITO

THE HOUSE WAS SET OFF from the road, sheltered by the papery fronds
of banana trees. A field of sorghum stalks stood next door, their top-
heavy red cluster of tiny fruit swaying in the breeze, ready for harvesting.
The MP—member of parliament—was rich. She lived in a cinder-block
house with glass windows on three out of four walls, metal latticework
covering them all for added security. She owned a small television and
there was a radio in every room. Family portraits and posters decorated
the walls: Ms. Kizito had both a cross and a crucifix in her living room,
just like in her office in town.

She introduced the O'Connells to Sister Evastina, the new director
of the RACIS clinic. The nun, a thin woman of about fifty, wore a simple
but full habit, black plastic-framed glasses, and an engaging smile. Their
conversation started with women's rights, as Stephen expected it would.

"The church is our strongest ally," Phoebe explained to him. "It is
the easiest way for us to reach the villagers." She was referring to the
work of the Women for Global Development, which she headed in the

Act II

district. The WGD was known for making small loans to women so they could make basketry or set up a beehive and sell the products to support their families. "So few girls are truly able to go on to secondary and post-secondary education. The average Ugandan woman has seven children, so their role in the home often keeps them back. But only seven percent of them even own the land they live on! The WGD is outspoken in its opposition to wife beating and adultery, both fairly common practices. There is so much work to do…"

The soft-spoken sister at this point introduced a local story, and her voice went into a more dramatic mode: "Nshaka's wife wanted to know his secret. He refused to tell her, but she insisted. Then he took a spear blade and beat her until her back bled. His wife wept and promised that she would never ask him again. Nshaka caught her blood in a cup and put it in an iron pot, and with it cooked dry leaves from the yard. They became beautiful clothes, which he gave to his wife. She was pleased, dried her tears and said, 'Nshaka, you are a great husband.'"

"What does *Nshaka* mean?" Stephen asked, somewhat familiar by now with the local practice of bestowing significant names.

Sister Evastina answered, "It means, 'I want.'"

"This is how values are passed on?" he asked.

"Of course. Storytelling is the most powerful way. Jesus used it often."

"It condones abuse."

"Of course it does," Phoebe said. "But you and I know that just because certain beliefs have brought about what people think are good results does not make them true."

After two steaming mugs of chai, Julie excused herself and went to the latrine for a short call, the Ugandan term for 'number one'. On her way back, Stephen saw her stand in the dirt yard watching Sam and Phoebe's grandchildren kick a soccer ball—a real one, not the usual plastic bags tied into a spherical shape with twine—around the enclosure. He could hear their laughter through the open casement.

"I know you advocate against abuse and promote the cottage industries," said Stephen, "but what other areas do you address?"

The Wrong Side of Eternity

"Women's rights advocates here address things you remain rather squeamish about in the United States. Female circumcision, for instance. Well, that is not practiced here, but it is not far away, in parts of Zaire. We have much more sexual dysfunction than the West is led to believe," she explained.

"There are still people who believe that having sex with a young girl will cure their AIDS," Sister Evastina said.

"You're joking."

"Not at all," said the MP. "They will not admit it, of course, but their behaviour tells a different tale. And some of the witch doctors recommend this abhorrent practice."

"Some?" asked Stephen, hearing Julie reenter the house.

"Some are more progressive than others, mixing their traditional treatments with decent medical advice. Not many, though."

"I knew that AIDS reached such high proportions here due to the trucking routes," said Stephen, "and that prostitution is an almost-acceptable diversion for men who commute for work to the capital. But it is so *wrong* when they bring HIV home, and their wives don't know enough to protect themselves."

"You mean, use condoms?" The MP laughed, and Sister Evastina frowned. "They know about them. But most would rather not even consider it, I think, than to show that level of distrust in their husbands."

"No wonder the infection rate is so high."

"It's down just below ten percent now, almost half of what it used to be, due to all the education programmes. But you are right: that is still too high." Apparently sensing that Stephen liked the historical angle, Phoebe added, "It was never considered a gay man's disease here, like it has been in America."

"You seem to know American history well," commented Julie, turning toward the conversation after perusing the large bookshelf.

"We study it thoroughly in secondary school. I would wager that some of us know it better than many Americans."

"I'm sure that's true," admitted Julie.

Act II

"And what is the local thinking on alternate lifestyles?" Stephen asked.

"Homosexuality, you mean?"

He nodded.

Once again she laughed, but the tone of her voice was serious. "They'll tell you it doesn't exist in Uganda. But it does, it does... Generations ago, Semahoro, the missionaries taught against polygamy all over Africa. Families were caught in a cultural crossfire: either the men reduce the number of wives they had to one, or they risk the disapproval—and likely the financial support—of the *bazungu*."

"And when they did that, what happened to the disenfranchised women?" He could use big words with Phoebe: she was educated and appreciated the banter.

"They were lost, either returning to their homes to take care of elderly parents or ill family members, taking the status of a shamed servant, or becoming prostitutes."

"All because we were so shortsighted and offered no alternative."

"The thing is, if the teaching had been presented more—ah—patiently, the practice might have died out on its own within a couple of generations."

Sister Evastina nodded at this and commented, "I have noticed the Protestant tendency to be impatient."

The MP continued. "But because the conformity to the—ahem—*biblical* model was so emphasised..."

Stephen kept up with her, reading the innuendos. She didn't mean the biblical model, she meant the Western example.

"It created a whole new set of problems," finished Julie, perched on the arm of the chair, next to Stephen.

"Yes. And if the preaching about homosexuality continues the way it is now, especially in the city centres..."

Stephen took a sip of the fermented sorghum brew he'd accepted in the place of the chai and swished it about in his mouth, waiting for her to finish her thought. Phoebe looked at him and shook her head.

The Wrong Side of Eternity

"I think it will formally become a capital offense. Anyone found practicing it will be imprisoned, castrated, or sentenced to death." His look of incredulity made her explain further. "People brought up under dictators think that is the only way to change behaviour: offer a threat of violence against it. Besides, for the past hundred years it has already been considered a capital offense on a less formal level. If your neighbours found out, they would arrange your murder, probably make it look like an accident."

"A death sentence would be sanctioned by the *government?*"

"Of course. Fear has proven to be the easy way to legislate changes of behaviour in this part of the world."

"It doesn't work, it doesn't last. It's not effective," he protested.

"Of course not. That's why the cycle repeats itself."

Phoebe walked with the O'Connells down the path that led from her house to the main road, greeting the watchman-driver who stood at the wrought-iron gate. Sister Evastina remained in the house, probably waiting her turn to give the director of WGD a piece of her mind.

"I am so glad to have met you, *Nyabo*," Phoebe said, shaking Julie's hand while placing her left hand on Julie's upper right arm and squeezing softly. "You would be welcome to come to the WGD meetings—they are held in my office once a month, on the first Tuesday. You might have some valuable ideas to share."

"I haven't been here long enough," confessed Julie, "but I thank you for the compliment. Give me a little more time and I'll certainly consider it."

Mrs. Kizito stood near the latching gate and nodded as they waved good-bye.

"Dat was fun," said Sam. "Can we get a football like dat?"

"No, Sam. The neighbors would just get jealous," answered Stephen. "What did she call me?" he asked Julie, as they walked homeward. "An African name."

"*Semahoro*. It means peaceful. They all call you that behind your back. I guess you've a talent for diplomacy, my sweet man."

Act II

"Huh."

"What do they call you?" asked Stephen.

"Me? Right now it's just Mama-Sammy. I guess they name a woman after her firstborn." She looked at the sky, heard the thunder. "It's going to pour soon. Come on, Sam, I'll race you home." And she and the boy ran laughing through the streets, oblivious to the many stares along the way.

44. THREE MONTHS LATER

Julie sighed with relief. So happy to have a long-drop instead of an inside toilet! The missioners in Kabiizi were always having their flush commodes break down or spring an unwelcome leak...The O'Connells made do at the guest house with an old-fashioned latrine. Stephen, that sweetheart, had endured some amused stares aboard the minibus when he brought back a toilet seat from his recent excursion to the capital. He'd bought it to attach to a sturdy bucket in their cement washroom— for night use. One daren't go outdoors at night.

She emerged from the outhouse, washed her hands in the outside basin, and entered the house to hear knocking at the front door. Insistent. Very unlike the locals. Pulling on a cardigan, she went to open it. Geoffrey, in his capacity as diocesan administrator, stood there, looking abashed.

"Geoffrey, what's up?" she asked, genuinely curious.

"Sorry to bother you, Mama-Sammy," he stammered. "We've scheduled a trip to the Twa village today, with important visitors from England..."

"Yes?"

"And Wilberforce is too ill to drive." He looked around, apparently for signs of Stephen. "Bishop told me that you, ah, can drive, that you grew up in Cameroon...that you might be used to our roads."

"Well, I never drove in Cameroon, Geoffrey, but I have driven on rougher roads. Did you need me to help out?"

197

The Wrong Side of Eternity

"If it is possible. The Land Rover is in the shop, but the double-cabin is free."

She thought. Sam would love an outing in a truck, and it would be an exciting diversion for him to visit the pygmy tribal group, the poorest of the poor. They still lived in dirt huts, smoking their long pipes and drinking banana beer much of the time, ever since their hunting rights had been withdrawn by the government, to free up space for the sake of progress. It wouldn't do, they'd been told, to have little dirty forest hunters terrorizing the tourists in the gorilla sanctuary. The Twa now made their living by begging and providing uninvited entertainment at any major event in town.

"I would love to." She could see the mixed relief and puzzlement on his face: relief that the problem had been solved, puzzlement that she did not need to ask her husband. He thanked her, bowed, and went back to the office to share the good news.

"Sam!" she called, interrupting her son from building a tower with Legos, the only toy they'd brought to Uganda. He came running down the hall, his feet slapping against the bare cement of the floor. She knelt to talk with him. "Would you like to go with mummy to the forest to see the Twa people? They would love to meet *you*, I'm sure." She would have to put deet-soaked socks on him to keep away the fleas. He nodded excitedly, and they went to pack a bit of travel food.

"And this is our driver today, Mrs. O'Connell," Geoffrey said.

"Julie," she corrected, extending her hand. The visitors had the air of project funders, dressed in their khakis and canvas hats, their belly bags strapped around their waists. She almost expected to see the bowl of a pipe protruding from the man's breast pocket. He looked skeptical.

"American?"

"Yes, from the West Coast."

"Your accent betrays you."

She could almost hear him asking himself, *Can such a small woman handle such a large lorry?* "Really? Shucks." She steeled herself for the next comment, and it wasn't long in coming.

Act II

"In my experience I've found Americans to be arrogant and selfish."

"Me too!" she responded, swatting him on the arm. "Every single one of them! And the entire country is full of bigots and prudes."

He didn't say one more word to her the rest of the journey.

The double-cabin pickup was monstrous, high off the ground, very impressive. Every cutting-edge mission project seemed to want one, they were such status symbols. An amateur hand had painted the diocesan seal on the door. Julie plunked Sam on the front seat next to Geoffrey, then she slid behind the steering wheel of the truck. She adjusted the mirrors and started the diesel engine, happy to be of practical use. The Brits sat in the back seat, taking in the countryside as they meandered between the cinder cones and around a myriad of banana plantations. Geoffrey provided a running narrative of the diocese, its projects and its history, and the conversation got stuck, as usual, on the differences between people.

"We hear there are tensions building in Rwanda between the two tribal groups there," commented the man.

"It is not a problem here in Uganda," Geoffrey explained. "We have many tribes here, so they do not oppose one another in the same way."

No, thought Julie, focused on the rutted dirt track in front of them. *They oppose one another in other ways. Competition for foreign-aid funding. Us and Them, again.* She wondered where it would lead and sighed.

"So why is it a problem over there and not here?" the quieter companion of the man asked, almost timidly. His wife, or a secretary? Her voice sounded so searching that Julie felt for her and smiled. She really wanted a better answer. Perhaps she was really the senior of the two, his superior...Julie nearly laughed aloud at the thought.

"It has become political over the years," explained Geoffrey. "The colonial power favoured one over the other, despite all the intermarrying. It was the Belgians who first formally issued identity cards with either 'Hutu' or 'Tutsi' printed on them."

"But Uganda was a British Protectorate, never a colony," added the man in defense. "Therefore the locals did not carry the same amount of, ah, history."

Baggage, thought Julie.

"Perhaps," answered Geoffrey. "But we have our own share of problems. The country next door blames us for the tensions."

"Why?" the woman asked.

"Because thousands of Rwandan refugees have been living here since the last set of troubles, and there is a force gathering to return when the opportunity comes. They accuse us of harbouring, what do you call it? Terrorists."

"And do you?" the man asked.

"I do not call them that. They are refugees." He paused. "Some of them, the RPF, live in the Impenetrable Forest, armed and waiting."

"Waiting for what?"

"An opportunity to lead the refugees back."

Julie put the enormous vehicle into four-wheel drive and coaxed it over some rocks; it was like driving over a dry riverbed. She geared down, then crept over some sharp outcroppings, capably plopping the truck down on the other side—although it wobbled ferociously. Sam was delighted with what he called "Mr. Toad's wild ride," but the visitors in the backseat looked alarmed.

"Woo-*HOOO!*" she exclaimed, increasing their speed. "Just like boony busting on the logging roads back home!"

Geoffrey laughed, and within minutes they had arrived at the Twa village.

The visitors took in the new huts and small water tanks their project had provided, and sat down to sample the local fare. Greasy plastic cups full of sorghum brew were set before them, with white bread, goat livers, and chai. *A veritable feast,* thought Julie. *These people really made an effort.* But the *bazungu* funders did not look so appreciative, though the woman nodded and smiled politely. A gray-headed elder stepped forward to spout some poetry. Then the Twa danced and sang; Sam slid off his bamboo stool to join them, to the immense delight of the villagers.

Act II

As they drove back down the road, some children ran close behind the truck as it bounced along. Julie scowled, considering what to do. She foresaw one slipping under the truck's tires. If she were to stop and get out to scold them, they would probably just mock her and continue. So she slammed on the brake, and two little boys crashed into the rear bumper. They picked themselves up and ran back, laughing in embarrassment. She heard the Brits in the back gasp in horror, but Geoffrey commended her for teaching "those little urchins" a valuable lesson.

On the way back, Geoffrey asked if the visitors would like some fresh air. Of course they would, came the answer: being with those rather smelly people made one long for a good wash. The clouds coming through the mountainous corridor from the east were not black with rain—yet—so they stopped at the foot of one of the more circular cinder cones for a bit of a hike. It looked like a miniature shield volcano. The woman passenger looked quite eager to stretch her legs, to Julie's delight. They went ahead of the men, who lingered to discuss the day's visit and walked more slowly. Sam had shot out in front and was two-thirds of the way up just as they began their ascent.

"I didn't catch your name," said Julie.

"Sophie. Sophia Grimes."

"So glad you could come."

"Me too. It's eye-opening," she admitted, smiling. The hill was steep, and they were getting winded.

The man asked Geoffrey, "What was that poem about?" Due to time constraints, no translation had been provided. Geoffrey stopped.

"It was about listening, listening to things rather than people. Things like the voices of fire, of water; the wind in the trees, the groaning rock. 'They are the forefathers' breathing. The dead are not dead,' in African tribal religion. They speak in a woman's breast, a crying child, a glowing ember."

The Wrong Side of Eternity

"They do, eh? That's preposterous," answered the man, and the translation ended there.

The wind whipped at the women when they reached the top of the cinder cone; Sophie had to tie down her hat to keep it from blowing away. Julie let her hair dance across her face, lifting her head in exultation. It was like being perched on the edge of a giant bowl, but green and lush, suspended halfway between the heights of the craggy volcanoes to the west and the undulating village land below, which was interspersed with banana plantations and wattle-and-daub huts, some with corrugated iron roofing, others with thatch. Moving along its round rim, Julie didn't seem to be going anywhere, except that the horizon changed from lake to mountain to cinder cone–strewn field stretching along the vast corridor. The distance around was deceptive and longer than she expected. While the women walked around the perimeter, Sam plunged down into the bowl to explore the puddles at the bottom.

"Will he have to watch for snakes?" asked Sophie.

"The snakes here aren't any danger," explained Julie. "No mambas, like in Kampala. The elevation's too high. That doesn't stop the locals from fearing them, though. Lots of myths and stories. Seeing a snake usually forebodes disaster."

"You know a great deal about the local customs, then?"

"Not a lot. I'm learning more all the time, though," Julie answered, smiling. "There's a lot to learn. The history books don't give these people much credit."

"I've noticed that," responded the woman.

You would, thought Julie with a smile. *Sophia. Lady Wisdom.*

45. ON HOLIDAY

The bus stopped, and vendors with meat on skewers and hot roasted maize appeared at the windows, hawking their wares. Several passengers stepped off and headed into the sparse bushes a stone's throw away, relieving themselves. Julie lifted her midlength skirt and squatted along with several other women; although there was only the space of a few meters between them, no one seemed to mind, and each provided a sort of privacy by looking into the trees rather than at one another. Feeling a need to stretch his legs, Stephen disembarked with Sam, and purchased a kebab of goat meat for them to share.

It was time to get back on. Sam ran to join his mother as she approached the bus. A crowd of twenty or so mobbed the door; a man elbowed his way in, just ahead of Stephen. The dry dusty field smell blended with the odors of unwashed bodies and gasoline. Stephen hated pushing.

"Hey, Julie, how'd you get way up there?" he shouted, amused. She was such a small wiry thing, and she was already climbing the bus steps, helping Sam up in front of her.

"Speed and agility, my dear. And a little muscle. Where's your sporting instinct?" She laughed back at him and climbed aboard.

"Just save me a seat."

"Yeah, right," came the muffled answer from the stuffy aisle.

The Thompsons met them at the bus park in Kabiizi later that morning to give them a lift to the most parasite-free lake in the district. A mass of borderland passengers spilled out of the bus into the space surrounded by rows of dark doorways: little shops all marketing the same inventory of washing powder, cigarettes, sodas, biscuits, and stationery supplies. The O'Connells looked a little wrinkled to Eva as they tumbled off the steps of the dusty bus with the bright VAROOM! painted on its side.

"You should really invest in a modest vehicle, Stephen. God knows what you could pick up riding on a crowded bus like that." Eva always had their best interest in mind when she gave counsel. "Not that we are bothered with taking you, not at all. But you could have some independence...The head nursing sister at the clinic is retiring next month and will need to find a buyer for her small jeep. Perhaps you could talk with her?"

The Wrong Side of Eternity

"We haven't minded going on public transport so far, but you may be right," he answered as they climbed into the Thompsons' Range Rover. "It would make it easier if ever we wanted to visit the game parks," he reasoned as Julie gave him a look. "Maybe she would be willing to meet with us when we come back?" They could spend a day or two, visit the new mission family at the bible college, do some shopping. *You could get decent cheese now, in Kabiizi.*

Julie did not want to buy a car: "It sets us further apart," she had told him. "Makes us the Haves." But Stephen would talk with her about it; perhaps they could share its use and cost with Pastor Ann, who had to schedule her visits to the back country through the diocesan offices and often ran into conflicts. She had told Stephen she was contemplating getting a motor scooter for pastoral visits. *That* would go over well.

They arrived at the lake well after lunch. Julie was glad they had brought the backpacks; it kept their hands free.

"When you get to the lake shore, pay them only three thousand shillings for the trip across—knowing you are visitors, they'll want to overcharge you," instructed Eva.

Two dollars and fifty cents for a canoe trip for three to an island. Such a deal. *And who exactly,* Julie wondered, *was being robbed?* She smiled at the Thompsons, who invited her to join them for a quick cup of tea at the lakeside kiosk.

Sam had run off and was squatting near the side of the road. Stephen walked over to see what had captured his son's attention.

A blue-green chameleon, its sides dappled yellow, slowly made its way through the brown dirt. It did not startle much when Sam's hand came within its view. Its volcano-shaped eyes turned in its head, apparently looking in opposite directions. Its tail curved wheel-like, a living spiral. No wonder the creature had magic, in the stories.

"Isn't it beautiful, Sam?" asked his father, crouching beside him. "It can change color to escape the notice of predators, other animals that might want to eat it. It hides that way."

Act II

"Don't it get dizzy, Da, looking in diffewent ways like that?"

"I don't know."

"I sure would!" Together they watched it laboriously make its way across the road. "Can we take it home to keep as a pet? Pwease?"

"No, Sam, we can't. I don't think it would be too happy living in any kind of cage." A glass case, heated with a lamp. No; it would not be happy. "But we can put it out of danger, where the cars won't run over it." Stephen picked up a stick and let the chameleon crawl onto it, its prehensile feet grasping the smooth wood, and then he slowly carried it to a dense hedge. The creature refused to let go of its perch, so he put the stick down among the gnarled roots, shaded from the sun. The Thompsons were just preparing to drive off, and Stephen shouted a hearty thanks to them, which was answered with a wave from Stan.

Julie stood negotiating with the boatman for a canoe ride to the island, and he went to join her. When the price quoted was for six thousand, he nodded, and Julie smiled at him with approval. Sam crawled into the middle of the dugout canoe, where the boatman had told him to go, and climbed onto the pile of rushes tied together to form a small seat. He spent the trip across the water watching his parents row with heavy, ancient paddles, miming their actions with an invisible oar.

The boatman joined them but mostly did the steering. Stephen caught him smiling, as if to say *What a couple, paying me so much, then helping to row.* His family would be able to eat meat this week.

The "resort" cook told them that although there were no dangerous animals in the lake—crocodiles or hippos or fish that bite—most of the people could not swim, so there were drownings from time to time. All due to luck, of course, and the weather. The O'Connells dropped their packs in a hut at the island camp where they would sleep under the ever-present mosquito netting, and Stephen headed off with Sam to make a tour of the little island. They arrived back at the dock to see Julie swimming, nearly a third of the way to the opposite shore, doing a steady crawl. A boatman stood up in his dugout to shout at her. *She must have competed in high school,* concluded Stephen, watching her smooth stroke. *It's a good thing there aren't any hippos, because if there were, she'd be toast.* Ten minutes later she emerged dripping and shivering from the water, and she gratefully accepted the beach towel he picked up from the pile of her cast-off clothes.

"That was *terrific!*" she exclaimed, and they headed off to a supper of crayfish masala.

A group of Peace Corps workers arrived just at sunset and sat around the fire ring drinking beer and talking loudly into the night. *At least they didn't bring portable CD players,* thought Stephen, trying to sleep. There was more peace at their tumbledown house in Rutoki.

But the morning was quiet, and after breakfast Sam spent much of the day playing at the lake shore, watching the canoe men make their trips back and forth as they pulled up wooden traps full of crayfish. Julie stood next to the dock, waist deep in the cool water, urging him to jump in. Why wait until he was six to give swimming lessons?

Stephen meted out their holiday funds carefully, so they had enough left over to hire a dilapidated taxi to cart them back to Kabiizi from the lake shore. The phones worked better on the Protestant hill: he would try to call St. Simeon's and arrange to have a bank draft sent out for the jeep.

They brought along a thank-you gift for the Thompsons: a black plastic sack filled with two kilos of crawling crayfish. The crackling of the bag made the driver look back into the rearview mirror nervously the entire half-hour journey. Julie wasn't at all sure if Eva would appreciate it, but she knew the Thompson's house girl had a love for cooking exotic dishes, and Julie wanted to give her something fun to do for a change.

On their way back to Rutoki four days later in their "new" used jeep, Stephen saw a billboard put up by the AIDS Education Counsel. LOVE SAFELY, it read, with a picture of a smiling doctor holding out small foil packages that could only contain condoms. That wouldn't go down well

Act II

with the Catholics, and the more conservative Protestants were preaching abstinence everywhere. The AEC had done a good job, dropping the infection rate down to 9 percent, but there must be a better way.

And the slogan? It carried a mixed message, as if mere intercourse implied love. And on top of that, "love safely" was an oxymoron: it was impossible. Loving at all, decided Stephen, carried a tremendous amount of risk. It was quite a dangerous thing altogether.

46. NIGHT

Words emerged from blackness. Years ago they were in the Northern dialect; then, a year or two later they shifted into Swahili. Then, circling closer, into English. "Move over, it's my turn," Charity heard the soldier say. "They're no fun once they're dead." This night the words trapped her, uttered in her own borderland dialect, her mother tongue: she awoke panting hard, damp with perspiration.

The nightmares had started up again. Charity could not quite pinpoint the cause; maybe it was because Peace was growing older and looked less like a little girl. Maybe all the "cultural questions" Julie was asking were opening a locked part of her, forcing her to face the buried past...No one ever had to warn her of the dangers of cigarettes or beer, for she could smell both, in the dreams. They re-emerged every three or four years, to make her sit bolt upright at night on the brink of screaming.

Perhaps she should see James or Dr. Nsekanabo, maybe ask for those pills that could make one calm. But at the same time she feared that such a remedy might lower her ability to stay in control.

A shadow moved between her curtained window and the moonlight outside. Were the night dancers out, trying to find ways to curse and ruin? *No wonder people go to the local healers to shield themselves from danger,* she thought. *No wonder people reach for anything that offers protection: a rosary, an amulet, a cross, a crystal.* Fear was such a powerful force!

Her heart was racing and on the edge of pain. She needed help with these night terrors before she woke Peace with real screams. *All secrets will come into the light,* she reminded herself as she rose to light a candle against the growing darkness. She opened her bible and found the verses she'd underlined about peace, love, deliverance from fear. They were just words on a page. What she needed, wanted, was a *voice.*

The nearest woman pastor she trusted lived in Kabiizi, but she had no excuse to go there: Uncle Asaph and his wife had moved away. There was Reverend Ann; but would she keep Charity's fragile confidence? Would she not pass along her concerns to the other pastors? But Ann was a woman, after all. She *might* understand. She had been inviting Charity to come over for tea as of late...Did God tell Reverend Ann the secrets of Ntambara Charity? *I hope not. I'd rather reveal them on my own.*

Tomorrow was Sunday. She sighed and decided to approach the missioner, ask to meet after all.

47. THE MODEST BRICK HOME OF ANN ROURKE

Ann had the O'Connells over for lunch and served a sort of tuna salad. No mayonnaise, but with diced pickles and vinegar atop homemade bread. Her house helper was a master baker, so Ann had had an outdoor oven built so she could enjoy her art. Sam ate the exotic food as if he hadn't had a huge bowl of *posho* for breakfast three hours earlier.

"You've been here a long time, Ann?"

"Only six years."

"Only?"

"Things take a while to catch on. You have to do things in little bits," Ann explained and turned to Sam, wanting to include him in the conversation even though his mouth was full. "If you take little bites, over time you can eat an elephant."

Stephen caught the photo on the front of the *New Vision* lying atop Ann's coffee table. A group of young soldiers were holding up severed body parts of a 'rebel'. He scanned the article. Their weapon: "intense personal discipline and a potion made from rinsing ink from copied verses from the Koran with water and applying it to self-inflicted wounds." It was, the article went on, effective in deterring bullets.

"Is that what I think it is?" he asked Ann, peering more closely at the photograph.

"Yiss," she answered, lowering her voice. "Someone's balls. Guess it'd be bist to throw that copy out, before some little man spots it, eh? Might scare him to dith." She whisked the paper away while Julie stood smirking at the shock that passed over her husband's face.

When they emerged from the brick house, a young woman stood before it, blocking their way down the path. She was well dressed, although thin, and she stared at them, clenching her fists.

"May I help you?" asked Stephen.

Her accent was negligible, her English very good. "No. You may not help us. We've come for you, for them." Her eyes darted past the steps to Julie and Sam.

"We don't need any more house help, thank you," answered Ann, approaching. "Please go now." The woman did not move an inch. "Where are you from?" Ann asked casually.

Her eyes narrowed at the sight of Ann's clerical collar. "Zaire. There are many of us." Tilting her head downward, she said in a growly voice, "You have no power to make us leave."

"No, I probably don't," admitted Ann. She looked straight into the woman's eyes, which were yellow and dull. Ann lifted her arm slowly and spoke clearly, raising her voice only a little. "But we—and this compound—belong to the Lord Jesus Christ, and in his name, I command you to go."

The woman turned mechanically and headed toward the gate. Charity stood there and moved aside to let her pass. She had seen the whole thing. Their eyes followed the woman toward town; she kept looking back as if a dog were chasing her heels.

That was so simple, what Ann did. So effective, thought Charity. Why didn't someone like that appear over twelve years ago, when she lay

The Wrong Side of Eternity

pinned to the dirt by those soldiers? But Charity already knew the answer: *they* were not possessed by demons. They were merely men taking advantage during a time of chaos. Opportunists. A simple command spoken in the name of God may not have worked. Hadn't she tried that herself? She sighed.

"Do you think she'll come back?" asked Julie.

"No. She won't be back. Not here, anyway." Ann motioned Charity into the house. "There might be others: young hoodlums breaking a window, stealing from the garden. Maybe even that crazy Twa woman who comes by every month or so to dance in the yard spouting gibberish, and urinate, and beg for old clothing. The cattle might even break in again. But not her. Come on in, Charity," she said, as she walked her colleagues to the gate and waved them off.

48. CHURCH OFFICES, RUTOKI

Stephen sat down next to Geoffrey's desk for their weekly meeting.

"Geoffrey, I saw the secondary-school drama production and the water project outreach. They are *brilliant* at theater. And everyone agrees on what the problems are: alcoholism, poor sanitation, poverty, lack of respect for women. Everyone wants to work against the spread of AIDS. We could build a troupe made up of Native Anglicans, Roman Catholics, and folks from the independent churches..."

"The Seventh-day Adventists, the Baptists, the Pentecostals... You'll never get them to meet under the same roof, Stephen my friend."

"There's so much talent in this town. The creative approach is *working* with the water project. We could combine resources, come up with more dramas, have a variety..."

"It could not be a church-sponsored project," the diocesan administrator pointed out. Too many players.

"It wouldn't be," admitted Stephen. "It would be a community project."

Act II

"You would have to include the Muslims, the pagans…"

"Of course."

Geoffrey was skeptical. Here was a Christian missionary wanting to mix people up. It was potentially explosive. There were bound to be battles, bullies…politics. Tribalism in Uganda wasn't dead. It had only taken on different names.

"I am not so sure. The funders, they hesitate to sponsor people, give school fees. It is easier to get help for materials, books, buildings…"

"But don't you see? The drama will pull them together in a team. We can write the script—well, the outline; they love to improvise—using medical facts, and extend the plot into life practice and behavior. It needn't turn into preaching."

"Ah, Stephen, I think I see. It is not the *words* themselves that will bring them together. It is *doing* the project."

"Yes, Geoffrey. Remember when you were at the ITS? Remember how people there would disagree but still be forced to collaborate on a team project? When they turned their efforts to the success of the project, look how well they worked together. Or at least they would try. We could do it here. We have a common language—mostly—and agreement that these are huge problems."

"Which word would you use for God? The Catholic one, or the Protestant?" *"Allah" is not even an option,* thought Geoffrey.

"We could use both, depending on the characters. Or neither. It could be a religious-free piece of drama."

I doubt that is even possible, thought Geoffrey. Did Stephen not realise that no one here considered himself an atheist? But he had another idea. "We could write a proposal under the RACIS."

"Yes!"

"You begin to write then, Stephen, and I shall start the talk going around."

"Deal."

They shook hands, and the Community Health through Drama Project was born.

211

49. LATER, AT THE HOME OF GEOFFREY MAHORO

The cooking fires were dying, the light fading. Grace was just getting out the kerosene lanterns, making sure they had enough fuel for the evening. Gideon, their night watchman, had just arrived. Geoffrey stood in the little screened lean-to, washing, when he heard the woman next door cry out. The neighbours were fighting again.

"Geoffrey!" his wife called. "It's gone too far this time."

Quickly he pulled on his trousers, grabbed a T-shirt, and called to the night watchman who was just passing by on his way to the diocesan offices.

"Gideon, come help me."

Crashing sounds were coming from the mud-brick house next door as two terrified children ran out to the kraal, where cattle huddled in the evening air. Geoffrey and Gideon moved past them to enter the house.

"Stop it, John," commanded Geoffrey, grabbing the upraised arm of the man, who brandished a *panga* at the woman cowering in a corner. Blood covered her left arm. Gideon wrestled the machete out of John's hand and sat him firmly in a chair. He began to defend himself, his speech slurred.

"She is a worthless, stupid woman. My food was *cold* when I came home tonight—"

"From the bar," Geoffrey finished his sentence. "John, your drinking is killing you, your family." He helped the woman up to a chair and saw that the cut on her upper arm was deep, although the blood was flowing, not spurting. If John hadn't been drunk, it would likely be even worse. He trusted Gideon to keep the man restrained while he bound up the wound, tearing a strip from the thin tablecloth to make a pressure dressing

"She *deserves* it, Pastor Geoffrey. It's her fault we are so poor. She wastes so much money, buying vitamins and other unnecessary things for the children. Their shoes will last another term!"

Act II

"And how will they survive at all if you kill her?" Geoffrey answered. He considered what to do. It was fast becoming night. "You'll come home with me, John, or I'll take you to the police."

"I can do what I like in my own home!"

"No, John, you do not have a right to harm your family like this. You are a Christian, and this is not what God wants from you."

"God has never married, how should he know?"

"Quiet now. Gideon, help me to get him to my house." Geoffrey would give him some medicine he kept on hand, to help him sleep off the anger and the booze—probably *waragi*, that poisonous stuff that made people mad. Would he remember any of it, come morning? He looked at the woman. "Keep your arm up on a pillow. I will send over James to do a better job at the bandaging. Tomorrow we'll take you to hospital. The church will cover the cost—this time." She looked up at him and nodded gratefully, cradling her arm, starting to whimper softly. *A machete.* What was happening to the world? Was not John an awakened one, touched by the revival? *It is too bad,* thought Geoffrey, *that the police will do nothing.* She was John's wife; legally, he could punish her for infractions in the home.

But a *machete?*

50. RUTOKI MARKET, A TUESDAY AFTERNOON

Peace, Charity Ntambara's young ward, found Julie in the market looking at the swaths of bright silk-screened cloth that billowed like a curtain of rainbows. "Julie!" she greeted her. Together they walked back to Charity's.

"So what did you think of our little hospital?" Peace asked. "Will you be training some of the dressers to do physiotherapy?"

"One question at a time, dear girl!" answered Julie. Was it the time to be brutally honest? *I almost gagged at the sight of the lab, with vials of blood practically falling over, open needles lying on the countertop...I admired the commitment of the nurses...* "I like the way you let the families in to take care of the patients," she responded. "The staff seems to really care."

"So will you be training them?" Peace knew that Julie O'Connell had been invited to. After all, she was a qualified physio, and there were only a handful in the entire country. News of the proposal had gotten around. Plenty of people would benefit, not least the ones who'd had polio, yet to be eradicated in Uganda.

"I would have to work with a nursing sister, I think, because I haven't mastered the local language yet." The *how* of the project still had lots of details to iron out.

"Your language is good enough to train the dressers. They're keen to have you teach them, Mama-Sammy. Dr. Nsekanabo is telling everyone that you will. Didn't he show you the plans for building a gym?"

Julie had taken in the physical therapy area, with its sticks pounded into the ground to keep a child's legs in line, useless in the rainy season when it became a muddy bog. She couldn't do it alone. She would have to spend some time in Kabiizi, at the hospital, observing their staff.

Kabiizi. They didn't think much of the borderland folks. Complained that they refused to learn a real Ugandan language, opting for the language from Rwanda. Complained that they self-isolated, that they were too proud to be either Ugandan or Rwandan, that they held on to ideas of still being an ancient kingdom, that they were backward, ignorant, and fickle. She smiled: the borderlanders had opinions of their own of the people of Kabiizi: sneaky, deceitful, snobbish.

It would have been funny if it wasn't so sad.

Perhaps one of the PTs in Kabiizi would consider a stay in Rutoki as a sort of outreach; she and Dr. Nsekanabo could benefit from the government training the certified therapists had, and their eagerness to help would offset the prejudice. Or, she could appeal to the mission to send one of their PTs over from Rwanda as a consultant. That might be better, less of a language barrier. There was a Catholic hospital only twenty miles from the border. She would meet with James about all the options.

Act II

"Well?"

"I would like to. I need to talk with some other people. If this is going to last, it has to be properly planned." They walked together in silence for a few minutes more. "And I don't want to be away from home more than three days a week, ever. Sam's doing well with the home schooling."

"I'm glad. Being only with our primary students would slow him down."

"He'll probably attend the local school for a few terms, though. He needs to be part of the community."

Peace beamed with pleasure. She practically skipped the rest of the way.

———◆———

In town, a panel of spiritual leaders had gathered at the office of the MP for a special meeting of the Women for Global Development. They had been invited there to contrast the tribal creation myths with the teachings of the Bible and the Koran. The imam from the mosque greeted Geoffrey warmly; the others maintained an air of aloofness as Phoebe introduced them to the growing audience.

Charity took a seat in the least-visible corner of the room in order to observe and take notes. She watched while an assortment of people came through the door to hear what these men would say: a man in a business suit, the woman who ran the tourist hotel, a teacher from the secondary school, two aid workers, an elderly woman with bare feet, some secondary school students. Charity would corner the speakers later if they quoted something relevant, to get their source. She'd thought about journalism, but it seemed so dry.

The speaker was reading from a pamphlet recently printed in Nairobi, although Charity noted that the paper had a brown-yellow tinge. How recent could it be? "It is clear from some of the creation stories that Man represents the spiritual aspirations of the human race: the devotion to the adoration of the eternal light, to study and reflection.

215

Woman represents the earthly wishes of people, the desires for lust and for the enjoyment of children. The adoration of God is a duty for Man—leading a spiritual life will make us happy. But following our desires for earthly satisfaction, for sex and satiety, will lead to endless unhappiness. If only Adam had persisted in his prayers and patient prostrations, centuries of suffering would have been prevented."

Written by a man, no doubt, thought Charity.

Phoebe stepped in to moderate.

"Very interesting, Caleb. Especially as the writer so easily makes 'man' and 'woman' symbols for two sides of the human being—sides each and every one of us knows so well." Some in the audience smiled at her comments.

Geoffrey sat more erect to respond; to Charity he looked distinguished in his clerical collar and black jacket, his gray hair complementing his gentle voice.

"I do not quote from a modern pamphlet, Madame Kizito," he began. "If we turn to the Old Testament, women were not representative of a type, but *people*, some who were good, some who were bad, just like the men. It is really not fair to lump them all together. And in the Gospels, we see that Jesus talked to women as individuals. He was not afraid to speak with them, either privately or in public."

"Sometimes I think our more interpretive writers were a little afraid of them," added the imam, and almost every person in the audience laughed.

Phoebe smiled, looked at the clock on the wall, and stood to make her closing statement. "People are talking to each other; this had been a really good meeting," she began.

Charity agreed.

———◆———

Julie kept going, past Charity's house, walking up the twisty path to Ann's place. James, the capable medical assistant, was just leaving. So good of him to make house calls like this.

Act II

"How's she doing?"

"Very good. She may not want to visit long, though. And you, Mama-Sammy, take care you do not drink the water or use the long-drop at present."

"I won't, James. Thank you so much for coming, taking care of her."

"We say the same about you *bazungu* who choose to be here with us."

Julie knocked timidly. "Ann?"

Her house helper answered the door. "She knows you are here but will be a few moments."

"Thank you." Julie was ushered in and sat down on the foam cushion, admiring the tidy garden outside the window. *What a failure I am as a gardener,* she thought. Ann shuffled in to sink into a corner of the wicker sofa.

"God, Julie, what a mess. All over the sheets...What a silly bird I am, to come down with typhoid. Don't get this, okay?"

"I'll do my best. James says I've got to keep my distance. But don't be too hard on yourself. They forgot to tell us in training that the vaccine is only 60 percent effective."

"It's a two-week incubation period, they say. God knows where I picked it up. Hurts like hell."

"Yeah?"

"Just above the arse, whenever I go. I looked it up. The lower bowel ulcerates and you shit blood."

"Yeah, I looked it up too. Nasty."

"I can't offer you tea."

"No problem. I just wanted to see how you're doing."

"Better, except for the pain. I've got to take it easy for another month at least, get my strength back. I actually sent a note to that husband of yours, see if he wanted to take my preaching this Sunday, at the English service."

"And?"

"And he sounds keen to do it—shy, but keen. If you know what I mean."

217

"He'll take it very seriously," said Julie.

"I like that about him." She put her head back and sighed.

"I'd better go, Ann. Do you need me to pick anything up for you?"

"That pink stuff, tastes like peppermint. It'd be worth a try."

"It's got salicylates in it, could make any bleeding worse. Sorry. Anything else?"

"Got any decent room deodoriser, maybe pine scent?"

Julie laughed. "As a matter of fact, I brought a fair bit of it for the loo. Reminds me of where I grew up, in the woods. I'll bring some up later."

"Can you let yourself out?"

"Sure thing." Julie walked over to Ann, then bent down to kiss her forehead. "You get better."

"So do you...bittah and bittah."

51. NIGHTTIME, THE O'CONNELL HOME

Stephen sat at the little desk in their bedroom, reading a letter by the light of the kerosene lamp. It had been more than two years since Bryce had written. Or maybe, just maybe, a letter or two had gone missing on the way.

Dear Stephen,

What a fantastic prayer letter you write! Your project sounds delightful. I always knew you had it in you to do drama. I can almost see you sitting with a pad and a pen, chewing on the cap while the young people rehearse their AIDS production. It sounds as if you've been able to encourage them to step up to their talents, instead of pushing some foreign script on them. As you Yanks say, WAY TO GO!

Madeleine is taking a bit of dramatic coaching in preparation for some upcoming TV appearances. I never thought I'd be married to a celebrity, but she is already approached like one— apart from people asking for her autograph. If you thought she

Act II

was polished before, HOLY COW. I'll never be able to express my gratitude for the hot tip you gave me, those long years ago, which led me to my present bliss.

As to your concerns about the struggles over there, it is an unfortunate turn of history, that the cycle of violence repeats itself over and over. The colonial shadow is such a dream stopper: where would these people have gone if we had not interfered? Of course, as you so rightly put it, the influence is a mixed one: you write of all the positive regard the Ugandans have for the British system of education, administration. But you also write of the high level of organization that some tribes showed before the arrival of Europeans. You make people *think*, Stephen, by putting forth both sides.

You asked about my work. I continue at the cathedral in the city, that is my most regular gig, but I've been collaborating on some minor-scale musical projects for both theatre and music graduate students at the university. I'm ashamed to admit that my spiritual life is not as sharp as it could be: when Madeleine gives me an important book to read, I normally fall asleep in the recliner. And the late-night gigs don't inspire me to get up as early as she. I'm afraid I've turned into a lazy, good-for-nothing doofus.

I need to get this into the post before I head out into the Wild West. Do be careful, my friend: the news from your part of the world is hardly encouraging. I do get concerned for your safety; it is one of the more regular petitions in my meagre prayers.

Cheers, and I mean that most literally,

Bryce

Stephen sighed. Such mixed feelings. How many aerograms had he sent to Bryce? Over a dozen, surely. And long ones, too. Maybe Bryce was just one of those people who could only love one person at a time.

In their washroom, Julie squatted in lantern light, scrubbing a filthy little shirt in a plastic basin. The rainy season relentlessly dowsed the

The Wrong Side of Eternity

green hills, sending field workers scurrying two or three times a day for the nearest cover. It had been raining too hard for Sam's small guest to go home, and now the orphan was asleep on their bamboo couch, tucked in with a thick blanket. It would be safer for him to go back in the morning anyway. She doubted if his uncle would miss him, except as a target of drunken fury.

Wringing the plaid shirt out for the third time, she went out the back door to hang it on the line; the rain seemed to let up at night for some strange reason. Not always; there were occasions when she would wake to a thin layer of hail on the grassy patch that served as a lawn. The moon shone over mottled waves of cloud, illuminating the volcanic hills in a faint luminescent blue. A pinpoint of light flickered halfway up the ridge: somebody's paraffin lamp.

Here, a child with a widowed mother could call himself an orphan, be eligible for sponsorship from caring strangers half a world away. In the West, he might be regarded as only having a single parent—deficiency enough, in some circles. Parenting was for pairs, these little lives being too precious to hang them upon one frail human guardian. But here the extended family stepped in with scarcely a breath to provide help. Usually.

"Julie, what are you doing out now?" asked Stephen from the doorway.

"Shh, there's a kid asleep on the couch."

"I saw him, sweet little thing. Looks to be about six."

"He's Sam's age, I think, or a little older. Just don't go in the washroom."

"Why?"

"He and Sam were collecting frogs today. They brought a bucketful home."

"Oh." He opened the washroom door to hear croaking coming from the cement cistern where they did their bathing. "Great." In the morning, they would find it covered with spawn.

"We'll set them all free tomorrow," she said, coming back in.

"And what if that shirt doesn't dry tonight?"

Act II

"He can have one of Sam's."

"Don't set a precedent: pretty soon we'll have street children lining up at the door for free clothes."

"We don't have street children here."

"Yes we do, and once they get the electricity in, there will be more."

"I see your point, and I'll be judicious." She smiled. He looked tired. All those meetings, running around in the rain. "The boys are both asleep. Let's go light a candle."

He knew what that meant, and he locked the door to night behind her, to follow her willingly down the hall.

In the morning after breakfast, it was quite a project setting all the frogs free, cleaning up. Stephen had taken his Chinese bicycle to the office as usual, despite the mud. They used the jeep only for longer treks or emergencies. Julie and Esther left the compound to take their little guest home. Sam stayed with Aunt Charity at the diocesan office, coloring; Julie was not sure that he should be along this time.

The orphan boy nervously held both the women's hands, walking between them, shielded and safe. Something he did not have at home. He had a sister, five years older than he, but she never spoke. She was too busy cooking and cleaning.

They approached a rectangular mud hut with a tin roof, built on a small shelf right next to an eroding hillside surrounded by the terraced fields checkering the steep slope. Esther called out a greeting, and they waited. The door opened and an unshaven and bedraggled man blinked in the bright morning light. He looked puzzled to have such visitors, two women—and then he saw the boy. Before he could grab him and pull him inside, Julie stepped across the threshold.

"Your nephew was safe last night. He is returned to your care." Esther translated as clearly as she could but stayed outside, still holding the boy's hand. "Take care you do not beat him, or hurt him in *any* way, or I shall have the police on you so fast you will not know what happened." She saw the boy's sister standing behind his uncle, staring

221

at Julie with eyes wider than she knew possible. *God, he's probably abusing her,* she thought.

The man swallowed and ran his hand through his unkempt hair, nodding. Although she stood shorter than he, this was more than a *muzungu,* this was more than a woman. An ancestral spirit, or an angel...Her hair shone like fire and there was fire burning in her face, her eyes. Her voice was as the sound of many waters, and it made his headache worse.

"I know your name," she said, "and you will be watched. So you had better make things better in your home, and soon." She reached for the boy and held him gently in front of her, with both her hands on his thin shoulders. "If you *ever...*" she continued, but he began bowing and nodding and talking with Esther in the borderland dialect, giving assurances.

On their way home, Julie would ask Pastor Boniface to follow up on this one.

———◆———

She stood at the heavy hardwood table, working with a hunk of goat meat. Slicing away the tough membrane was a challenge, reminding her of anatomy class and dissection. But picking out the bits of splintered bone, hair, and dirt was more tedious still. Julie smiled to recall Stephen's initial revulsion when he went with her those first days to the butcher shop, how a blood-spattered fellow had hacked a chunk of meat off a suspended carcass with a dull *panga,* and how the goat's head on the counter had seemed to stare back with its clouded eyes.

Now, a few years later, cutting up meat was a mere inconvenience, a normal task. Letters from home were full of admiration for what the O'Connells had chosen to give up, and also pity for the poor Ugandans who had so little. Well, it wasn't fair. She had *chosen* to come, and it wasn't bad at all, not in comparison to the rat race that tore you up on the West

Act II

Coast. The Ugandans were the ones who should be admired; she was merely a privileged guest, an honored visitor.

At this point in her reverie, Esther walked through the door with the supplies from market; she ducked through the doorway with the basket of sweet potatoes still perched atop her head. Julie rinsed and dried her hands and went to help her unload, but she just couldn't help but hug the woman, offering wordless thanks for all the help Esther so cheerfully gave them.

INCURSION

Violence is a way of proving that one exists,
when one believes oneself to be insignificant.

—PAUL TOURNIER, *THE VIOLENCE WITHIN*

52. FURLOUGH

THE PLANE LEVELED OUT AT 35,000 feet. The second movie was playing
on the small monitor in the aisle above Stephen's head; he could hardly
see the screen but it didn't matter. He dangled between worlds, between
Africa, and America, and England. Ah, but there were more than two,
or twenty, or two hundred. There were worlds between people, even individuals in the same family.

How well did he know his own mother? He'd been too busy distancing himself from the culture that his father found so embarrassing.
Look what he might have missed! The fantastic spicy food, the mariachi
band some of Cipriana's church friends had rented for the reception
welcoming them home from the mission field. He was so glad they'd
bothered to spend a week there, with his mother, and even cornered her
to apologize for having taken her love so for granted. She'd just smiled
up at him and patted his cheek.

Once upon a time, Stephen thought, his mental current a distant tangent
from the night flight back to England, *missionaries used to travel across the wide*

sea in ships. They would have time, then, to be in between worlds. Time to leave one behind, time to know yourself again before being hurled into another world. Now—he glanced around the dim cabin, where passengers read or slept or watched a movie—*a credit-card phone can keep you in touch with a frenetic world 35,000 feet below. You never have to leave, just bring one world along into another.*

A businessman lit by the focused spot of overhead light pecked ideas into a tidy laptop, while a woman in front of him showed snapshots of her children to an uninterested neighbor. Stephen shivered: how many worlds were there on this very plane? Crashing worlds, with nobody bothering to take time to even think about how his actions or words impacted someone else. *God forgive us,* he prayed, staring out the tiny window to where a line of pink light showed on the eastern horizon.

———◆———

He sat on the sofa at the London guest house and opened the letter, recognizing Madeleine's elegant handwriting at once. She had sent it to him care of the mission office.

Dear Stephen,

I'm sorry we weren't able to see you Stateside. It just didn't work out. And even though we happen to be in England the same dates as you, Sir Thomas (Bryce's father) has got us on a busy schedule; he'll be introducing us to some of the gentility around the Lake District. Bryce is also booked to discuss some of his show ideas with some fellow musicians and I'm lined up to speak in several venues in Mayfair, where they hold a regular prayer breakfast for members of Parliament. It would have been nice to meet Sam.

My best to you and Julie.

Madeleine

Oh, Maddy, he thought, *couldn't you have spared a single "God bless you" or "We're praying for you"?* He knew that she opened all the mail. *Did you even let Bryce know our itinerary?* He felt slighted, and sighed. *Give it up, Steve. Your friendship with him is over.* Stephen let his head fall back against the sofa, while a tear slowly emerged from his eye.

Julie found him five minutes later, asleep. She took the letter and read it, smiled sadly at him, and extracted the page from his hand to throw it away. *Ouch,* she thought, leaning over to kiss his wet cheek.

Tk—tk-tk-tk Tk—tk-tk-tk...Stephen closed his eyes and imagined the train wheels' clacking as percussion notes, increasing in tempo as the engine sped forward. Church visitation was so different from work in the field, pretty much the same intensity but with a very different angle, talking about your work rather than *doing* it. Their photo album was showing the wear of being handled by many interested hands. Julie, to his great relief, seemed plenty happy to share the presentations, and she spoke quite capably at every other church, while he concentrated on keeping Sam in line with the seemly standards of proper British behavior.

Taking the train through London environs provided a welcome reprieve from talking with people. Julie and Sam formed a unit, staring out the rain-spotted window. She, pointing out landmarks ("That's Saint Paul's, isn't it *huge?*") while Sam *oohed* and *ahhed* at all the sights; he never seemed to tire of the passing parade of new things. He especially seemed to like going through the tunnels.

Stephen pulled out the newly published travel guide to Uganda, and a paragraph in the introduction caught his eye:

An estimated million Ugandans met a violent death between 1966 and 1986, some brutally tortured...

Political violence has been succeeded by the worst AIDS epidemic in the world. There are tens of thousands of orphans in the country, many of whom have seen or experienced suffering and brutality that is beyond the conception of most westerners...

Act II

After all they have been through, it is remarkable that Ugandans are still regarded by most travelers to be among the friendliest and most welcoming people in Africa.

He could hardly argue with that; nowhere else had he felt so comfortable just being himself. But somewhere beneath the surface, all the pain had to emerge, somehow…

PKhhhhHHhhhHHhhh. Another train sped by in the opposite direction, startling Sam and pulling Stephen out of his reverie. One week to go, then back to Uganda. He looked forward to returning to the slower pace, where nothing happened until It Happened, where people looked one another in the eye and grasped hands, genuinely happy to have survived another day.

53. RUTOKI ENVIRONS, LATE FEBRUARY

The O'Connells were back. Charity's feelings were muddled. She had missed them both more than she thought she would. To talk with them, Julie about life in general, about being a woman and what that meant, and Stephen about his ideas, about art…it was so enriching. And they seemed genuinely interested in what she had to say, both during and apart from the meetings. That, for some reason, brought tears to her eyes. Julie had given her a beautiful book by someone named Amy Carmichael, a single woman who'd spent decades in India rescuing abandoned babies. The language was so deep, so beautiful! She loved the poetry in it and read it every night.

She was walking home from Julie's, and Julie went with her. A sign of friendship, to provide an escort. How far one went showed how deep was the friendship, she'd taught her pupil in their early days of language learning. They wound their way through the forest path in between the brief episodes of pelting rain. The sun had dared show his head, and he mingled with the drops to mist the world in glory.

The Wrong Side of Eternity

Julie stopped, admiring a dark snake gliding across the path in front of them.

Charity pulled up short and touched her arm.

"It's harmless," Julie reminded her.

"I know. I'm not afraid of it."

"But you fear *something*."

"I fear...I do not know what." She changed into teaching mode. "Traditionally, it forebodes something."

"Only for those whose path it crosses, or for everybody?"

"This time, for everybody."

"Charity, tell me what you know."

"There will be trouble. I have been listening to the radio programmes from Rwanda. The Arusha peace agreement they signed while you were away, it will not last."

Julie considered, then pointed to the snake. "What if we kill it?"

Charity knew she was joking but answered, "It does not change the situation."

The air grew warmer of a sudden, and the two women let the snake slither away, and hurried on.

Charity turned on the radio and flinched at the mention of cockroaches and "clearing the bush." Tonight the Thousand Hills Radio hosts were using a new expression, warning their countrymen to "kill the snake before it bites." She shuddered. She knew the broadcasters were using code, referring to people, not insects or snakes—preparing an entire population to do the unthinkable. It happened over and over again, twenty years ago, and six years ago, and decades and centuries before that. In Asia, in Europe, in Africa. One group set up against another, no one meeting to compromise, only engendering violence to prove which group was the better. She'd read the news analyses: exacting revenge and controlling the exploding population were among the reasons listed by the experts. She heard the stories her aunt told, about the growing opposition to the moderate Hutu government, about grenades openly on sale at the market, stacked in little piles right next to the mangos and tomatoes.

The breaking out of genocide would not shock her like it would so many of the borderlanders. They hadn't been watching. They weren't listening carefully to the radio propaganda. And why had the church over the border delayed in using radio, the same media? They wrote pamphlets and articles and sent them to the newspapers. Too late, and besides, not enough people in the villages knew how to read. They were at the mercy of the broadcasted voice. *Stupid church.*

As the contentions rose, Charity would not be surprised at the cruelty around her. At the same time, she would wonder how she could possibly have been spared, why the disease that ate one's morals away had failed to catch hold of her as well. Was it just latent, like syphilis, coiling around her soul, biding its time? Would it strike, like a green mamba hidden in the grass, when some circumstance set off a chain of fateful events and stepped inadvertently on its tail?

Meetings with the bishop were going nowhere. They were all too busy looking at the past, at the Arusha Accords, to anticipate the present. She knew they would step patiently aside and deal only with the aftermath, waiting until *someone else* took action. No one could prevent this volcanic explosion now, but they *could* have, if they'd let the revival seep into their homes and hearts and not just made a lot of noise about it in the churches and in the streets. Maybe. She hadn't herself, and she knew it. Would it have been enough to stop it, if the revival had gone deeper? Could she, with her hidden feelings of self-disgust and guilt, be driven to do what her neighbours in Rwanda were being urged to do?

Peace, now a teenager, sat down next to her on the slatted wood frame with foam cushions that was their sofa, and snuggled into the crook of her arm. An orphan, both her parents dead from AIDS. Together, they two were a family. Outcasts, both. Charity gazed into the dim light of the paraffin lantern and leaned forward to switch off the radio. Usually she turned the dial over to Radio Muhavura to get another perspective, but it, too, would be full of the threat of outright war. *Enough war.* A quiet evening was in order. Not even praise music from the portable cassette player—it was running out of batteries anyway. But she could not shut out her thoughts. It would take hours to fall asleep that night.

She looked up at the woven mat that hung next to the door. JESUS IS THE ANSWER, it proclaimed in dark brown letters against a light brown background. *The answer to what?* she thought, and she closed her eyes to give all her attention to the chirping of the crickets outside, trying hard to shut out further speculation and fear.

54. CHURCH OFFICES, APRIL 1994

The reports were not good; the talk reached Rutoki before the radio news did. The president of Rwanda had been killed in a plane crash, with no witnesses. There had been no warning.

Charity sat typing in the small office next to the bishop's when shouts erupted at the door. She stood to investigate, and found her uncle leading his brother-in-law, Paul, into the meeting room, where a thermos of tea stood at the ready. He was disheveled and shaking, and she noticed that he had on only one shoe. She *knew*, before he began talking, and steeled herself to hear his news. But before she turned back to the shaded confines of the building, a small pickup hurtled past, packed with women in religious dress. They clutched at one another to keep from falling off as the driver took the curve. On their way to the Catholic offices to tell a similar story, no doubt.

"They will kill us all!" the man shouted. "You must hide Grace, Geoffrey, they will come across the border for her!" Charity pulled the lightweight blanket off the sofa, which had been put there to conceal some holes in the cushions, and threw it around him, while the diocesan administrator took hold of his shaking hands.

"Paul, calm down. They will not pass the border. They know the RPF will stop them."

"They had lists, Geoffrey, the *interahamwe,* and they started last night. This morning there were groups of men with *pangas* gathering in the streets, beginning to break into the houses. I had Francis with me, we were out behind the house. I just grabbed his hand and ran into the bush as quick as I could. On the way, I heard my wife scream...She has a Tutsi registration card."

"You did the best thing you could," Charity offered, worthlessly.

"We ran until he was practically collapsing. He is too big to carry. When we reached the road to the border, we saw the UN patrols heading inland and knew it had begun again. She has perished, I know...I should have gone inside to stop them!" He bent over and began rocking like one possessed.

Geoffrey caught Charity's eye. *Slaughter.* The wholesale slaughter of human beings, their relatives, their friends. It would not make any difference, even if you were Hutu, not if you had a thin nose or a tall build, not if you owned many cattle, not if you had spent time lately with friends who carried the other identity card, or voiced a moderate, tolerant point of view. Unless you chose to take up the mob mandate of murdering your own neighbours, you were already on the death list.

The match that was the president's death had lit a well-prepared bonfire, and it was already out of control. *They will pray,* thought Charity, *but it will make no difference.* Her memory tried to drag her into the past, but she would not let it; she would not be pulled down into that black hole again. If she did, she would be of no use to those who were sinking into it now. Geoffrey had propped Paul upright. With trembling hands, the Rwandan reached to take the cup she had poured. His voice shook violently.

"I held my son up to the UN troops, passing by on their patrol vehicles, Geoffrey, but they would not take him. They just drove past. A sedan car stopped, with a frightened family inside—rich people, it was a new Mercedes. They were on their way to the border, to Kabiizi. I begged them to take Francis, and they opened the boot. There was hardly room for him in there amid their suitcases, but they stuffed him alongside of them. I hope he did not suffocate on the journey, I hope he is safe...but the rest of my family..." He broke down, dropping the cup of chai just as the bishop appeared in the doorway.

The Wrong Side of Eternity

"Radio Muhavura is reporting what this man is telling us, that killing has begun in Rwanda." The border was only four miles away. "We shall close the offices."

"But, Bishop," protested Charity.

"No, the staff need to go to their homes. We will be more useful there than here. Other relatives might be coming this way."

Geoffrey did not know if this was at all likely, but held his peace. Bishop had family of his own over there. Many people in the borderlands did. They were lucky to be on this side of the border.

"I will alert Reverend Ann and the O'Connells. They will want to listen to the BBC. The mission may wish to evacuate them."

Charity knelt on the floor, wiping up the spilled tea, and realised that he too was in shock. *How could they not have seen this coming?* She stood as Geoffrey gathered up his brother-in-law to guide him out the door. The bishop had picked up the telephone and was trying in vain to reach the operator in town. He would not be searching out the *bazungu;* he would stay here, to use the phone. Was it her job to alert them? She should collect Peace at the secondary school, take her home, lock the door.

Let the missioners find out on their own, she decided. *We have enough to do.*

55. THE PROTESTANT HILL, KABIIZI

The town was choked with people fleeing the bloodbath in Rwanda. Every house on the hill was either readying space for guests or sending someone to the shops for supplies. There were rumours that they would close the border soon and accept refugees only in Goma and Rutoki. No one in Kabiizi knew how true it was; there had been tensions and back-and-forth emigrations for years.

It couldn't be that much worse, this time around.

Stan came home early from the secondary school to find Eva seated at their table with a crying pastor's wife. He caught some details of

Act II

her choking story, that mobs were running about Rwanda with *pangas*, hacking people to death. People targeted only because of the shape of their hands or the label on their identification cards had run into the churches, where they had always found refuge before. But this time the *interahamwe* had shown no respect, following them inside to shoot them all, or locking them in to burn the entire building down. There was no sanctuary, no mercy. Killing women, children, priests, pastors, doctors. There, in that country so full of Christian revival, they were running mad.

He'd been following the stories in the *New Vision* and the *Guardian*. With the UN peacekeeping force practically sidelined, the RPF had responded almost immediately, because no one else in the global community would. A mass exodus had begun of every civilian who had not been enlisted to join in the slaughter. The rich ones got out with bribes and had connections, but the poor sometimes fared better in the camps: they came with cooking pots and mats, while the wealthier came with nothing but their wallets. Their suffering was, by contrast, greater. *The French Revolution*, thought Stan, *in another dress.*

OCA had missioners over there: had they gotten out in time? Would the British Consul or the Red Cross be able to help them? The clinic at Ntabgoba must be overrun by now, if it were operating at all…would the staff there succumb to the madness, or would they hold together? And what about the O'Connells, so close to the border? Were they safe?

Not knowing what else to do and feeling nauseated, he went to the latrine and began both retching and praying his heart out.

56. INSIDE THE O'CONNELL HOME, 3:00 A.M.

Stephen awoke, sweating beneath the mosquito netting that draped their bed. The darkness outside the window was complete. So was the silence, although he listened for footfalls. He'd heard about the night

The Wrong Side of Eternity

dancers, and he wondered if they could be congregating in the small yard out back, but nothing seemed to be outside.

Something invisible sat atop the wardrobe, not so dense as the imp from Blake's painting but substantial nonetheless. Something black, shadowy. Julie lay beside him, unaware of any danger, breathing peacefully.

He stood and held his hand over her sleeping form. "Lord Jesus, protect her, protect us this night from all harm, fear, and darkness. Let your light fill this room." He half expected something tangible to happen. Nothing did. Stephen tiptoed up the hall and opened the door to Sam's room. The demon-thing had followed him there—or was there a second one?—it sat perched on the window ledge. Talons. Dry, piercing eyes. He prayed the same words, with the same negligible effect.

Without knowing why, he gathered up the boy into his arms and returned to his own bed. He would not leave either of them alone. Carefully he placed Sam under the mosquito net and covered them. He lit no lamp. He did not need to. Somehow he knew what to do. He began to pray in a whisper, using words of warfare: *Begone, evil thing. I plead the blood of Jesus over us. By the power of God I tell you, get out. We do not belong to you.* On and on he prayed, moving his lips in words that even he could not recognize.

Speaking in tongues? Never mind. To be doing something, anything at all, felt good. Something primal, perhaps: standing between a nameless terror and your family. Calling out to heaven for deliverance. He kept at it calmly, despite his heart pounding, and the thing squatting atop the wardrobe began to fade. He'd never actually seen it, but his spirit perceived it, clear as vision.

Stephen never could define what this ability in him was; he had tried to at a youth meeting once, when some shiver went through him and he fled the room to sit on the steps outside the kitchen door. He'd tried to tell the youth leader that something evil was there in the living room, he could feel it. The man had placed a humoring arm around his shoulders and said that he needn't fear, nothing bad would happen in a righteous home. He'd practically patted Stephen's hand, making light of it.

Act II

It had not been a light feeling, back then, but a heavy black one, dragging downward. He was glad he had snuck off, after that, to read those Pentecostal books on spiritual warfare. He was glad that he took the African stories seriously. *Because if you didn't*, he thought, *you'd think you were going crazy.* And maybe the enemy would win, if you did nothing. Maybe you would go crazy.

Maybe that was what was happening in Rwanda.

57. RUTOKI ENVIRONS, JUNE 1994

People were nervous, glancing over their shoulders, fidgeting during meetings. Radios broadcast news in every home: the *bazungu* in Rwanda had all been evacuated…The UN peacekeepers were being ordered to do nothing but observe…

The younger people looked on in shock, the older ones haunted by memories of Amin and Obote. How could it happen all over again?

It was Ann's turn to take a crack at the monster; the Ugandan pastors had preached to an audience whose ears were stopped up with too much trauma, too much fear. She had a challenge all right, trying to even capture their attention.

Instead of sitting at her writing desk, she walked miles into the hills, eavesdropping on the radio broadcasts as she passed house after house. She let the wind whip her brown hair and the scriptures seep into her senses. She could feel the sparks of fear and did not greet her neighbours with the usual smile. The estimates of people killed had climbed from an initial three hundred thousand up to thrice that amount. Almost a million people! Abandoned, deserted by such as herself: well-intentioned foreigners who thought they could make a difference. She could repent on their behalf.

No, it was too raw, too soon for that. A cheap apology.

During her walk she ran into Phoebe Kizito, whose lips were pursed with disappointment.

"Good morning, Ann," she said, an edge to her voice.

The Wrong Side of Eternity

Ann reached to take the MP's hand; they stood in the middle of the dirt road, which was empty except for cow dung splattered in foul puddles every fifteen metres or so.

"Phoebe. What news?"

Phoebe stared at her. "No news but the old news: Tragedy. Chaos. Hatred."

"Yiss, all of that."

"It is all so unnecessary, and yet..."

Ann waited, and seconds went by. Phoebe went on, continuing to hold Ann's hand. *A new and novel behaviour,* the priest thought.

"And yet, the statisticians are beginning to make guesses. One is the scarcity of land, overpopulation control. It is about survival: 'Food comes first, then morals.'"

"Local proverb?"

"No: Bertold Brecht. Another theory is that it is repression on a massive scale. Did you know, Reverend Ann, that some are blaming the colonial imposition of Western Christianity?"

"Yiss, I knew that. I'm not sure how that works, though. Perhaps you could enlighten me?" She sensed that Phoebe needed the analytical escape hatch, and listened.

"Instead of the ecstatic possession by the *imandwa* spirits, they've been put under so much pressure to 'be good,' to bear their poverty, to keep quiet despite the political circus and human-rights abuses. They've had to make do with the gloomy virtue of Christianity in place of the 'pagan' drama."

Gracious, thought Ann. *We're the scapegoat again.* She let Phoebe keep talking, because Phoebe needed to unload, and Ann needed to hear it.

"It must be a great emotional release for them," the MP went on, "to let it out, to participate in the cleansing of the land, as the radio broadcasts urged them to do—to welcome the Final Judgment. Well, the Last Judgement happens every day," she added bitterly, quoting Camus this time. "Women, children, all involved in killing their own neighbours, whom they'd known for years...They shot the prime minister, right along with her UN guards, in her own home!"

"You'd think they'd have some respect for the prime minister..."

"Why? She was a woman! Did you know, Ann, that the daily killing rate is five times greater than that of the Nazi concentration camps? That garbage trucks in Kigali have picked up sixty thousand bodies and that over forty thousand corpses have been hauled out of Lake Victoria—so far?"

"No, I didn't know," answered Ann, tears now spilling. She did not let go of Phoebe's hand to wipe them away.

"They say we are lucky here in Uganda, but it has crossed over to us. The incidence of rape is on the rise. The camps are sheltering thousands of *interahamwe* who are hiding among other Hutu refugees in order to escape the RPF. Many are here, in Rutoki, at the camp near the airstrip, Ann. Amnesty is reporting that genocidal thugs have taken over the leadership of the camps in Tanzania and Goma, to threaten and brainwash the hundreds of thousands that have gone there." She looked straight into Ann's eyes once more. "It will happen all over again."

"It may. I hope it does not." Reverend Ann thought it worth taking a risk. What was there to lose? "Phoebe, will you be attending any worship this Sunday?"

"Can you give me any reason why I should?"

"I'm working on a response to what you're telling me, and I'd like it to cook a little longer to make it palatable."

"I might be there. I'm on the way to the mosque now, to see if they have anything to say that makes any sense at all."

At this, Ann smiled despite the churning in her gut. Phoebe was a powerful woman—strong enough to want to hear what other people had to say, keen enough to sort it through. This was a very good thing.

Days later, she stared into the hungry faces of the small congregation of the English service. Teachers, office workers, project developers...the

The Wrong Side of Eternity

more educated of the lot, at least by Western estimates, because they spoke better English. James had posted notices near the doors that cautioned against shaking hands, due to the outbreak of cholera from the refugee camp beginning to spread into town. They obeyed, touching one another's elbows instead, craving the habitual physical greeting. How noble they were! How ignorant she was. How *dare* she stand before them to proclaim a word from God! *Little by little,* she coached herself, *if you take one bite at a time, you can eat an elephant...*

With a heavy sigh and a silent swallow, she began.

"My brothers and sisters, I need not repeat to you what has happened in our part of the world. You have all heard it over the radio—if not the truth, then someone's version of it. God knows what has been going on next door. I cannot at the present time convince you that God *cares*, for your faces are all full of question marks. Let us, for the sake of simplicity, assume that he does care. That all this evil destruction matters to him. And let us turn our hearts to the actions that all of us—and each of us—can take as God's obedient children."

With the one exception of the honourable Phoebe Kizito, they nodded, dully it seemed. Was there a breath of relief that she wasn't going to try to prove things they could not yet believe? Or offer some theoretical explanation for the madness of neighbours killing one another in a Christian country a mere four miles away?

Stephen leaned forward in his seat. Julie held Sam close to her side, while Ann caught the glint of a single tear slipping down her face. Boniface, in his robes, looked out the open casement of the window. And Charity Ntambara looked into Ann's face as if to dare her to go on.

"It was Bishop Festo who taught us that violence begets violence, that a bullet can kill but a bullet cannot heal. It was he who urged us to love our neighbours as ourselves...as Jesus taught."

Oh no, their faces said, *do not tell us that: we are not ready,* and she had expected that.

"Those words seem far away, even empty, now. Even farther away than the words written by another Christian more than fifteen hundred

Act II

years ago: 'Force is no attribute of God.' In the shock that has come upon us, I am going to be more simple, for I am not Bishop Festo and I have not lived through what he did."

Once again, they relaxed a little.

"What is happening is painful, sinful, evil. To kill another person is to crucify Jesus all over again, for is not every person made in the image of God? Imagine finding yourself guilty, after the noise has died down. Imagine the suffering you would bear, if you had a conscience and had taken part. Imagine how you would hurt, like Peter, like Judas, if you had done such things. How could you bear that kind of pain? It would be as hard as if you were a survivor. Perhaps worse." She paused briefly.

"Let us go back to what we understand of Jesus's sacrifice for us. We know that he bore our sins, yours, mine, and everyone's." A few nodded, very slightly. "We are told that he bore our griefs and sorrows, too, to bring us healing. We are not told *how*. Perhaps it is in the fact that he *shared* them with us, that he, too, suffered like we do, that the healing comes. For the sorrows, the griefs are not taken away: that is obvious. They are still there, repeating themselves in our lives over and over again. Perhaps as we come to realise—that is, actually *perceive*—that Jesus is alongside of us, understanding our pain, suffering with each one and offering his peace in a mysterious way in the middle of it all, perhaps it is there that we find healing.

"All that is too distant, mere words, ideas. We need something more real, simpler, more concrete. So I will suggest that we undertake, with all our hearts, to do three things.

"First, that we allow ourselves to hurt. That we allow ourselves to be the weak human creatures that we are. Festo said, 'Only bleeding hearts can heal bleeding wounds,' and I think this is a good place to start. We must not fault or condemn one another for feeling hurt, pain, and anguish at what is happening to our neighbours next door—we must not become angry with those who dare to express anger or doubt, with those who cry or break down in grief. That in itself will take plenty of willpower, plenty of discipline. To allow the pain to sink in, as it were, to allow ourselves to even acknowledge it, to not try to cover it up with nice words."

Several faces showed tears now, but no one wept aloud. At least three amid the seventeen, though, were stone hard, their jaws clenched in brittle defiance.

"Secondly," Pastor Ann went on, "we can go out of our way to be kind to one another. We can fight the hatred by showing the opposite spirit of courtesy and respect. We can soften our voices as we talk to one another. We can offer a cup of chai or stand a little longer on the road while our neighbour talks about his or her loss. If this sounds impossible, it is simple, because each of us can do what is right in front of us, each moment, and not try to stretch our faith or our love where it cannot stretch. God can and will help us in the here and now, in each waking moment, to achieve a victory far greater than merely proclaiming bible verses or empty comforts."

The defiant heads snapped up.

"And thirdly, we can become ready to forgive. I do not say 'we *can* forgive,' because to even be *ready* to do that may take much time. But we can prepare a place in our hearts for forgiveness, just like you prepare your fields before you plant seeds every year. You know that those who make the best preparations—removing stones, putting in fertiliser, grinding up and airing the ground—have a better harvest, even if their seeds are not the highest quality.

"That is what I, your sister, am asking of each of you. I do not tell you to do these things—that is for the Holy Spirit. I do not ask you to understand what is going on, because I do not think any of us can. There will be many who claim to, who will try to explain it all like a history professor looking back through time. But no: it is too soon, we are still in the midst of it. And so is our Lord Jesus, suffering still.

"So, to sum up: let us not try to understand or make sense of the madness of our world. Let us not try to explain it, but let us make every effort to *feel* it, not shielding our hearts from the kind of pain that led to Calvary. Let us *show* one another care, and courtesy, and kindness, despite every temptation to do otherwise, because that would only allow the evil to win. And let us begin to make a place in our hearts for forgiveness, the forgiveness that God's grace will give to us when we are ready, when the ground of our hearts is prepared for the holy seed that may, in time and with great patience, become the harvest that will stop people from harming one another, that will stop the destructive cycle forever. Amen."

It was the hardest thing she'd ever done, using words like that, flimsy words, in the face of such enormous evil. In another hour, she would preach half of it in the local dialect, allowing Geoffrey to translate the more difficult parts. God, she must be mad to tell them what to do. She sat down to give them all some moments to reflect, and consulted her watch. The second hand moved around its little face, and she could not budge from the high wooden chair.

Three full minutes of silence passed before she stood again to resume the service.

That afternoon, Pastor Ann slept like a stone.

58. TWO WEEKS LATER

Julie could tell something was wrong, the way Stephen came storming into the house. He was returning from the refugee camp, which now burst with ten thousand people. It took so much to get him *angry*.

"Stephen?" She dried her hands on a dishtowel and went down the hall in search of him. He sat on the edge of the foam mattress, holding his head in his hands. "Were you able—"

"No." His jaw was clenched. "The whole place is sealed off. They wouldn't let us past the gate." He looked up. "From the first minute we get here, the children want stuff. They hold out their hands and beg. Now, when they've got nothing...*nothing*..."

"Maybe they think you just want to look, and that feels humiliating."

The Wrong Side of Eternity

"No. There's more to it. Geoff was with me. It was a good-will gesture. The whole parish contributed."

"Would they have let just him in, if he'd gone alone?"

"He told me no. It was their policy: no refugees allowed to mix with the townspeople. But they do. They get out to trade stuff. There's UNHCR products all over the market. They bring it in to swap for beer, or blankets, or cigarettes."

Julie knew already. Esther had brought a gallon of USDA cooking oil home from the shop: a donation to the survivors of ethnic cleansing. She felt awkward even opening it; it wasn't meant for Americans to use. The senders felt sorry for the poor Africans and had sent *stuff* again. The poor refugees didn't want American cooking oil.

He was getting agitated, but he needed to keep talking. "Geoff says that these refugees may not even be Tutsi—they're probably *bahutu*, scared for their lives that the RPF wants them dead, wants revenge. And it doesn't even matter, this side of the border," he rattled on, the sociologist in him trying to contain the passion. "Different history, different politics. The borderlands used to be part of Rwanda, seventy years ago. Some official drew a new dotted line across a map, and now they don't even speak the same language."

As Julie stepped closer to comfort him, the smoke and the smell from the kitchen reached the bedroom. The meat for the day's lunch lay smoldering in a saucepan. Esther was out back, hanging up laundry. Julie hurried down the hall.

Precious beef, and she'd spoiled it. Stephen followed after her, yelling, "Don't you know how valuable that is? That would have cost Esther three days' wages!"

"You needed to talk. You're upset," she called back.

"Damn right I am!"

He caught her arm and jerked her hard as she entered the kitchen to whisk the pan off the propane stove, enfolded in smoke. She lost her footing and whirled against the wall on the way to the concrete floor, grasping for balance and looking up at him in pure disbelief. He bent

Act II

over her, his fist over his head, unable to stop the impulse. She cowered and flinched, and he pivoted just before fury drove his arm down—onto the edge of the hardwood table instead of into her face. The table shook with its impact. His eyes were fixed on her, afraid.

It took another eternal second before she realized that he failed to hit her. *On purpose.* And now he bent double, suffocating a scream.

Sam stood unblinking in the doorway, and Esther hurried in from outside.

"Da?" Sam asked.

"Daddy's hurt," explained Julie, on her feet in an instant. "He fell hard on his arm. We need to get him to the doctor."

Stephen heard her defense of him through the cloud of pain. Pain he deserved. He hadn't hit her, it was true, but he doubted he would ever be worthy of her. *Ever.*

———◆———

Almost a compound fracture but not quite. Two bones above the wrist. He deserved worse. He rationalized and felt reprieved, although his lower arm throbbed incessantly within the heavy plaster cast. He lay on his back, staring beyond the mosquito net at the ceiling. Moonlight drifted through the sheer curtains at the window; the night was calm. The night dancers would be out beneath the shadows of scraggly trees, casting their spells. Julie's arm wandered his way, and he almost threw it off. He swore he'd never hurt her. And he didn't—this time. But he knew that he was capable of it. That knowledge tormented him, worse than physical pain. She mumbled and raised her head.

"You've got to get your mind off it."

"I can't."

"Yes, you can." Her hand slid down his front and nestled in his groin. *She can't be serious,* he thought. But after a few seconds, her fingers began

243

The Wrong Side of Eternity

to move in slow, light circles, descending farther, until he was enveloped in her embrace. *God, Julie, how can you possibly love me?*

"Mmmm." He turned slightly toward her and let her.

"Close your eyes. Just feel." His thoughts intruded, once or twice: Was she doing this for her? For him? For the both of them? He drifted again, waves of pleasure drowning out the sharp ache. He lifted his left arm and gently touched her face. He opened his eyes to a vision that stayed with him a long, long time.

She bent over, astride him now, her nightgown draping her like a gossamer tapestry. Her hair hung down, a luminescent burning water-fall in the moonlight. She moved slowly, smiling softly through parted lips. His arm fell back to the mattress, overcome by gravity and passion. Surrounded by her in every sense, he could do nothing but receive— and he felt awkward.

"It's okay, Stephen, just stay with me."

"I'll stay with you," he murmured, as the beams of moonlight mixed with his drifting and they rode the curling wave together.

Not long after, spent and satiated, he murmured, "You should write a book. With your expertise."

"Mmm?"

"Call it *Sex as Pain Management*. I'm sure it would sell. You could make a mint."

"I don't want a mint," she answered. "I want you. Safe."

And off to sleep he drifted, no longer afraid.

59. A BORDERLAND VILLAGE, FIVE WEEKS LATER

They had been invited to a family wedding. Stephen's forearm itched inside the cast, but next week he had an appointment to have the plaster cut off. What a relief *that* would be! Julie helped him dress, as usual, the day before, to attend the giving-away ceremony. Sam, that sweet boy, had knelt down to tie his daddy's shoes. They walked past more than a dozen trucks parked on the main road of Rutoki, stranded so close to the Rwandan border because it had been closed again. All the aid supplies were held up for at least the third time, and there was nothing the Red Cross or the UN could do about it. And the clouds of diesel fumes had driven off all the nesting storks from the towering pine trees. If the environmentalists knew, they would be furious.

Rutoki had become a very crowded ghost town on the African frontier.

The final contract making took place the day before the church marriage service, in the compound of the bride's aunt, on an area of fairly thick grass. Drinking gourds sat placed at strategic intervals, ready to seal the occasion once the formal hand-shaking had been done.

The bishop's niece sat on a woven mat along with her bridesmaids, wearing traditional but formal dress. The group of women had their feet in front of them, their legs together. Julie figured they would have quite a backache when the ceremony was over, but then again, they were all so used to carrying heavy baskets on their heads and hoeing in the fields… They all looked down, making eye contact with no one. It was obviously a solemn occasion.

In front of them, on chairs, sat the groom and his parents, the district commissioner, and the bishop—in a suit and not his church robes. Along the side of the square sat other witnesses, also in chairs: Pastor Boniface and Joy; the community health outreach officer, James, and his wife; Geoffrey and Grace; Phoebe Kizito and her staff; the O'Connell family; and Ann Rourke. A small group of Twa stood outside the perimeter of the square, ready to sing and dance once the ceremony concluded. The Roman Catholic guests, it was explained to Stephen, would be joining them for the festivities after the wedding tomorrow. Neither the bride nor Reverend Ann looked very happy about what was to take place.

Phoebe quoted, to Ann, "'Brides' tears are not just water.' Local proverb."

And Charity leaned over on Ann's other side to add, "When you're a woman, life is a sacrifice."

The district commissioner stood to begin, and speeches were made as usual. The bride sat still, looking somber and downcast. A woman getting married had no reason to rejoice. She was leaving her family, and to honor her parents, she had to look as sad as possible. She was also taking on the burden of being a rural Ugandan housewife, which often meant working up to sixteen hours a day while her husband worked eight or nine. The conversation prior to the ceremony had been about how in love the bride and groom were.

She looks like she's headed to a funeral, thought Julie, who perceived something other than celebration in the proceedings. She noted with a sinking feeling that the bride was not allowed to speak once during the hour-long rite.

The older men haggled about the final bride price and shook hands with the groom, while his parents nodded and witnesses signed a contract. Two cows, less than the cattle herders in Kabiizi would ask. The men smiled. Anyway, commented Geoffrey to both the O'Connells, it was no longer about buying a woman; they had progressed way beyond that. The bride price was merely a symbolic assurance that the groom would take care of his wife, that he was willing to make sacrifices on her behalf.

Ann looked as if she was trying to maintain her composure. This traditional wedding ceremony would definitely trouble her.

Stephen, sitting near Phoebe, leaned over to check his comprehension, as the groom stood to tap the bride's bare shoulder with a forked stick and spoke some words.

"*What* did he say?" Stephen asked with disbelief.

"What did you hear?" Phoebe whispered.

"Something about speaking once, twice, and cutting."

"You heard right, Stephen." She translated the local proverb for him, sotto voce:

Act II

"'You must speak once while I speak twice. If you speak again, I will cut off your ears.'" She resumed her regal neutral look.

"Lovely, in't it?" whispered Ann from the other side of Julie.

"God help us," he answered.

The bishop asked everyone to stand and ended the ceremony with a final proverb, holding his arm extended with hand palm down as the bride stood to take the hand of her future husband. "A home built by God is not destroyed by wind." Then the bride's family escorted her away, followed by her bridesmaids, while the men congratulated one another with loud pats on the back.

"I hope the wedding tomorrow will be more cheerful," Julie said as the *bazungu* walked homeward together.

Don't count on it, thought Ann, but she smiled grimly instead of saying it aloud.

———◆———

Charity and Peace put the finishing touches on their outfits and headed toward the cathedral. Such a fine couple, such a lovely day. Although it was too bad the people of Rutoki had adopted from the British the white frilly bridal dress of the Victorian era and the excessive makeup and hairstyling. Charity preferred the elegant simplicity of the sheer and sparkling *kitenge*, fastened at the shoulder instead of around the waist, with a white or pale blouse and skirt underneath. The drums had been sounding for ten minutes now, and she found that she missed Stephen's solid rhythm under Boniface's choreographed drumming. He wouldn't be drumming for another month yet, after his injury.

She and Peace entered the large church and caught sight of Julie sitting with Sam about a third of the way back, with ample space beside them. She opted to join them; Julie looked delighted to have company.

"I like what you're wearing," she said. "I wish the bride would wear that style too, like she did yesterday. That lacy wedding gown looks pretty out of place to me. And she would be beautiful enough without all the makeup."

"It's in imitation of what they see in the Western magazines," explained Charity.

Peace sat next to Sam, but not too close. She would have to bear the taunts of the other children at school, calling them "salt and pepper," but she didn't mind: when Charity had gone over to give Mama-Sammy language lessons years before, Julie had allowed her to play with Sam's plastic Legos with him, and she felt privileged. Although she would never marry a *muzungu*. Salt and pepper made for nice flavouring of food, but it would never work with people, Peace decided.

Stephen joined them just as the choir lined up at the back, and they patiently sat through the Anglican wedding service together, marveling at how different it all was from the day before. Except that the bride did not look any happier.

A traditional reception meal was served beneath a blue canopy of UNHCR plastic tarps. Twenty-gallon drums full of bubbling sorghum brew stood ready for the servers to ladle the drink into the usual plastic cups. Everyone ate with their fingers, plastic bowls on their laps. The only big difference in the feast was the addition of a very sweet wedding cake, baked in the O'Connell's propane oven and covered with a heavy marzipan frosting. The children, who until that time had behaved with impeccable manners, began to giggle and slip away to run and play in the adjacent football pitch.

The *ntore* dancers appeared in their amazing costumes. It was the first time Julie felt like she had actually slipped between the pages of a *National Geographic* magazine. The seven men wore a *kitenge*-style kilt, with cowry shells draped diagonally across their bare chests, and headdresses made of long white fibers, which they shook in circular patterns. Strapped to their ankles were heavy round bells, the kind used as sleigh bells at Christmas concerts in America. As they stepped in a complicated time signature, the bells kept the rhythm, speeding up and slowing down according to the drama required. A few of the

Act II

men carried ornate spears and at intervals the leader would launch into a lofty speech, brandishing his weapon at the bridal couple at the head table.

"It's a kind of epic poetry," explained Ann to Stephen. "The Rwandan war dance. Except that the leader recites verses of praise instead of threatening the couple, telling about how brave the husband is, how lovely the wife…"

"It's beautiful," Stephen said, as the leader swayed his torso and rotated his sculpted shoulders, moving the spear as if it were a beautiful baton, directing the tempo as the chorus of bells resumed. He recognized the head dancer as the night watchman for the diocesan offices—such talent, right under their noses. He could do this professionally at a hotel in the capital and make a lot of money…What was his name? Gideon, that was it. His teeth flashed white in the late afternoon light, the almost iridescent light of an equatorial sky, while the volcanoes stood sentinel on the western horizon.

How brave of them, Stephen thought, to get married, to continue living life when thousands of refugees huddled under the tents and mud huts a mere mile away, perhaps among them some *interahamwe* hiding from RPF reprisal. He looked overhead, where bamboo poles supported the blue aid-agency tarps, probably traded in town for *waragi,* that strong drink that turned gentle farmers into madmen, or for thicker blankets. The nights were getting cold again.

In the thick of this darkening night in the borderlands, while the world just over the hills in front of them churned and tumbled in an ever-tightening circle of horror and brutal destruction, they dared to dance.

60. A Field Outside of Kigali, Rwanda

The field inspector from the UN contingent surveyed a marshy field strewn with maggot-infested bodies; only his nausea convinced him that he was not asleep and merely dreaming a scene from Dante's *Inferno.*

The Wrong Side of Eternity

Three corpses, mutilated not only by machete but by the ravaging of the dogs, lay at his feet. A male and two females, judging by the remains of their clothing. One's severed arms lay alongside of her. Their dead faces were frozen in horror and pain; they seemed to be looking up through the branches of the towering trees, begging the sky beyond them to bear witness. The women's legs were spread, their knees bent; instruments of torture lay on the ground between them.

And where were you? the field inspector asked the sky, *when they cried out for help? And who will ever believe us? Those who could have stopped all this, they will want to come and see it for themselves,* he realized, shuddering.

61. OCA CONFERENCE, AUGUST

"Ready?" asked Stephen at daybreak.

"Everything's packed—you can help me load it in," Julie said to Sam, who picked up a duffel and struggled to carry it out the door. They were going to the OCA conference, halfway to the capital. To save on the high cost of petrol—people in the States got it for so *cheap*—the O'Connells had agreed to meet the Thompsons and share the second half of the journey together. Ann, who was on a short holiday, would meet them there, and the borderland missioners would return from Kabiizi in their jeep after the long weekend.

The trip from Rutoki to Kabiizi took over four hours, thanks to the condition of the roads, so torn up from all the aid trucks climbing up through the bamboo forest and inching their way down between the cinder cones. The little jeep sputtered around the sandy turns, through the impenetrable forest, and along the shores of the lake, where half the track had been washed away with the seasonal rains. Sam loved to stare out the window at the cluster of baboons that gathered—just like tourists—watching the strange noisy beast roll by. A boulder broke through the sand-colored roadway like a breaching whale, and the little vehicle with its high axles gingerly climbed over it, tilting precariously. At one wide stretch in the road, the little family stopped to take a potty break.

250

Act II

Julie always voiced her envy at the guys, herself heading off into the bushes to squat out of sight of the passing lorries and buses.

"Oww!"

"You okay?" asked Stephen, zipping up his fly.

"No, dammit." She emerged, her face red. "I sat on something. A hairy caterpillar, or some nettles or something."

"We left early enough to have you seen at the clinic when we get to Kabiizi."

"Great. What a way to start a missionary conference," she answered, not protesting, which meant that she was really hurting. Julie seldom complained.

They drove into the mission compound forty minutes later. Sam wiggled out the door, glad to be free to run on the softness of manicured grass. The Thompsons met them with some enthusiasm, wanting to know all about life closer to the border, curious about the troubles in Rwanda. Stephen asked if he could fill Stan in while they took Sam on a short hike to the waterfall.

Eva looked puzzled.

"Julie needs a medical consultation," he explained. "Do you think the clinic staff would have time to take a look at her injury before we take off again?"

"Of course. I'll walk her over. They'll let us jump the queue. Stan can update me later." She turned to Julie. "How did you hurt yourself?"

"I sat on something."

At this point Stephen motioned to Sam, and they went with 'Uncle Stan'. They walked a third of a mile to where a cataract of water fell from a high shelf in the forest. Stan explained that, in the old days, unmarried women who were pregnant were tied hand and foot and pushed off the top. A deterrent to hanky-panky, he said.

"Well, in the borderlands they had a different approach."

"Really? What was that?"

The Wrong Side of Eternity

"They would take them into the forest and tie them to a tree and leave them for the animals."

"Oh, dear Lord. That's worse." A pause, while Sam went down to the river's edge to pitch stones into the water. "Stephen, you've not been here long, but you've seen much. The genocide and all."

"I've seen none of that—only the side effects. Cholera, refugees by the thousands pouring across the border. Lorries carrying aid tearing up our mountain roads."

"You weren't here in the days of Amin, but they were similar. A lot of innocent people dying for no reason. Violently." He sighed. "Do you, a relative newcomer, feel there's any real hope for these people?"

Stephen shook his head and laughed sadly. "I think about the way Americans have treated blacks and natives...and maybe why so many people left England during the days of Cromwell...Do you, a seasoned missionary, feel there's any real hope for *us*, Stan?"

"I have to believe that, or I wouldn't still be here."

"Then if there's hope for *us*, there's probably hope for *them*."

"You sat on a *what?*"

"I don't know, a hairy caterpillar or some nettles...I was squatting to pee. It's not as if I can *see* what's going on down there."

"You've contact dermatitis, at least," spoke the capable British nurse. "Very red. Does it itch?"

Julie laughed. "More than itch!"

"Probably the hairy caterpillar, then: *Lepidoptera noctuidae.*"

Show off, thought Julie, but smiled instead.

"I'll give you some cream, but let me see if I can get a better light on this and try to extract some of these fibers...and you can take some oral antihistamine, in case there's an allergy."

"Well, it's more exotic than a plain ol' yeast infection," said Julie, knowing that Eva could hear her from behind the screen. "Something for the prayer letter. We'll put it under the Local Humor section."

Eva Thompson was horrified. "You'd put *that* in a prayer letter??"

"Sure," she said, laughing. "One of the challenges of life in the bush. You're a real pal, Eva." Although she couldn't see the response, she felt Eva cringe.

So reminiscent of our first journey together, thought Julie, *when Sam was small enough to sit in my lap.* Over six years ago now. Eva trying to knit, Stan driving, Stephen and Sam looking out opposite windows. There was a man sitting along the edge of the road, not far from the quarry, pounding a pile of rocks into smaller stones with a hammer. He seemed to have developed some sort of rhythm.

"There's a soul-destroying job for you," remarked Eva.

"Oh, I don't know," said Stephen. "You could make up some pretty good poetry or maybe write songs while you do it." He winked at Julie, and they smiled as Eva fell back into quiet, her lips pressed together.

The Range Rover skidded to a halt. Up ahead, a lorry lay on its side, spewing petrol. The vehicle looked like a beast shot, its blood draining into the red dirt while it gasped its last breath. Chickens flapped across the road, and the driver and his helper were trying to remove the remaining crates before the tank burst into flames and fire devoured the lot.

"We'll be late," remarked Eva.

"So let's pitch in," said Stephen, opening the door and rolling up his sleeves. Stan stepped out to offer some translation, because the borderland dialect and the one spoken near Kabiizi were so different. He didn't run forward, as Stephen did, to grab the makeshift and splintered cages, but the men were grateful for any help they could get.

"Praise God," they shouted back and forth. Did they sound a little drunk?

"Praise him," answered Stan. "You could have been killed or hurt." He evaluated the space between the truck and the far edge of the road, mentally calculating the space required for their Range Rover to pass. While he was doing this, more men had emerged from the brush to help. In another hour, the crates had been loaded onto a pickup that appeared from nowhere, and the Thompsons were passing by on the other side.

The Wrong Side of Eternity

"You smell of petrol," said Eva as Stan got back into the driver's seat.

"I'll shower when we reach the resort—it's mostly on my shoes, dear."

Stephen, still standing outside, sniffed his clothes and made a face, brushing off some stray mites that had landed on his forearms when he handled the chickens. "Am I allowed in there?" he asked, embarrassed. He lifted his eyes toward Julie in the back seat.

"Just stomp well, Stephen, before you climb aboard," answered Stan. "You'll leave most of it behind. And we'll keep the windows down."

Sam had been carted off by the teenagers to play games, giving his parents a little respite. To distract her from the severe burning in her crotch, Julie sat watching a line of ants march in a diagonal line across the heavily varnished tabletop. The round tables, replete with huge thatched umbrellas, looked like hairy mushroom islands in the sculpted garden. The paths were straight but slippery; she wondered why they hadn't put down some gravel to prevent injuries. Prevention was a foreign concept here. She snickered.

"This is a *Bazungu* place."

"Yeah, Europe in an African frame," answered Stephen, taking in the bird feeder attracting little chirpers who flitted about like arcing jewels.

Just the spot to come if you were tired of too much Africa, Julie thought. *Hot water showers, table service...* She realized she needed it, but she didn't like it. Instead, she wondered through the next two whole days how the locals who worked there could stand all the civility.

After dinner and much small talk, she and Sam stood by the terrarium, watching a turtle clamber up a slanted rock only to fall and bash itself on a sharp stone at the bottom, and then climb up all over again. Pull, strain, move...somewhere else, perhaps more comfortable, closer to the sunlight? Finally it succeeded, lying on a warm stone,

Act II

exhausted—sporting a grim smile? She wondered if it knew that a bigger creature than itself was watching, admiring its tenacity. She patted Sam's shoulder, and he turned and followed her, ready enough from the day's adventures to go to bed.

In the lounge area, missioners were catching up on one another's news. The genocide, although it was officially considered over, was a hot topic; several of them related stories of neighbours and friends who'd lost just about everyone they knew. The round-table discussion scheduled for the next day was to address some of the ongoing grief issues. One of the nursing sisters was circulating among the families, making notes and checking that everyone's HIV kit—the bag of equipment and fluids they all carried when they traveled—was not out of date.

"So, Ann, how are you holding up with all that refugee traffic in town?" asked Eva. "Are the figures reported in the *New Vision*—over ten thousand people in a little town like Rutoki—exaggerated?."

"The authorities do their level bist to keep them cordoned off. Cholera's broken out at the camp in Zaire, since it's difficult to dig latrines into hard lava. The locals have kept it in check in Rutoki, despite the thousands of refugees we've got...tons of trucks parked along the main road, though, since they keep closing the border."

"Do you ever get nervous?"

"Not as much as some people," said Ann. "Do you?"

"What do you mean?"

"Well, you've had your share of excitement, with Mr. Kituma and his 'God's Guerilla Army' burning down schools, kidnapping young women to provide brides to the young soldiers in the bush..."

"They're nowhere near Kabiizi, they're farther north," answered Eva, dodging the question.

Julie listened with interest to some of the other missioners.

The Wrong Side of Eternity

"The British High Commission contacted us right away in April, just after it started."

"Really? We've heard nothing from the embassy," she replied, and was met only by blank stares. The O'Connells were the only Americans in the group. Julie knew the embassy would be concentrating on military and the more political matters. And that the separation between church and state often led them to ignore missionaries. "They were probably too busy with the evacuations," she offered. Or was it possible that despite her family registering twice, the embassy had no idea that the O'Connells were even there, practically sitting on the border? In any case, it was too awkward to begin explaining it to her colleagues, so she left it at that.

Half of the conference attendees had turned in for the night, but a small group gathered around the fireplace where Stephen and Stan sat, books in hand, to provide some cultured entertainment. *Bryce would have called this readers theater,* thought Stephen. Stan had selected a passage from John Milton, a conversation between two brothers. He of course took the role of the elder, and Stephen adapted his accent to a more English cadence, pretending he was reading Shakespeare:

Brother: Will Danger wink on Opportunity
    And let a single helpless maiden pass
    Uninjured in the wild surrounding waste?
    Of night or loneliness it wrecks me not;
    I fear the dread events that dog them both,
    Lest some ill-greeting touch
    Attempt the person of our unownèd sister.

Elder: My sister is not so defenceless left
    As you imagine; she has a hidden strength,
    Which you remember not.

Act II

Brother: What hidden strength,
                 Unless the strength of Heaven, if you mean that?

Elder: I mean that too, but yet a hidden strength,
                 Which, if Heaven gave it, may be termed her own.
                 'Tis Chastity, my brother, Chastity.
                 Yea, there where very desolation dwells,
                 By grots and caverns shagged with horrid shades,
                 She may pass on with unblenched majesty,
                 Be it not done in pride, or in presumption.
                 Some say no evil thing that walks by night,
                 In fog or fire, by lake or moorish fen,
                 Blue meagre hag, or stubborn unlaid ghost,
                 That breaks his magic chains at curfew time,
                 No goblin or swart faery of the mire,
                 Hath hurtful power o'er true virginity.

Out of the corner of his eye, Stephen could see Julie stepping silently into the corner of the room. He wondered how she might take this particular section. He nearly missed his next cue, thinking about how he might offer her comfort for the sting of memory that the poetry incited. Stan kept going, oblivious.

So dear to heaven is saintly Chastity
That, when a soul is found sincerely so,
A thousand liveried angels lackey her,
Driving far off each thing of sin and guilt,
And in clear dream and solemn vision
Tell her of things that no gross ear can hear;
Till oft converse with heavenly habitants
Begin to cast a beam on the outward shape,
The unpolluted temple of the mind,

The Wrong Side of Eternity

And turns it by degrees into the soul's essence,
Till all be made immortal.

I'm glad Charity's not here, thought Julie, sipping some white wine and ap-preciating her husband's fine talents.

"Do you have any idea why Stan chose that particular reading?" asked Julie later, as they lay together on a too-hard mattress under clean sheets.
"Not really," Stephen answered. "But I have a guess."
"Yeah?"
"We've got so many unmarried ladies in the mission, serving all the way from Burundi and Zimbabwe. I think he was trying to assure them of their safety apart from a male companion."
"You're putting me on."
"No. Stan's subtle that way. And old fashioned."
"Do you think it worked? I mean, his intention—if that's really what it was?"
He turned toward her. "Anytime we gents can encourage the gals, my dear, in any way, it would count for something."
You guys think so highly of yourselves! she thought, kissing him. *And a fat lot of good it did for the women in Rwanda.*

Julie overheard a conversation about national politics during breakfast the following morning. Speculation was tossed back and forth about how much the various home governments knew about the genocide, both now and before it had begun. Opinions like badminton shuttle-cocks flew sailing over her head, and the volley settled into what the missioners thought of the host countries.
"The president of Uganda has been lecturing his citizens on their re-sponsibility," Eva stated. "He keeps saying they should be able to sort out their own problems, since the colonialists have been gone for decades." She sounded quite proud of his insight.
Gone for decades? Julie thought. *So in what box do you put aid workers and missioners?*

258

Act II

"He's been saying that for years now, dear," reminded Stan, helping himself to a third cup of tea.

They were all late to lunch on Sunday; the discussions and healing-prayer time provided by the OCA leadership after the morning worship took much longer than planned. And just before they adjourned, Julie O'Connell stood up to make a contribution.

"This might seem out of place, but I don't think so. The night before last we were treated to some classic poetry—I want to read you something written by a neighbor of mine in the borderlands, because I think it fits with what we've been talking about." And without awaiting permission, she pulled out a yellow piece of lined paper and began to read.

"I with reluctance give myself away
    —I have so little left of aught that I may call my own—
So great a debt, so much there is to pay
I empty start, and find a hard, grey stone
Is all that's near to hand.

"The waves pound endless on the sunburnt coast
    Where shell and rock fall prey to tidal force and shifting sand
That pound and batter into lifeless dust
What once was sturdy, solid, faithful land
And the foundations move.

"A never-failing Treas'ry bright, a Rock
    Which anchors life to Life is what my soul so thirsty seeks.
If after Source alone I stealthy stalk
The grace eludes my grasp and, towering, peaks
The One who fills up all."

She sat down, and silence filled the meeting room. The visiting counselor closed with prayer, and they filed out to share a last meal together.

259

The Wrong Side of Eternity

A seasoned mission partner who'd had to flee Rwanda caught her up on the way to the dining room. "Where'd you get that from, a British aid worker?" she asked.

"Nope. One of the villagers."

"That was written by a *Ugandan?*"

"Yup," answered Julie.

Eva overheard the exchange and thought it highly unlikely, but she kept her peace. She was still reflecting on what Sam had shared during the children's ministry time, when they were telling stories of sickness and injury: all MKs had something to add.

"My da broke his arm on the table."

"How did he do that, Sam?"

"He got angry with Mum and almost hit her, but he missed." Some of the children giggled, but he turned to 'Aunt Eva' to say, "It's kinda like sin, huh?"

"What is?" She peered down at him.

"When you are bad and try to hurt somebody, your badness comes back and hurts you instead."

"That's right. And your daddy must have felt awful."

"He didn't let his badness hurt her." Sam smiled. "God is making my da good."

Poor fellow, to be so young a theologian and from such a dysfunctional family, thought Eva, wondering what she was going to say to the OCA leadership about it.

62. RUTOKI SECONDARY SCHOOL, WEDNESDAY

Stephen, newly back from the conference, came to see an early draft of their AIDS production. A nail hole pierced the iron sheeting above his head, letting an arrow shaft of sunlight in to make a bright mark on the cement floor. *That's my prayer life*, he thought. *So minimal, so inadequate.*

Act II

A makeshift stage had been set up in the main hall of the secondary school, complete with curtains draped over ropes running between brick pillars. Phoebe Kizito sat in the front row, and several teachers from the secondary school were in attendance, along with the Catholic priest, Sister Evastina, the Baptist pastor, a regional development officer, the imam from the small Rutoki mosque, and members of the Mothers Union.

Like he'd seen in the safe water show, Stephen expected a certain amount of coarse humor. But he was not prepared for the second act, in which a philandering man—who just happened to be an influential businessman in the play's fictitious village—was just tiptoeing out of the shamba of a young woman. A sign hung on her fence: PICK UP AFTER YOURSELF—OR ELSE. Her laughter poured out the open window of the prop house, a painted piece of thick cardboard supported with wood slats.

"You forgot something!" she called.

He hurried back to the window, still tiptoeing. "What?"

"This!" A withered condom, slick with vegetable oil, dropped to his feet, just before the prop shutters closed so that he would not be tempted to throw it back.

It was a scene right out of Chaucer.

Geoffrey laughed. "He is getting what he deserves," he explained to Stephen.

"But—"

"Shh—you should see what happens next. It is educational."

The man uttered some expletive in the borderland dialect, pulled a white handkerchief from his trousers pocket to wipe his face, and was just about to kick the slimy thing into the bushes when two primary school children came around the back of the house and stared at him, then at the condom, then back at him.

Being a community leader, he was now trapped into providing some sort of good example, so he reached down, picked it up in the handkerchief, and began to look around. The children pointed him toward another prop, an outline of a latrine. He made a face full of embarrassment

261

The Wrong Side of Eternity

and defeat, and, holding the handkerchief at arm's length, opened the door and went inside. A loud plop could be heard, made with a bucket of water offstage.

The test audience roared with laughter.

Stephen looked around. The only officials who did not seem amused were the Catholics, which was understandable. But, as Geoffrey explained once the show ended, they had allowed the content to remain as it was, because the amount of shame linked to both the naughty behavior of the man and the disgust he showed toward the used condom offered a message in keeping with their policies—just. The team had made other concessions, in the final scene, implying that abstinence was indeed the safest approach, and in the end, all parties agreed that the show could go on.

"Geoffrey, they could go on tour," said Stephen, once the set had been packed up. "It's so much better than the clinical diagrams they publish in the *New Vision*. They've managed to make believable all sorts of things: that no matter how important you are in the community, you could get caught, and that just because a woman allows you into her home, she might not respect you and doesn't want your problems. That she can actually stand up to you, that school children are smarter than we think, and that there's a best way to dispose of a used condom. And they actually put aside some trying differences to pull it off."

"Your encouragement and direction gave them the start they needed," answered Geoffrey.

Stephen wondered if that were true. And how in heaven's name was he going to write a report on the production's inevitable success to the project funders without explaining some of the inside jokes? *If I use big enough words, they'll never know,* he decided.

63. RUTOKI, MARKET DAY

Julie and Sam were on their way back from their weekly date, a walk to town to buy a bottle of soda and watch the villagers. Men getting their

Act II

hair cut under the tall canopy of trees, women sporting baskets heavy with sorghum balanced on their heads, bicyclists heavy-laden with burlap bags full of charcoal. It was better than a parade in America.

From the mud-brick house next to the post office, a woman stepped out of her front door and pointed at them. She spoke in Swahili, motioning Julie to step inside. Julie only caught the words 'hello' and 'malaria'—the rest was Greek to her.

"Parlez-vous français?" she asked the woman.

"Un petit peu."

The rest of their conversation would hover between the two languages—not the native tongue of either of them, but it would have to do. Julie and Sam were led into a bedroom, where an unconscious man lay on a bed beneath an IV bag and tubing. The woman pointed at him and then made gestures of prayer, folding her hands, crossing herself.

Stephen had suffered the usual kind, and she had nursed him while his fever spiked and retreated over days, leaving the bed linens soaked. *Cerebral malaria, that's rough,* she thought. When it went into the brain, the prognosis was always poor. She swallowed.

Julie asked in French, "Do you want me to pray for him?"

The woman nodded vigorously in reply.

"Okay then." She took Sam's hand and the woman's in her own. Keeping her eyes open, she prayed, "Dear loving God, you know what it is to suffer. You raise people from the dead, you cure fevers, you release the tormented from fear... Help this man. Heal him, restore him to his family, in Jesus' name. Parce que Tu les aimes. Amen."

"Amen," echoed Sam and the woman.

Nothing happened. The woman smiled and led them back to the meager porch, uttering thanks. They took their leave, Sam smiling at his mother with confidence.

A week later, the woman came by the guest house, chattering loudly. Her son had fully recovered: it was a miracle.

Hmm. "I'm happy he's better," was all Julie could say in reply.

RIFT

Who can attain to anything great if
he does not feel in himself
the force and will to inflict great pain? The
ability to suffer is a small matter...
But not to perish from internal distress and doubt
when one inflicts great suffering and hears the cry
of it—that is great, that belongs to greatness.

—NIETZSCHE IN *THE JOYFUL WISDOM*

64. INSIDE A BUS HEADING SOUTH

THE PACKET OF GROUNDNUTS WAS stale. Innocent Habimana finished them off and threw the wrapper out the window. He then pulled out the large Bible from his rucksack and started to read. The fellow in the seat next to him noticed.

"I used to be an awakened one," he said. Someone touched by the Revival.

"When did you stop being one, and how?" asked Innocent, putting his finger in the passage from Judges to keep his place.

"When my mother became sick and all the prayers didn't help. I went to the witchdoctor, and his treatments worked. So I stopped going to all the meetings. I'm happier now."

"Are you truly?" asked Innocent. "Knowing that you have dishonoured the king of heaven?"

Act II

"Dishonoured?" His seat mate laughed. "No, hardly that, my friend. I just took a shortcut. The Christian way was too hard: getting up at all those early hours, trying to figure out what the Bible meant…I still believe, in my own kind of way."

"A mixture of beliefs, some traditional, some Christian?"

"Yeah, like that. My business is doing good, my wife is fruitful, and my children have shoes on their feet. And I have time to enjoy it." He smiled and pulled out some headphones and a portable CD player, closing the door to evangelization.

Innocent sighed. If people didn't know they were in need, they would not listen. Compromise was all around him. Thank God the *bazungu* missionaries up north had spent hours with him after his rescue, once he left the bush. He became a house boy for one of them when he got saved, and by now he knew the Bible as well as many so-called pastors. He'd heard the shared concerns of his brethren as they told about other groups who were coming to distort the true meaning of the gospel, mostly along the southern corridor between Rwanda and the capital. He was traveling to see his sister in Mukezi, who had come into their blasphemous clutches and had decided to get her degree at the university. Maybe he could set her straight. He would tell her his testimony, about how God had delivered him from the grips of Kituma's forces and into holier warfare. The hymn started to sing itself inside his head:

We want to fight, we want to fight,
Look, Jesus stands to give us the victory.
Fighters, do not fear this battle;
Fighters, do not be discouraged.

It played over and over again inside him, to counter the up-tempo Zairian radio music piped through the bus, as he considered his next step.

After visiting his sister, he would head to the borderlands, where, the rumours said, certain ruinous things were going on. And there he would do as the Lord bid him.

265

65. O'CONNELL HOME, 7:30 A.M. TUESDAY

"You seem tired, Emmanuel," Julie observed.

The young man stood just outside the door, yawning. "I did not sleep last night."

"Why's that?" Julie had never mastered the art of subtle conversation, but no one faulted her for it. The Ugandans loved her direct simplicity, and she knew it. It seemed to work well enough, so she'd decided early on to not fix it. He looked a little sheepish.

"We were up all night, praying." She tilted her head and let him continue. "A village family wanted to destroy their shrines." She nodded: ancestral spirit worship lingered in the most Christian corner of the diocese. "So a group of us went over to help."

"You knocked down their shrines for them?" she guessed, and he nodded. She was curious at first, then grew more alarmed. Stephen and she had been talking a lot lately. "Why didn't they knock them down themselves?"

"Because they were afraid."

"And you weren't."

"No."

She deduced the rest. They hadn't asked the pastor or Geoffrey or the bishop to come over. Those who wielded church authority. The youth had gone themselves. *They are brave. Maybe ignorant, naive—but certainly brave.* Julie smiled and took his hand, pulling him inside for a cup of strong tea. She knew he had to go to work, teaching at the primary school, and may not have had any breakfast. She would offer him some bread and jam, a banana...

"What do you expect will happen to this family in the long run?" she asked.

"I don't know. They agreed to come to worship more." He beamed.

"I hope they do." *Or something worse might happen to them,* some bible passage whispered. Worse demons might replace those who'd been booted out. She thought of the genocide, the more recent bombings at the American embassies, and shuddered.

And what have you replaced your demons with? asked her conscience.

Motherhood, she inwardly answered, satisfied. Her period was over two weeks late, and she had yet to tell Stephen. She smiled, pushing darker thoughts away, and busied herself with Emmanuel's poor breakfast.

Esther sat Sam down on the countertop so she could better reach his foot. Julie handed her a safety pin, just sterilized from the propane flame of the stove, and watched as the house helper patiently dug out a sack of *jiga* flea eggs from Sam's third toe. Either her technique was gentle or Sam was used to it, because he didn't even whimper. Julie had tried to do it once or twice, managing to break the sack and smear flea eggs all over the counter. This was *art*, she decided, thankful for such a house helper.

Ann came by to thank them for the new foam mattress she found at her house. The O'Connells had bought it for her during a shopping trip in Kabiizi and had hauled it over the mountains tied to their jeep, as a surprise birthday present for her.

"So, Sam, what kinds of exciting things did you find in the big town shops?"

Ann always talked to Sam as if he were a friend. The boy hopped off the countertop and went to the pantry to look on the high shelf. He found what he wanted and asked his mother to reach it down for him, then he ran outside.

Julie shook her head and smiled: what child could get so excited about a box of Cheerios? *So nice,* she thought, *to have an adult who's not a parent to befriend my boy.*

"Look, Ann! We got these!" she overheard him say.

"Oh, those are fintesstic!" Ann looked around, as if they were discussing hidden treasure. "Would your mum allow us to have a bit?"

"Yes, she got them down for me, although I'm almost tall enough myself." He put his hand inside the box and took out a handful. "We can share these. I told mum that I would make them last a long time."

"Very generous of you, Sam, my man." They savored the round cereal bits, sucking on them like bits of hard candy, and looked over the

The Wrong Side of Eternity

bamboo fence where they could see a boy herding some long-horned cattle along the road. "Save three or four."

"Why?" he asked.

"So we can plant them."

"Plant them?"

"Yiss—if you plant them, they will grow up into a doughnut tree."

"Really?"

"What do you think?"

He looked *very* skeptical. "I think I want to try and then wait and see."

"You are a clever boy."

Julie opened her arms to the both of them and invited Ann to stay for tea.

66. THE HOME OF CHARITY NTAMBARA, LATER THAT DAY

Peace had taken Sam to climb up the ridge where they could see all three mountain lakes, so Julie took advantage of the opportunity for a private visit.

"Why would you bring me flowers?" asked Charity, greeting her at the door.

"I just felt like it," answered Julie. "And I'm proud of myself for growing them! I usually kill any kind of plant in the garden besides grass."

"You're in time for chai," said Charity, who'd just gotten home from the office and had yet to begin preparing the evening meal. She headed to the kitchen to pour the steaming drink from an aluminum saucepan into two enamel mugs.

"I wanted to talk with you about something," said Julie, latching the door behind her. She laid the bright posies on the table.

What have I done wrong? thought Charity, growing anxious. *She's come to point something out...*

Julie washed and dried her hands in the simple kitchen and accept-ed the hot cup. The afternoons were cool, and the warmth felt nice against her palms.

"I took the liberty to read your poem to some of our missioners."

"Why?" she asked in alarm.

"Because it's that good. All the reading you've done, it shows, Charity. But more than that, you've taken some of your own life, your own thoughts, and turned them into something really beautiful."

"But I didn't even get past my A-levels."

"So? You have so much to offer, my friend."

At this, Charity changed the subject and shared news that Aunt Grace's brother Paul had gone back to Rwanda to try to find out what happened to his wife and daughters. She hoped that the news would not destroy him.

Small talk gave way to concern.

"Julie, there was a letter on the bishop's desk. I am hoping that he spoke to you about it."

"Oh?"

Charity looked around the kitchen and lowered her voice. "Some people are making *bazungu* their targets...probably some of the *intera-hamwe* in Zaire, it is not known for certain." She looked up at Julie with concern. "They are offering money."

"Really? A bounty?"

"On Westerners, especially Americans. You remember the tourists who went missing in the gorilla park a month ago? And the bombings in Kenya and the capital?"

"Yes, of course—it was all over the papers."

"That is why. When a *muzungu* is involved, the media wake up."

Of a sudden, tears sprang up in Julie's eyes. Tears of anger. "And so many injured at the embassies were *Africans*, Charity! And during the genocide, the victims were *just* Tutsi, *just* Rwandans. Oh, God! Charity, they have lived through so much to be counted so worthless. It is not *right*."

Has she no concern for herself? thought Charity. "Julie, I wanted you to know, so that you, and Stephen and Ann too, can be careful. Do not ride in open taxis. Do not talk about being from America." *We all know anyway, you can't hide it.*

"Maybe I'll have Stephen teach me how to speak in an Irish accent," Julie answered, lightly. She put her cup down and reached for Charity's hand. "I'm hearing you, Charity, and we'll take precautions. Thank you for letting me know."

Half an hour later, Julie steered the conversation to another topic.

"Charity, the bishop keeps trying to set you up with one of his deacons."

"You are a bright woman, Julie, to notice. They can't be priested, in his diocese, unless they are married."

"How do you feel about it?"

"What do you mean, how do I feel?"

Julie was silent, knowing that Charity understood the question. *Was a woman allowed to feel?*

"Having Peace in my home is not just a protection for her, or a favour to her parents, God rest their souls. Having her gives me a little bit of regard. People who avoid marriage, Julie, they are despised, they have no respect. That is why the bishop requires all his priests to be married. In our culture, if you do not have a child, you are not a real woman."

"But Reverend Ann—"

"Reverend Ann is a *muzungu*, like you. She is allowed to be an exception."

"You would still be considered a *girl*, if it were not for Peace?"

"Yes. That is what some of them call me. Girl, not woman."

You're kidding, thought Julie, *you're the same age as I am.* But she could see that it was the truth. "Were you never attracted to a man?" she asked, sincere.

"No. No. Not after…"

"Charity, did something terrible happen to you? Something in the past. Did it involve men?" Charity hung her head and her tears fell

Act II

silently to the floor. Julie had never seen a Ugandan cry before, except at funerals, where there was often loud mourning. This was different; this was like a watercourse had emerged from an underground spring, silently. She pulled some toilet tissue from a pocket and handed it to her.

"You did not choose it."

Charity shook her head violently. "I was seventeen years old."

"You cannot punish yourself for something you could not help."

No response; Charity just stood there, head bowed, in silence. A minute ticked by, measured by the battery-powered clock on the wall.

"No one here wants a used woman, Julie."

"I do. I want you as my friend." This was not going as she had hoped. *Time to take a risk.* "Something terrible happened to me, too, Charity, but I *chose* it."

"What terrible thing did you choose?" sniffed Charity, softly.

Julie swallowed. "I was with a man, long ago. I was not married, and he did not wish to claim responsibility. So I did, Charity. I chose to end a pregnancy." Julie knew by now that abortion was as bad as practicing infanticide, here. Worse.

"You?"

"Yes, me."

Unexpectedly, Charity reached for Julie's hand. "I am so sorry."

"I am sorry too. I have to forgive myself over and over again."

"But you are so happy."

"Not always. And I can only be happy when I remember that I am forgiven. If I forgot that, Charity, I would not be here today." *I would probably have killed myself,* she didn't add aloud. "Except for my family," she confided, placing her hand discreetly on her lower tummy.

"Then let me remind you," offered Charity, totally missing the nonverbal message. She looked up, her cheeks still wet. She had not used the tissue at all. She looked Julie full in the face. "You are forgiven. God cannot help loving you: it is his nature."

"Oh, Charity, coming from another woman, one as dear to me as you are…" Julie stood to enter her friend's embrace, soaking up the strong

271

The Wrong Side of Eternity

comfort, hugging back. "Thank you. Thank you for speaking those words...I will remember your voice saying them for a long time. They will *keep* me, I'm sure. But Charity," continued Julie, gently, "do not be so proud as to think you are beyond God's love yourself. Please."

Charity smiled sadly, shook her head, and pulled Julie toward her once again. *We are the same,* she thought. *She is my sister. She understands. Oh, God.*

67. THE BORDERLANDS, A HILLSIDE

People appeared from nowhere. Julie had not seen so many outside of a market day, when up to four thousand people could materialize on the streets of Rutoki. Was life in the borderlands so boring that an open-air worship would attract this much attention? Apparently so, because they stood twenty thick, surrounding the little mound that Boniface had chosen as Reverend Ann's speaking platform.

Or perhaps it was the fact that the preacher was a woman, a *muzungu*. How common would that be in this backwater of Africa? As one of the honored guests, Julie was given a wooden chair, and she sat with Sam in the front row. She had tried to decline this on other occasions, but the church leaders insisted. She sighed and took the position of honor reluctantly. Someone standing behind her began to play with her hair, even though it was braided down her back this time. They always did. It had happened since childhood...she was quite used to it. In another setting, she would have turned around to grin at the girl twirling her locks and maybe even reach up to play with the tightly curled hair on *her* head. But the atmosphere was somber today, so she tried to look dignified She squinted toward the stage, where the driver was setting up a makeshift microphone and speaker, powered by the Land Rover's spare battery.

Ann wore her clerical collar under a cable-knit sweater and a silk-screened *kitenge*, an odd but beautiful blend. She took off her battered canvas hat—probably, surmised Julie, to let the crowd see her face better. Before she stepped onto the little knoll, she crossed herself, like a baseball player just stepping up to the plate. "Go for it, Ann: hit a homer," mumbled Julie, while the crowd sang the last verse of a local hymn:

I praise the cross;
I praise the holy way;
but more than that, much more,
I praise the Lord Jesus.

Ann's dialect was nearly flawless, but every once in a while she would let Boniface translate a phrase or two. Sometimes he wouldn't quite catch her meaning, and she would correct him, which always brought laughs from the audience and a blush from the pastor.

"Today I want to talk about scars," she began. "The marks that set us apart from other people, the marks we get as we live this life: scars from knife cuts, from accidentally stumbling over a stool in the dark house; scars from a dog bite or from climbing over a barbed-wire fence..."

Julie looked around. Each example landed on an individual in the crowd. There were real stories behind these phrases. Ann carefully avoided locking eyes with any specific person, but let her eyes roam freely across the crowd.

"Each and every scar has a story, and some of the stories we tell with great drama and gusto. Some are embarrassing, so others tell them while we hang our heads. Some we do not tell at all. Some come from deep pain and cast the looks of other people aside..."

Ah, thought Julie, *the deep cuts from the machetes, or the missing ear. From Amin's time. Or more recently.*

Ann continued. "Each scar has an experience behind it, each and every one. But there are other scars we carry, not in our bodies but in our souls, in our memories. Scars of hurt, where someone has called us a bad name. Scars of humiliation, where someone we trusted passed the point of love to abuse or to take advantage of us."

Julie felt a sudden stiffening at her left and caught Charity out of the corner of her eye. *She's on target. Way to go, Ann,* she thought, while the

The Wrong Side of Eternity

emotion of exposure caught up with her as well. Ann had stepped off the mound and approached the crowd, softening her voice and extending her hand.

"Scars of anger, where someone has done us wrong and then turned the finger of blame upon us...Scars of sorrow, where we have lost a child, a husband, a mother...These are the scars we don't talk about, the scars we keep hidden. But they are real, and they affect how we treat other people, how we treat ourselves. They are just as real as the scars in our bodies we tell all the stories about.

"God bears scars, too. Not only the physical scars from his time on earth, when he came to us in the person of Jesus. But also the scars borne of the pain of loving us, of seeing his people turn away again, and again, and again, in spite of his calling and wooing and loving. The scars of rejection." She turned to Boniface, who restated the last two sentences for clarity or good measure or both.

Innocent had heard of such things, these usurpers of God-given authority. He had never seen one until now. She was preaching! How *could* she, when the very scriptures she quoted forbade it? It was blasphemy; she must be silenced. How?

"The big difference between the scars we have and God's scars," Ann went on, "are that his have the power to heal. They do not form calluses that drive others away, like ours do. The ancient writers used to talk about hiding themselves in the wounds of Christ...of slipping into the scars of God just like doubting Thomas put his hand into the open wound in Jesus's side, after Jesus had been raised from the dead. They remembered the verses about Moses hiding in the cleft of the rock while God passed by him, proclaiming himself as 'rich in compassion, gracious and forgiving, slow to anger, merciful and kind.' They linked that to the image of hiding inside of Jesus's scars, seeking and receiving protection from the enemy, the evil one."

Act II

Sam started fidgeting, so Julie nodded at him, and he wandered off to play football with some children on the periphery of the crowd. She kept her eye on him for a few minutes and so lost the thread of the presentation. She glanced sideways, carefully, and noted that the crowd was riveted on the speaker. Ann had touched a nerve: she was brilliant. Some guy standing near the back did not look happy, and Julie wondered what scar he was trying to conceal. But most of them were nodding, or had tilted their heads, fascinated and engaged. Ann would give an invitation soon, and people would come up to Pastor Boniface for prayer. Her language fluency had not yet reached that conversational level. *But it's getting close*, thought Julie.

Innocent clenched his teeth. He was so tempted to cry out, "How can you stand there and listen to her? She is a Jezebel, she will lead you away from the Righteous One!" but now was not the time, and here was not the place. He had his orders. Just speaking out would not stop her—she who was supported by so many local church leaders! Something would have to be done, something that showed her true weakness.

He would meet her alone and challenge her authority. She had been consecrated, ordained by somebody: it would have to be undone. He would have to act under cover of darkness, letting the ends justify the means. In such a way as brought discredit and shame to the Native Anglican Church, who dared to support her. Did not Ehud use a sword to kill the usurping king of Moab? Did not Samuel hew Agag in pieces before the Lord? Other prophets had acted, and so would he. He would come prepared, and he would not be made unclean by her. She would need to be humiliated, shamed. He knew how to do that; he had seen so many women humbled by the soldiers. But he himself would have to remain pure. A punishing husband could use a stick, the handle of a wooden spoon. He need not defile himself.

His body unstiffened, and his face relaxed. He even began to smile a little as Ann began her altar call, and people began stepping forward

The Wrong Side of Eternity

for prayer. He crossed his arms and watched as another pastor nodded to the drummer to begin another song.

He would use a knife.

68. Church Offices, Friday Afternoon

Joseph and Sarah, illustrious visitors from the Outreach to Central Africa, sat at the bishop's conference table, sipping from ceramic cups. They exchanged glances and each got out a lined notepad. Tensions could be high, but today they were not: the Christians of Rutoki liked the OCA. They made fewer demands compared to other mission agencies.

"I like her," Joseph confided to his colleague. He was referring to the woman who had met them and poured water over their hands into a plastic basin before serving them chai. "She takes care."

"She's sad, Joseph," remarked Sarah. "Grieving. Over something."

At that moment the bishop entered with his administrator Geoffrey in tow. Charity followed them and sat at the other end of the table, prepared to take minutes. Everyone shook everyone else's hand; Charity looked reserved.

The four discussed the projects administered by the diocese and funded by OCA; the bishop presented his five-year plan, complete with budget information, project descriptions, and lists of needs. Goat husbandry, clinic outreach, literacy classes held at the cathedral. Joseph seemed impressed.

"It's very organised, Bishop." He smiled.

"Thank you. I have capable helpers."

Sarah noted that the bishop glanced briefly at the woman taking notes—the one who'd served them earlier and now kept her head down—then looked toward Geoffrey. *He appreciates both of them,* she guessed, pleased.

Geoffrey spoke up. "The missioners have given us so much," he began. "Our project funding has tripled, with Stephen helping to write the project proposals. He is a good listener, able to translate what we want into language that the funders like. His wife has been helping twice a week at the local hospital as a volunteer; Dr. Nsekanabo tells us that when she walks through the door with her physiotherapy jacket on, everyone smiles. She has been working with him to improve their facility."

Sarah answered, "And I thought she was just homeschooling their son."

"Oh, no. She is very active in the community."

Why wouldn't she tell us all this? thought Sarah, who hadn't had time to read the O'Connells' prayer letters. She hoped that Joseph had.

"And Pastor Ann is nearly fluent now in the borderland dialect."

"She visited Rwanda recently, didn't she?"

"Yes, along with Mrs. O'Connell, who speaks some French, and myself," answered Geoffrey. "Julie asked to go, to also act as our driver since she is used to driving on that side of the road, and to see how the people there had gotten along. So many of us have—had—relatives there."

"I see." *The things you learn on a field visit!* thought Joseph. "I'm glad to hear that they are of help to you."

Charity sighed deeply, put her pen down, and raised her head. Everyone turned to look at her. Without asking leave she rose to speak.

"You people are all leaders," she began, "and all of you deserve respect. You take time to listen to the people, you come and observe and report. But I will offer you some thoughts—if I may." She looked to the bishop, whose wide eyes had calmed a bit since the start of her interruption. He nodded and sat back, folding his hands across his stomach, his large pectoral cross glinting from the rare sunlight streaming through the window. Charity now addressed the visitors.

"You are kind, and you send kind people. You visit in our homes, and you walk miles to the distant villages. You plan and you organise and your help is most appreciated. You set great store by numbers... But you overlook your most valuable assets: the people themselves. Each has a story, each has a gift—I mean one to give, not just what they have received from you. You have helped them, and they are grateful. Now, they ask that you let them help *you*."

She paused. She was making this up as she went along, wanting to say so much, afraid it would not come out right. It had been building for some time. Were it not for her friendship with Julie O'Connell, she would never have the nerve to speak up like this. She maintained her composure.

"Some of us have suffered greatly." She looked at her uncle Geoffrey, whose eyes brimmed with tears at her courage. "Some of us have stood by and allowed great suffering to happen." She intentionally looked at no one person. "Some of us are broken, some have been silenced altogether by their sufferings: of what consequence is one person's pain when there is so much? I read about the UN plans to send trained counselors, about the Rwandan archbishop's desire to set up a truth and reconciliation committee like the one his grace Bishop Tutu set up in South Africa. I hear about many plans. Plans and projects take time, my brothers, my sister. But there is one thing—no, two things—that work better than plans and projects."

She had gotten their attention now. All four of them had been wracking their brains, trying to streamline the resources, to make them go further, to economise. Planning and efficiency, everyone knew, saved money.

"They are forgiveness and friendship. That is all. If every Christian were to practice those two things, practice them until they became a habit, then we could have hope for growth, for improvement. For relief from our suffering." She sat down again, with elegance, but she was not finished.

"You have sent to us a precious gift: people who really care about us. People who not only work alongside us, but who are willing to even be friends with us. People who come into our homes not as visitors, but as coworkers, to fellowship, to share. We do not feel our poverty when they are with us. They treat us as if we mattered. *We*, not just the projects or the funding. It is in their friendship, their willingness to share with and

Act II

accept our own suffering, that we find hope. I do not know if anything more is needed. It is like the story of Mary and Martha: the gift of listening is more cherished than all the busy actions." She was overstepping her boundary now, and she felt the limit line. So she took a deep breath and finished. "If you wish more details, I can give them to you. My own story. But that is a more private matter, and I should not take up any more of your time. I thank you for allowing me to speak."

She looked down at her notepad and took up her ballpoint pen once more.

No one spoke; they could hear the clock ticking just before the wind stirred at the window, begging to enter. The sky clouded over again. The room was suddenly close and stuffy.

Sarah asked politely, "Do you mind?" and Geoffrey went to open the shutter. The bishop looked in shock, and he reached out to touch his five-year plan. Joseph leaned forward.

"Nyabo," he addressed the woman, who as of yet had not been introduced by name. Neither Geoffrey nor the bishop tried to correct him. Having never married, she would still be considered a girl. "I thank you for being so brave. And so positive. I'm sure you could have said things in a much different way…Many have been hurt, and when we come from the West wanting to help, sometimes we go too fast, or in the wrong style, and cause more hurt. I do not wish this to continue. It is as you say—that friendship will make a difference in our work. I have heard from the O'Connells that people here have been so welcoming, so generous. They will never be the same."

"They are doing good work here," Geoffrey interrupted.

Joseph fell silent, leaving Sarah to respond with words of steady encouragement. Ann Rourke had always been above reproach, but she was seconded from the Tui Mission Society. A light had shifted in his head. All the negative comments made by others about Stephen and Julie seemed so trivial now; they paled in comparison with this report. Yes, they were human. Yes, they made mistakes. And that is why the people

The Wrong Side of Eternity

loved them. They were fallible, fallen, in need of compassion, in need of friendship. The new brand of missioner should surmount his role and actually engage with the people he has come to serve. As had begun, fifty and more years ago, in revival days. Not patronise Ugandans with put-on humility, then grumble about others' attitudes and behaviours to mission overseers.

Missioners, from countries other than Britain, certainly differing in their approach and home culture, yet making some kind of difference. Refreshing.

The O'Connells would stay.

69. RUTOKI SECONDARY SCHOOL, WEEKEND REVIVAL CONFERENCE

"You know Bishop's not keen on overnight prayer meetings," said Stephen as he and Julie left the youth meeting.

"So we'll split it up—we need to support these people. They pray, and it matters. They don't get caught up in church politics or local politics, they just pray for blessing, for healing. We could be seen as a sort of chaperone with our presence there, for the bishop's peace of mind."

"You're right, and I like the idea of splitting it up. I'll do the second shift."

"No, Sam and I are really into his bedtime story right now."

"And I can't pinch hit?"

"Of course you can, but it's kind of a gushy section, and he likes the mom voice."

"Uh-huh. So I'll go until midnight and walk you over then."

"Sounds good to me. I usually pray at night anyway."

"Yeah—too many visitors interrupting you throughout the day." He winked.

The small group had prayed quietly, earnestly, for several hours, and a lull settled into the small brick-lined room. The kerosene lantern burned with a surreal light; no angelic or demonic presence interrupted its steady glow. Boniface, Esther, and Emmanuel had their eyes closed, but their bodies remained in an attentive position. Receptive, calm.

Julie, on the other hand, felt stiff and sleep deprived. She could not stretch there without disturbing them. She needed to walk a bit. She reached quietly into her cloth bag for a pen and paper and jotted a quick note: GONE TO THE CHURCH, BACK SOON. Slowly, she extricated herself from the little room and tiptoed out into the night. Once outside, she breathed deeply and looked up. Cold wind blew her to wakefulness. Mottled clouds had stolen silently over the moon; the sky's light was dim, but the buildings were silhouetted enough for her to glide around them. She smelled rain, close. She only wondered how long it would be until the clouds began to empty: she had no umbrella and storms moved so quickly through the volcano-laden corridor. Gray dawn was within an hour at the most. Well, she would only be gone for a few minutes.

Flexing her shoulders and swinging her arms, Julie headed through the enclosure toward the church. Its doors were always open, but at this hour the gaping windows were black. She stepped inside. So quiet. It took her eyes a few minutes to adjust to the dark; approaching rumbles of thunder did not surprise her.

He watched her go inside. The sudden predawn storm drowned out all sound in the vacant cathedral, as rain pelted the corrugated iron roof with spear-shaft force.

It was the perfect opportunity.

Julie missed the red glimmer of a sanctuary lamp and knelt on the concrete step in front of the altar, willing herself into the warm embrace of St. Simeon's. She pictured the vestments, the colors of carpet and window, and recollected the smell of incense...

A very hard something smacked her head from behind, and she pitched forward, seeing a blazing mass of white light. Someone was grabbing at her, trying to lift her up, and struggling to get a good hold.

The Wrong Side of Eternity

She fought back and felt her flailing hand slap his face. Seeing nothing but red flashes of pain, she couldn't get her arms to cooperate, and she couldn't get her footing. The someone dropped her and pushed her face down to the floor, wet shoes stepping on her legs; a hand grabbed her hair and banged her forehead down onto the smooth cement, once, twice...

She felt her arms pinched, her body flipped over and dragged a few feet. Then she heard a distant ripping of cloth, and from somewhere far away felt her legs forced apart. Sheets of rain pounded the metal roof overhead, drowning out all hope of rescue.

Oh God, she thought, as sharp bolts of pain rammed into her and tore her world in two.

Innocent panted with relief: at last she had gone slack. Smaller than he remembered, but stronger as well. Too bad he couldn't get her on top of the altar—that would have been best, defiling their holy table. But what he had done would serve a sufficient warning to those who would desecrate the word of God. May she burn in hell.

He was too smart to wipe the knife on his trousers; he held it away from him and left through the same side door. Happy he had planned so carefully, rolling up his sleeves earlier, he let the pouring rain wash the blood off his hand as he continued to the nearest latrine, where he dropped the knife into the filth—a fitting place for it. Despite the deluge, the sky lightened. He would just have time to gather his umbrella and dry off before finding a *matatu* in the market square. He hated to travel on a Sabbath, but circumstances being what they were, there was no other choice. Jesus had dared to work on the Sabbath: he could too.

He would return to serve his missionary family in the north with pride, knowing that he had made a real difference. He would find out later that it was not the woman pastor after all, but someone else. Maybe that other *muzungu* he'd seen on the hillside. He excused himself: his act and her death would still give a warning. And besides, how was he to know? Especially in the dark—all *bazungu* look alike.

Act II

The midnight prayer team found her at dawn. Esther ran to the house to get Stephen, and Emmanuel hurried to find James. Geoffrey got there ahead of the rest, still adjusting his clothes. Ann arrived in the jeep disheveled but with an IV bag and setup. Her farm background prompted her to improvise a tampon; she applied it, hoping it would act as a pressure dressing to staunch the worst of the bleeding. James used a strip of cloth as a tourniquet, and he had the needle placed in no time despite her falling blood pressure.

"You *bazungu* are so soft, it's like poking a hole in butter," he managed to joke. It also helped that Julie's skin was so pale, he could see the veins underneath, even in the dim morning light. So many people gathering, crowding around, many with an idea of how to help. Their words collided in midair.

"We could get MissionAir to fly her to Nairobi."

"That will take hours." Charity looked at Stephen. "Do we have hours?" The look in his eyes told her everything.

"Could the mission hospital at Kabiizi manage her?" asked Ann.

"It's a long bumpy ride, and she's got a head injury. We can't chance it."

"Has somebody gone for Dr. Nsekanabo?"

"Yes, Mugisha's gone on his motorbike to collect him."

Geoffrey gazed at Stephen, kneeling at the head of the basket-stretcher where they had placed Julie, his hands slippery with clotting blood, cradling her head to the side, keeping her airway open, speaking softly to her, watching her feeble carotid pulse. They were scrambling to stay inside the country. But Kigali was closer by far. There were UN troops there still, and *Médecins sans Frontières* doctors. What were the chances...?

The bishop was standing, staring in horror at the bloody mess that was Julie. Geoffrey ventured to direct, appealing to the one person present who had the most power:

"Your grace, could we get the border guards to radio Kigali, check on the possibility of an air evacuation there? A helicopter would be safer

283

The Wrong Side of Eternity

than an aeroplane, and going to the airstrip..." He couldn't say it might kill her. "I'm afraid if we take too much time..."

"You're very right, Geoffrey. The doctors there have more practice with this." He turned to his driver and barked some orders. Wilberforce took off sprinting toward the village, and Charity ran to the office, hoping that the telephones worked.

70. KIGALI HOSPITAL MEDICAL WARD

She slept, ever on her side; the bandage was so thick it reminded him of an old leather football helmet. Stephen watched her ragged, shallow breathing. Cups of chai appeared, small bananas were handed to him; someone picked up the empty cups, someone else knelt to pour warm water over his sticky hands after he'd gulped the food down. People came and went like shadows in a play that dragged on and on and on. A curtain of rain passed over the capital on its way east. The light changed, the shadows lengthened, the kerosene lanterns were lit.

A gaunt French doctor stood next to him.

"She's very strong," he ventured in a beautiful accent.

"Tenacious," answered Stephen. The doctor sat down gently on a bamboo stool. He held a clipboard; his clinic coat was khaki colored, and his name badge read M. FOUCAULT, MÉDECINS SANS FRONTIÈRES.

"Monsieur O'Connell, her vital signs look good. We cannot tell until she wakes up what damage may have been done, by the injury or by the loss of blood. We had to give her several units." A gentle man, exuding compassion, tired from tragedy, exhausted. How much trauma had this man seen, tended to? More than Stephen could imagine, two lifetimes' worth. More. "What questions do you have that I may be able to answer?" His English was very good, practiced, clear. Stephen reached into his thoughts and hoped he wouldn't sound selfish.

"The source of the blood supply, Doctor?"

"We did the best we could."

Meaning it could be local, tainted with HIV. *Oh, God, must you?*

Act II

"The other wounds, Doctor." He meant the deep knife cuts, below. "Your prognosis?"

"There is much scarring—her cervix was damaged too." He paused, searching for a way to extend hope. "She will have to see a gynaecological specialist about whether or not she can bear more children, or comfortably be intimate." He paused, and Stephen had the impression that he had something else to say. The doctor tapped his pen very softly against the clipboard, while the rain began pelting the thick leaded window above his head. "The bruises will heal fine. As I said, she is very strong."

They sat together in silence, waiting for inspiration or something to continue the conversation. Stephen veered toward the practical as a way to cope.

"How long do you think, before she is able to travel?" He was jumping way ahead, en route to a specialist's office in London or America, and once he said this he knew it, but the doctor, bless his heart, met him.

"I don't want her moved until she is more stable. The radiograph of her skull shows what could be a hairline break in the base. Too many nerves there. I would rather evaluate her again in a day or two. In the meantime, we will give her IV medicine to reduce any swelling in her brain. And of course morphine."

"Thank you so much for your time." It sounded so hollow. This doctor had given everything to come out here, his wages insufficient, made up for only by the looks of gratitude from grief-stricken Rwandans—what was left of them.

"I am sorry it happened." He slowly rose and left.

"Ungh…" Julie moaned from beneath many waters of pain.

"Julie." He jostled himself awake, to see a furrow on her brow, her eyelids clenched.

"Ow," she grunted.

"Don't try to move. You've got a head injury."

"You had to tell me?" She licked her lips, and Stephen reached for the Chap Stick in his pocket. As he applied it, she winced and struggled

The Wrong Side of Eternity

to open her eyes. She gave up after a few seconds and let him sit next to her, holding her hand. "Where's Sam?"

"Staying with Ann."

"That rhymes."

The heavy rains began to fall, pellets of water drowning out conversation. A nursing sister stopped to check Julie's pulse; she wore a starched pinafore and a veil-like head covering. Stephen caught her eye. She nodded professionally. Had they seen so much that they were inured to all suffering? Were they numb? He thought of nurses back at the university, back in the war zones of Europe, long ago. Tough gals with hearts of gold. She reached into her uniform pocket, pulling out a small rosary. She draped it gently over Julie's limp hand.

"Thank you," he said in Kinyarwanda. Loudly, because of the rain.

The nursing sister sighed and continued her rounds.

In the lantern light, he watched Julie's bruised face contort with pain, and he went to find help. Twenty minutes later, a white-coated junior doctor usurped Stephen's seat at her bedside; he was young and brandished a vial of medicine. He felt her pulse and frowned.

"It was right to call me—this could not have waited until morning," he told Stephen. He loaded a syringe and jabbed it into a port in the IV line without wiping it with alcohol first. Of a sudden, Julie's labored breathing slowed like a satin wave smoothing into glassy calm. The resident smiled. "Valium's a wonderful drug," he stated. "Works every time."

Stephen did not hear him as he headed back to the sofa to continue his sleep. He talked only to himself. "Stupid missionary neocolonialists. She probably had it coming."

The clock read 2:30. Stephen blinked and looked out the window, where the sun was emerging from its rainy holiday. He remembered nothing of the night, only the evening before, when she woke and talked with him. Joking. She would be all right. When he directed his gaze to the bed, she lay quietly, her eyes open.

286

Act II

"Stephen? Are you there?"

"Yo." Her eyes drifted upward, toward his face, but began to jerk.

"Nystagmus," she said, letting her eyes fall back toward the window. "Gosh it's dark."

He sat forward. The day was bright, bright enough to make him squint. Slowly, he moved his hand in front of her face. She stared straight ahead. He waved it. Nothing.

God, he thought, sickening. *She's blind.*

71. THE O'CONNELL HOME, THREE WEEKS LATER

That day, in the middle of trying to pack with a migraine, Julie received two visitors.

Sam had been following her around, asking so many questions, some of them painful. "Why did someone hurt you, Mum? Didn't he know it was wrong, 'specially in God's house? Why didn't Jesus stop him? Can our friends come visit us in America?" Her head pounded and she fought hard to keep her temper. When Esther arrived, she saw what needed to be done and took Sam's hand to give Julie some respite.

Ann came in the morning, while Esther and Sam worked together to clean up his room. It always needed tidying, and his mother insisted that he pick up after himself. The house helper had finally relented and allowed him to help her.

After gently knocking, Ann let herself in.

"Julie?"

"In here." She emerged wiping her hands on her *kitenge*. "Tea?"

"Sure, but you need a rist. Let me make it, okay?" She glanced at Julie's face, still yellow from the fading bruises, and thought it beautiful.

"Fine with me." She sat at the table, pressing her hands against the sides of her aching head while Ann lit the propane burner. "Bishop wants us to come back."

287

The Wrong Side of Eternity

Ann sat down, touching Julie's shoulder. "Sure he would. You're such an asset."

"But we might need a longer furlough. My vision is still terrible, the headaches are getting worse, and depending on what happens…"

"You're afraid you'll get stuck in the States and not return."

"More than afraid," Julie admitted.

"You know more than you're letting on."

"Yeah. They're practically airlifting me to Nairobi for a consult with the ophthalmologist. The docs didn't want me bouncing along the rough roads." She put her head down on the table. "I'll miss seeing the countryside."

The kettle boiled and Ann stood to prepare the tea. As she stirred sugar into her cup, she broached the subject.

"No, I don't mean about your medical status. I mean about the attack."

"I can't figure out why someone would hurt me like this."

"Julie," she said, as softly as she could, "I wanted to tell you that the day of the open-air meeting, one of the men in the audience approached me. He said he was interested in my teaching, asked if I'd be around during the conference. I told him I'd be in and out. His English was pretty good. I had no idea he was dangerous."

Julie lifted her head, which was pounding. "How could you know, Ann?"

"You suffered a beating intended for me."

"There's no proof of that. And it's not as if I meant to. I mean, it's not as if I volunteered or something. God, I need to take some medicine."

"Can I get it for you?"

"Sure. It's on the nightstand, in the bedroom."

Strong stuff, thought Ann, retrieving the bottle, reading the label. She watched as Julie downed two tablets. *She'll be in pain the rest of her life.* Ann didn't know what else to say.

"You can't take any blame," said Julie. "And promise me, Ann, that you'll be careful, not go out at night, avoid being alone…"

Act II

"I will. I came to thank you for more than my life. I came to thank you for being such a friend—no, more than that. A saviour." The word sounded so cheap in the Julie's simple kitchen.

"Oh, Ann, cut the crap. I had no such intentions. It was all a mistake. I was in the wrong place at the wrong time. That's all."

"I'll miss you."

"Yeah, well, that makes two of us. I wish you could stay, and you can, if you just sit quietly, but I've got to get to bed. It's all getting to me, the packing, Sam's questions, the pain..." She stood and swayed, grasping the table top as Ann seized her hand to keep her from falling. "Sorry. Doctors say that will last awhile, but it might get better. I hope. Do come again—I'd like to end on a happier note."

"Let me at least walk you down the hall."

"Sure thing. Stephen'll be home in a minute. Let him walk you out." The shutters in the bedroom were closed against the light, and Julie fell atop the foam mattress that served as their bed. She curled into a fetal position as Ann covered her with the duvet before going to find Sam. Julie trusted her to give her son good counsel. The 'bist'.

Charity came by in the afternoon and stayed three hours.

OPENING NIGHT

WEST-COAST AMERICA, THE YEAR 2000

House Lights Down

The thing on the blind side of the heart,
On the wrong side of the door,
The green plant growth, menacing
Almighty lovers in the Spring;
There is always a forgotten thing,
And love is not secure.

—G. K. Chesterton

72. Gilded Lily Café across the Bay, Tuesday, Noon

Madeleine daintily stabbed the romaine of her Caesar salad. "I used to find it so intriguing, doing the research, anticipating the comebacks. And because I never took a caustic approach, not directly to their face anyway, I was getting invited to all sorts of gatherings. Lately, though, I've been getting rather nasty e-mails." She kept her eyes down and lowered her volume. "There was some talk of my going political…"

"I know. I heard it too," Elisabeth Hardesty answered in a neutral tone.

"You did?"

"Even Keith mentioned how you would put a fresh new face on the religious right." Elisabeth had become a good friend, a confidant.

The Wrong Side of Eternity

"I thought he supported a more...*private* role for women in general."

"Christian women, certainly. But as long as a public role could be one of *representation* and not of *teaching*, he might be supportive." There was an edge to Elisabeth's tone that Madeleine had not noticed before.

"Is something going on with Keith?"

"Keith is true to himself, as always," answered Elisabeth, looking away.

"And to you?"

Elisabeth laughed. "True to me? In what way? You mean, is he faithful? Of course."

"Then what is it?" They had always seemed like the model couple, Elisabeth with her love of homemaking, the professor with his old-fashioned values.

In answer, Elisabeth rolled up her silken sleeve. A gauze bandage encircled her left forearm. Madeleine winced.

"What happened?"

"Oh, Maddy, don't tell me you've never noticed my penchant for long sleeves?"

"I thought it was a reflection of your modesty."

"Everyone probably thinks that." She sighed. "It's probably just as well."

Madeleine put her fork down and leaned forward, folding her hands in front of the china plate. "How did you hurt yourself?"

"I didn't. *He* did." Elisabeth corrected. "I'm not asking you to publicize it. I just wanted to tell someone I trust."

Such a gentleman, Professor Hardesty, thought Madeleine. Always opening the door for his wife, placing his hand gently on her back to steer her into a room. Always so proud of her. The only evidence to the contrary being the penetrating gaze of Elisabeth—and now a gauze bandage.

"Let me see it."

"Here?" She looked about them and quickly buttoned up the sleeve.

"In the car. I'm serious, Elisabeth. I need to know."

"I'm leaving him, Maddy," she said, taking a sip of water. "It's not the first time."

"Have you sought counseling?"

Opening Night

"Is that second-person singular or second-person plural?" Elisabeth asked, sounding sincere.

"Either."

"Yes to the first, no to the second."

"And?"

"It was a Christian counselor. What do you *think* he told me?"

"To hang in there?"

"Something to that effect. And then he made excuses for my husband. Almost to the point of insinuating that I had triggered it, the violence, somehow."

"Did he by any chance quote the rabbinic arguments?"

"Only the ones that support total submission. I know there are others, from the more reformed branch." She smiled at Madeleine's surprise. "You're not the only one who reads theology," explained Elisabeth. "I just do it on the sly."

Madeleine knew her friend was intelligent, judging from their stimulating conversations. But she never would have suspected...She needed to see, to be sure. And even then, would some accidental loss of temper justify the breaking of a marriage? Her aunt had confided to her once that her home was full of all kinds of abuse, but she'd proudly stated she'd never leave. Even if it killed her. Aunt Trudy hadn't the heart to call her husband's bluff, to bring shame on him in the community where he stood as a pillar. Elisabeth seemed to be of similar ilk but not to the point of self-sacrifice.

Madeleine reached to pick up the check, pursing her lips. *If it could happen with the Hardestys...*She shook her head. Elisabeth went to the ladies' room, looking slightly nervous, as Madeleine picked up her purse and stood, straightening her blouse and heading to the counter. They would exit separately and meet at the car.

She started the engine as Elisabeth slid into the passenger seat and closed the door, then turned on the air conditioning. It was a hot day, but she also did not want to risk any chance of being overheard. She saw that the windows were tinted and sighed.

295

The Wrong Side of Eternity

"You'll have to help me do it up again."

"Because you're left handed." Something Madeleine had not noticed before.

"Yes." Elisabeth gingerly unrolled the dressing to reveal a brown-stained rip in her forearm with black stitches zig-zagging across the purpling skin.

"Did he push you against something?"

"No, Maddy. He just twisted my arm until the skin tore open. A laceration, they called it at the emergency room. He's never broken a bone or touched my face, only parts of me that were easy to hide."

"Oh, Elisabeth, I never imagined."

"Not something I was ready for when I married him, I can assure you. Anyway, Maddy, I plan to just sort of disappear. Not make a big stink about this. But I wanted you to know, in case..."

"In case he tries to search for you?"

"No. In case he tries to find another wife. You've got to warn her."

73. THE EVERETT TOWNHOUSE, THURSDAY EVENING

They returned from the lecture together. Madeleine threw her bag at the foot of the coat-stand.

"'Deconstructing the Mythologies of Sacred Scripture'. That's like pouring acid over a Michelangelo," she complained, opening the fridge to see what was there. Bryce poured a cup of cold decaf and placed it in the microwave.

"Oh, I don't know. We all have our mythologies, sacred or not."

"They have theirs in plenty. Like the ancient need to tear down someone else's tradition. As if the word of God could be *demythologized*."

"Whether it can or not, people think it's worth their effort to try."

"They want no authority in their life," she said, bitterly.

"Why would they want an authority like the stereotype many of them have of God? The frowning father or a harmless celestial Santa Claus.

No, dear Madeleine, it's up to folks like you and me to challenge their tack, to pick up the gauntlet they throw down."

"We just do it in such different ways, Bryce," she said, softly. He stirred cream into his coffee. "People say you compromise."

He smiled. "They've no idea what a tightrope it is, being orthodox and artistic at the same time," he said to the kitchen light fixture, a tasteful stained-glass piece that he thought would look better over a billiard table. He looked at her weary face, trying to cheer her. "You did a phenomenal job in the last TV interview. You know I fully support you in your crusade."

"Yes, I know that."

"And that I think you're horribly good at deconstructing those erudite mythologies of theirs."

She faced the sink. "Thank you." She turned her head toward him. *So handsome.*

"Just don't let them catch you doing it," he warned, winking, before putting his cup on the counter to get cold, while he moved closer. She was not very surprised when his arms circled her waist.

"I've already closed the curtains," he murmured, close to her ear. His hands crept upward.

She almost resisted, then thought better of it. He was virile enough—even though, after four years of trying, the doctor had told them he was shooting blanks, his sperm count too low to make a natural family likely. It had been no real disappointment, leaving her free to pursue her career. But tonight, she was so tense; she needed the release that Bryce's affections would bring.

She needed him, she admitted, as his caress lifted her beyond herself, and that thought nearly scared her as he led her up the winding staircase and to bed.

In the morning, she woke to Bryce whistling some baroque concerto down in the kitchen, but she was hardly prepared when, half an hour later, he walked in with a breakfast tray, complete with red rose.

The Wrong Side of Eternity

"You didn't have to do that."

"That's what made it so pleasurable. That I didn't have to. That's where the joy is, *chère* Madeleine."

She ate while he sat in the upholstered chair and admired her.

Later, they went downstairs, preparing to head out into the busy day—in separate directions, as usual.

"I read the aerogram," she said.

"The one from Stephen O'Connell?"

We don't get aerograms every day, Bryce, she wanted to say. *And when we do, they're always from him.* "That's the one. Postmarked in Nairobi. What's going on?"

"I don't know. The politics over there have been getting rough..." He frowned. "It would have to be something serious to warrant such a sudden return."

Maybe he finally fell apart, she thought.

"Anyway, my love," he went on, "I went ahead and phoned their mission office in London, gave them our address and number."

"Why?"

"So he can reach me when he gets back here. I'm sure he could use a friend, regardless of the situation."

"He's *got* friends, at that liberal church. He doesn't need you—I do."

He smiled. "Do you really?"

"Yes, really." She grabbed his hand and held it, staring directly into his eyes, before they went out the door.

74. Re-Entry

It was raining outside.

"So good of my folks to keep him another week while we get settled."

Julie always found the good in every situation. Sometimes Stephen wondered if she ever suffered, because she didn't talk about it much. But he knew she did; he could see it in the dullness of her eyes.

Opening Night

Their time with her family was peaceful and at the same time strained. No one knew how to talk about what had happened; they *almost* discussed it, more than once, but the conversation slipped out of reach like a moth. She walked in the forest, sometimes by herself, or with Sam to divert her. Stephen watched as she pointed out the tall trees and taught their son how to kick pinecones.

"Time heals all wounds," commented her father, while they were there. Bonnie, who was clearing the table at the time, looked at Stephen with an unreadable expression. The only translation Stephen could come up with was, "Maybe; maybe not." He returned her gaze with his own weighty look, one that read "I shall do everything in my power for her security and safety."

He felt completely powerless nonetheless.

During the second week up there, they had received a phone call from Rev. Margaret informing them that an elderly parishioner, Lillian Seaton, was going into a nursing home, and her son was trying to find a house sitter. "It's available for you," she had said, "and will be free for several months at least, while he has it on the market. You'd only have to be willing to keep it tidy for when potential buyers come to look. Are you interested?" Of course he was interested. They could be at their home church again. The Everetts lived near there...

Then he remembered who Lillian was, the lady with lavender hair who always smiled flirtatiously at him during service. *Poor Lil.* He smiled to think of the pranks she might play in a nursing home. A woman like her would be pinching the orderlies on their bottoms. Did they still have orderlies these days?

The house sat conveniently next to a small Italian market. Julie could walk there, since her vision stubbornly refused to improve well enough for her to drive. Diplopia, double vision, with half the visual field missing. The doctor had explained it to them with anatomical charts showing where the optic nerve had been damaged by the underlying skull fracture; he doubted it would heal. She would have to turn her head

The Wrong Side of Eternity

anytime she wanted to see to her right. The prescription glasses were thick, with built-in prisms. They were also costly, but the mission had paid for that. Her balance had improved since they'd arrived back in America, although she still stumbled now and then.

Stephen noticed how differently people treated her now. Not out of pity, because she wasn't quite legally blind and used no white cane. They just talked with her as if she lacked intelligence, as if a visual deficit amounted to retardation or stupidity. He jumped to her defense often, until she stopped him.

"They don't understand, Stephen. How can they? Look where they've been brought up, the shows they've watched, the news they read. They can't help thinking the way they do."

"It's not Christian."

"No, but when did we ever live in a Christian country?" Julie asked.

He did not say that the guys at SBC would insist it was Christian at its inception. They would fault those foreign immigrants for ruining it, by importing paganism, Hinduism, Buddhism, Islam. *It was all their fault, as usual*, his former classmates whispered in his memory.

"Rwanda was supposedly a Christian country," he answered instead.

"How fragile we all are," she concluded. "How easily turned aside from doing the right things."

He led her to a chair and sat her down, then knelt at her feet to gaze up into her face. "Miz Julie," he drawled in a southern accent, "you is so *wise!*"

She laughed and stroked his hair, then let him make her a superb cup of coffee from the French press he'd bought in London.

Now they wandered between living room and bedroom, putting things away. Mrs. Seaton's son had packed up the more personal items into boxes, which were neatly labeled and stored on shelves in the garage. He'd given them use of Lillian's Buick. The house was nicer than anything they could have afforded to rent, a godsend in their time of need. The elementary school was a block away; they could report back to their supporting churches without having to put up in dingy hotel

Opening Night

rooms, and they had time to consider what to do next. Best of all, there were friends in the area. Stephen would see Bryce soon.

"It's been months," he said, gently, when she sat on the bed and sighed. She looked past him, stood up, and went to resume her unpacking. The very old-fashioned house phone rang. Stephen debated about answering it, since it wasn't their home. He opted to pick up the receiver.

Julie cocked her head to eavesdrop. Her hearing had become phenomenal, now that her vision was a mess.

"Hello? This is he...Oh, Reverend Margaret, it's perfect. Everything we need...well, more than that. Vince said we could use anything we like, even the car...Yes, there are several meals in the freezer. They're for us? The ladies' guild, of course. We'll send a wordy thank-you note...I'm so glad you're still at St. Simeon's. A safe harbor, yes, that's it...Yes, I'm sure she will. We both will, if you're up to it. I'll discuss it with her, and we'll get back to you to schedule...Thank you so much... You too. Good-bye."

"Saint Margaret extended an offer for pastoral counseling," Julie guessed as he opened the refrigerator to survey the supplies.

"Anytime, she said."

"I'll go tomorrow, if you can take me."

He nodded in reply, and they set their hands to making dinner.

75. MONROE ELEMENTARY SCHOOL, A THURSDAY AFTERNOON

The sky had turned cold; autumn was wearily preparing to surrender to winter. They sat across a large desk at the public school. Sam's artwork was spread out before them: idyllic scenes, someone lying in bed with Xs for eyes, lots of trucks.

"He's very vivid."

"He lived in Africa," Julie said, as an explanation.

The teacher, showing concern, probed a little. "I was surprised at how mild these were. I understand you lived very close to the troubles."

301

The Wrong Side of Eternity

Yeah, thought Julie, nobody ever called it what it was. America had officially objected to the use of the term. "The genocide," she corrected.

"Was not your son exposed to any of that horror?" Mrs. Kelly asked, in that patient and gentle tone that teachers use so well.

"No, thank God, he was spared," answered Stephen. "We lived across the border. Hutu and Tutsi were not an issue, the history was different. The adults in our circles talked carefully in the presence of children, and when they were graphic, they used the local language."

"Which your son did not understand."

"He knew the appropriate greetings," he said.

"And a few choice swear words," added Julie, smiling. Then her demeanor changed. "But the bullying he's seen here far surpasses anything he witnessed in Uganda."

This brought the teacher up short. "What do you mean?"

Stephen answered on Julie's behalf. "She means that people in general, whether they are children in public schools or tribal leaders in Africa, call one another names. They just do. Do you have a remedy for the trauma it causes, Mrs. Kelly?"

Stephen, you are so full of it, thought Julie, and swatted his arm to shut him up. The teacher looked relieved and went back to the conference.

"He's very, very bright. I'm afraid a little precocious, socially. He seeks out the ones who are different and befriends them. Seems to like their company."

"Different? How so?"

"Anything coming close to fitting a type: the Asian nerd, the black gang member..."

"You have black gang members in sixth grade?" asked Julie.

"No, but kids watch a lot of TV, and they jump to conclusions."

"That's why we don't own one."

"Well, I would like to involve Sam in as much art and drama as I can. It seems to be a good outlet for him, and he has talent that way."

"Does that mean his fundamentals in math are weak?" asked Stephen, who had tutored his son.

Opening Night

"No, not at all, he scores just fine. He's just so good at putting sentences together. I'm thinking if we can get him going in a creative-writing or storytelling project, it would give him a way to review his memories without—ah—upsetting the other children."

"He thinks like an African," answered Julie. "A reverse Oreo."

"Oreo?"

"That's what they called the black kids where I grew up who thought and acted like privileged whites. Sam's the opposite: white on the outside, African at heart."

"Oh, I never thought of it that way."

"Why label him at all?" asked Stephen. "Why not just let him be himself, an international child with a lot of promise?"

Mrs. Kelly leaned back in her chair. "What a good idea. Mr. O'Connell, you're so right. I can be his ally. And he'll be Sam."

"Thank you for understanding, Mrs. Kelly."

"Oh, I hardly understand," the teacher said. "But I'm not above learning, either."

76. THAT EVENING

"It's been months," Stephen said again, very gently this time. They sat together on the seventies-era sofa, drinking cheap Chablis. Late-autumn rain softly pelted the roof overhead. A recording of Schubert wove a symphonic tapestry in the background, and two candles burned on top of the short bookshelf. In lieu of a fireplace. It was cozy enough. He turned his head to kiss her neck and lingered there.

"Months..." she murmured. She set her wine glass down on the heavy coffee table, next to his. He took off her glasses, and she closed her eyes, letting him touch her face. A tear overspilled one eye, then another.

"My hand's cold."

"That's all right." She unbuttoned her blouse, and he reached inside.

"Is it?" He slipped his palm over her bra. She gulped a quick breath.

303

It was cold all right. The shock of his touch mingled with the warmth of the wine, opening a crack in a long-locked door to a place of both comfort and pleasure. If he kept at it, his hands would warm soon enough.

"Yes," she answered. He had been so careful not to intrude, almost as if he himself had suffered the assault. As if he, not she, were afraid of being touched again. "Stephen, don't...come inside. The scars are still thick. And tender."

"Do you want me to stop?"

"No, please. Just...no penetration."

He leaned back and smiled gently, with care. "I've had lessons from an expert, a famous author...*Sex as Pain Management*. There are ways..."

Her capitulating laugh was a murmuring brook.

She let him caress her as he would the keyboard, coaxing out tunes so beautiful they could make you cry. And he did, playing a concerto—the word whispered "teamwork"—his instruments being fingers and lips, hands and tongue, the middle section deliciously slow... They moved to the bedroom, where she waited, and he began again. To his surprise and relief, she responded, echoing his touch and rising to meet him. The finale building up *accelerando poco a poco, con moto*, and the last lingering note drifting off like mist toward an unseen horizon.

Come morning, he woke first and noticed that their pillowcases were wet. *That's right*, he mused, *we both cried*. A long time. And how good it felt, to cry together. *The pain of joy, the joy of pain*. He got up quietly, softly kissed her hair, and stole off to the kitchen to make coffee.

OFFSTAGE

Whom the gods wish to destroy they first call promising.

—JOSEPH CONRAD

77. FACULTY OFFICE, SCHOLARS BIBLE COLLEGE

TWO WEEKS LATER, PROFESSOR HARDESTY found a blank business-sized envelope atop his office desk. Unsure if it were even meant for him, he turned it over; the flap had not been sealed but merely tucked inside. He took out a piece of white copy paper and read

> "The LORD was witness to the covenant between you
> and the wife of your youth, to whom you have been
> faithless, though she is your companion and your
> wife by covenant…For I hate…the covering of one's
> garment with violence, says the LORD of hosts."

MALACHI 2:14–16.

You who so capably teach the Holy Scriptures, how could you have missed this message? How could any of us have missed it??

The Wrong Side of Eternity

He stared at it. It was not signed. He sat down, his hands shaking. But other verses came flooding into his mind, verses that justified him. Whoever had written this had neglected to include the part of the passage right before it, about divorce...*Shame on them, taking verses out of context like that!* If push came to shove, he could defend himself, both practically and scripturally. But it irked him all the same, that some coward would accuse him—falsely—with a Bible passage. Elisabeth had been a rebellious woman who warranted correction. *Good riddance, Elisabeth: you should well have kept your pretty mouth shut.*

Deciding to say nothing but to bear himself righteously and let his deeds do all the talking, he pitched the page into his freshly lined trash can and pulled out the day's lecture notes.

78. AN APARTMENT OVERLOOKING THE BAY, WEDNESDAY EVENING

Every time he opened a new envelope, he was back in another adventure of the old *Mission: Impossible*. Studying the photos, reading the details of the lives of his targets always gave him a thrill.

He always wore camouflage to the rifle range and made sure it looked tattered enough, even if he had to roll around in the dirt of his driveway. He'd learned to talk the hunting lingo as comfortably as any of the guys or gals that hung out there. His apartment was even strewn with hunting and ammo magazines, giving his "hobby" of gun collecting and cleaning a respectable air.

Hell, his girlfriend had complained that he came to bed smelling like a paint-by-numbers set, after he'd spent an hour and a half dissembling and oiling his NATO Special, as he fondly called it, that 5.56-mm beauty of a piece. There were so many of them floating around out there, harder to trace that way. When someone admired the rifle, he'd generously let them know where they could get one too: they weren't available at Big 5, but you could pick one up at Andy's Ammo or the swap meet easily enough.

He caressed the matte black metal finish as he laid out his jag and patch. He would use a soft-tip bullet for maximum damage...Better to

Opening Night

take the .22 with him, though, when he trailed his quarry, just in case there was a close-range opportunity.

Such an attractive person: he liked those. People who impressed others, who'd gotten a good deal out of life. They were the most fun to blow away. The articles had gotten longer lately, the target more notable. Life was good. This one enjoyed a bit of a public persona. Well, a public figure warranted a public execution, something more dramatic than the standard brake failure or household gas leak.

He would hang out at the theater, maybe pose as a student techie, until he knew the lay of the land, the accessible corridors of the lighting scaffolds, the more invisible exits. He would take his time, fill in as an apprentice stagehand maybe...The silencer would mean extra bulk, but all students carried enormous daypacks these days, and no one would notice. Like many of the druggy students, he would socialize little and melt away into the night when rehearsals were still winding down.

This was going to be good.

79. LEAVING THE UNIVERSITY LIBRARY

Madeleine felt suddenly tired and looked at her watch. Plenty of students still around, taking advantage of the library's extended hours before exams. The preparation had taken her too much time; she should be getting home. Madeleine sighed, gathered up the copied articles and her notebook, and organized them into her canvas tote. Bryce always had such good input, but he was occupied with his production. She should show more interest in his work for a change. The thought fatigued her even more: she wasn't sure of its success. But he was after a different audience from hers, she reminded herself. "God," she muttered, as she left the library. "Help it to work."

What she'd read that evening troubled her; she couldn't shut out her thoughts on her way out to the car. The "welcoming" churches were finding a voice in the media. URBAN GOSPEL CHURCH OPENS ITS ARMS, read one title.

Mix it all up, God and sin, right and wrong, and you'll have a mess someday. They might as well hook up with the Universalist Unitarians; everything's okay as long as you're sincere...what a load of crap, she thought, as she drove right past her exit from the freeway. A minute later, maybe two, she realized her mistake.

I'll just exit here and double back on the surface streets, she reasoned, as the hour had struck for the emptying out of theaters and restaurants, which meant the freeways were far from empty. She consulted the local map, the one inside her head, and knew she could find her way. It was just a few miles...Foothill Avenue south, then a left onto Canyon...*No problem.* The streetlights and bright billboards made her blink: she was more tired than she thought.

She pulled out her cell phone to leave a message for Bryce. It was dead. She'd forgotten to charge it during her stint at the library. *What now?*

Did they still make pay phones? She'd seen one or two in restaurant chains...Ah, there was the Upper Crust, a ubiquitous pie shop, coming up on her right. She pulled into the parking lot and hurried inside.

A black pickup pulled in behind her.

80. THE TOWNHOUSE, THE SAME EVENING

"I'm having a hard time believing that you really want my opinion," Stephen confessed. He'd been gone nine years and felt out of sync with everything. He sat in the leather recliner, closed his eyes, and drifted back to their coastal hikes and the youthful sharing of dreams. Bryce was close to fulfilling his, and Stephen felt honored to be pulled into his confidence again. Did his thoughts actually *matter* to this gifted friend of his, whose genius outdistanced anything Stephen would ever achieve?

"But I seriously do, mate." Bryce played through the main songs and provided the synopsis. He saved the most vulnerable piece for last.

"This is Roger's song," he explained. "Which means it isn't really in my range. It'll sound a bit growly..."

"That's okay. Go for it."

Opening Night

Bryce played some dissonant chords and a rocky beat and launched in:

I can do without them, I can do without them all
Don't need anyone to tell me what to do,
To pick me up, help me out when I fall into the mud
I can climb out myself, It's in me—leave them on the shelf
Got enough will to survive, to come out more alive than before
Gotta go through this door, alone…

"What do you think, Stephen?" Bryce asked. He sat at the piano, looking over his shoulder.

It was a driving rhythm with the lyrics in the right place for the tune, but Stephen couldn't venture to guess if the music were good—by current standards—or not, so he focused on the story line.

"It's pretty obvious that it's the parable," he offered gingerly. "I mean, you've got a father and two sons, and one of them rebels and the other stays loyal at home."

Bryce nodded and didn't interrupt.

"You've got a fairly strong subplot, with the girl and the mugging and all, but…"

"Go on, I need to hear your most basic thought."

You do? Really? You who give the world brilliance and depth, polish and beauty, need to hear something from me? "Okay. What if you ditched the whole patriarchal thing—it's so *Dallas*—and made the father into a divorced woman? Or, if it seems more moral, a widow. You could keep her character as it is, and the reconciliation at the end might be the more powerful, with the empathy factor thrown in. And it would break up all the male singing…"

His voice trailed off because instead of a scowl, Bryce looked past him, out the window toward the bay. He finished Stephen's sentence.

"…and make the parable much less obvious."

"That too."

Bryce's fingers drifted over the keys, playing an arpeggio with a Celtic lilt.

The Wrong Side of Eternity

"She'd have to be feisty, to manage two such ox-headed fellows."

"You could have some fun with that…"

"Fantastic," he said, and stopped playing. "My God, look at the time. The library's closed by now. I wonder what's become of my darling wife?"

"I'd better go home too. Julie gets nervous when she's left alone for long." He took his canvas jacket off the coat tree near the front door, admiring Bryce's new woolen pea coat and its dashing lines.

"And who could blame her?" Bryce filled in the awkward silence politely. "She's a brick, your wife," he added, quoting a line from an old film. "An absolute brick. Let me not keep you from her one minute longer." He strode to the door to see Stephen out. The night outside was black velvet, some storm snuffing out the stars.

"Thanks for letting me hear your work, Bryce. It's…it's wonderful. I don't know how to tell you decently. I've been speaking Ugandan English too long."

"You do have an accent now. Someone might think you're from Britain, if they didn't know better."

"It probably won't last."

"No, your ear is too good—you'll adjust back into West Coast slang in no time."

"Thanks." He paused at the threshold, then stepped back in to wrap his arms around Bryce, who reciprocated. Stephen found himself beginning to weep, silently, and rather than linger there, slowly pushed away. Bryce released him, and he slipped off into the night, like a dinghy casting off from shore.

"Bye."

81. THE UPPER CRUST RESTAURANT, 10:35 P.M.

She'd been to the ladies' room and found the payphone in the hallway just outside the door, where she expected it would be. *Fifty cents for a local call. My, how times had changed…* Bryce picked up on the second ring.

"Hello?"

310

Opening Night

She kept the conversation short, aching to get home. "I'm sorry I'm running late. I missed my exit, and I'll be coming home via Foothill." She checked her watch again.

"Everything all right?"

"Yes, I'm okay—you don't need to send out a posse..."

"Where are you now?"

"Not far, I know my way. Should take me no more than fifteen minutes." She took in the Monet print that probably covered an electrical fuse box and glanced at her manicure out of habit.

"Be safe, then," he told her.

"I will. See you soon...bye." She replaced the receiver and turned around to find a dark-complexioned man blocking her way out. He wore a leather jacket, and gold jewelry sparkled from his collar and wrist. She looked him straight in the eyes. "Excuse me."

"Excuse *me*, miss, but you were followed in here," he said softly and carefully. He had an accent of some kind...Middle Eastern? Armenian? She had no idea whether to believe him or not. No idea at all. "Let me walk you back to your car. I'll make sure he loses you."

He who? Was this for real? Or was it a ruse, a trick to corner her? Suddenly she was aware that she knew this particular neighborhood much less than she wanted to, about now. And that she had no desire to know it better, about now. She had parked directly under a streetlight, as always. Should she decline? Something in his look warned her. She took a gamble and decided to trust him—to a certain degree.

"All right...Perhaps you could pretend to know me."

"Good idea." They emerged from the hallway together. He spoke louder. "Imagine meeting you here! I'm glad that mister of yours is expecting you soon, or I might be tempted to steal you away!" He hammed it up. She pretended to look delighted; inwardly she was terrified. "I'll tell Maha I saw you...boy, will she be surprised!" he ranted on until they spilled out the restaurant door. He looked back as he bustled her over to her BMW, and he kept his eye on the entrance as she opened the car to hurry inside it, heart pounding, half expecting him to yank the door open and drag her to the ground.

311

The Wrong Side of Eternity

But he didn't. He just stood by until she'd closed it, always looking back toward the restaurant to make sure. She pushed the electric door lock and heard its welcome click. Then she thought of her manners and lowered the window, just a little.

"Thank you," she said, and made a wild guess, starting the engine. *He must be a believer, to be so helpful.* "Where do you fellowship?"

"Fellowship?" He seemed puzzled. "Oh, you mean pray. I go to the Sunni mosque on Sycamore. Have a nice evening, lady. And watch yourself."

"I will." She closed the window tight and pulled out of the parking lot onto the street, watching him in the side mirror as she drove off. He remained in the parking lot until she lost sight of him two blocks later. "Huh," she said, as a Bible quote floated to her consciousness: "for as much as ye have done it to the least of My brethren, ye have done it unto Me."

"Whatever he did, just now, if it was a good thing, Lord, bless him for it," she prayed, and sped her way home.

CURTAIN

———

I've been living to see you; dying to see
you, but it shouldn't be like this.
This was unexpected. What do I do now?
Could we start again, please?

—TIM RICE

82. THE TOWNHOUSE

"I'M NOT SURE WHY YOU pulled Stephen O'Connell into the critic's seat," Madeleine commented after dinner the next night.

"Stephen's got a knack for knowing what works," Bryce answered. "He watched some of my earlier stuff, remember, and had brilliant feedback. Why wouldn't I want his input?"

"And Roger, playing the prodigal? Are you sure that's going to go over very well?" She could imagine conservative Christians picketing the theater, holding signs that read NOT ALL SHALL INHERIT THE KINGDOM OF GOD...

"But don't you see the magic of it, Madeleine? Roger's the best for the part. He's got the range and the acting experience. He's even got his doctorate. So what if he's gay? He'll communicate better than anybody else. And, if you want to assume a logical argument, who better than a gay man to play the prodigal son? It will work for everybody."

313

The Wrong Side of Eternity

She wasn't sure he was right this time but decided to press him no further.

82. University Auditorium, Tuesday Night

Rehearsal hadn't started yet. Roger approached him with two cups of latté, offering one. "Hey, Stephen, got a sec?"

"Sure. What's up?"

Roger sat down congenially next to him in the fourteenth row, house left.

"Wanted to bounce something off of you regarding Bryce."

Stephen felt a surge of anxiety, remembering the gossip at SBC surrounding this special friendship he had with Bryce, which no one, including himself, could really understand.

"Yeah, sure."

"I'm wanting to provoke some feelings of jealousy in the guy, I mean *real* ones. He's acting well enough, but I'm not sure he's really connecting. I know he envied you..."

"Me?"

"He never told you? About how he wished he had your freedom from such a driven life, your freedom to go home during the shorter term breaks, even your freedom to date whoever you wanted."

"You're kidding." *What a remarkable voice Roger has,* he thought. He could talk with you and convince you beyond all doubt that he really cared about you as a person. No wonder he was an assistant pastor as well as a first-rate actor.

"Nope, not at all. So how can I tap into that, to draw it out in a performance? This jealousy thing."

"I have no idea. I'm not the consummate professional you are, Roger." *Far from it.* An ignoramus when it came to all things theater. Then a second thought occurred to him. "What about this dissertation of yours? Where you underlined the audience's role in performance quality."

314

Opening Night

"What about it? I finished it two years ago."

"Well, why don't you try to tap into the *audience's* feelings of jealousy, maybe somehow get them to project onto Bryce?"

"I never thought of manipulating it like that."

"Is it manipulation or just some sort of subliminal appeal to them?"

"Aren't the two the same thing?"

"I suppose it would depend on one's motives…"

The director clapped twice, summoning the cast onto the stage.

Madeleine stepped inside to see how it was going. The cast members were on a break, munching energy bars and sipping from multicolored thermos cups. She loitered just within hearing.

"It's *brilliant*, Bryce. You and Roger really capture the tension of the moment," Maureen said.

Maureen MacLaren, the venerable actress from ACT. She'd played Lady Macbeth, Golde from *Fiddler*. Strong, endearing, and utterly professional. *Does she really have that Irish an accent, really?* thought Madeleine, as the actress wandered away to schmooze other cast members.

"Roger's the professional—he's making it happen," offered Bryce. "Like when your tennis game improves when playing with someone far above your capabilities."

"Don't let him off, Stephen," scolded Roger. "Bryce is plenty convincing. I'm not sure if it's the playwright or the actor in him that's bringing the inspiration."

"How did you get Maureen to stoop to this ragtag production?"

"Maureen's got a soft spot for the underdog," explained Roger, winking at the dowager queen across the room. "She liked the script, loved the lyrics—and she's a sucker for good music."

"What a great voice," Stephen said.

What a mutual appreciation society, thought Madeleine, shaking her head. These artistic types, all scratching one another's backs. She'd given input too, mostly for content, to make sure the story line didn't spin off into sensuality. It was tricky, staging a PG production that appealed to believers and nonbelievers alike. A fine line, a tightrope. There were going to be people that were not amused, others who would feel it was way, way too tame. The potential for disaster was great. With all his talent, *their* talent, she wasn't convinced that her husband could pull it off. She noticed that Stephen had approached the older actress and that they had struck up a pleasant conversation, but she could overhear none of it, and she excused herself to go home and make a very late dinner.

"So, Miss MacLaren," Stephen began, "how Irish are you, really?"

"About as Irish as yourself, Mr. O'Connell," she answered with a twinkle in her eye and a Dublin accent thick as Celtic fog. Then she switched to West Coast American. "My parents came over, poor as church mice—they still use that expression, don't they? Well, I knew I could with *you*, after all...My father took a job aboard a fishing boat, doing the heavy work, and my mother, God rest her soul, found herself singing in nightclubs. She managed to maintain her dignity, though, and stumbled into small-time theater just when it was starting to pick up here. I caught the acting bug from her."

"I sure like what you're doing with the part. I'm curious, though: how did you know my name?"

She laughed. "That dear boy Bryce is crazy about you, says you've got the best intuition for story writing he's ever encountered. Must be the Irish blood, eh?"

"Must be." He looked down at the floor. *That, and living in Africa.* The stage manager was calling the troops together to give some notes before they went into the second act. "Back into battle," he said in parting, tilting his head toward the stage.

Maureen MacLaren smiled broadly and blew a kiss at him as he exited a side door.

83. THE O'CONNELLS' TEMPORARY RESIDENCE

REVIEW by Arthur J. Sadler, theater critic for the *Chronicle:*

Composer and playwright Bryce Everett ambitiously has undertaken a new view of parent-child tension in his cutting-edge modern musical, *The Lodestone.* He has succeeded against all odds, for at the play's end we are truly convinced that a redemptive family story is not only possible but (with an enormous amount of sacrifice) the achievable ideal.

Family dynamics prove to be an eternal wellspring of inspiration for drama, and the play's premise sets us up with what we think is a predictable story, akin to the plot of an epic novel. Set in an impressionistic seaside port city, *The Lodestone* chronicles a brief period in the family saga of the widowed Judith Wade and her two sons, Jeremy and Benjamin. The time is more or less the present, and that the play succeeds in wooing the audience is a wonder, for one would expect the story to be set in the turbulent nineteenth century or the speakeasy days of Prohibition rather than in the complex and postmodern world of contemporary America, where the entire concept of family is in question. The success is partially attributable to the deft use of modern music, a combination of abstract fusion and classic rock forms. Since the composer was schooled in classical and church music, this writer assumed the writing would be predictable and cliché, but from the outset the production delights in proving those expectations dead wrong: Mr. Everett is a true musical chameleon, convincingly changing style and color to not only suit individual characters but to become a perfect vehicle to convey their innermost feelings.

The story follows a path suspiciously similar to Brecht's *Mother Courage*, to the extent that the audience is nearly duped into labeling the show a rewrite. But Judith steps widely out of that opportunist's boots when she risks everything for her wandering son's welfare. Her audacity in letting him have his own way seems at first foolish, but by the end we wonder if she knew in advance what would happen, or if she secretly holds an advanced degree in psychology (or led a previous life as a wise empress), for her parenting skills are a marvel. She spends little time in the spotlight; we are not treated to most of her inner thoughts, and yet she emerges as not only the play's real protagonist but its heroine as well. Maureen MacLaren, despite meager stage time, steps up to the echelons of Judi Dench's performance in *Shakespeare in Love,* creating a powerful and memorable character that practically follows us home, with her fearless and tenacious belief that children can be really messed up and really worth loving at the same time.

The composer tells the tale mostly through the first-person views of the two sons: the loss of their father in a boating tragedy is barely hinted at, but subtle lyrics clue us in. The two young men are nearly opposites; they do not think alike, live alike, or sing alike. One is a paramount of virtue, focused on the family business, faithful, consistent, and inwardly angry as hell; the other, a wanderlust, self-centered, insecure, lost. The only way either can come to fruition and completeness, in this production at least, is through a working relationship with his mother. The shock is that the final relationships are not dysfunctional. Although the play's ending is left up to the viewer, one feels almost certain that things will work out and that these wildly differing young men will come to not only understand but embrace each other in the best kind of family way.

Roger Morris plays the younger son with frenetic power, his ample baritone clear and beseeching for acceptance. His performance is marked with the success of subtlety too, because

Opening Night

although the lyrics are excellent, he makes them believable. The composer himself plays the older, more stable brother, a veritable tenor Javert in focused intensity. Mr. Everett's reversal of the "higher voice, younger age" standard jars expectations but serves the story line most effectively: we wonder who these people are rather than settling into comfortable stereotypes and biases.

Something about *The Lodestone* cries that we've heard it all before, and rebukes us for not believing the message that reconciliation within one's family is indeed possible. It begs us to take hopefulness out of the theater and onto the street, into the office, or into the home with us, where the searching, waiting heart of Mother Judith will always welcome us home. Not to a punishing bowl of soggy corn flakes and cold coffee, but to a gourmet feast lit by candlelight, complete with hearty red wine and homemade bread.

"Nice review!" exclaimed Julie, after he'd read it to her. "Can we go to the dress rehearsal together?"

"It's all set, darlin'," he answered, kissing her head. "Gwen's set up to watch Sam for the evening. I'd hate to go all alone..."

"I'm proud of him. That Bryce of yours. He's had an uphill battle with this, I'm sure."

Stephen nodded. What was with her? She had no such intimate friend that he knew of, but she never begrudged him time with his. Well, perhaps she did have such a friend, over in Uganda: he read Charity's letters to her. It was as if Julie had nothing left of herself but the solid gold core. But maybe it was his idealism speaking. Maybe she was just too tired to do anything but drift with the current that was life, after braving the rapids and crashing into the rocks and being crushed by whirling water to the bottom...

"Does Madeleine like it?" she asked.

The Wrong Side of Eternity

"Huh?"

"Does his wife like the piece?"

"She *looked* interested but not enthralled. Maddy's a deep well, Jules—she thinks a long time before she ventures an opinion."

"But can she ever venture an opinion!" Julie laughed. "I heard her speak once: so classy, so confident. Eloquent, I guess. I saw you, you hung on her every word. It was beautiful."

"That's what makes the two of them such a grand pair," concluded Stephen. *Not that you'd ever see them on the same stage.*

84. UNIVERSITY LIBRARY

Madeleine sipped cappuccino from a paper cup as she scanned the university paper and found a small article in the theater arts section. Some academic thespian had penned a review:

> Mr. Everett's extraordinary composition is a remarkable blend of classical and modern musical styles, demanding the richness of tone and fluidity from others that he is himself so capable of as a performer. The content of his modern parable, however, is about three hundred years past due. His passionate portrait of a loving but firm parent belongs in the historical period preceding the Enlightenment, and a contemporary audience will find it a strain to accept such a portrayal of a deposed deity. There is a high degree of appeal to the imagination, and a challenge to logic, considering the more idealistic tendencies of the lyrics. On the whole, Mr. Everett is spending an immense treasure of musical and dramatic talent to convey a message that will fall upon a host of deaf ears.

Her heart sank. They had already deemed it a failure before it even opened.

85. Dress Rehearsal, the Following Week

He settled Julie next to him under the overhang of the balcony. They'd had trouble finding a parking spot and had made it into the auditorium just as the stage manager finished his introductory remarks, reminding everyone to turn off cell phones and beepers. Stephen looked around; the house was about a third full. Reporters, theater and music students, the understudies, and a smattering of family members. Madeleine sat close to the front, on the right side of the house, her ever-present stenographer's pad poised and ready. She could write in the dark, he knew, and she would, pulling out her notes at the earliest opportunity so she could to let Bryce know exactly what she thought. Stephen had always admired her for that, never taking someone else's word as seriously as she took her own.

From the moment the music started, he sat rapt in the presence of his friend's greatness. Better than any Andrew Lloyd Webber thing he'd ever heard, the composition grabbed his attention, transporting him to the gritty world of the wharf. Halfway through the overture, the scrim at the back of the stage lit up, revealing a silhouetted scene of someone perishing at sea, the dissonant chords sufficing for a man's cries as dark waves pulled him under. A rock-jazz fusion with modern overtones and classic Broadway musical structure. Not that he was qualified to offer any real critique. He was far too involved in the process: he'd listened to Bryce dream this for years.

Stunned by the quality, the O'Connells remained in their seats while the audience ambled out to the lobby during the intermission. Julie wouldn't trust her compromised vision to negotiate the crowds; she always chose either a late or early entrance to church services now. She nestled up to him.

"It's brilliant. I'm enraptured."

"He's worked so hard, pulling it together."

"And he'd have given up, if it weren't for you."

The Wrong Side of Eternity

"Ha."

"No, really, Stephen. You kept up his interest, nurtured him into this. You showed that you believe in him. That's all it takes, really."

"We've hardly talked, the last decade," he answered, with a tiny hint of bitterness.

"It doesn't matter, the quantity."

He looked over at her, feeling small. She was right. Quality. Had he done for Bryce what she'd done for him, just by believing? The house lights flashed their summons, and people responded: no one appeared to have left early. A good sign.

Thirty minutes into the second act, Julie gave his forearm a little squeeze and quietly got up to exit. Of course, she needed the restroom. He motioned to help her but she waved him off, pointing toward the stage. She knew how important this was to him. He smiled and let her go. *I mustn't baby her.*

Stephen leaned forward, his eyes drifting not only across the stage but over the entire house as Roger, downstage right, worked up to his intense soliloquy, deciding whether or not to return home. Bryce stood dimly lit upstage left, where a villain would normally be placed. It leant a gothic air to the jarring notes that elevated Roger's solo above the small pit orchestra, cordoned off with a wooden screen from the audience's view. Every single person in the audience was giving full attention. He could almost hear their heartbeats racing...

Something felt amiss. He got up to find his wife.

Opening the foyer door as softly as possible, even though the music was increasing in volume, he emerged into the lobby. To his right, a little flash of movement caught his eye. The chain across the entrance to upstairs, along with the sign BALCONY CLOSED, was swinging slightly. Just like her, to impulsively go up to check out the change of perspective. Looking around for a censorial usher and seeing no one—they must have all gone inside to watch the show—he followed. Not wanting to attract anyone's attention, he stepped over the chain and tiptoed up the steps, which were not lit, and entered the walkway just behind the upper-level seats. The aisle lights were off; the only glow came from the dim EXIT signs above his head and to his left. He had to squint to look around for Julie.

A theater tech in a black hooded sweatshirt had set up a tripod just behind the banister below him and was fiddling with the videotaping equipment, standing now to pan across the stage, where Roger was lit from above with a column of high-beam magenta. A neon blue light beam overshadowed Bryce, standing with his fists clenched and raised. They had discussed this at rehearsal. The scene had been written to subtly show the older brother's intense anger even though Roger was the one singing. As if they felt the same but from widely differing points of view. Stephen anticipated the loud train whistle that would end the song, symbolizing the decision made by the prodigal to go back. Stephen's search for Julie was, for the moment, thwarted by the high drama of the story unfolding on the stage below.

The techie stepped back just long enough for Stephen to notice that the tripod was empty: there was no video camera perched upon it. The guy was looking at the stage, then down, adjusting something. He lifted a long, thick cylinder to his right shoulder and Stephen's breathing stopped short. An assault rifle of some kind.

"DON'T!" he heard himself shout, drowned out by the reverberating train whistle that shook the building, obscuring even the music. Roger had covered his head with his hands in surrender, and the techie whirled around, catching sight of Stephen at the back of the balcony.

"Shit," Stephen heard him say, as quick footsteps and another blur of motion filled his peripheral vision, but something slammed into his stomach, burning a hole through him. Julie flew down the other aisle and hurled into the assailant, knocking them both off balance. Stephen pitched forward, and time slowed. Between the shot and the time he hit the steps of the aisle in front of him, the train whistle stopped and a thudding crash sounded from below.

Madeleine heard the crash just as the train whistle ended, and whirled around. A scuffle was going on just below the edge of the balcony, and

The Wrong Side of Eternity

she saw someone pick up a rifle of some sort from the aisle. She dropped to the floor, where Bryce joined her five long seconds later.

"You all right?" she asked him.

"Yeah, fine. You?"

"Just shook up a bit. What's going on?"

"I'm not sure," he answered, his hand on her shoulder. "Roger says he heard gunfire up in the balcony."

"How would he know? He was singing."

"He's so tuned in to the audience, Madeleine—he notices everything."

Bryce stood up to survey the scene, and she pulled him back down. Her heart was pounding inside her blouse, and she closed her eyes to slow her breathing.

"Wasn't there any security at the door?" she asked, wondering how something like this could happen, how someone could spoil the show so awfully.

"Same as always: students."

"Goddamn fucking bitch, I'll *kill* her!" a man at the back shouted.

Bryce lifted his head to see some guy wearing black, thrashing but restrained by three men; he glared at a limp form draped over the edge of a seat just below the balcony.

A woman, Bryce realized, *with red hair.*

Stephen lay unable to move, his body a slab of concrete, telling himself it was a good thing that his feet were higher than his head, it would help with the shock...

He remembered his father taking him to a magic show when he was about seven, and watching a woman being sawn in half—this is how it must feel.

Beyond a cataract of burning pain, he heard someone scream. Seconds ticked by as the music faltered, the house lights flared up, and bustling noises rose upward from the main floor of the auditorium. A rivulet of blood splashed on the tiled step in front of his face; the metallic smell blended with dust from the floor. It took a moment for him to

Opening Night

realize it was his own. *Oh God*, he thought. *Where's Julie? Bryce. Sam, with Gwen...Maddy. God, no.*

Somewhere in the far distance, almost in the realm of his imagination and just before he lost consciousness, Stephen heard a man's furious shout mount up from the abyss: "Goddamn fucking bitch, I'll *kill* her!"

He would not know until much, much later that it was too late, that Julie had gone over the banister with the thwarted assassin, that she had landed on the back of a metal theater seat, breaking her neck.

86. UNIVERSITY HOSPITAL, INTENSIVE CARE UNIT

Some woman's hand held his. It was warm and firm.

"Julie?" he mumbled.

"I'm sorry, no," came Reverend Margaret's voice.

Of course. Julie's hand would be cold by now. Hot tears spilled out of his closed eyes, and he squeezed back.

That night during shift exchange, he lay in agony, burning alive in a hospital bed. All he wanted to do was to pass out, to sleep...it would end, eventually, somehow. The pain of loss wouldn't. It hurt longer and deeper than a gunshot wound. The surgical scars would be visible, but they would stop hurting.

By the time the nurse checked him, he was panting and sweating, clenching his teeth and groaning out loud.

He drifted in and out of consciousness, and when he approached twilight, he often heard the Voice. Melodious, it flowed like river water over smooth stones and held the words from the Psalms: "Have mercy upon me, O LORD, according to Your loving-kindness..." At times he felt a tear coursing down his cheek; when the Voice was there, a gentle hand would brush it away.

325

The Wrong Side of Eternity

"Where's Sam?" he asked the Voice.

"With Gwen, Bryce's sister. She's the best thing in the world for him. But he misses his dad."

"I miss him too. Stuck here for a while, I guess…Bryce okay?"

"Yeah, he's fine. Sends his love."

Stephen asked no further questions of the Voice, and he drifted again.

Kate, the ICU nurse, asked her supervisor, "Who's that in twenty-seven?"

"Oh, the regular visitor? Says he's the patient's brother."

"Odd," said the intern, who leaned against a counter writing notes in a chart. "They don't look a thing alike." His tone indicated that he suspected they were lovers.

"Maybe half brother, then." Billie, the charge nurse, had a reputation for being generous. Although hospital policy forbade visits from anyone except immediate family and the clergy, she screened all comers and allowed in anyone she felt would bring comfort or support. Related or not.

Kate ventured, "As long as his visits don't upset the patient or other family members…"

"…we'll let it go," Billie replied.

It's time to operate, decided Madeleine. The liberal cancer had spread and would kill Stephen's soul soon, if it went unchecked. The experience in Uganda, running into all those zealous missionaries, apparently hadn't done it. She couldn't imagine his being so dense, with all the trauma, the plagues, the fiery preaching he must have heard over there. It seemed God had left it up to her.

Boundaries. The relationship needed to be severed. The sharper the scalpel, the less the bruising, the less the pain. Madeleine would be merciful; she would be sharp. It was the only way. She must act now, while he was vulnerable enough to really take in what she had to say. Her heels drummed a soft rhythm on the thin carpet of the hospital hallway.

She turned a corner and ran into Roger, who was just leaving Stephen's room.

"Why, Madeleine! Glad to see you. He's waking up a bit now and seems to like having company. Although he's hurting quite a bit." He paused. "Where words are scarce, they are seldom spent in vain," he quoted, "for they breathe truth, that breathe their words in pain. Go easy on him, Maddy."

She smiled weakly and forced politeness. Roger was not the company that Stephen needed right now.

"How's Bryce?" Roger asked her.

"You see him as much as I do—you should know."

"Ah, but we're not so intimately acquainted. He seems to be coping. The show's going well...I've only seen you at two performances, though."

It *was* going well, she mused. The reviews were favorable from every quarter. Even the conservatives were willing to concede that the contemporary medium and setting, although not recommended for the edification of Christians, might draw some lost souls to the light. Pre-evangelism, that's what they called it. Preparing the soil for the seed of the gospel. Someone had to do it.

"I've been working."

Roger's face crinkled with concern. "Something wrong with your voice, Maddy? It sounds hoarse."

She opted to not tell him that Bryce was pushing her to see a doctor about it.

"Just a frog in my throat, Roger."

"Hope it doesn't keep you from speaking—you're awfully good at what you do," he said, lifting his eyebrows twice. Which she found unsettling, knowing his affiliation with the Urban Gospel Church. He glanced at his watch. "Uh-oh. Got to get to the theater, I'm almost late for call. Hope to see you again soon." He nodded politely, as if he wanted to shake her hand but was unsure if she would find that acceptable, and headed briskly down the corridor.

The Wrong Side of Eternity

She entered the room gingerly, hoping Stephen was awake. His expression was blank, his breathing shallow.

"Let me guess: his sister," said Kate.
"So she tells me," answered Billie.

"I need to make something clear, Stephen."
"Mmmm."
"More than a request. For Bryce's sake."
He opened his eyes, even though the room blurred. "Hello, Maddy. Nice of you to come," he slurred. He sighed and waited. He never knew what Madeleine was going to pull from up her sleeve.
"You sound like you're on narcotics."
"I am. Can't quite see you clearly."
"Then let me talk. Bryce can't be here for you right now. We weren't expecting you to show up so soon in the States."
"I know that."
"Stephen, your letters upset us both. He's lost sleep trying to understand, praying for you. Your life has been too different—we can't expend the energy trying to relate to what you've been through. You can't be his hero, he'll tear himself apart thinking he owes you his life. You've got to seek comfort, get support from some other quarter. I'm only trying to be honest with you, for your own good."

Bryce's sake, Stephen's good—who was it for, really? *"For God's sake, Maddy, Julie's dead,"* he murmured. What kind of cruel game was she playing? It was a test, right? To see how he would respond. In his condition. He was hardly capable of thinking, much less taking on a debate queen. And she didn't *know. She needs to know.*
He would tell her; he obviously had nothing to lose.
"Maddy," he sighed, his mouth dry, his speech slightly thick. He licked his lips and tried his best to articulate. "Bryce was not the target." He paused, and thankfully she waited, primly perched on the bedside

Opening Night

chair, clutching her purse. "I was above and behind him, I saw over that gunman's shoulder," he pressed on, taking in a quivering breath. "He wasn't aiming at the stage." The words were slurred but comprehensible, to his relief. "He was aiming at *you*."

"You're not listening, Stephen." She looked backward, over her own shoulder toward the door. Then at her watch. "The hospital chaplain is heading this way," she observed. "Perhaps he can give you the support you need right now. I can't, and Bryce can't. We aren't your kind of people. But it's not too late, Stephen. We care about you. We want you to surrender to God's will for your life."

The words hung in the air like dust motes. He tentatively changed position; her composure ruffled at his weight upon the bed.

"You need to know, Maddy."

"Know what? I know enough already. The police report gave both you and Julie credit…"

"Julie didn't save Bryce's life."

"No. She acted on impulse, after she heard you yell. She couldn't see the stage. She didn't know what she was doing. You'd like Bryce to be in your debt, I know, but…"

"She saved *yours*."

At first she didn't hear him.

The words would haunt her later when she got undressed for bed, alone. A gunman. Stalked to the café parking lot, to the theater. Saved by a Muslim, then a fallen, liberal woman. *No. It can't be possible*, she would tell herself. But for now, she had to fulfill her mission.

"Don't contact us, Stephen." There. The surgery was done. He would be cast upon the grace of God now, if only some Ms. Reverend didn't undo it all with worthless comforts. Her heels clicked their way down the hall, an angry rhythm.

She fled.

Exit Music

Out-worn heart, in a time out-worn,
Come clear of the nets of wrong and right;
Laugh, heart, again in the grey twilight;
Sigh, heart, again in the dew of morn.

—W. B. Yeats

87. The Theater, after a Performance

Bryce was ready to head out the door, when Roger walked up to him.

"Have a minute?"

"Sure. Why?"

"We need to talk. About something other than the show."

Bryce scowled. *Yeah? Why does Roger look so miffed?* "Okay." He sat down.

Roger launched into his concern. "About Stephen."

"He's my best friend," Bryce explained.

"Seriously? You were his best man, I know *that* much. What's wrong?"

"What do you mean?"

"The guy almost died, Bryce! I heard his voice, up in the balcony. He took a bullet meant for someone here. Maybe *you*. Why haven't you gone to see him?"

"Roger, I hardly think..."

"He *loves* you. Not like Ben and me, maybe, but definitely."

330

Opening Night

"And?"

"What keeps you from giving something back? Your time, your interest, your *anything?*"

Bryce paused. *What to say, how to say it.* The artist's call was always the priority. One couldn't be distracted. He answered carefully. "Maddy's wondered about his stability, maybe his life getting derailed during his time overseas."

"What about *you?*"

Bryce answered with silence.

Roger pressed on. "Look, Bryce, I know you love your wife, but *you* lived with him, you know him better than she does. Have you ever thought she might be wrong? You're perfect, mostly: you're rich, you're successful, you have a formidably gorgeous wife, you're idolized... and you're a rotten friend."

You don't get it, Roger. You don't understand. "This is rude of you, Roger. Stephen respects my time commitments, my priorities."

"—And loves you anyway. Or is that what bothers you? Being loved by another man? If it's about the art, Bryce, relationships are art. Love is art."

"You're getting too personal."

"You Brits! So repressed, so innocent..."

"That's enough, Roger. I didn't have a brother growing up, like you did."

"*Poor Bryce.* Of course you did: Stephen's been there for you, for *years.* You just never admit it. *What are you so afraid of, Bryce?*" After a moment, Roger turned and strode away, his hands falling to his sides in defeat.

88. THREE BLOCKS FROM THE EVERETT'S TOWNHOUSE

Bryce looked up at the hospital façade, brightly lit against the scrim of a foggy night. *I should have come sooner.* He went through the automatic doors and smiled at the receptionist.

"Am I too late for visiting hours?" he asked.

331

The Wrong Side of Eternity

"No, they end at nine," she answered.

"In what room is Stephen O'Connell?"

"Let me see..." She peered at the computer screen. "I'm sorry," she said. "He was discharged two days ago."

89. SPECIALTY CLINICS PARKING LOT, EARLY MARCH

Bryce parked his little Nissan and warily approached the clinic. Madeleine had phoned him to let him know she had a follow-up appointment with the specialist she saw only a week ago. It was too soon for a follow-up. Something was not right. Not that she routinely invited him to sit in on her doctors' appointments. The only time they'd gone together was during those weeks of trying to find out the source of their infertility. They'd each weathered invasive tests and ended up sitting on one side of a walnut desk, holding hands, while the doctor sat on the other side, explained the problem, and reviewed their options.

Driving here, he had begun to speculate. A benign result on a biopsy wouldn't warrant more than a phone call, would it? Didn't they just send you an "It's all fine, have a nice day" letter? Or did they add appointments on top of appointments because the docs only had twenty minutes for each patient—one problem at a time, please—and some required forty-five? Or were they all just greedy—more visits, more fees? Medicine was so secretive! The experts had you over a barrel; one's whole life could revolve around medical appointments. His father had told him things weren't much better in England. Different, but not better.

The past few weeks had been so rough. Maddy not being able to talk, giving her voice a rest. Writing everything down, using improvised mime in lieu of sign language.

She'd hit the wall of frustration on the second day, throwing her shoes, grimacing, shaking her head. He'd had to lead her to the garage and show her how to pound on the wall with her fists. Then he'd gone

Opening Night

back inside to cook dinner while she pummeled the sheetrock for the next ten minutes straight.

She was so strong, so determined. Whatever it was, she would beat it. His job was merely to support her, give her space and provide enough diversion to keep her mind off it. He took her to the zoo, out on picnics, to the planetarium, to a movie.

By the end of the week, she had begun to brighten a little. She had smiled when he poured her a glass of chardonnay, when he sat next to her on the sofa and picked up her feet to massage them. But she hadn't smiled that morning. And she didn't tell him, until she left a phone message that afternoon, that she had an appointment.

Halfway across the parking lot, he saw her exit through the double glass doors, walking slowly in a state of utter shock. He hurried to the steps and looked up; she saw him and descended, still slowly. This was so unlike her. When she reached the level of the sidewalk, he tilted his head to ask her.

Madeleine began to shake, there in broad daylight. He stepped forward to take her hand, but she fell against him instead, sobbing silently. Her inner dam broke, and her voice, scratchy and pitiful, howled in anguish. He ignored the stares of people passing by and enfolded her in his arms.

He thought about whether he should lead her to a bench, sheltered by tree and hedge apart from the crowd, but something stopped him from exerting pressure on her to do so. *Right*, he answered the prompt, *she needs to stand*. She needs to keep standing, just with support.

They stood that way for a long time, and finally, without a word, Bryce escorted her to the waiting car and home. He would return that evening to collect the BMW.

The next day, she sat down at the kitchen table and took up a pen and notepad.

She's so pale! she could almost hear Bryce thinking as he sat down across from her, ready for their now-usual conversation.

333

The Wrong Side of Eternity

B, where r those aerograms from Africa? I want 2 read them over again, she wrote.

"My desk, top drawer. Help yourself, darling. I've no secrets to hide from you," he said, taking her hand and kissing it.

That makes one of us, thought Madeleine, *but I hope to change that soon.*

90. St. Simeon's Parish Hall, Late March

Rev. Margaret approached Stephen as he sat distancing himself from well-wishing mourners in the parish hall. She took Sam's hand and placed it on his father's shoulder. Sam left it there and stood. Margaret knelt down to catch Stephen's lost gaze. She let him speak first.

"I liked that prayer."

She handed him a card, and he read aloud the sentences that had spoken to his heart: *"LORD, vouchsafe her light and rest, peace and refreshment, joy and consolation, in Paradise...in the ample folds of Thy great love. Grant that her life—so troubled here—may enfold itself in Thy sight, and find a sweet employment in the spacious fields of eternity."* His eyes were dull as he looked at his priest. "You called her a saint."

"She was. In every sense of the word. I might have added martyr, but it's lost its meaning."

He nodded. "How did you know?"

"You aren't the only person in the room to have known how special she was."

"Is."

"*Is.* I stand corrected."

"So many misjudged her. So many. Christians. How could they not know?" He looked into her gray eyes.

She sat down next to him. Gently. "Saints scare people, Stephen. They're like mirrors: they show us where we've gone wrong. If you look

Opening Night

deep enough, you can see the reflection of the sky behind them. If you look deep enough. Which you did." She handed him a paper plate laden with finger sandwiches, olives, tuna-covered crackers. "Eat."

Blinking through tears, he wanly smiled and nodded, taking the plate.

Later, Bryce stepped gingerly up to him as he stood staring out the window, put his hands on Stephen's arms and turned him around.

"I'm so sorry, mate," he said. Stephen stood statue-still, his face a blank.

Madeleine watched from across the room. She wondered if he'd make it through this. Of course he would: he'd lived next door to a genocide, gone through malaria. He saw and heard horrible things over there. And she'd always thought him so weak! She couldn't go up to him to talk, because she was on strict orders to not use her voice. They'd scheduled surgery and more specialist visits for follow-up. But it was probably just as well: she didn't know what to say to him anyway. She wished some relevant scripture would pop into her head, so she could write him a note, but nothing came. Except a verse from an old legend—she'd memorized it in grade school—which she couldn't get to shut up inside her head:

'In former times it was my fatal chance
To be the proudest maiden even known.
By birth I was the daughter of a king,
Though now a breathless tree and senseless thing.'

That's me, all right, she admitted, and she took Bryce's arm, motioning with her head that it was time to go.

91. The O'Connells' Temporary Residence, a Week Later

He sat in the dark with red wine in his glass. Alone. Earlier he and Sam had been at Gwen's watching *Toy Story Two*. That song would not

The Wrong Side of Eternity

leave his head; it played over and over, and he remembered during the film how his heart rate had sped up, how he sweated when the lyrics described a little girl growing up to leave her doll behind: "when she loved me..." But it was not Julie that met his memory's gaze.

It was Bryce.

The world was wrong. He threw the glass against the cream-colored wall. It shattered, and a purple stream, like a tear, ran down into the carpet.

92. Mercy Cathedral Reception, Holy Week

Stephen nervously tapped his finger on the lamp table; the dean entered with an air of graceful humility. As the occasion warranted.

"Good afternoon. I understand you were inquiring about the quilts." The cathedral was famous for its stylized memorials of those who had died of AIDS. "How can I help you?"

"I know, sir," began Stephen, not knowing how to address a dean. *Your worship? Too African.* "I know all about confidentiality. I've worked in health care. I lost a friend some time ago and was hoping to find her name on one of the quilts."

The dean listened carefully.

"I lost touch with her in the early eighties. I know that's a long time ago. I've been praying for her ever since."

"We keep the older quilts on rods, much like carpets are displayed in the furniture stores. If you'd be willing to be accompanied by the sexton, I have no objection to your looking them over." He did not smile, and his voice was gentle.

Stephen offered his sincere gratitude and stood up. The dean shook his hand, and the power of the man's touch nearly made him cry. How a simple handshake could be so embracing...a mystery.

The sexton led the way, and they walked along several hallways to a large room. It could have been a banquet hall or a basketball court; it

Opening Night

seemed to have gone through several remodelings. At the far end hung the quilts. The sexton, a man who seemed dressed in worldly experience, asked if Stephen would mind if he sat near the door while he looked, an unexpected offer of additional privacy. And the rather elderly gentleman seemed to welcome a break.

Stephen stepped up to the hangings, feeling like he was entering a morgue to identify a body. For he knew, deep down, that she was dead. He'd felt it, early in the Uganda days. And his last phone call with her had haunted him, prompting prayer. He'd entirely given up on content, recently, and just spoke her name to God, sometimes with a question mark. No answer had come; he did not give up praying.

He reached up to open the great book made of fabric, turning the "pages" from left to right, like reading Hebrew or Arabic. He scanned the names and felt waves of memory and love and sorrow cascading down on him...

JIM NOVAK—WHAT A GUY!

SALLY Q, I LOVE YOU.

JESSICA, NOW WITH JESUS INSTEAD OF ME, I'M JEALOUS...

The messages rained down and the room lit up with holiness. Stephen blinked and turned another fabric page. He scanned again.

On the fourth quilt page, he saw her name. DIANE SHAW, HEART-BREAKER, it said. And in the center of that gorgeous piece of artwork, full of color and love, were the words, cross-stitched in heavy silk, like a sampler, TEARS ARE THE JEWELS OF SORROW. He touched her name, touched his breast, touched his lips. He must have stood there another five minutes, before turning back to the sexton, who slouched comfortably in the chair by the door.

The wind hit his face when he exited the cathedral.

"Now we can talk, now you're beyond all the shit. Mine and everyone else's. Someone called you a heartbreaker, but we know, Diane, that the biggest heart you broke was your own. Now you know, now you understand, and if it weren't for you, I wouldn't have a clue...I never would have gotten it." The tears were running down his cheeks, but he didn't bother to wipe them off; his hands remained deep in his pockets, trying to find warmth. He didn't care if someone saw him talking to the air and suspected he was another homeless madman. "Thank you, love," he said, hoping that the gratitude would find its target. "Thank you so much. May you know joy and fulfillment and all good, now and evermore." It didn't seem quite enough. "And if you meet Julie, and I hope you do, say hello for me. Amen."

The wind died suddenly, and he looked up to see a stream of light piercing the edge of a very dark cloud. He kept an eye on that streak all the way to the transit station, putting all fears for her finally to rest.

Late that evening, the telephone rang. Who would call after nine? His heart beating rapidly, he rose to answer it.

"Hello?"

"Stephen? Stephen O'Connell?"

"Yes?"

"This is Sam Stuart—from SBC, long years ago."

"Sam...Oh, Sam!"

"Uh-huh." He cleared his throat. "I was at the funeral the other day..."

"You knew Julie?" He hadn't seen him there, but he had been pretty out of it.

"Not as well as you, but we'd had some pretty remarkable conversations."

When she was dating that SBC guy, before I came along, Stephen guessed.

"Special gal."

"Very. What prompts the call, Sam?"

"Obviously, to offer my condolences, although that's putting it way too cheaply." Stephen sniffled; there was a longish pause. "I've sort of kept up with you through the years, and sadly enough never put pen to paper to let you know how wonderful your prayer letters were. I was thinking about you, wondering if you have any plans."

Opening Night

"Well, I'm still convalescing, if that's what you mean," Stephen said. "Beyond that, I've no clue."

"Can I ask you something personal?"

"Sure. I've nothing left to lose."

"What do you love to do? Think. What have you always loved to do?"

"You caught me off guard, Sam. Hold on a minute." He squeezed his eyes shut and tried to sort through pounding waves of thought. Names, faces, conversations... "I guess I really enjoy listening to what people want to do, then encouraging them to do it."

"Bingo. Would you like to turn that into a career?"

"What?"

"Would you like to make a living doing just that?"

"I think you know I would, once I'm up and running...it'll be a good couple of weeks yet. What exactly did you have in mind?"

"There's a position open at Millennium College, where I've been the last eight years, which would suit you perfectly. You'd have to start in on a doctorate, but you could work with undergrads, entry-level course teaching. A pushover for you. They'd love you here."

"I haven't many answers, Sam, to offer *anybody*."

"That's exactly why it would work. This place is a refuge for earnest, honest seekers of truth with good hearts. Shit, that sounds so pious and trite. But it's true. Eclectics and scholars, and humble ones for a change. And the culture's quieter than where you are..."

"Where in Sam Hill *is* Millennium?" He'd never heard of it.

"Central Oregon. Hill country. Lots of fishing. Very pretty. Mountains on one side of you, high desert the other."

"Can I have some time to think it over?"

"Absolutely. Just call me when you want to talk—*whenever* you want to talk. And come up and see us when you're up to traveling."

"My in-laws live up there. We were planning a trip during spring break."

339

The Wrong Side of Eternity

That namesake of his, Sam, could be close to his grandparents. Heck, Stephen needed some family too. "Perfect. We'll put you up." Sam crossed his fingers.

"We?"

"Yeah—I surprised myself by getting married, kind of short notice."

"She must be wonderful, Sam. I look forward to meeting her."

"You already have."

"I have?"

"Her name's Elisabeth Hardesty. She remembers you."

93. Gateway Park, Mid-June

They'd gone to the aquarium to see the octopus and the seahorses, walked in the park and fed birds. Time had not stood still like this since he was in Uganda. Sam was happy, shockingly enough, surrounded by a beautiful world once again. He'd seen lives end abruptly before; why should he not think it normal to have his own mother snatched away?

"Da?" asked Sam, quietly. They were sitting in front of the aquarium glass, watching bright fish swim around the coral.

"Yeah, son."

"Now that Mum's a spirit, can she go wherever she wants?"

"Well, Sam, I'm not altogether sure how it works, once you die. Maybe."

"Because I think she'd like to take an adventure tour, go swimming with the fishes, even the whales..."

"Yeah, she'd like that."

"And she wouldn't have to worry about breathing underwater or drowning, because she's already died."

Stephen nodded, imagining and envying such freedom.

"And she wouldn't ever get too cold." Sam looked up toward his father, who had closed his eyes. "She kind of went out like a supernova, huh?"

Stephen looked back at him. "And not like a black hole. Yup."

Sam put his arm around Stephen's back and they sat there together. Even though he was almost thirteen, Sam fell asleep on his father's lap when they got home, and Stephen carried him to bed. Then he went back into the living room to look at the photo albums, hungry for Julie's face, the light of her hair, her laughter, her touch. He pulled the envelope from his pocket, then he picked up the bamboo letter opener from Rutoki and slid its blade along the top edge. The familiar handwritten scrawl on the paper sped his heart rate.

Dear Stephen, my dear friend,

PLEASE forgive me for taking so long to write. Roger informed me that you were moving north. Just when I could use a really good friend...I realise it's been quite some time since we sat and talked. I've been distracted with the show (sorry about that, really) and time just slipped away. If it weren't for Roger, I wouldn't even have known what all came down during dress rehearsal; so much mayhem, so many uniformed fellows running about. I'm sure he told you that all action stopped right there and the show was postponed for two days. Well, all the publicity certainly didn't hurt the turnout on the actual opening night. We had a sell-out crowd, and within the week we were moving to ACT. Lucky for us it was their off-season and they could clear space. Had to practically bribe several stage carpenters to whip together the required sets. We've settled down into only two shows a week now, giving us a breather and letting us return to our other lives. Except Maureen. Theatre always was her other life, so she just gets time off to roam the countryside and play tourist in the art galleries.

I managed to show up on the periphery of Julie's funeral, but I had no idea what to say to you. I know now that I should have stayed longer and stood by you, like you have done for me so many times. Stupid of me, I can't think why I didn't. Maybe I just needed to hang onto Madeleine, hoping that she wouldn't go away...Although she and Julie weren't very close. She came with me to offer you support. I don't believe you even recognised her when she shook your hand. In shock, you were.

I am botching this letter, but since you and I have been such close mates, I know you'd prefer my awkward language to a mess of false sentiment. I'd rather be stupid with you than false. Although sometimes I'm not sure myself when I'm being authentic or not. That's a toughie, as you told me once.

I'm writing to let you know that we've had some bad news. Maddy would probably write herself except that she's much too distraught. Remember the missive I sent you in Uganda, when we found out we were sterile? This is worse, and I do hope you're sitting down. When you've digested this letter, perhaps you can telephone me at your convenience, because it would do me so much good to hear your voice.

Madeleine's got laryngeal cancer, Stephen. Surgery will be bad enough, but the loss of her voice and hence her career has put her deep into the dumps. You know—you of all people—how hard she can be on herself. Now, with this happening at the peak of her influence, she's taken to doubting everything. Her worth to me, to God. She won't even put makeup on, for God's sake— or mine, or hers. When I walk near her, she just reaches out and grabs my hand, and then the tears flow again. What's scarier even are the days when she doesn't cry at all, when she just sits and stares at the wall. I wonder at times if she contemplates do-ing herself harm.

The dean of Mercy's been good to sit and counsel with me. First he grants me a leave of absence for the show, and then he gives me freely of his precious time. Mostly he listens, but every now and then he's helped me know what to do. Like nothing. Give her space to mourn the loss, he says; give her time to grieve. Lately I've been able to get her outside for maybe a half an hour at a go—we walk around the block, holding hands. So much like the old days, when we had time to do that sort of thing! Why do we ever stop, Stephen? Why do we ever take it all so for granted, as if being healthy and whole is our right in this broken world? When so much of the world is—as you well know—fallen. So arrogant of us!! No one is exempt—sometimes I think Madeleine's despondency comes from that expectation, and then she berates herself for having had it in the first place.

I'm hoping to take her home to the Lake District once the treatments are over. Give her some space and privacy to think, have her all to myself for a change. We could use some time apart: the show's taken its share of me, God knows.

I hope with time that she will feel inspired to write. She's so good with words! Sometimes she tries to write me poems, and they are so raw and small, almost like a little girl trying to fit rhymes to little events. I think someday she'll move beyond the rhyme to reason again, but it will be a seasoned reason—there I go being clever—thoughtfulness. And dare I say? It takes some amount of hurt to make sense of anything.

Remember when we walked all night through the city? It's as if our whole lives were summed up in that visit, because after that I never felt the same about you. To be tender as you are tender, and strong as you are strong...I could never, never be enough of a husband to Madeleine if it were not for my friendship with you. It sounds so cliché to say that, but I would not risk it if it were not so. You taught me so much, just being there to listen to me and all that.

Perhaps we could meet before you go? We needn't say much, words are inadequate, but just to look at the sea together again? Maybe when I have the luxury of another holiday we will come up to the forest lands of Oregon and drop in on you. Maybe we will be able to laugh again, the four of us, because we would want little Sam (not so little anymore, is he?), to feel some of our enduring friendship for you, with you.

The Wrong Side of Eternity

Listen to whimsical me! Sounding like the idealist! Oh, Stephen, I never had a brother, I didn't know how to relate with men. I faked it until you came along. Thank God you did, or I would not be up to the challenges rolling my way.

Love, Bryce

Sam found Stephen asleep on the sofa the next morning, the letter on the floor. He covered his father with the quilt, then went to the kitchen to make him coffee.

94. MILLENNIUM COLLEGE, SEVEN MONTHS LATER

They sat in the fourteenth row, stage right, with Stephen perusing the program of the college's production of *The Fantasticks*. (*"The Fintesstics!"* Ann's voice corrected in his head.) He put the low-budget paper on his lap and glanced to his right, where Cipriana and Sam were taking in the hall. The house was modest but nicely designed, with just enough décor to break up the utilitarian lines of the modern architecture. He turned around to take in the small curved balcony, but the chill that came with memory forced his gaze back to the front, where a heavy curtain hung in front of the stage.

So good of Mama to come here, to give Sam a woman's point of view. He realized that his mother may have had motives of her own, her own need for family, and smiled. Then he shook his head. He seemed always to be sitting on the audience side, always watching someone else's show. Always lending a supportive role offstage. He felt insignificant. So passive! "Unstable as water," the bible verse taunted him. Plain, clear, more-or-less tasteless, having no qualities of its own. Except that it was foundational for life. Just a drop of water, just a cog in the wheel, just a member of the audience.

They were early, and the house lights were good, so he pulled the two letters out of his jacket pocket. He unfolded the four pages of lined paper and soaked in each word. Charity had such beautiful handwriting.

344

Opening Night

Dear Sam,

We miss you here in Rutoki. You were eleven when you left, and now you're a teenager. The children ask about you all the time. I still have your poem tacked to my wall, along with the school picture your father sent me. I hope you will always write to me. Someday, if God gives me the grace (and the air ticket!) I shall fly over to America to see you.

Are you reading all those wonderful books we talked about? You are a really smart boy, so I hope you get good marks and go to university. I think you could be a great scientist, with your curiosity about everything. Keep asking questions: your mum taught me it is safe to do that. She was a wonderful person, Sam. I loved her. When I think of her, I think of you, so please know that you will be in my mind and heart always.

Please write to your Aunt Charity, let her know what you are up to. And if the wind ever blows you back to this part of the world, know that you will always be welcome to stay with me and Peace. Our home is always open to you.

Love, (Aunt) Charity Ntambara

Dear Stephen,

Life in Rutoki is not the same without you. I pass the old guest house, and it will always be *your* house to me. I miss your family more than you will know. The new guest house is full of visitors from abroad—when it is deemed safe for them to travel. The region has not had the stability it hoped for—every now and then the *interahamwe* make an appearance, coming from the bush and killing a few people before going back into hiding. We hope and pray that they will not grow again to create a new wave of hatred among the young people. It seems that when youth are bored or frustrated, they become easy targets for those people to spread the hate of others. It is too sad, that it doesn't seem to ever end.

Reverend Ann continues to become more fluent and preaches entirely on her own now. She will be travelling to New Zealand

The Wrong Side of Eternity

soon, for six months, and we pray she comes back to us. We pray that for you, too, if it is right, some day. Although it may be a painful thing to consider, you would be welcome, and we will be kind to you in your grief. Do not forget us.

I have some happy news and some very sad news. The happy news is that I have received a scholarship to study literature at Makerere University, in the capital. I won the scholarship by submitting some of my writing, a collection of poems I have written through the years. I titled it "The Disappearing Watercourse." I did not have the qualification required to go abroad to study, as Uncle Geoffrey wished, and besides I am getting too old for that, but I can have access to great literature among our dusty books. Foreign donations have fully stocked the library shelves again, they are no longer practically empty as they were in Amin's time. But they are still dusty. Not enough people *want* to read the old classics. They do not think them relevant. Thanks to you, I have seen their value.

Now for the sad news. Your friend my uncle Geoffrey has disappeared. He was going to the airport on his way to the Anglican Conference of Bishops, and he never arrived at the guest house in Kampala. Stephen, it is terrible. He told me about the pain my parents felt during my days of being delayed—I told you why—and now I am feeling some of that emptiness and fear for him. The police do not show much concern. They took a report and assured us they would try very hard to locate him. But I fear he is dead. You know that if you take a stand on anything here, you are putting yourself at risk. And if you are a poor pastor, even a diocesan official, they know you are not worth much of a ransom, not as if you were a *muzungu*.

Stephen, pray for him, and pray for us. The pain is around every turn in the road, every step toward progress is slippery. Some pastors in Rwanda are even urging a return to tribal religion, the appeasement of spirits. How can this be? Is it because

346

Opening Night

they are not paid enough to serve God through the church, that they have been practically reduced to begging for their living, that they can say such things?

I do not see any way forward for us. But God, who has met us in the past, will also meet us in future, so I can sleep at night. The meetings for reconciliation and forgiveness over in Rwanda have petered out. We have gotten quiet again, since Uncle went missing. The awakened ones sing and meet to pray, but never at night now. The situation here is too tense, according to Bishop, for the OCA to consider sending someone else out. Rev. Ann will stay because she wishes to, she has made Rutoki her home.

Please know that my thoughts and prayers are with you, as you move into your teaching position. I wish you the best, in every way. I hope you will become happy again. But I understand completely if that does not happen for a while. Julie was the best person I have ever met in my life. If it were not for her, I would be going nowhere, and growing bitterer by the day. She was my best friend. One could feel loved just being with her. You must miss her terribly. The books she gave me are my most treasured possessions, and I offer you this quote from one: "For truly lovers are near to one another; years make no difference, nor country, nor climate, nor colour. This kind of loving laughs at all dividing things."

With affection in our Lord Jesus Christ, I am your sister,
Charity

Sam wiggled up to him, wrapping his arm around him, so unself-conscious for an adolescent. Like his mother. Stephen's eyes stung; he was glad the lights were beginning to dim as the overture started, so his son couldn't see him crying.

Just before the curtains fell open, at that moment between where the real world ended and the world of Story began, he was comforted by a voice. It was like Roger's voice, but deeper, and it came from someplace

The Wrong Side of Eternity

distant and immediate at the same time. It was like a line from the list of performers in a program: "Witness/ Catalyst: Stephen O'Connell." And just before the show began in earnest, at the moment the stage lights illumined a tattered, hand-lettered banner, he finally understood that life wasn't over, not yet. He might still have a role to play on this side of the curtain.

Encore

We may ignore, but we can nowhere
evade, the presence of God.
The world is crowded with him. He
walks everywhere *incognito*.

—C. S. Lewis

Three Years Later

"Da, just to let you know, I invited someone from out of town to come to my graduation next week," Sam O'Connell said in his most normal voice.

"Who?" his father asked.

"It's a surprise."

Gwen? Margaret? That amazingly wonderful teacher Mrs. Kelly? Who else was he close to, besides the grandparents? Stephen tried to guess, then gave up.

"Staying with us?"

"No—at Sam and Elisabeth's. Our place is too small."

"Nice of them."

"Yup. Well, I'm off to rehearsal."

"Drive carefully."

"I will."

The Wrong Side of Eternity

"Before we dismiss for the year, I want to read you again the passage I started with, back in September," Stephen told the class. "And I want you to carry it into your lives. The social sciences tend toward the analytical, as you have seen, and we need to find balance and wholeness apart from all the statistics."

He could see that this time, they were grasping it. Well, most were.

"Because mystery is horrible to us, we have agreed to avoid it by living in a world of labels and by forgetting that they are mere symbols. We judge by what we see or can name. A wider, sharper, deeper understanding lies right outside our door, but we cannot take it in: except in abnormal moments, we hardly know that it is there. Models and categories do serve a vital purpose. They set boundaries for communication and provide handles for understanding. The difficulty is that they spill over into the world of things that one cannot easily define. In a world that is more and more educated, it is amazing that we so quickly resort to name-calling for either self-promotion or self-defense." He paused, wondering if adding further words would help them at all. "Have a great summer."

And they spilled out the door, clutching their final marks, many of them with smiles of relief on their faces.

———◆———

He walked into the evening air to smell the pines and watch the twilight colors bloom and fade in the western sky. He always went to Julie's grave at this time of day.

Someone was there, wearing a long trench coat, stooping down next to the small brass cross—its green patina blended with the moss—where he'd placed her ashes. A woman. It was hard to see—the light was fading. She had heard his footfalls and held perfectly still.

"Hello?" he said, softly.

She slowly stood and turned around. The tunnel of time enveloped him, her gentleness surrounded him. He recognized her, and she

Encore

smiled. "Your family, they asked me to come," she explained, looking down at the forest floor.

"I'm glad you did, Charity," was all he could say, then.

ACKNOWLEDGMENTS

(AND APOLOGY)

I AM DEEPLY INDEBTED TO many people, especially those who entrusted me with their stories and who shared their memories and feelings in the face of terrible tragedy. Others allowed me access to pertinent information in their archives, particularly the staff at the Makerere University library in Kampala, Uganda, and the Graduate Theological Union library (and the Center for Women and Religion) in Berkeley, California. Former missioners of Mid-Africa Ministry (CMS, London) provided needed hospitality, input, and friendship: David and Cynthia Andrewartha, Marg Walker, the Rev. Sonia Barron and her wonderful husband, Tom. My Ugandan sources were both generous and gracious; some of them lived through circumstances described in the book: Lydia Benda, Grace Baganizi, Agnes Tumwizeere, George Dutki, church canons Fred Mugenge and Zephaniah Mikekemo. Others inspired specific characters, and for obvious reasons they shall remain anonymous.

Stateside, I am indebted to Rev. Cully and Julie Anderson, the Rev. Meg Decker, and dramatist Cass Ludington and her journalist husband, Nick. They provided much encouragement as well as invaluable feedback. Little but important details were furnished me by the Rev. Lee Kiefer, Carmen Guerrero, gun expert Kelsey Hilderbrand, the late Dr. Frank Winter, and my New Zealand acquaintance Jessie Wigzell. I also thank my past AIDS and hospice patients, and those medical

The Wrong Side of Eternity

professionals dedicated to their care, for sharing with me the present-day passion so dismissed by contemporary values.

Many people read and offered feedback on the manuscript, but special attention was provided by Carrie Tucker-Pollard and Dr. Maureen Gatt.

As to the numerous technical errors contained in this book, I take full responsibility for each and every one; some are made in ignorance and some for the sake of brevity. My use of the English language got pretty messed up during all my years abroad, so I'm very grateful for the help of CreateSpace editor Andrea in polishing my many rough spots. Finally, after the example of Robert Louis Stevenson, I beg the reader to allow some leeway in my renaming geographical places and changing dates to suit the story line.

Finding "sermons in stones…and good in everything" might express kernels of Idealism in Shakespeare, but it is essential to my models, who live (and die) in hope despite tragedy and terror. When we ignore them and what is revealed through them, we find ourselves on the wrong side of eternity.

GLOSSARY AND ABBREVIATIONS

ACT   American Conservatory Theater (San Francisco, California)
AEC   AIDS Education Council (fictional)
Aerogram   a lightweight paper, usually light blue, folded into a letter
Ankole   region in Western Uganda
Bazungu   Westerners, white people
Bickies   New Zealand term for cookies (American) or biscuits (British)
Da   an Irish term for father
Data weh Kinyarwanda exclamation, can translate loosely as "my God"
Diocese   an Anglican word for a region or collection of churches
Horchata a beverage from Mexico made from rice, vanilla, cinnamon, and sugar
Ibirunga also *Virunga*, chain of volcanoes straddling Rwanda, Uganda, and Congo
Ikidongo Ugandan folk string instruments
Imandwa   ancestral spirits, African tribal religion
Interahamwe civilian perpetrators of the Rwandan genocide
ITS   International Theological Seminary (fictional)
Kabiizi   trade town in southwestern Uganda (fictional)

Kigali	Capital of Rwanda
Kitenge	a rectangular cloth, often used as a wraparound skirt
Koran	the Qur'an: Muslim holy book, archaic spelling (still used in Africa)
Kyrie Eleison	Greek for "Lord, have mercy"
Lugandan	the language spoken by the Baganda, a Ugandan people group
Magnificat	the Song of Mary as recorded in St. Luke chapter 1
Matatu	a taxi, usually a small minibus
M. Div	Master of Divinity degree
Médecins sans Frontières	Doctors without Borders, a medical-aid society
Missioner	a more current word for missionary
MK	missionary kid, a child who grows up in another country
MP	Member of Parliament, a political office
Mukezi	town in south-central Uganda (fictional)
Muzungu	Westerner, white person (singular)
NAC	Native Anglican Church (fictional)
Ntabgoba	town in Rwanda where OCA has a clinic (fictional)
Ntore	name of a men's dance troupe, based on Rwandan warrior culture
Nyabo	madame, title for a married woman
OCA	Outreach to Central Africa, a mission group in England (fictional)
Panga	machete
Posho	porridge made from corn flour
PT	physical (physio) therapist
RACIS	Rutoki AIDS Counseling and Information Service (fictional)
RP	religious pervert/prostitute/pagan, a term of derision (fictional)
RPF	Rwanda Patriotic Front
Rutoki	Ugandan village near the border of Rwanda (fictional)

SBC	Scholars Bible College (fictional)
Twa	loose designation for 'pygmy' people groups in Western Uganda
UNHCR	United Nations High Commission for Refugees
USDA	US Department of Agriculture
WGD	Women for Global Development (fictional)

Quotation Sources

MANY QUOTATIONS IN THIS STORY are paraphrases incorporated into the dialogue and thoughts of the characters. They are listed by page number (on the left). If the source is given in the text or if they are created fiction, no reference is provided below. Nearly all details in the story were furnished by *individuals* rather than books.

21	Ambrose Bierce, from *Cynic's Word Book,* 1906
26-27	from *Newsweek,* vol. 89, no. 10 (March 7, 1977), pp. 28–35
32	lecture notes adapted from Henri Nouwen, *The Wounded Healer*
39-40	extract from a theology text in the GTU library, Berkeley
53	Archimandrite Sophrony, from *His Life Is Mine*
56	Alfred Adler, in *Problems of Neurosis,* 1929
59-61	Sigerson Clifford, "The Ballad of the Tinker's Daughter"
72	from the hymn "Like a River Glorious," words by Frances Havergal, 1876
80	Dan B. Allender, PhD, from *Bold Love*
89-90	from "They Were You," *The Fantasticks,* lyrics by Tom Jones, 1960
105	Festo Kivengere's comments derived from his book *Revolutionary Love*
105	plainsong hymn from the *Mass of St. Gregory the Great*
123	Shakespeare quote from *Othello,* act 3, sc. 3

125-126	Governor John Winthrop, from the Trial of Anne Hutchinson, 1637
133	Teresa of Avila, from *Cartas*
137	Martin Buber, from *Werke*, vol. 1, 1962
137-138	Irish poetry by Padraic Colum in *The Irish Reciter*
144	Robert Frost, "The Secret Sits," from *The Witness Tree*, 1942
159	Carl Jung et al., from *Man and His Symbols*, section 3
192	MLK quote from a speech given in March 1964
193	statistics from the Ugandan newspaper the *New Vision*, June 18, 1996
193	original story "The Arrowheads" is found in *Myths and Legends of the Swahili* by Jan Knappert, 1979
201	adapted from a poem by Birago Diop
215-216	pamphlet excerpt from the section on creation myths in *Myths and Legends of the Swahili*
226-227	travel book excerpt from Philip Briggs, *Guide to Uganda*, 1994
236	Bertoldt Brecht in *Three Penny Opera*, act 2, sc. 3, 1928
236	comments on the *imandwa* spirits adapted from Gerald Prunier, *The Rwanda Crisis: History of a Genocide*, 1995
236	Camus quote adapted from *The Fall*, 1956
237	genocide statistics from R. Dallaire's book *Shake Hands with the Devil*
239	"Force" quote from Ignatius of Antioch; Bishop Festo's quotes are derived from his biography by Anne Coomes
256-258	John Milton quote from *Comus*
258	from *What Is Africa's Problem?* by Yoweri Museveni, 1992
273	hymn lyrics from the Kimbanguist church in Zaire, trans. Nsambu Andre
293	Chesterton quote from *The Ballad of the White Horse*, bk. 3, 1911
305	Joseph Conrad, from *Under Western Eyes*, 1911

Opening Night

305	Malachi quote from *The New International Version* of the Bible
313	from *Jesus Christ, Superstar*
327	John of Gaunt in Shakespeare's *Richard II*, act 2, sc. 1
330	stanza from Yeats's poem "Into the Twilight," *The Celtic Twilight*, 1893
335	Eglantine's lament from *L'histoire de St. Denis*, W. H. G. Kingston, 1861
344	the phrase "unstable as water" is spoken by Jacob in Genesis 49:4
347	Charity quotes Amy Carmichael, *Ploughed Under*, 1934
349	C. S. Lewis, from *Letters to Malcolm: Chiefly on Prayer*
350	Stephen paraphrases Evelyn Underhill, *Practical Mysticism*, chapter 1

The author welcomes feedback and correspondence. She can be reached through her website at www.marymendenhalletc.net.

Made in the USA
San Bernardino, CA
04 August 2018